THE EMPERORS
AMERICAN

THE EMPEROR'S AMERICAN

BY

ART MCGRATH

Fireship Press
www.FireshipPress.com

EMPEROR'S AMERICAN : By Art McGrath
Copyright © 2013 Art McGrath

ISBN-13:978-1-61179-259-1: Paperback
ISBN 978-1-61179-260-7: ebook

BISAC Subject Headings:
FIC014000FICTION / Historical
FIC002000FICTION / Action & Adventure
FIC027050 FICTION / Romance / Historical

Cover Work: Christine Horner

Address all correspondence to:
Fireship Press, LLC
P.O. Box 68412
Tucson, AZ 85737
Or visit our website at:
www.FireshipPress.com

DEDICATION

To Christina, Connor and Ethan, the best family a guy could ask for.

ACKNOWLEDGEMENTS

Writing the acknowledgements is a difficult task, especially for a novel that took so long to get to print.

First and foremost, I would like to thank my wife, Christina, for her encouragement and close reading of the text.

This book would not have been possible without the help and advice of two men in particular: William "Cassius" Bradford and Christophe "Albucius" Puissant. Will was one of the first people to read pages from the book when I had barely started, and from then on he was there every step of the way, offering advice, suggestions and encouragement. He was my first reader, my first audience.

Christophe was my eyes on the ground in Boulogne and elsewhere in France, going to Ney's chateau, investigating in detail the positions of people and items in Notre Dame. His knowledge of the period, Napoleon and the Grande Armée was invaluable, as was his close reading of the text.

The members of the Brigade Napoleon reenactment group, particularly the *3me regiment infanterie de ligne* have been invaluable, especially Victor Eiser and Erik Gram.

I also want to thank interlibrary loan specialist Angie and the rest of the staff at the Littleton Public Library in Littleton, New Hampshire, for their tireless work in seeking the most obscure texts from across the country.

A thank-you to Duncan McKee for his wonderful map at the beginning of this book, my editor Jessica Knauss, editor Pat Washburn, and author Kim Rendfeld for referring me to Fireship Press. A thank you also to everyone at Fireship Press for making this book a reality.

PROLOGUE

August 15, 1822
New Jersey

For over ten years I fought for Napoleon Bonaparte, Emperor of the French, rising to the rank of general.

Napoleon died last year on the barren rock of St. Helena, in the South Atlantic, where he was banished by the perfidious English. Today would have been the Emperor's birthday, and I marked it by visiting his older brother Joseph, who lives on a 2,000 acre estate in southern New Jersey. He too is in exile from France, though always he works towards his eventual return home and the return of his family to prominence.

Sitting in his ornate study, surrounded by artwork brought from Europe, Joseph begged me to write my story.

"Your story is unusual, Burns," he said. "You must tell your countrymen. It will help keep my brother's legend alive." Silently, I listened to his plea. It did not carry the weight a request from his brother would have. With black hair, dusky complexion, and similar features, Joseph may have looked a lot like his younger brother, but he was no Napoleon.

I insisted I was not so unusual.

"I was not the only American to serve in the Grande Armée; I know of many other officers and men," I said.

"Yes, but none served as long as you or were as close to my brother," Joseph replied quietly. "And even if you could find them, none of them are here today celebrating my brother's birthday. The memory, the sacred fire, still burns in you, Monsieur le baron."

1

I looked closely at him, smiling wryly. No one had addressed me by that title in almost seven years.

"It's just Burns, or Mister Burns, Your Majesty. The United States recognizes no title of nobility."

Joseph smiled ironically. "You're quite right. And it's no longer 'Majesty.' Now I am just Mister Bonaparte, or as the locals call me, the Good Mister Bonaparte, as opposed to my brother, presumably." There was a trace of sadness in his eyes. "That does not change the interest of your story, of a man who landed penniless on a French shore and left a baron ten years later."

I thought of the sequence of events that brought me into Napoleon's army, looking for a chance to kill Englishmen. Eventually I got my wish, not only killing English in droves, but Spaniards, Russians, Austrians and Prussians too. Enough killing for several lifetimes. More than anyone should see.

The former king of Naples and Spain looked at me intently. Once one of the most powerful men in Europe, he was far removed from that now, not that he was ever up to the responsibility his brother gave him. Some blamed him for mishandling the debacle in Spain, where I served him for a time, even saving his life once. It was funny, but the way he was making the request it was as if I were indebted to him, rather than the other way around. Perhaps it is true that once you save a life you are bound together.

Looking at him brought back echoes of those lost years, when Europe quaked at our approach, when no one could stand in the way of our army, when over the sound of cannon and musketry could be heard the cry of thousands of men, a cry that chilled the courts of Europe and sent terror through armies that tried to stand against us.

"*Vive L'Empereur! Vive L'Empereur! Vive L'Empereur!*" Long Live the Emperor...

For all his faults, Joseph was right. Coming out of my reverie, I looked at him.

"I'll do it."

A LETTER

May 5, 1823
Joseph Bonaparte
Point Breeze
Bordentown, New Jersey

Your Majesty,

Forgive the formal address, but I cannot bring myself to address you as simply Mister Bonaparte, despite your state of exile in my country.

In response to Your Majesty's request, I have sent the first volume recounting my ten years spent in your brother's service. It has been seven years since I left France, and I will be frank, I had not given much thought to those events in some time. There was so much blood, and I became so good at killing, that I prefer not to dwell on it; though on occasion, the moments of glory wash the blood away and I am left with the memory of thousands of us trampling the thrones of Europe and offering them to the Emperor. It is hard to forget such things.

At first I was hesitant to consent to Your Majesty's request to write these memoirs. To have fought for Napoleon is not a great mark of distinction, even here in the United States. Many officers and soldiers of the Emperor's *Grande Armée* fled here after his defeat, unable to bear living under the Bourbon family's rule again. Louisiana is full of such refugees. And of course many, such as Your Majesty, fled on pain of death. But however much I share the contempt you and others hold for them, I did not come here after Napoleon's fall just to flee the Bourbons and their puppet-masters, the English. I was returning home. After all, I am an American.

THE EMPEROR'S AMERICAN

I was not the only American to serve in the *Grande Armée*, but I concede your point of the potential interest of the story.

It seems somehow fitting I send you this on the anniversary of the day our Emperor died in exile on Saint Helena. If I can do anything to keep his memory alive in the face of such infamy, then it is my honor and duty to do so.

I remain, your loyal and obedient servant,

Pierre Burns
Baltimore, Maryland

CHAPTER 1

May 11, 1804
Off the northwestern coast of France

The ship was ablaze.

Thick smoke made it impossible to see, and I stumbled over wreckage strewn across the deck. The smell of burning timber mixed with the stench of seared flesh and acrid gunpowder. The screams of the dying and the panicked survivors filled the air. *The Bedford* was doomed.

We were a sixteen gun merchantman out of Baltimore and had been outclassed from the first shot fired. The English frigate that had pursued us since dawn and dismasted us—we believed it to be the 36-gun HMS *Doris*—continued to shoot, though its fire had slackened. We were helpless, and the English were likely expecting us to strike our colors. They would be waiting a long time for that, dying ship or not.

I slipped on a viscous pool of what I quickly realized was blood. There was an arm in the pool, looking pale and rather incongruous all by itself. I had no idea whose it had been or where the body was. Fighting back bile, I continued on.

A cloud of smoke enveloped me and I began coughing. I was overwhelmed for a moment by the sweet, pungent aroma of longleaf tobacco, which was our cargo. The fire had to be in the guts of the ship.

A gust of wind cleared the air around me. Some of the men were heading towards a boat on the landward side. I went to Captain Rankin to convince him to leave. He was trying to load one of the few functioning deck guns. A piece of burning rigging crashed, causing us both to jump out of the way. His white beard was crusted with soot.

"No, my boy, I'm not leaving, at least not until everyone else is gone. Get to the boat and get it to shore. Take this." He took a pistol out of his belt and handed it to me. It was an elaborate, handmade weapon, with an unusual rifled barrel. He had once said it was his favorite possession.

Before I could say another word he shoved me away. "Get going! Save who you can!"

With that, I left behind the man who had been a second father to me since I was a boy. He was the only true family I had.

Choking back tears, I headed towards the boat, feeling my document packet with identity papers safely around my neck. Obadiah Cushman, the second mate, waved me in the right direction. He began lowering the boat while I grabbed several more men and pushed them towards it. I looked around once more but couldn't see anyone else through the smoke.

The boat descended to the water, but caught in some ropes. I tried cutting them but my knife did little to the heavy, tar-encrusted lines. The same material that protected it from the elements was now preventing us from getting off the ship.

Drawing my cutlass, I hacked furiously. A weapon best for slashing, it was perfect for cutting rope. I made progress, but the ship listed as another shot from the frigate hit us. Wood splinters, some of them longer than my arm, sailed through the air above our heads, scattering on the water like a fall of spears. We were fortunate the bulk of the ship protected us from them.

One of our deck guns responded when the craft righted itself. Someone was still manning it—probably the Captain. As I cut the line, the ship shuddered under another shot and I slipped. My cutlass went flying into the water, as did my hat, and I dangled off the side. I grabbed another loose line, likely cut by a load of British grapeshot, used it to swing into the boat, and immediately took an oar.

We rowed hastily towards shore, looking about for the English frigate, which continued to fire at our ship, even while it drew away from us. They could have come closer and finished us off.

"Pull!" Cushman shouted, steering towards the shore, which was more than a half-mile away. A wave washed over us as we pulled on the oars in desperate fury. I spat out cold seawater and kept rowing.

"Did any other boats get away from the ship?" I asked, trying to catch a glimpse of it at the crest of each wave, hoping against hope that Captain Rankin had managed to leave the ship.

Cushman, still at the rudder in the stern, stole a quick glance back. "I can't tell for certain, but I think not," he said. "Maybe a boat got off the other side, in which case the English will likely capture it."

"Bloody bastards," said a seaman from Rhode Island named Adams. The sentiment echoed from man to man.

The rest of us said nothing else but continued to row. The ship had been my home for well over a year, a refuge where I fled to escape the pain of losing my young wife, Catherine. Now, just past my twenty-fourth birthday, I once again had no home.

Water splashed my face, sharp features crusted with salt and gunpowder. Hazel eyes looked out from under a shock of dark brown hair. Unlike most of my shipmates, I did not have a beard, though several days worth of stubble were starting to itch. I had preferred to waste water on ship or even use seawater shaving to set myself apart from the others, even the other officers. I was no sailor, though I was third mate because of my family connections to Captain Rankin. I was a competent enough seaman and could fight, which earned me the grudging respect of most of the crew, but for me the sea was a temporary refuge, not my future.

As we drew nearer the shore, Cushman stood up to get his bearings, bracing himself against the movement of the boat, and then aimed us towards an open stretch of beach, only a few hundred yards away now. Shading his eyes from the sun, he scanned the low rises and a small hill not far from shore. Running a hand through his thick beard, he looked at me, then at the crew.

"I think I know why the English didn't pursue us to shore," he said. He nodded towards the rises, keeping his hands on the rudder. "There are fortifications up there, cannon and all. And they're manned with troops."

As we crested another wave, he looked again.

"Don't look, keep rowing, but we're going to be welcomed," Cushman said, indicating a troop of men and horses moving toward the spot where we were about to beach.

7

The boat scraped bottom.

"Stand by to exit port and starboard and pull the boat ashore," Cushman said. "And for God's sake, no weapons. Any that you have, leave in the boat."

Another wave washed over us, propelling us forward, and we scraped bottom.

The ten of us jumped out on our respective sides of the boat into the crashing surf and pushed it high up onto the sand, helped by another wave. Out of breath, we clung to the boat as a group of forty or fifty soldiers in uniform—dark blue coats and white trousers—approached us in a half circle, muskets at the ready. They made no move to help us with the boat. Five mounted horsemen were behind them. There was silence as we stared at each other. Beyond the sandy beach we could see stone and wood fortifications, from which the black maw of cannon jutted.

A young man, an officer, approached from one side of the soldiers and went up to Cushman, as he had been giving us orders and was the only one of us in uniform. Cushman was also still wearing a sword, the only one of us so armed, though we had left a few cutlasses and pistols in the boat.

The officer was dressed like his men in a red-faced blue coat, white trousers, waistcoat and black felt bicorn hat. A sword remained sheathed at his side. He approached Cushman and addressed him.

"*Qui êtes vous? Qui commande ici? Identifiez vous!*"

Cushman's puzzled expression annoyed him.

"*Parlez vous Français?*" When he received no response, he addressed all of us. "*Parlez vous Français?*"

None of us said anything. Though I knew what he said, I was so fascinated by the entire event I couldn't speak.

Cushman turned his head toward me. "Pierre, you speak their lingo, say something before someone gets shot."

I shook myself out of my reverie and walked slowly around the boat, arms at my side and raised a little, with palms up to show I had nothing in them and meant no harm.

"*Je parle Français, Monsieur,*" I said to the young officer, who turned his attention towards me. "We are Americans come to trade

8

with France, but were waylaid by the English," I explained in his language.

"Then what are you doing here, rather than out there, Monsieur?" the officer asked. "A merchant ship would not have fought as you did, but would have submitted."

"We kill the English, we don't surrender to them!" I said more fiercely than I intended. A few muskets rose at my tone and the officer took a half step back.

I was sure I wasn't speaking for the crew: they would have surrendered if it hadn't meant certain death, hanged as pirates, as we did not have a letter of marque granting us protection. I *was* speaking for myself, however, as I loathed the English, a trait I had shared with Captain Rankin.

The officer's eyes narrowed a bit. "Are you pirates?"

I looked at him. "To the French people and their consul, Bonaparte, no. To the English," I shrugged, "on occasion, but we usually get more out of running their blockades than fighting them. Until today..."

I suppose the British would indeed have called us pirates, which is why we didn't surrender. Our ship was a heavily armed merchantman that took the occasional English trading vessel when the opportunity arose. On this trip we were trying to smuggle tobacco past the English blockade, but apparently the bastards had been told to keep an eye out for us.

One of the mounted soldiers observing the scene had moved closer to listen. He dismounted and walked through the semicircle. They parted for him, and the officer I had been addressing deferred to him immediately and came to attention.

"General Ney," the young officer said to the newcomer.

I turned my attention to the general, who was watching me with eyes like those of a bird of prey. Hatless, his dark blue uniform had a high collar with gold braid on it, with gold epaulettes on his shoulders. It seemed as if it were a part of him. His left hand was on his sword hilt, not in menace, but simply at rest. Around thirty five years old, his hair was dark red and his expression was one of bemused curiosity. Something I had said had seized his attention.

9

There was a striking sense of self-confidence and boundless energy about the man. His bearing was military, yet open at the same time. There was definite amusement in his eye.

Here was a man who could laugh.

"What was your cargo, American, that you fought so hard to keep it from the English?" Ney asked in a deep baritone voice, looking at us and then at our burning ship, which was now fully engulfed. The English frigate was still visible beyond it, as were a couple of boats it had launched towards our ship.

A few shore batteries from the fortifications beyond us suddenly fired some shots in the direction of the English ship, causing all of us to look at the cannon and then out to sea. Ney turned to an aide.

"Tell those fools up there to cease firing; that ship is well out of range. We've made our point for them to keep their distance."

The aide spurred his horse and galloped away, kicking up sand as he went.

"Now, you were saying, Monsieur....?" Ney said.

"Pierre Burns, *mon général*," I replied. "You asked about our cargo. Our cargo was tobacco from Virginia."

A gasp of dismay escaped Ney and several of the soldiers, including the young officer.

"*Mon Dieu*, what a waste," Ney said, looking towards the burning hulk. "The damn English have no appreciation for fine things." He looked back at me. "Still, I suppose it is better destroyed than in the hands of barbarians."

I nodded. "My thoughts exactly, Monsieur, though I assure you it was not our intention to get caught and see the *Bedford* burned to the water. We got some fair shots in before they overtook us, though we never stood a chance fighting a frigate."

"We watched much of your battle. You fought bravely. All of you," Ney said, addressing the remnant of our crew. I translated his comments to the crew, who smiled nervously.

Then, taking in at a glance our nervous crew, the burning ship and the semi-circle of French soldiers still watching us, he smiled, a broad smile that could melt the heart of Lucifer.

"But where are my manners, standing here, chatting on the beach?" he asked, more to himself than anyone else. "Let's get you out of those wet clothes, get some food in you, and then we can talk more."

Turning to the young officer, a lieutenant, he told him to have his men pull our boat far up on the beach and to find some kind of conveyance for our crew. The lieutenant saluted briskly and turned to give the requisite orders to the soldiers.

We walked away from the beach towards the low mounds and hills where the fortifications stood. I walked with Ney while the rest of our crew followed at a distance, accompanied by about twice their number of French soldiers.

We weren't prisoners, but we weren't going to be allowed to wander around at will either.

CHAPTER 2

"Your French is very good," Ney commented as we walked off the beach. I didn't realize until much later my good fortune that day, landing not far from where General Michel Ney was conducting an inspection of coastal fortifications. If not for his intervention, we might have languished for months in a French jail until some official could be bothered to check our papers.

I glanced at him. Ney's own French, while excellent, had more than a hint of German in it.

"Thank you," I said. "My mother was French and insisted I learn the language. We often spoke it at home after my father died."

Ney smiled. "She was a good teacher. Your father was not French." It was a statement rather than a question.

"No, Scots, though he was born in France, near Paris—his family fled Scotland when we lost at Culloden. He married my mother and moved to America when he was twenty. I've always thought French and Scots quite a combination."

Ney laughed. "Indeed. We have quite a few Scottish soldiers in our ranks, many the descendants of the Jacobites, who like your grandfather, escaped after the failed revolt of Bonnie Prince Charlie fifty years ago. A friend of mine, Étienne MacDonald, is an excellent soldier and general—" Ney paused a moment "—retired at the moment, though I suspect he'll be back when the shooting starts again."

"Shooting? I thought France was at peace, or relatively so," I said.

We were off the beach and approaching a group of horses, held by several soldiers. Two wagons were there also, with boxes piled next to them, which had been hastily offloaded.

13

Ney nodded. "Yes, for the moment things are peaceful, except at sea where our old enemies the English give us trouble, but that will change again. For the past fifteen years, France has been almost continuously at war with one European power or another because they despise the Revolution and our First Consul, Bonaparte, for making France peaceful and prosperous without the Bourbons."

Ney stopped and looked at me. "So, yes, the shooting will start again, and France will be ready. We beat them and beat them and yet they keep coming." Grasping my shoulder, he said, "And any foe of England, as you clearly are, is an ally." Looking at the horses, and then at me, he asked me if I could ride.

It had been several years. I had last ridden when I left Maryland, after burying my wife, and soon after, my mother. "Yes, I can ride, *mon général.*"

"Excellent!" Ney put on a bicorn hat, of the type Napoleon would soon make famous, and mounted a horse in one well-practiced motion. "Ride with me to my camp."

I looked at the remainder of the crew of my ship, who had been following at a distance and watching us curiously.

"What of my shipmates?"

Ney indicated the nearby wagons. "They will have to ride in those. Unfortunately, I don't have enough spare horses with me for them." He looked at me with a glint of amusement in his eyes. "And likely they can't all ride anyway, eh?"

I accepted the reins of the proffered horse and mounted with only a little difficulty. The soldier who had been holding my horse handed me a canteen. "Some wine, Monsieur? It's a long way to the general's headquarters," he said. I accepted gratefully and took a long draught.

I walked the horse over to the crew and addressed Cushman. "These wagons will take you to the French camp, sir. General Ney has asked me to ride with him."

Cushman nodded sullenly. I understood his point of view—he was the senior man present, and should have been the one to ride with the general, but for his failure to speak French. Still, he made no protest.

"See you there," was all he said.

ART MCGRATH

The horse was a spirited animal and gave me some trouble, testing out the new rider. I gently pulled the reins, talking to it, which only seemed to irritate it more.

Ney watched with the barest of grins on his face. "Try speaking French to the horse, Burns, you might have better luck. I think you're scaring the animal talking English." Of course he was right. I switched to French and the animal calmed immediately.

Ney spurred his horse down a road that led inland. I galloped to catch up, as did his aides, the wagons trailing.

We rode in silence, settling to a pace not much faster than a walk. By now it was past noon and the weather was perfect, hardly a cloud in the sky and warm, though not as warm as Maryland at this time of year, and certainly not as humid. Farmers tended fields, and in the distance I could see church spires and villages. There was a sense of comfort, of life moving along as it had for centuries. These lands had been civilized since becoming part of the Roman Empire nearly two millennia ago.

Of course, I knew things were not as calm as they seemed. Those steeples belonged to churches that quite possibly no longer had priests in them. They might have been killed or fled for their lives during the Revolution, when thousands of priests and nuns were guillotined during the Terror.

Like many Americans, I both admired and was repulsed by the Revolution. We had gone through our own revolution, but it was not as violent as France's. Their resentment was much deeper than ours had been. We changed governments but they changed their society. When Napoleon Bonaparte had come into power as First Consul four years earlier, he curbed the excesses of the Revolution, allowing the churches to reopen and the clergy to return, while solidifying the gains ordinary people had made.

It was taking me a little time to become accustomed to riding again, even at a slow pace. Instead of moving up and down with the horse, I kept moving opposite to it. I tried not to let Ney see my trouble and prayed I would catch on soon.

We passed groups of soldiers marching towards the beach, or peasants leading flocks of animals, all of whom moved aside to let us pass. We, however, stopped on the side of the road to let a convoy of ten wagons and an escort of troops pass us in the direction of the fortifications.

15

THE EMPEROR'S AMERICAN

Soon we came to a fork in the road and turned north, on a road parallel to the beach we had left behind. Here was constant movement, both civilian and military. I was astounded.

"There are so many troops here," I said to Ney. They were the first words we had exchanged in awhile.

"*Oui,* this is the coast road. It connects many of the villages south of Boulogne and our camps south of the city. Our camps are spread out for many miles on either side of it. Mine, which contains the VI Corps, is the farthest south, on the far left of the French forces," Ney said as we rode along.

So, we might make it to Boulogne after all—although without our ship, our cargo, or most of our shipmates.

"Do you expect trouble along this stretch of coast?" I was amazed at the sheer number of troops I had seen. More were evident in some of the fields we passed, marching and drilling.

Shifting in his saddle, Ney took in all the activity.

"It's no secret we plan to invade England. Boulogne is the port from which the army will embark when it is time. In and around the city we have 200,000 men training and waiting for that day. There has never been an army as well trained or as well led as this one. When we land, the English army will crumble before us." Ney chuckled grimly. "Of course, we have to get there first, and that has been something of a problem. While the French army is the finest in Europe, our navy, alas, is not. We have enough landing craft and transports in Boulogne to get the army to England, but we have not been able to find a way to deal with the Royal Navy. The English know how many of us are here, what we intend to do, and what is stopping us. Read any of their newspapers and you'll hear what I just told you—except they usually exaggerate our numbers."

We continued north in silence for a time again, Ney returning the salutes of officers and men we passed, even greeting peasants with their flocks. The greetings of the troops were not perfunctory. They clearly admired the man, one group shouting out "*Vive le Rougeaud!*" Long live the red-faced one. With his red hair and ruddy complexion, it was evident where Ney got the nickname.

At one point, we came upon a field where a regiment of infantry was conducting maneuvers. Drums beat and a band played a march as the unit went about its drills flawlessly.

16

I had seen units of the United States Army as a child after the American Revolution, and in the years since then. I had even served in a local militia unit, but all of them, even the professionals I had seen, were rank amateurs compared to these soldiers. I had never seen or even imagined anything like it.

I looked at Ney. He was scrutinizing me while I watched the maneuvers.

"It can stir the blood." Ney spoke quietly.

I nodded. We sat on our horses watching a few minutes longer. My clothes had pretty much dried, between the heat of the sun and the horse beneath me. The wagons had caught up and my shipmates were also watching the spectacle.

Ney called an aide over and sent him to the colonel of the regiment, who looked, saw the general watching, and ordered a change in one of the formations.

"It really was nothing," Ney said, smiling, "but it's always best to keep the officers on their toes, holding them to the highest standard."

Pulling out a telescope from his saddlebag, Ney watched the regiment as they formed in a line before a low hill. Commands echoed across the field and the men raised their muskets. The first rank fired, followed by the second. The men then began to fire at will, shooting as fast as they were able to load, aim and fire.

The musketry reverberated across the field; the band still played and drums rolled out commands.

"What are they firing at?" I asked, seeing no targets before the soldiers.

"Nothing in particular," Ney replied. "A tree, a shrub, whatever they see in front of them. This is an exercise in firing as quickly as possible while remaining in formation. The officers try to have the men do this occasionally while on maneuvers to keep their musketry skills sharp. We must march fast and shoot straight."

Snapping his telescope shut, he put it back in a case on his saddle, and gently spurred his horse back onto the road. The rest of us followed, with the wagons again taking up the rear. We went another mile and turned right, off the road to Boulogne, onto another road that headed east.

"We are not going to Boulogne?" I asked, disappointed. I hoped to see the city we had been aiming for, and also hoped to see the French invasion armada.

"No, not today," Ney said. "We are heading to Montreuil, where my headquarters is located. It is only a few miles ahead, and there we'll be able to get you some food and a change of clothes."

I nodded, looking at the road, which went through some gently rolling hills, trying to glimpse our destination. The thought of food made my stomach growl. It had been hours since I had last eaten.

"I should tell my shipmates where we're heading and what we're doing," I said.

"By all means," Ney agreed.

I turned my horse and walked back along our convoy, made up of Ney's mounted aides and an escort of around thirty infantry.

Cushman was in the first wagon and had seated himself next to the driver, a French civilian.

"Where are we heading?" Cushman demanded as I pulled my horse alongside the wagon, walking my animal at the same pace.

"To General Ney's headquarters at Montreuil, a few miles ahead, where we'll get a hot meal, a change of clothes and a bed for the night," I said matter-of-factly.

Indicating the road we just came off, I told Cushman that Boulogne was in that direction. "Hopefully we'll be able to get there soon, though probably not today."

Cushman nodded, looking back the way we had come. "No hurry, it's not like we have a cargo to deliver."

I was relieved at his practical answer and nodded. "We're lucky to be alive. We could have drowned, or been burned to death, or hanged by the English."

"True enough. Still..." and here Cushman turned sullen again. "You don't seem to be doing so badly, consorting with a French general, and you barely an officer on our ship."

His resentment was understandable, but I didn't care to be on the receiving end of it, considering I had almost died, too. Besides, one of my jobs on the *Bedford* was as interpreter, so this situation shouldn't have been strange to him.

"Mere luck, Mr. Cushman. My mother was a Frenchwoman, but I have never looked to gain advantage from the fact. Let me see if I can learn more about what the general plans for us."

I spurred my horse to a trot before he could reply and rode back up to the head of the column, where Ney was riding. I noticed he had turned his head to watch part of my discussion with Cushman. I think my voice carried.

"Trouble?" Ney asked.

I was reluctant to speak ill of my shipmate but also knew much depended on the generosity of this man, who had been so forthcoming to a man of a considerably lower station.

"No trouble, *mon général*, it's just that Monsieur Cushman resents that I am here on a horse talking to you, when he outranks me," I replied.

Ney looked annoyed. "I will decide to whom I talk. The man doesn't speak French or German, does he?"

I shook my head.

Ney laughed. "Then we both would be bored."

We rode along and I rubbed my horse gently on the neck. We were getting used to one another, and I regretted not asking the animal's name.

"So tell me, Burns, what are you doing with this crew? You are no sailor, are you?" Ney asked, watching me ride.

How had he known that? "My parents are dead. I have no family except a sister whose husband is not fond of me, and I wanted to see more of the world. And, I thought, at sea I might get a chance to fight the English.

Looking at me, Ney said, "I do not mind your dislike of the English. Most French share it. I was wondering about the intensity of it. I didn't think Americans had such a hatred of England."

"My father was killed by the English. Not just shot, but brutally murdered and scalped by Tories and British soldiers with Tarleton's Raiders."

"Scalped?"

"A practice common in frontier warfare, especially among the Indians. The scalp is removed as a trophy, sometimes while someone is still alive."

Ney didn't look at first as if he believed me. "That's barbaric."

"Yes," I agreed. "Yet still common." I looked away for a moment before turning back to him. "I was only a year old, so I never knew him, but my mother kept his memory alive, and the memory of how he died. She never failed to remind me of that heritage and of my French blood."

There was no response from Ney.

"*Mon général*, I don't mind answering your questions, but I find it odd that a general, someone close to Bonaparte and the highest levels of government, would be so curious about an American of low rank and background," I said to Ney, adjusting my legs in the stirrups of the saddle. I finally seemed to be getting accustomed to riding again.

To my surprise, Ney laughed. "Low background? My boy, just what do you think *my* background is?"

I shrugged. "I don't know. You are a general, you're dressed magnificently, and you command an army corps. I assumed an old, distinguished military family of some sort."

"*Mais non*," Ney said turning his piercing eyes at me. "My family is German from a border town called Saarlouis. I didn't even speak French until I went to school. I am the son of a barrel cooper who served as an enlisted man in our war against Frederick the Great and Prussia before returning home to make barrels. He enrolled me in a law office, hoping I would rise that way, but it was a trade I despised, and I ran away to join the army. I was a private with little hope of rising beyond sergeant or lieutenant because of my background. Then the Revolution made anything possible for a man of ability. No my friend, this is the France of 1804, not 1774. Your background doesn't matter. Anything is possible now."

He adjusted his reins. "So the interest I take in you is natural. I see a man of ability wash up on shore nearly in front of me, a man from America, another country where anything is possible. A possible ally. At the very least, I anticipate an interesting story from someone who has been places I have not. And, I saw you personally fight well against the English—that has to count for something. You saved the lives of several of your men, including your second mate when you freed your boat. And last but not least, Pierre is my father's name."

"How did you know I wasn't a sailor by profession?" I asked.

"You didn't look like one. And you don't ride like one, despite your troubles when we started," Ney replied.

We crested a hill and before us lay a river, and beyond it, on another hill, a walled medieval town, with other buildings at the base of the hill outside the walls.

"Montreuil, my headquarters," Ney said.

.

CHAPTER 3

It looked like a town from above, but as we drew closer I saw the signs that marked Montreuil as a military camp. There were hundreds of whitewashed buildings with walkways, streets, and gardens, all filled with soldiers.

The soldiers had been told they might be here a while, and like soldiers everywhere, these troops showed a talent for making themselves comfortable. The smell of food cooking drifted over us, reminding me that I had not eaten since breakfast that morning on the ship, except for that long drink of wine that soldier had given me on the beach. Laughter, music and singing came from several buildings, as did the sound of children playing. There were even chickens running around between some of the buildings.

All the comforts of home, indeed. On the outskirts of the camp, on either side of the road, were dozens of women of varying age who appeared to be offering all kinds of wares, including themselves. Some even had on uniforms. As we approached they looked up. Seeing Ney at the head of the column, they drew back, but still looked at us boldly.

"Who are those women?" I asked Ney.

I received an incredulous look from Ney. "You do not have whores in America?"

"Well, umm," I sputtered. "Yes, but not in such numbers in one place, I'm sure."

Ney laughed. "Wherever an army goes, there will be women. Not all of them are prostitutes. Some are *vivandières* and *cantinières* who do laundry for the men, cook for them, serve them drinks on and off the battlefield and tend them when they are sick. Usually they are attached to one man exclusively in a kind of marriage, though rarely is there a ceremony of any kind. Most are

23

faithful, some are not. They can make a lot of money, as do the whores."

I thought I had seen much of the world, but really I had not. I said nothing more for fear of being thought naive. My shipmates doubtless were not surprised by the women.

I later learned that one prostitute in Boulogne became famous and beloved of the army, earning the nickname "Madame 40,000." I don't think I need to explain why.

I was less naive when I left Boulogne.

We rode through the camp on the main road, with Ney stopping to speak to soldiers and officers along the way. I received curious looks from some, but they received no explanation. I was not a prisoner, yet wasn't a soldier either.

We crossed the bridge and rode up the hill into Montreuil. The town and buildings were old, far older than anything in the United States.

"The town is ancient, built by the savage Gauls, tamed by Roman genius," Ney said.

Ney's headquarters was in a citadel on the western side of the town, built right into the ramparts. Before we reached it, we stopped at a structure guarded by soldiers. Ney inquired of one if a Captain Reille was inside. When the captain came out, Ney indicated us and gave him several orders.

Ney turned to me. "I know you need a bath, clean clothes, food and some rest. Captain Reille will put you and your officer in officer quarters, while your men will be billeted nearby in one of the enlisted huts we saw on the way in. I hope both of you will join me for dinner tonight at my house at seven o'clock."

"Of course we would be honored, *mon général*." I answered. I hadn't consulted Cushman, but I knew he wouldn't dare refuse.

With a quick nod, Ney turned his horse and rode off towards his headquarters, accompanied by his group of mounted aides, one of whom took my horse.

I dismounted and introduced myself to our escort, Reille, who was a company commander in the Sixth Légèr—Light Infantry— Regiment, part of the First Brigade of the Second Division of Ney's Corps.

I walked to the wagons with my shipmates in them. The men were already out and stretching their legs. I joined Cushman, who had finished checking on the men.

"So what's going on, Pierre? What are they doing with us now?" he asked, while looking around.

I repeated what Ney had told me, including the invitation to dine.

"Well, we probably can't refuse," Cushman said, stretching, and then rubbing his jaw. He eyed Reille and some of the French soldiers.

"No, and why would we?" I asked.

It was well past three in the afternoon and a well-appointed dinner sounded like just the thing to me—after a bath, of course.

"No reason, Pierre; I was thinking out loud. So what did you learn? Anything useful?" Cushman asked, looking at me intently.

"Useful to whom? Our ship is gone, all that remains of our crew is standing here," I said to Cushman.

"Useful to our *survival*. What have we gotten ourselves into? We landed on a beach full of soldiers, and have seen nothing but soldiers since we left that beach three hours ago. And what is this French general's intention towards us? He seems to have taken quite an interest in you." Cushman said and paused, waiting for an answer.

I nodded. "We've landed in the midst of French preparations to invade England. These soldiers are part of 200,000 men training to take part in that invasion."

Cushman's eyes widened but he said nothing.

"Apparently it's no secret in England. It would be hard to keep such a secret anyway. As for Ney's intentions towards us, I think we'll find that out at dinner. I suspect he's being hospitable. We're likely an interesting distraction from the current military situation. We'll probably be able to go on our way soon, to wherever that will be..."

Reille and a group of French soldiers were waiting politely for us to finish talking but were obviously ready to take us to our quarters. No doubt they had other things to do.

I introduced Reille to Cushman, and then explained to the eight crewmen that they were being taken to a nearby barracks, where food and other comforts would be available. They left accompanied by five French soldiers, while Reille took us in the opposite direction, to a nearby inn.

Like so many other buildings in the towns around Boulogne, the army had taken over the inn and was paying a good price, so there were no complaints by the landlords, who continued to serve meals and wait on officers staying there. The prostitutes weren't the only ones in the area to welcome the army.

Captain Reille gave instructions to the owner to give us a room, hot baths and a meal to tide us over until our dinner with Ney.

"Also, wash their clothes, if they are salvageable," Reille said. He turned to me. "Even if they are, we'll probably have to find clothes for you if you are to have dinner tonight with the general." He looked me over. "We're about the same size. I have some that might fit you."

I wondered if he was joking. It's true Reille was of average height and thin, of very similar build to me, but he was quite dashing, with his perfectly fitting light infantry uniform, complete with red-faced blue coat and trousers, and white waistcoat. He sported a somewhat bushy mustache. His face was serious, but there was a sparkle in his eye. Somehow I was amusing him, I just wasn't sure why. Probably the thought of me in his extra clothes, as I didn't look the least bit elegant in my crumpled rags from the ship.

I wasn't about to give him the satisfaction of commenting, but simply thanked him.

"Very well, I'll be here at half past six." With that, he left.

Pacing around the room, Cushman looked on shelves and in jars, trying to find tobacco and failing. "God, I wish we had been able to save some of the cargo. That was a good load we had."

"I wish we could have saved more of the crew," I said, unsympathetic. Though I occasionally indulge in it, I have never understood the appeal of tobacco, though many men my age are devoted to it.

Cushman was fifteen years older than I, around forty, and a career seaman. He had taught himself to read and had worked his way up out of the ranks from seaman to being an officer, second mate on our ship. I always got the feeling he resented me, starting my career as a junior officer because of my education and because the Captain had known my family. I knew Cushman would be able to find a ship easily after we left here. It was his life, and he was one of those who are never happy on land. But what of myself? The sea was not my calling, nor had I any home to return to. The *Bedford* and Captain Rankin were the only ties I'd had to home, and now they were gone.

At half past six o'clock, there was a knock on the door. Reille was back with an orderly and two sets of clothes, including well-polished boots.

Cushman was dressed in a brown jacket and trousers of fine quality—far better than he was used to. When I put my clothes on, it was the blue trousers and blue coat of a French light infantry officer, but without any insignia.

Reille smiled. "I told you I had clothes that would fit you. I just had them made not long ago and have not had my insignia and piping put on. Keep them clean."

I started to protest but he held up his hand. "There is no time to argue, you are expected for dinner."

As we left the room, Cushman stared at me. "The uniform suits you," he said before going out in the hall.

We left the inn with Reille, who led us to Ney's large house on a street not far from the citadel, skirting part of the ancient fortifications that surrounded the town. Though the walls were ancient, they were kept in good repair with modern additions.

A few people watched us inquisitively.

"The general made this his headquarters when arriving in Montreuil five months ago. Sometimes his wife stays near here, or in a house a few miles away which he has bought, but she is in Paris for the month," Reille said as we mounted the steps. At the door he dismissed the orderly. "Soon they will move into a chateau in Recques, northeast of here, though he will keep this house so he can sleep near the troops when necessary."

After being admitted past several guards, we entered a well-lit dining room, not as grand as I expected, considering the size of the building.

"The general uses this room for small, more informal dinners." Reille explained. A servant informed us the general would be along momentarily and asked Reille to wait.

I looked at some of the paintings on the wall, including a copy of the famous *Oath of the Horatii*, by Jacques-Louis David. In it, the three Horatius brothers take an oath before their father to fight three men from Alba Longa to determine whether Rome or Alba would be supreme in central Italy.

On another wall was a copy of another painting by David, this one of Bonaparte from 1800, a much reproduced picture of him on a horse crossing the St. Bernard Pass into Italy to attack the Austrians. I studied the man on the rearing white horse. He had changed France and would soon remake the face of Europe. He held the reins with one hand, and with the other outstretched, was pointing onward, asking the viewer to follow him.

There was a sense of energetic majesty to the picture. David had caught the moment, though from what I heard from people who were there, the crossing was more prosaic: Napoleon walked or rode a mule, which was more reliable in mountain passes. That didn't matter. The picture wasn't trying to portray the actual moment, but the spirit of the event and what it meant for the future.

"David truly captures how remarkable Bonaparte is in that painting," said a voice from behind us. Ney had entered the room, accompanied by two other officers. I had not noticed their arrival, I was so engrossed by the paintings.

"I generally do not pay much attention to art, but David is different and I had these copies of his works made. If you ever get to Paris, you should try to see more of his work and meet the man if you can. Remarkable."

There were introductions all around, and Ney presented the two officers with him. One, Antoine-Henri Jomini, a Swiss mercenary who was an aide-de-camp to Ney, was just a few years older than I. Jomini had intelligent eyes, a constant wry expression, and somewhat aristocratic looks. A vain man, I could tell immediately.

The other officer was a colonel, who appeared at least ten years older than Ney. He was a holdover from the old French Royal Army who had served in America during our Revolution. A rather nondescript man, with somewhat long, graying hair, I quickly realized he was there because he spoke English and would give Cushman another person to talk to. I can't even remember his name.

When Reille asked permission to leave, Ney asked him instead to join us for dinner, bringing the total up to six. After we sat down and a servant brought wine out for all of us, Ney proposed a toast.

"To our American friends, washed up on our shores: long life, success, glory and more battles to fight."

That was Ney's attitude toward life. He didn't care so much about money—though he was coming into a lot of it. Military ambition and glory drove him, but he was almost always boisterous and smiling.

Dinner was filled with small talk, but the conversation inevitably turned to war and politics, both American and French. For the sake of those who had not witnessed our arrival, I recounted our flight and subsequent battle with the British frigate, with Ney interspersing comments about what he witnessed from shore. Occasionally, I would translate part of the conversation for Cushman, but the old colonel sitting next to him eventually took on that role. "France has been in a precarious position since the start of the Revolution," Ney said. "The courts of Europe view us as a threat to their thrones, if only because by our very existence we inspire their citizens to look beyond the rule of kings to something better."

I knew this was true, but I also knew the violence of France's Revolution inspired fear in the monarchies and many ordinary people throughout Europe. Thousands of people had died under the guillotine, often for little or no reason. Many of the clergy and nobility were killed because of their status, not because of anything they had done.

"But what of the thousands killed during the Reign of Terror? All killed without a trial, or only a show trial. I think that might have something to do with why they fear you," I said tentatively.

"That was ten years ago. The mass killings stopped in the summer of 1794, when Robespierre was guillotined," Ney said, sipping his wine. "Without a trial," he added, with an ironic smile.

Before I could say anything else, Ney continued, "They were horrible times, when no one was safe from the blade. You never knew when someone might make up something that could send you before a tribunal and immediate execution. Those times are behind us, however. They were growing pains, as France learned to live without a king."

At that moment, several servants came in with heaping plates of game birds and vegetables, along with plenty of bread, cheese and more wine. In the center was a steaming pot from which wafted delicious aromas. After so long on ship eating bland food, my stomach was ready for a change, though I hoped I wouldn't make myself sick.

"A meal born on a battlefield," Ney said with an enigmatic smile, noting my interest as I watched the servants arrange the dish in front of me.

"On a battlefield, Monsieur?" I said, looking at him, then back at the dish.

"Indeed, as is so much of our modern France. It is Chicken Marengo and was concocted by Bonaparte's chef after the Battle of Marengo in 1800 when he defeated the Austrians—thus the name," Ney said, drawing out the tale. "I was fighting the Austrians in Germany at the time, not having met our First Consul yet, but the story goes that after the battle, he ordered his chef, Dunand, to cook him a meal, as he was famished. In near darkness Dunand gathered what ingredients he could from the surrounding area. The man turned out to be a culinary genius of sorts. In the dish you'll find chicken, of course, tomatoes, garlic, onions, mushrooms, crayfish and truffles. It is cooked in olive oil and white wine, all topped with fried eggs."

"It sounds delicious, General," I said, accepting another glass of wine from a servant.

"It is delicious, Monsieur Burns. The least we can do after the uneven fight you had with the English today," Ney said, lifting his glass in an informal salute, which I returned. He returned us to recent French history, where we had been before the food was brought in.

"Things are much more peaceful here now since Bonaparte came to power," Ney said. "He made peace with the Catholic Church, allowing priests and nuns to return to their churches and convents, bringing religion back to public life. Even thousands of the *émigrés* have come back."

"Émigrés?" Cushman asked.

Ney looked at him, then at me. "What we call an émigré is someone who fled France during the Revolution, usually someone of noble birth who thought his life was in danger if he remained. Certainly some of them were right, their lives *were* in danger. I have heard estimates that almost 100,000 people fled the country during the Revolution. Bonaparte issued a general amnesty so that most could return safely, unless they had served in the armies of France's enemies."

"I can't blame them for leaving, the Revolution had killed their king," Cushman said to me.

"What did he say?" Ney asked, glancing at the sour-looking Cushman.

"He said he couldn't blame them, as the king had been killed," I said.

"Indeed. It is ironic, then, that we are on the verge of having an emperor."

I wasn't sure I had heard right: France, which had killed its hereditary king, was to have an emperor?

"Emperor? Who? How and what will the people think?" I blurted out, all at once.

Ney laughed. "I thought you knew, but of course how could you have heard the news in America? The decision to elect an emperor was only made in the last few months. Who? Why Bonaparte, of course, though from now on, like any monarch, he will be known as Napoleon, or the Emperor Napoleon. No more Bonaparte."

I was stunned and fascinated at the same time. "Did you say 'elected,' General?"

"Yes, elected. Very soon the Senate will declare Napoleon emperor, but he insisted the French people also ratify his nomination. The plebiscite is being prepared as we speak and will be held in a few months."

"Electing an emperor? Kind of an oxymoron," I said, quickly trying to eat some of the Chicken Marengo while the general answered.

Chuckling, Ney nodded. "I can see why you would say that, but if the French people want an emperor, elect an emperor, what is undemocratic about that? Besides this will be solidifying, protecting all the gains ordinary people made during the Revolution."

Catching my quizzical look, he described the numerous attempts on Napoleon's life, the most recent and daring of which had been uncovered just a few months before. A Royalist named Georges Cadoudal had planned on killing Bonaparte during a review of troops, when conspirators would have surrounded him and killed him with daggers, much in the way Julius Caesar had been killed.

Cadoudal had been captured and revealed that his plot was not to be enacted until a royal prince arrived in France. A Bourbon, the Duc d'Enghien, was suspected of being the plotting prince and was captured—essentially kidnapped—outside of France in the neighboring German principality of Ettenheim. He was taken to Paris, tried, and shot the same night he arrived. To this day I do not understand the violent reaction of the monarchs of Europe, unless they didn't like the reminder that they and their families were no longer sacrosanct. Perhaps, being an American, I took a less involved view of the whole affair. As for the French people, they were generally supportive of Bonaparte for dealing with the nation's enemies in this manner.

"This was not the first time Cadoudal tried to kill Bonaparte. On Christmas Eve four years ago, his men exploded a bomb in a cart near his carriage on the Rue St. Nicaise as he was going to the opera in Paris. Bonaparte was unhurt, but ten civilians were killed, including a little girl the plotters paid to hold the horse pulling the cart," Ney said, anger filling his eyes at the image.

I was trying to tie all the threads together and failing. "General Ney, this is interesting and I understand the concern for Bonaparte's life, but what does that have to do with France choosing an emperor or solidifying the gains of the Revolution?"

A servant came in and started lighting more candles. Dusk was turning to dark as Ney answered my question.

"I was getting to that, but I wanted to explain the background of these events, their impetus. After that attempt on Bonaparte's life, people began to fear what would happen to France if he died.

Chaos and the Terror again? The return of the Bourbons? To prevent that, it was decided in the highest levels of government to make First Consul Bonaparte into Emperor Napoleon I, a hereditary ruler who can appoint his successor. The Empire will preserve much of what has been gained for ordinary people, keeping them free from the almost feudal system that existed until the Revolution and protecting the freedoms and changes to our society, such as the new civil code Bonaparte has been enacting. In essence, we will be a Republic with imperial trappings."

Ney looked at me, as if waiting for a protest.

"Or an Empire with Republican trappings," I said. My mind was weighing everything Ney had been saying and its implications.

"Or an Empire with Republican trappings," Ney nodded in agreement, calling over a servant to bring another bottle of wine. "Better that than the return of a Bourbon king. The empire really will preserve much that has been gained, while the Bourbons would turn the clock back one hundred years. And believe me, they are waiting to return, and they constantly work to undermine France—with the help of English gold. We will have to fight again to maintain this empire, I am certain of it."

For the first time, Jomini spoke. "Our invasion of England will put an end to their plotting. Six hours of favorable weather will see us on the shores of England. *We* will change the political dynamics of Europe."

A theorist of war, who had written much about combat, Jomini was eager to put his theories into practice. His ideas were sound, but in the years that followed it seemed to me that he was never on hand when his ideas were put to the test, though he did see a lot of action over the years.

I smiled grimly. "Six hours of good weather and a way to deal with the Royal Navy. General Ney was telling me today they are your main obstacle, and believe me, I can tell you firsthand, they *are* formidable."

Jomini leaned forward, warming to the topic. "Yes, yes, I agree, and that is a problem to be worked out by the combined French and Spanish navies. But even without invading, our presence here on the coast forces them to react to us and change their strategy."

"Yes. It's quite an undertaking. I have to admit, I'd love to see it happen," I said.

Ney and Jomini exchanged glances.

"Actually, that may be quite possible," Jomini said.

"I'm not sure I know what you mean"

"Join us, Pierre, be a part of this undertaking," Ney interjected quietly.

My wineglass stopped halfway up to my mouth. I looked around the table. Cushman was no longer paying attention, deep in a conversation with the French colonel about games of chance. Reille, who was sitting across from Cushman, was listening to our conversation but hadn't said a word. It was quite possibly the first time he had ever sat down to dinner with his general, and he was probably wondering why he was there.

I finished taking the sip and carefully placed the glass on the table. "Just what do you mean? What are you offering and why?"

"I am prepared to offer you a commission in the French Army as a full lieutenant, with promotion to captain just before the army prepares to invade England. You would be on my staff as an aide-de-camp. As for why, because you are fluent in both French and English, have nothing but enmity for the English and are intelligent. I would make you a captain because it would give you more authority parlaying with the English and interrogating English prisoners." Ney said.

Stunned, I looked at him to see if was joking. He was not.

"But General, my military experience is rather limited," I said, rather weakly.

Ney smiled, perhaps sensing victory. "That is why Captain Reille is here. He would take you under his wing, teach you the ins and outs of command and of being an infantry officer. There is an opening for an officer in his company, and you would be on loan from my staff until the invasion is imminent. Jomini would help fill out your education, both through recommending works to read —his own included—and through discussions several times a week."

"But I am American, not French." I was protesting, but at the same time I sat up straighter and leaned forward eagerly.

"That does not matter to me. You are a man of quality. We have many foreigners in our ranks, from many countries, including Jomini here. He is from Switzerland. And besides, you are half French, though I would make this offer even if you weren't."

I was having trouble finding objections to the offer.

"Why should I fight for France?"

This question was clearly anticipated. "Why not? Many Frenchmen fought for the independence of your nation, like the Marquis de Lafayette. France went bankrupt supporting your revolution, which made France ripe for its own. One good turn deserves another, perhaps? Your father was even born here; in a sense you would be returning to fight for your fatherland. It's not as if I am asking you to fight for an enemy nation—France is your country's oldest ally. And our foe is yours, Pierre."

I was still confused. "General Ney, you're offering me a great deal, considering you've just met me. There must be French officers who speak English who would be suitable as aides-de-camp for you, without the risk of taking in a foreigner you first laid eyes on today."

"I am a quick judge of character. A general has to be," Ney said. "I think you would make an excellent officer, motivated to do his job and able to think on his feet. Yes, there are French officers in my corps who speak English, but you are an American, which means you understand the English better than a typical Frenchman—your country was English not that long ago. As for taking a risk, the invasion isn't for some months, perhaps longer. My officers and I will be able to evaluate you in the coming months. If I've made a mistake, I'll find out and we'll part company, no harm done."

He paused to take a sip of wine. "This is an unusual opportunity and I decided to seize it before you leave, perhaps on another ship where you don't belong." I didn't even deny that last assertion. He was right.

"Just think of the tales that will be told of you back home when this is over. Think of the adventure you can relate to your grandchildren and how posterity will view you," Jomini interjected —he seemed to be always thinking of posterity and assuming everyone shared his long-term vanity.

My ties to home were broken, my prospects there were slim to say the least, and my most recent venture was at the bottom of the ocean. Why not indeed?

I was about to answer when Ney shook his head. "Don't give me your answer tonight, no matter what it is. Sleep and tell me tomorrow."

With that, a servant came in with pipes and brandy. While I rarely touched tobacco, I did that night.

"Not as good as ours," Cushman said to me, almost wistful.

"How your cargo would have been welcome in Boulogne," Ney said as he lit his, wisps of smoke drifting lazily in front of him. It was as if he understood Cushman's lament.

We finished our pipes, then Ney excused himself, saying he had to check on the dispositions of troops and meet with some local officials. He left, accompanied by Jomini.

By torchlight, Reille guided Cushman and me back to the inn. Before retiring, we asked to check on the rest of our crew.

CHAPTER 4

The men were in good spirits, sharing several bottles of cheap wine with some French soldiers around a fire when we checked on them.

"When are we shipping out again, gentlemen?" they asked us.

Cushman shook his head. "I don't know, lads, but keep your eyes open and your wits about you until then. It should be soon—will be soon, I hope."

The men had been drinking a while but hadn't completely lost their wits. One of them, Sherman, looked at me across the fire, squinting to get a better look.

"Why Mr. Burns, that almost looks like one of them Frenchie uniforms. What, did ya go and sign up?" He and several of the men laughed uproariously at this.

My expression must have said something, because before I could say anything, Cushman spoke up.

"We had supper with a bigwig French general tonight and they dug out some fancy clothes for us to wear. It seems the best they could come up with for Mr. Burns was that uniform. How does he look? Makes you want to salute him and parlay fransay, eh?"

The men thought this great fun and started laughing again while I grinned, trying to make light of the whole affair. One of the sailors jumped up and gave me a drunken salute.

Cushman had accepted a bottle from one of the sailors and was taking a drink, but I noticed him peering at me closely over the bottle. I wasn't sure how much I had given away in the moment after the sailor's comment. I continued to laugh with the sailors and also accepted a drink from the bottle being passed around.

"Well, they may have given me someone's old uniform, but Mr. Cushman got some fancy clothes. I don't think he's ever been so well-dressed in his life, just feel that material!"

After a few more minutes I was ready to make my excuses and leave. "I'm going to get back to the room and go to sleep, Cushman. Goodnight. I'll ask Captain Reille to send a man back with a torch to get you." I started to walk away from the fire. Reille was waiting nearby with a torch.

Unfortunately, Cushman quickly said his farewells to the men and ran to catch up. We walked in silence up the hill into the walled town and through the dark streets, just Reille's flickering torch to guide us.

Once back in our room, it seemed Cushman wasn't ready to sleep, either.

"What's going on, Pierre? I saw your expression at Sherman's comments. What did I miss in that long talk you had with the general?" I could barely see Cushman's expression in the light of the single candle we had lit in the room, but there seemed to be genuine concern in it—a rare thing.

Out with it, no sense in avoiding it, I remember thinking to myself. I was also thinking maybe he would say something that would help me make a decision, bring up some point I hadn't thought of.

"Ney offered me a position as a French officer. I would be a captain once the invasion started. This uniform, or one like it, would be mine." Straightforward answer, though I wondered what the reaction would be. I expected anger, shock, or some kind of emotional outburst. Instead, Cushman was calm. Surprise, perhaps, disappointment, yes, but no anger or sense of betrayal was immediately evident in his countenance.

"That could be conceived of as treason, joining the armed forces of another country," he said quietly.

Treason. That was something I didn't expect. "How so? France is not at war with the United States. I would be fighting England, which our country fought to get its independence. Besides, I haven't even said I was going to do it, only that I was offered the position."

Cushman was visibly relieved. "Good, I'm glad you turned it down."

Now I was getting annoyed. "I also didn't say I had turned Ney down, only that I was offered the position. I am to give him my answer tomorrow."

"Surely you're not considering it?" Cushman asked, finally allowing an expression of shock to creep into his face.

"Yes, I'm considering it. I admit it's rather sudden—to say the least—but it is also a unique opportunity, certainly it's a once in a lifetime offer. Think of it. In the morning I'm on a ship that's forced to run from a British frigate. We're attacked and run aground, wash up on the shores of France, and later that night I'm offered a military position in the French army training to invade England." Cushman was listening silently. "And you know how I feel about the English, Mr. Cushman."

Cushman nodded, but took his time before answering. He was surprised by this turn of events and was stepping cautiously.

"Even if it's not treason, you would be turning your back on your homeland to serve in the army of another country, perhaps never to see home again, possibly to die for another country. What would your family think?" Very still in his chair, Cushman watched me carefully as he spoke.

"My family is mostly dead, you know that. My mother was French, she would probably approve. I never knew my father, but I think he would understand my motivation if I accepted the position." I sat down at the table opposite Cushman and poured a glass of wine from the jug on the table.

"And your shipmates? What of us? And your life at sea? You've barely been a ship's officer a year. Just because we've lost the *Bedford* doesn't mean your career is over. On the contrary, you're now an experienced junior officer. You could get another position and it wouldn't be dependent on family connections with the Captain." Cushman's last remark sounded blunt and cutting, but it wasn't meant to be. That was just his nature.

"My contract ended when the ship sank. If we were in trouble or facing some kind of danger, then I wouldn't consider abandoning you, but as it is, it's every man for himself. The remainder of the crew will likely separate, go their own ways looking for their next ship. Possibly go to a French port looking for an American ship, and if you don't find any, then where? On to

England to find a ship, right? Maybe you'd even sign on to an English ship?" Cushman nodded in agreement.

"No thank you, I'd take my chances here or try to find my way back home before doing that."

This plainly was not going the way Cushman intended and he scowled.

"I could order you to go with us, Pierre."

I was flabbergasted. "Order me? You could try for all the good it would do you. If I go with you, it'll be because I want to, just as I'll stay if I want to. We have no ship, you have no commission." All I could think was that he was just an old, resentful, stranded sailor with no power to order anyone anymore.

Cushman stood up angrily, knocking over his chair. "Damn you, Burns! You're still under my command and will obey any order I give!"

"Your command ended when our boat landed on that beach." I was on my feet now too. My blood was up now and I wasn't going to put up with anything from Cushman, especially an order.

Coming round the table, Cushman stood in front of me. "I could have the men hogtie you for the trip tomorrow."

I chuckled mirthlessly. "Try it and I'll gut you or anyone else who tries to touch me. Besides, try explaining to the French why the man Ney has offered a position has suddenly been tied up and is being forced to leave. You can't even speak their language. I could tell them I discovered you're an English spy and that's why you tied me."

Clenching his fists, Cushman stood staring at me in the dark, with the single candle creating sinister shadows on the walls.

I took a step back and shrugged. "Besides, as I said, I'm not sure what I'm going to do, this whole thing is so sudden. Let me sleep on it."

While he looked like he was ready to argue some more, Cushman nodded reluctantly.

I headed towards the door. "I'm just going to get some fresh air outside the inn before trying to sleep." Cushman started to join me but I waved him back. I didn't want his company. "No, I won't be long. I just need a few minutes alone before trying to sleep."

40

I lit a small candle on a brass holder and left the room, working my way back towards the main room of the inn. A fire was lit in the stone fireplace and I noticed a few tables were still occupied, one by what appeared to be civilians, the other by a few French officers. I blew my candle out, left it on a table by the door and stepped outside.

It was a beautiful night, quite clear, with a spangle of stars above. I looked both ways down the darkened street and knew I wouldn't be wandering anywhere. I would get lost. I just wanted to think. So much had transpired that day and the offer by Ney was so unexpected, yet compelling. It was nothing I'd ever imagined myself doing.

The door opened behind me. I turned, ready to tell Cushman to get back to the room, but it wasn't Cushman, it was Reille.

"Good evening, Captain Reille," I said, wondering what he was doing. He must have been part of that group of officers talking at one of the tables.

"Good evening, Monsieur Burns, almost good morning in fact. It must be near midnight." I saw him smile in the darkness. "I imagine you must be having trouble sleeping after the day you've had and General Ney's offer."

I chuckled. "That is an understatement that would be worthy of an Englishman." I wondered if he were simply chatting politely on his way back to his barracks or if he were trying to figure out what the American was going to do. After all, if I said yes, I would be under his tutelage and command.

"Not that it's my business of course, but it seems to me you are thinking of accepting the offer, otherwise you would have said no outright. I watched you, you were trying to find reasons to say no and unable to come up with any. Any ally is welcome, especially one who could be useful when we invade England, but I think such an offer would not be considered by the average man thrown in such a situation, to be so far from home and to accept the offer of a complete stranger to join an army that until that morning you had only the vaguest of ideas existed."

I could deny none of what he said.

"Are you running to or from something, Monsieur? I understand you dislike the English, but is that enough to turn your world upside down?"

"It's one reason. It certainly makes my decision easier. Fighting the English has been in the back of my mind since I was a child and is one reason I signed up on the ship, though I never imagined it would lead me to this. And how upside down would my world be? My father was killed by the English. My mother, French at her core, died of disease, as did my wife. In some ways I've been looking for a home, maybe for something larger than myself, for several years now." I shivered. It was getting chillier.

Reille nodded. "I understand looking for something larger than oneself. Certainly the army, especially this army, is larger than any one person—except possibly Napoleon Bonaparte. Just don't lose yourself in the process." Reille looked at his watch in the faint light. "I must check on the sentries and the men before going to bed. Goodnight, Burns." With that, he started to walk down the road.

"Captain Reille," I called to him quietly and he stopped and turned. "What is your first name?"

"André."

"Good night, André, and thank you."

"Good night, Pierre." André started walking briskly down the street to check on his sentries. I stood alone, looking at the stars, wondering at the speed of it all. Even twenty years later I marvel at it, both at Ney's snap decision to offer me a commission and that I accepted so quickly. It all happened in barely a day.

I was looking for something greater than myself and knew right away I'd found it. Ney saw a man in search of a cause, in search of a purpose. He seized on that need and gave purpose to me. From that day on I never turned my back on that cause, even when I left France for good eleven years later—even today as I write these words.

I went back inside and went to bed, fully expecting to lay awake all night thinking of my decision, but the events of the day caught up to me and in moments I was asleep.

CHAPTER 5

May 12, 1804
Montreuil, France

The next morning, Cushman and I ate breakfast in silence in the main room of the inn and meandered around the camp. We separated not long after. He went to check in on the men while I wandered around the town, the citadel and the camp.

It was another clear, sunny day and I wanted to see more of my surroundings.

The ramparts completely enclosed the town and had sentries on them, though no one approaching Montreuil would have got anywhere near the village itself because of the camp around it, which held many more soldiers than the few hundred villagers. The view from the walls of the surrounding gently rolling hills was stunning.

I was back in my clothes from the ship, which I found waiting for me when I woke up. Reille's extra uniform had been given back to him. I wondered if its loan was Ney's idea, to encourage me in my decision, which, as I thought back to our meeting and ride from the beach, must have occurred to him early on.

I wandered through the citadel and the camp outside the walls, talking to soldiers and officers alike. They told me that while Montreuil was Ney's headquarters, his 20,000 men were in semi-permanent camps throughout the area, between there and the village Étaples, about seven miles down the Canche River. Ney had focused the entire area on training the men for the invasion of England.

THE EMPEROR'S AMERICAN

The camp was more like a small city, and just one of many along the coast. There were regularly plotted rows of white wooden huts and straight roads between them which even had street signs, usually the name of a famous battle, sometimes of a city or a famous soldier. At some of the intersections were ten- or fifteen-foot high wooden columns surrounded by low fences on which were placed several tricolor flags. At the top was a bust, I presumed of First Consul Bonaparte.

Spirits were high, especially when the prospect of action came up. Like all soldiers, they hated inactivity, and waiting was the hardest part. The army was made up in large part of conscripts and drew upon all levels of society. Though conscripts could pay another to take their place, only the highest strata of society could afford to do so—and as the years went by the prices rose ever higher.

There were cook fires everywhere, as meals were being prepared. Some of the *vivandières* were collecting laundry. Many of the soldiers were cleaning their weapons. There is no activity a soldier hates more, yet is more important.

I watched the soldiers being drilled by their officers, learning drill movements through constant repetition so they would become second nature. Some units practiced aiming and firing their muskets without any ammunition—dry firing. Lead and gunpowder were expensive and weren't always available for live firing, which was generally only done once or twice a week.

Surprisingly, few people questioned my presence. Some had heard of the American who accompanied Ney back to camp the day before, while others just accepted my company.

Some of the older men, enlisted and officers alike, had served in America during the Revolution twenty years before, when France sent thousands of soldiers and a large fleet to help us gain independence from the British. These men greeted me warmly, like an old comrade, and spoke fondly of their time in the United States, especially watching the British surrender at Yorktown.

Walking alone through the camp, I felt a sense of camaraderie and purpose, each man a part of something much larger than himself. I suppose it is the same with most armies or other great ventures, but the Grande Armée, then still called the Army of England after its intended purpose, drew you in like no other.

ART MCGRATH

There is nothing like a history of victory and knowing you are led by the greatest general of the age to create something almost unstoppable.

This army of the people was unique among the armies of Europe, which up until the French Revolution had consisted for the most part of small professional armies, often made up of the dregs of society. During the Wars of French Revolution, when France was beset on all sides by countries trying to destroy the Republic, the ragtag peoples' army first learned to hold its own against the professionals, and then consistently beat them, becoming a professional army in its own right. Napoleon took that core of veterans and on the coast, in sight of England, trained them into the greatest army Europe had ever seen.

I remember being in awe of some of the men I met. These were not militia coming together for their monthly drills as I remembered from back home. These were consummate, well-ordered professionals, who had fought, worked and trained together for years. If I accepted Ney's commission, I would have to lead some of these men. I wondered if I were up to the task.

For a time I watched fencing and bayonet practice. Noting my interest, several soldiers spoke to me and let me handle their weapons. I felt awkward, especially after watching even some of the privates handle their muskets, which they wielded as easily as I did a foil. The musket was five feet of steel and wood that weighed ten pounds. Add a twelve inch bayonet and you have a long weapon, taller than most of the men who wielded them.

Embarrassed, I handed the weapon back, but my efforts had earned me compliments and slaps on the back, with no suggestion of condescension.

"You would learn quickly, Monsieur," one grizzled old sergeant said with a wide smile. "And there's nothing like aiming at a redcoat to encourage you!"

It was around noon. I slowly made my way back towards the barracks where my shipmates were staying. I found them gathered with Cushman. Reille was there too.

"There you are," Reille said when he saw me. "General Ney has arranged for transportation to Boulogne for you and your men. There is a convoy of wagons preparing to go. Meet them at the north end of town in fifteen minutes."

Before I could say anything, he turned and headed back into town. I wondered if Ney had changed his mind, and decided to say nothing.

"Well, it looks like you might not have to make that decision after all," Cushman said, watching Reille leave.

"So it seems," I said quietly. I felt disappointment in my gut, more than I would have thought. "Let's get going, Obadiah."

The men gathered their few belongings from the barracks. All anyone had were the clothes on their backs and whatever they had on them when they left the ship, mostly a few weapons, which the French had allowed us to keep. Besides my former Captain's pistol, I had a knife that had belonged to my father and a crucifix my mother had given me, which she insisted I always keep on me.

Dead several years, I still respected her wishes.

We made our way through the camp towards the northern approach to the village. There the convoy of mostly empty wagons gathered to make the trip to Boulogne and possibly beyond.

Reille was there and directed us to several wagons. The convoy was under the command of a gruff lieutenant who must have been fifty years old and looked like he never took his old crumpled uniform off, not even to bathe. He was yelling at his civilian drivers to line their wagons up. He gave us barely a glance except to make sure we were in our vehicles.

There was a clattering of horses' hooves from the rear of the column as Ney and several aides, including Jomini, rode up. The old lieutenant stopped yelling to salute Ney, who returned the salute and addressed me.

"Burns, sorry to cut this so close, I was delayed inspecting some of the units. I assume you have considered my offer?" He patted his horse, calming it after their ride.

I climbed out of the wagon and stood by Ney's horse.

"Yes, General Ney. I accept."

"Excellent!" Ney's horse whinnied and raised its head a bit at its master's tone. "Short and to the point, I like that. I think we both have chosen wisely." He turned to Reille. "Captain Reille! Burns is now under your command, as we discussed. Start teaching him the basics of command, and give him some manuals to read." Addressing me again, he continued, "I am off to my camp at Étaples and then possibly to Boulogne. I'll be back in several days and we can talk more about your duties. *Au revoir.*" He turned his horse and started heading down the road towards the coast and Étaples.

Jomini trotted his horse over, took a package out of his saddle bag and threw it to me.

"I had a feeling you would say yes. A present to start your education. The more you learn about war, the more useful you will be on the battlefield. We'll talk more when I get back with the general." Then he too spurred his horse and galloped to catch up with Ney.

I opened the package. It was a book written by Jomini about war.

While I was looking at the book, Cushman got off the wagon and walked over to me. "What was that about? A parting gift?"

I had forgotten all about Cushman and the men during the exchange. I turned to him. "No, it's a gift to welcome me aboard. I'm staying."

For a moment Cushman was angry. "What? Why? You can't!"

"Yes, I can. You already know why. We discussed it last night. There's no point in arguing. I'm staying. Wish me luck, Obadiah, and let me say goodbye to the men." I held out my hand to him.

For a long moment he looked at me and the proffered hand, then took it. "Good luck, Pierre." I wasn't sure he entirely meant it.

I thanked him and went to the wagons, and said goodbye to each of the men. None of those who survived from the ship were my close friends, but they were comrades and we had shared many privations and close calls. They had known all along I wasn't a seaman at heart but had put up with me just the same. None of them questioned my decision. They simply wished me good luck.

One of the sailors handed me Captain Rankin's pistol, which I had left in the boat and forgotten. It felt important to have it with me now that I might need it.

The old French lieutenant yelled from the front of the convoy and the wagons and carts got under way. I stood and watched them leave with a lump in my throat. I waved to them, hoping their next voyage was better than their last and thinking my future —even more than theirs—was an uncharted sea.

"Lieutenant Burns." There was a voice next to me, calling me out of my reverie. "Pierre." I turned to see Reille next to me.

"What did you say?"

A smile spread across his face. "I called you Lieutenant Burns. It sounds strange, doesn't it? Get used to it. Let's go."

We walked along the walls of the town through the streets of the camp to one of the whitewashed huts. It was Reille's quarters, where the three officers for his company were billeted. It was to become my home for over a year.

A short, pudgy, rather nervous civilian waited there. He proved to be a tailor, there to take my measurements for a uniform. He left as nervous as he had been when we got there, after saying my uniforms would be ready in a week.

Reille watched him leave with a bemused expression on his face. "Probably an English spy."

I didn't reply, but wondered if he were serious.

"In the meanwhile, my uniform you wore last night is yours. I took the liberty of putting your insignia of rank on it. Next, we pick out a sword for you."

I dressed in the blue trousers, white waist coat, and red-trimmed blue coat of a French officer of the Sixième Légèr—the Sixth Light Infantry Regiment—which I would wear while training with the company. A black felt bicorn hat, with a round blue, white and red cockade, topped off my regalia. There was a single silver tassel hanging off the center of each black leather boot. I wore a sword belt in loops in my trousers, but there was no place to carry my pistol other than to stick it in the belt, which was somewhat unwieldy.

"If you don't want to carry that in camp you can lock it in the strongbox," Reille said, indicating a large, locked box along one wall to put our valuables. I locked the pistol in there but kept my crucifix on me. My father's knife, in its rather rough sheath, I attached to my belt under my jacket, out of sight.

I turned to Reille, who said I looked almost complete. The high collar of the jacket prevented slouching and made me feel the part as much as anything else. I looked at myself in a cheap mirror in a corner of the hut. I gasped, wondering who I was looking at. Clothes may not make the man, as Shakespeare said, but they help. My stubble from the ship was gone, my hair trimmed. My face was framed by the blue jacket, high red collar and black hat. I looked different, I felt like a soldier. I think it will always remain the image I have of myself when I think back on that period.

Before we left the barracks Reille explained the basics of saluting and watched me practice until he was satisfied. Fortunately, I was familiar with saluting from my time in the militia at home, though precision there had been somewhat lacking.

We walked back into town and into the citadel to a heavily guarded stone armory, newer than the rest of the buildings. There, I was given a number of swords to choose from.

"I would have picked one out for you, but a sword is very personal. Better you find one that fits you," Reille said.

I had fenced at home but was far from being an expert. I hefted several weapons, slashing, thrusting and feeling their balance in my hand until I finally chose one I liked, a straight infantry officer's epee.

Reille showed me how to hook it to my belt and then the basics of walking with it dangling at my side, bumping my leg and hitting me.

"Well, now you look the part anyway," Reille said, looking me over from head to toe. "It'll take awhile before you fully act it. Let's go introduce you to the regiment's officers."

CHAPTER 6

Outskirts of Montreuil

Outside of town, in one of the huts in the camp, the commander of the 6th Légèr—Colonel Jean-Gregoire-Barthelemy Rouger de Laplane—was meeting with some of his officers, including his three battalion commanders.

The men looked up when we entered the hut and stopped what they were doing. On the table was a map they evidently had been studying earlier. They watched me with undisguised curiosity.

Reille saluted. "Colonel Laplane, this is Lieutenant Pierre Burns, the American whom General Ney has taken on as an officer."

Colonel Laplane returned the salute and looked at me. I made my first salute as sharply as I could. "Bonjour, Colonel Laplane." I held the salute while he studied me, hands clasped behind his back, looking severe in his immaculate blue uniform, hair somewhat long and pulled back in a queue.

Around forty years old, Laplane was a veteran soldier, whose service extended before the Revolution to the army of Louis XVI. He was probably wondering why Ney had saddled him with me. He returned my salute.

"Bonjour, Lieutenant Burns. You've had an eventful few days, I hear, going from ship's officer, to castaway, to an officer in the French Army." He smiled. "Welcome aboard. I hope we can keep your life as interesting as you're accustomed to."

I relaxed. "Not that interesting, if you please, *mon colonel.*" Laplane and the other officers chuckled. "Unless we are ready to invade England, that is. That kind of excitement I am ready for."

The colonel nodded approvingly. "I hope we'll find lots of work for you then. It shouldn't be for some months, however. Let me introduce you to my officers."

The commander of the third battalion, my unit, was Chef de Bataillon, or Major, Jean Ledoyen.

Ledoyen was rugged looking, less refined than his commander, but a confident looking man nonetheless. Short and stocky, with graying hair, despite appearing no older than thirty, he moved like a fighter as he came over to greet me. He had the grip of a fighter, too, which I withstood without complaint.

"We'll be seeing a lot more of each other in the coming months, and I'll make sure you earn every bit of your pay," Ledoyen said, not as a threat, simply as a statement. "You'll have to tell me about America sometime; I've always wanted to go there."

I nodded. "Gladly, Monsieur."

Laplane continued. "Before you came in we had been discussing England. Though things can change between now and the invasion, right now, if we invade, we are to be assigned to the far left flank of the army, both circling to approach London from the west and to screen the army from interference from the flanks." Laplane indicated London and our route on a map of southern England. Leaning over to look at the map, I nodded, thinking I could add little with my limited tactical experience.

"How do you think the English people will react to having the French Army on their soil, in their villages?" Laplane asked, looking at me from across the table.

I thought for a moment. "With barely disguised hostility. We can't expect much cooperation from most ordinary people."

"Will the *rosbifs* fight? The ordinary people, I mean," asked Ledoyen. "We understand they have organized many militia units in the towns along the coast."

It was the first time I had ever heard the French nickname for the English. The French often referred to the English as *rosbifs*— roast beefs, just as the English called them frogs. An odd set of dueling food nicknames.

I considered his question and thought back to stories I heard and read about the American Revolution.

"I can't predict with certainty, but if unmolested I think they might leave the army alone. They have an innate sense of respect for authority and if the French Army is the local authority, they will be treated with respect. The English upper classes are not well loved by those below them—the ordinary people might welcome us to an extent." I said, looking around the table. The regimental commander caught a nuance the others missed.

"You said if unmolested. And if they are mistreated?" Laplane asked.

I looked at him squarely. "Then we'll be shot at from every tree and rock, like my people did to them at Lexington and Concord."

"And the response to that?" Ledoyen asked.

"The response to that will be to kill every Englishman we see. Even I don't relish that thought," I answered calmly.

Laplane and Ledoyen exchanged glances. "Then we'll have to see it doesn't come to that. The idea of killing militia has no appeal, no challenge to it," Laplane said. He turned to another officer. "Make a note to issue orders before the landing that no civilians are to be harmed. All foodstuffs taken are to be paid for."

That echoed an order Napoleon had already given. He had no intention of letting the army loose to forage and pillage as they had throughout much of the rest of Europe, not while they were on a foreign shore.

I stood and listened for a while longer as the colonel and his staff discussed the tactics needed for protecting the flanks of the attack on London. It was clear they expected to win once they reached English soil; it was also clear they expected the British to fight like the devil.

For the moment, I had nothing more to contribute. I paid attention, trying to absorb as much as possible about my new profession of arms.

During a pause in the discussion, Reille excused us and said he was going to introduce me to the soldiers of our company, the First Company of the Sixth Légèr's Third Battalion, which Reille commanded. It was a company of chasseurs, light infantry who, when they weren't skirmishing, were expected to stand in line and slug it out with lines of enemy infantry—the equivalent of the fusiliers in the line infantry battalions.

In a few minutes we were at the huts that belonged to the company. Soldiers there said the rest of the company had gone to a nearby field to practice drill.

At the practice field, we saw the company's other officer drilling the one hundred forty man company with the assistance of the NCOs. The officer was Sous-lieutenant, or Sub-lieutenant René Monge. He was around my age, tall, with a fair complexion and wisps of blond hair coming out from under his shako. Saluting Reille, he shot me a contemptuous look.

In retrospect, I can't really blame Monge for his attitude. The open officer's slot should have allowed him to move up to the number two slot in the company. Instead, a foreigner who became an officer that very morning was to usurp his place, at least until I permanently assumed my duties as Ney's aide-de-camp, which might not be for some time, unless the invasion commenced sooner than everyone thought.

While I technically outranked him, I was for the moment to defer to Monge for tactical decisions and look to him for assistance in learning my duties. The arrangement galled both of us.

Looking at him, I could tell he would be trouble but kept my own counsel for the moment.

"René, assemble the men in line, at attention," Reille ordered.

Quickly the men were marched in front of us and halted at attention. I examined them closely. Unlike the line infantry, which wore blue coats, white trousers and black bicorn hats, these light infantry wore blue coats with red facings with a white waistcoat underneath, blue trousers and high cylindrical hats called shakos. They wore white cross-belts across their chests, on which was carried their equipment such as bayonets, cartridge boxes and short sabers. Their modified Model 1777 muskets, generally known as Charlevilles after one of the manufacturing depots, gleamed in the sun. They were an efficient looking body of men. Reille addressed them.

"Citizen Soldiers! This is our new officer, Lieutenant Pierre Burns, here from America to help us in our fight against the English. He is helping repay the debt to the thousands of French soldiers who fought for the independence of the United States. *Vive l'America! Vive la France!*" There was an answering cheer of

"*Vive la France*" from the company. "Lieutenant Burns is rather new to that uniform. Try to be gentle with him."

There were a number of guffaws from the ranks at Reille's last comment. He ignored them, which surprised me. The French Army had an attitude towards discipline that took getting used to. Sometimes men would occasionally speak out towards their officers. Even Napoleon wasn't immune if his men thought he was placing himself in danger needlessly.

The officers were expected to earn their soldiers' respect by leading from the front. This was not the English Army, where commissions were often bought; they were assigned by merit, though doubtless most of the company was questioning my merit at that moment.

Reille turned the company back over to Monge and told him to prepare a line combat formation.

"First lesson, Pierre, learning to keep your position in line in a formation," Reille said as the company moved into position. "Remember, not only do you have to keep your position, but you have to ensure the men do as well. Keeping the men lined up shoulder to shoulder is a vital part of your job in combat. If they break formation they become more vulnerable to flanking fire and an enemy counterattack."

With the company lined up, Reille explained where each of us stood. As company commander he stood at the far right of the front line, exposed to enemy fire like any other soldier.

The second command, the full lieutenant—me in this case—stood left center behind the last rank, while the sub-lieutenant stood behind the last rank, right center. Reille was to lead from the front; we were to make sure the men stayed in ranks and didn't bolt. From where I stood there wasn't much to see except the backs of the men in front of me. To see ahead, I had to look over their shoulders.

As the company went through its paces, I stayed in ranks, hardly saying a word. The men had probably done this hundreds, if not thousands of times and they didn't need someone telling them to stay in ranks during his first day on the job.

It was an odd sensation. The unit had a life and spirit of its own which you could feel, a collective morale which rose and fell with circumstances.

The company went through its drills flawlessly, except for the newcomer, of course, who knew he had a lot of catching up to do.

After the line formation, Reille led us into an attack column formation, a much narrower and longer formation meant to punch through enemy lines by concentrating tremendous force on one point of them.

The next day, Reille decided the company needed to go on a cross country march of ten miles. It was the first but far from the last of these long distance marches for me. Sometimes the battalion or even the whole regiment would go on them. On other occasions, we would be part of much larger marches and operations, when the division or even corps would participate, which entailed many thousands of soldiers on the march.

Though I would go on many longer marches in the coming years, none hurt as much as that ten-mile company march. After so long on ship, I was not used to long walks, not to mention I was breaking in new boots.

By the time we got back in the late afternoon, cook fires had already been started. The company was dismissed for the evening meal and I hobbled off to my quarters, to the snickers of some of the men.

I dined with Reille and Monge that night, joined by three officers from another company in the battalion. Over several jugs of wine I regaled them all with the tales of my adventures leading to my arrival on the shores of France. They responded by saluting my good fortune, all except Monge, who glowered at me over his drink. Not only did I annoy Monge because I took the place he felt was his, but he also thought my origins beneath contempt. A member of the pre-Revolution nobility whose family returned to France under Napoleon's amnesty, he had not shaken the sense he was superior to the rest of us because of his birth.

CHAPTER 7

The next several days were very similar: drill, bayonet practice, drill, fencing, drill, dry firing of muskets, drill, live firing of muskets, drill, weapons cleaning, drill, five-mile hike, drill, inspections, drill, meals, drill, sleep, and yet more drill.

Drill was generally split between company level maneuvers and battalion drill, with the occasional regimental and brigade exercises. Not only is drill important to inculcating automatic obedience to orders, which is vital to any military organization, but the maneuvers themselves are essential to success on the battlefield. A unit must be able to quickly respond to orders and get in a specific formation without hesitation: sometimes a three-deep line, sometimes a column, sometimes a square, depending on the dispositions of the enemy and the terrain. With cavalry charging upon a battalion of infantry, hesitation in forming square could mean the destruction of the entire unit.

In any formation, the men marched shoulder to shoulder, while we, their officers, looked to their alignment and morale. It was a daunting task, but slowly I was learning to march as a soldier, all the while trying to keep an eye on the men and my surroundings, and an ear open for commands on bugles or drums.

All my senses were put to the test.

Some days we practiced skirmishing, a tactic small units often used to delay larger enemy units. Skirmishing would be familiar to my American readers. The men, often working in pairs to protect the other while reloading, were a yard or more apart and used every bit of available cover and concealment to protect themselves while firing at the enemy. Though each battalion had a company of *voltigeurs*, infantry who specialized in skirmishing, all infantrymen were trained to perform this task.

Some days I spent time in the ranks drilling as an ordinary soldier, learning all the drill movements. Other days we would put our weapons aside and picked up shovel and axe, building fortifications and roads. Ney believed the infantry must be able to do its own engineering out in the field and not depend on engineers.

At night, my time was often spent reading the *Règlement* —the Manual—of 1791, which laid out official French tactics for the infantry, as well as various treatises on which formation was better for the attack, the line or the column. These arguments had raged within the French Army for decades, especially after France lost the Seven Years War—the French and Indian War as we call it. There is nothing like defeat to make an army stop and think about what it did wrong.

The argument between column and line was never completely put to rest, though officially in the French Army, columns were for maneuvering, lines were for fighting.

I had never realized how much there is to learn about the art of waging war. It's not as simple as killing the other fellow, though in the end, that is the basic of it.

Other manuals I read were those on martial courtesy, drill, tactics, and military history, as well as Jomini's book on military operations. The importance of the infantry was stressed in all my studies. While cavalry might be more glamorous and artillery more dramatic with the noise and smoke it makes—not to mention carnage—in the end it is the infantryman, the *fantassin*, that is the backbone of any army. It is infantry that takes and holds territory. All other branches are there to support the *fantassin*, however much that might pain an elegantly uniformed hussar or cuirassier.

Ney himself had written a training paper for officers of his corps. My aching feet after one march screamed at a line in Ney's paper, that success or failure depended on quick, skillful marches. The French Army was known for marching farther and faster than any other army, and it never failed to live up to that reputation.

I didn't either, but I had to drag my feet along kicking and screaming until I was in better condition.

A few days into my training, Monge was showing me how to change the company's direction of march while in line and was getting frustrated at what he considered my slow pace of learning the movement. Reille was not present and Monge had me all to himself.

"Clumsy idiot!" Monge shouted at me, as I again gave the wrong command. "Don't they teach you to listen in America?!"

I was mortified. This was not a private rebuke—he said it in front of the entire company of one hundred forty men. It was humiliating and a violation of one of the most basic rules of leadership: praise in public, punish in private. Public dressing downs should only be done on rare occasions, and an officer should never rebuke a fellow officer in front of the men. He was going to affect my ability to lead the men by his outburst if I didn't react.

"Lieutenant Monge, thank you for your help, but this is neither the time nor place." I thought perhaps I could direct him back onto our training. Unfortunately, he was having too much fun for that. For days he had used every excuse to harass me. This was a God-given opportunity for him.

"Are you afraid of a little humiliation in front of the men? They might as well learn the kind of man you are now before you end up leading them into battle—if one could call you a man!"

This was getting out of hand and I had to do something. Unfortunately I made a bad choice. I tried to pull rank.

"Sub-Lieutenant, we are going to continue our duties. Now!" My command was barely above a whisper.

The expression on his face was shock mixed with incredible mirth. Bursting into laughter, he could barely speak. Even some of the men started to laugh.

"Listen to the mouse squeak! Don't let that uniform fool you into thinking you're a man, you little son of a whore! I wonder, did your mother even remember which of her customers your father was?" He laughed uproariously at that as I took several steps towards him, anger starting to well up in me.

Monge stopped laughing and looked at me with a look of utter contempt on his face. "Do you intend to use that on me?"

I was confused until I realized one hand was on my sword. Not knowing what to say, I stood there practically shaking with rage, my hand holding the hilt of my unsheathed sword in a death grip.

"I think perhaps we need weapons training today. You actually haven't had any practice with that sword," Monge said quietly.

Turning to a sergeant, he dismissed the company.

"I think we can practice over there," Monge said pointing to a nearby clump of trees.

We walked over to a dirt patch near the trees, took our coats off and hung them on a branch of the tree, then drew our swords.

"Of course, in battle, you wouldn't take your coat off, but no sense getting blood on it during an exercise," Monge said grinning.

We began, thrusting and parrying, testing each other's skill. After a few minutes, it was clear Monge was a far better swordsman than I and was easily starting to drive me back. Many of the men were watching, though mostly from a distance, pretending they were attending to other duties. The audience did not seem to bother Monge—no doubt he thought it better they were there to watch my humiliation.

Already I had received a few nicks without so much as scratching Monge. It was clear he was toying with me.

"Had enough, American?" he asked, enjoying himself.

"No," I said, lunging and slashing, both of which he parried and blocked easily. I feinted and managed to nick his arm, drawing blood.

A few of the men let out some calls of encouragement, which we both heard. I think that infuriated him more than the blood I drew.

"No more games," he growled, attacking swiftly. He drove me back easily. I no longer tried to counterattack, as I was doing all I could to block his blows. I stumbled over a root and as I was recovering, he cut my forearm and knocked the sword out of my hand. He punched me in the face with the guard of his sword, knocking me to the ground. Moving to stand over me, his sword tip hovered between my breast and chin, about six inches away.

"So sorry, I tripped." Standing over me, Monge looked at me smiling wickedly.

I may not have been the swordsman he was, but I had learned some dirty tricks back home, not to mention in more than a year on ship.

In my right hand I had already clutched a handful of dirt and sand, which I threw full in his face. He screamed, his eyes closing involuntarily. I rolled under his sword and, in a move I learned from Cushman, kicked his legs out from under him, leaping on him as he fell to the ground, driving an elbow into his sternum to knock the wind out him. As he gasped for breath, I held his sword hand down with my knee, my other knee on his chest. I had already drawn my knife from the small of my back and held it to his throat, the edge digging into the soft skin there.

I whispered quietly, just loud enough for him to hear me. "If you ever speak about my mother again, I will scalp you and slit your throat—in that order. Do you understand?"

I had his attention now. Terrified, he nodded desperately. I had never scalped anybody nor even seen it done, but many Europeans seemed to think it was a skill Americans acquired at birth, and it made a good threat.

Suddenly, someone pulled me off Monge and struck me in the face with great force, sending me flying to the ground. It was our *Chef de Bataillon*, Ledoyen. As Monge moved to rise, Ledoyen knocked the sword out of his hand then kicked him in the chest, sprawling him on his back.

"Pick up your weapons, sheath them and put on your jackets." Ledoyen ordered quietly. Monge and I caught each other's eye, both afraid to get up.

"Do it, on your feet." Ledoyen said again. He then ordered the soldiers mingling nearby to disperse.

Dressed, we walked under the nearby tree where Ledoyen was waiting. We stood at attention as he looked coldly at us.

"What was that about? What an honor you've been given in such a short time, American, and you seem ready to throw it away brawling. What could be worth it? And you, Monge, what disgrace you seem intent on bringing to your family. Why?"

Neither of us spoke.

"Say something, or I'll have you before the colonel and out of those uniforms in fifteen minutes. Junior officers fighting in front of the men is not behavior I will tolerate." Anger was evident in his quiet voice.

I spoke before Monge could. "It was training, Monsieur. The lieutenant felt I needed remedial sword training. He was right, look at how many cuts I have."

The slightest expression of surprise crossed Ledoyen's face. Clearly he hadn't expected this answer.

"Training? How is it you were on top of him with a knife at his throat?"

"I got the better of him. I was showing him some tricks I learned on ship, what to do if someone disarms you." I was starting to warm to my story.

Ledoyen wasn't convinced. "Is this true, Lieutenant Monge? This was weapons training?"

Monge hesitated before answering. "Yes, Monsieur, we stopped the drill and came over here to practice with our swords. Burns' technique is raw and needs improvement but his last move showed quick thinking."

While Ledoyen didn't seem entirely satisfied, there was nothing he could say. He dismissed us to return to our company. As we assembled the company and got into our places, Monge looked at me coldly. The hatred I had seen there earlier was gone but the resentment still lingered. We continued our drill and he drove us hard.

May 19, 1804
Montreuil

Nearly a week after I joined the army, the camp awoke to the sound of cannon fire. We tumbled out of our huts to find bands playing and drummers and buglers sounding assembly.

As we fell into formation, I saw Ney, Jomini and other mounted officers nearby. They had just gotten back from Boulogne with news.

The 5,000 men in the camp around Montreuil fell into a large box formation, facing the center. Ney rode his horse alone into the hollow in the middle of the square. Making a circle, he looked at the soldiers surrounding him.

"Citizen soldiers of the Sixth Corps!" Ney shouted out to us. "Napoleon Bonaparte has accepted the Empire to which the will of the people has called him. A new era starts today and the happiness of France is guaranteed forever! *Vive L'Empereur!*" He reared his horse at this and the cry slowly began to be repeated, louder each time as more soldiers took it up. "*Vive L'Empereur! Vive L'Empereur! Vive L'Empereur!*"

I stood there, at first saying nothing, the cry thundering in my ears. While I knew this had been a possibility when I agreed to join the army, I was still torn. I was an American, from a country with no king. Now, I was part of an army serving an emperor elected by the people. It was a contradiction I was wrapping my head around.

I noticed I wasn't the only silent person. There were a few grumblings; I heard references to the Republic and complaints about the title "emperor," mostly from older soldiers who had fought during the Revolution.

Ney called for silence and signaled to drummers to sound attention. Slowly, the clamor died down and he spoke again.

"We will now swear an oath, which will bind our hearts to the father of our nation. We swear obedience to the constitution of the Empire and faithfulness to the Emperor! We swear it!" At the last words, Ney unsheathed his sword and thrust it towards the sky.

Thousands of voices echoed Ney's. "*Nous le jurons!* We swear it!"

Cannon began to fire off in salutes and bands played "La Marseillaise." Thousands took up the cry, "*Vive L'Empereur!*" again and again.

Even I joined in, caught up in the moment. I had only been in the army a week and in France barely a day beyond that. Some things were taking getting used to, though I had no second thoughts about my decision.

Ney rode off with his staff.

The French senate had declared the empire. The results of the plebiscite were not released until later in the year—3,572,329 voted in favor of Napoleon accepting the crown of an empire, while 2,569 voted no. It's hard to argue with a majority like that.

An officer also announced a new title for Ney: Marshal of the Empire. He was one of eighteen generals who received this title.

THE EMPEROR'S AMERICAN

From now on he would be addressed as *Monsieur le Maréchal* Ney, or Marshal Ney in English.

We were dismissed to march off to training.

The next day I received a message to report to Jomini. Our talks on war were to begin.

I won't reminisce long about my talks with that Swiss soldier. They had little to do with tactics. Jomini was a theorist of war, not a battlefield tactician, as I reminded him on occasion when the shooting started. Our talks were about strategy, the science of war, and the interaction of war, diplomacy and politics. They weren't necessarily something an infantry officer would need to know but a staff officer would, and I was being groomed to be an aide-de-camp for the invasion.

I may not have liked Jomini, but I did learn a lot from him.

"War is just politics by another means," Jomini told me during one of our first sessions. "You should not view it as separate. They may be separate to the soldier fighting on the battlefield but to a general commanding an army, the relationship and the effect they have on each other is obvious. A political blow sometimes can do as much damage as a severe military one, just as a military victory or defeat can have lasting political repercussions. A staff officer often plays in both the political and military realm and can with a word have the same impact as thousands of men. He is also a jack of all trades. Able to ride and fight, fearless in carrying out his commander's orders—stepping into the middle of a battle if necessary if he thinks he can turn a situation around. One moment you may be a courier, the next your general may order you to prepare a defense or lead a battalion or squadron in a charge. You must be ready for literally anything."

The following week, I finally received my own uniforms and coincidently, or not, was called to see Marshal Ney. Instead of going to his headquarters in the chateau, I was told to visit him at his house, a few miles out of town.

It was a gorgeous spring day and I was intent on walking alone. I was now more accustomed to long walks and the thought of a stroll alone was pleasant. Jomini told me to borrow a horse, however. A staff officer always rode, he said, though in reality, I was an odd mixture, neither infantry nor staff officer yet. Be that as it may, Jomini said I should ride and sharpen my skills.

Riding alone was still a wondrous experience. I hadn't really been alone for any length of time in many months, first on ship, then in the midst of the French Army. My horse was a lively roan mare who seemed as delighted by the jaunt as I. Bouncing up and down on my mount, I began to feel the chinstrap of my shako digging into my chin. It was the first day I had worn the tall, cylindrical hat instead of the bicorn, thinking perhaps with its dark green plume it would look more dashing on me as I rode through the country, peasant women admiring me. The price of vanity.

Following the directions I had been given, I rode by houses and fields, with only the occasional soldier in sight. I waved at the farmers.

My vanity was stroked as, riding by a small clump of houses, I noticed a group of girls washing clothes. They looked to be around sixteen or seventeen years old. I slowed down and one waved me over, offering my horse and me a drink of water.

A vivacious lass, she was trying to convince me to follow her to her barn to show me a newborn calf, though her hand on *my* calf convinced me bovines were not on her mind. She had almost convinced me to dismount and accompany her when a grim-faced older woman came out of a nearby house and shouted at the girl.

Seeing the game was up, I thanked her for the water and continued on my way.

Being in no hurry—my orders said to report at my convenience —I dismounted a ways past the village and walked, leading my mount. For the first time in weeks I had time to reflect on the change in my station and my life. It was stunning how quickly my life had changed but what was just as startling to me—and still is— is how readily I accepted the change. Even though I was learning new things everyday about being an officer and living in France, I had rarely felt as at home.

Two things were truly strange and took getting used to, however. The first was the French Republican Calendar. During the Revolution, when God was banned, so was the calendar. Time started over, with the Year I being the start of the Revolution. The weeks grew to ten days and the months were renamed. The new year didn't even fall on the same date every year. Instead of riding out to see Ney on May 29, 1804, my orders said it was the ninth day of Prairial in the Year XII!

Napoleon abolished the system a year and a half after I joined the army, thank God. I was still having trouble fully understanding it.

The other strange thing was speaking French all the time. Even though I had learned it at home, it was not second nature to me and I had rarely spoken it during the previous couple of years. Soon I would be thinking in the language with ease, but it was awkward in the meanwhile.

As I walked my horse, I came upon a small, well-appointed house with a low fence in front of it. A woman was picking flowers in front. This was not a peasant woman. From her dress and mannerisms this was clearly a lady of quality.

"Bonjour, Mademoiselle." I said, bowing. She was the most exquisite thing I had ever seen. I stared in awe, as she gently pushed dark brown curls aside. She appeared to be about my age and had the most dazzling of smiles.

"Bonjour, Monsieur." Green eyes sparkled and the corners of her mouth turned up in a slight, curious smile as she waited for me to speak.

She had to wait, for I was unable to.

"May I help you, Monsieur? You look lost."

"No, Mademoiselle, I am not lost. Forgive my lack of manners. I am Lieutenant Pierre Burns, of the Sixth Léger. I was traveling to Marshal Ney's house when I was struck by your beauty and was unable to continue." I had found my voice at last, even if I sounded more than a tad maudlin.

"A young romantic out for a ride in the country." Her laugh was the most beautiful sound I ever heard. "Burns, did you say? Ah, you must be Michel's American."

I must have appeared dumbfounded, for she laughed again. "It seems now I have forgotten my manners. I am Aglaé Ney, Marshal Ney's wife and this is his house. He is inside and is expecting you."

Wife? This graceful flower was the marshal's wife, who moments before I was waxing poetic to? I stood at attention and bowed.

"Please, forgive anything I may have said to offend you, Madame Ney."

Again that beautiful, delicate laugh. "There is nothing to forgive. You were simply complimenting a young lady you met on the side of the road."

The door to the house opened and Ney called me inside for a brief interview in his study. He said so far he had received nothing but good reports about me, and heard I seemed to have an aptitude for soldiering.

"You are learning your trade quickly and are a natural leader. The men like you," Ney said.

He cautioned me against fighting and dueling.

"Not that you would engage in such behavior, Pierre, but just in case." Ney said this levelly but with a hint of amusement in his eye.

In his earlier years, Ney had engaged in a number of duels and fights and understood fighting for one's honor. As a commander, he also understood that discipline comes first and that officers must maintain a level of decorum, though even marshals weren't immune to fighting among themselves.

"No news on the invasion, though it's coming, fear not," Ney said, after I asked if we would be embarking on ships soon. In the meanwhile, we were to practice embarking and disembarking on the ships as part of our training, so when the order came we would be able to embark with ease.

When I left the house I looked for Aglaé and didn't see her. I felt a pang of disappointment.

Upon my return to camp that afternoon, I could not get Aglaé out of my mind and mentioned it to Reille.

"Why, you poor fool. Get over it. If you think Monge is a good swordsman, Ney makes him look like an amateur."

After I told him about the girl in the village, Reille burst into laughter.

"I think we've discovered your problem. When was the last time you were with a woman?"

"Months? Likely a whore in Charleston before we last left the United States." I grinned sheepishly. "At least I think that's where.

I had been drinking quite a bit with some of the ship's officers and had some problems remembering that night."

"Well, my friend, I think we'll have to find somewhere to spend your pay." What a wicked look of amusement he had on his face.

"What, you mean one of those women on the outskirts of camp?" I stammered.

Reille laughed again. I certainly was amusing him, and I wanted nothing more than to punch him at that moment.

"No, not one of those women at the edge of camp—unless you want to catch a disease. You are an officer, Pierre. We can find you, let us say, a somewhat higher quality companion for an evening. We'll have to go to Boulogne for that, however."

He may have only been a captain, but Reille had connections. The next day he was able to get us passes to Boulogne, leaving Monge in charge of the company—to the chagrin of both Monge and the soldiers.

We borrowed horses for the ride and arrived at dusk, pausing to look at the city from the low hills that ringed it and its harbor. It was my first visit to Boulogne, which had been the destination of the *Bedford*. It was the first time I had thought of the *Bedford* in weeks, and I wondered how Cushman and the men were faring.

Looking into the harbor I could see hundreds, perhaps thousands of small vessels. These were the boats and ships which were to carry the army to England. I sat on my horse looking at the ships and then out to sea. Out there was the English coast, faintly visible over the western horizon. I got restless thinking of how close we were, yet what obstacles kept us from getting there. Sensing my impatience, my horse grew fidgety as well, thinking something was afoot.

Reille was next to me on his mount, silently looking in the same direction. With a sigh, I spurred my horse a little more roughly than necessary and shot off down the road.

Once in the city we slowed and threaded through narrow streets. Eventually we came to a large house right on the street, much like the others next to it. There was light coming from the windows, the sound of laughter and talking and music.

Judging by the ease he displayed moving through the place and the greetings he received from the women inside, it was apparent this was not Reille's first trip to this brothel, for brothel it was, though finely furnished and with elegantly dressed ladies. It was all very tasteful, though I think my New World prudery was somewhat shocked. To me, a brothel was supposed to be a dark, hidden place, not a place with music, laughter, refined conversation—and of course exposed flesh, but only enough to titillate. This room was for inspecting the merchandise, not sampling the wares. There were other rooms for that.

Not all brothels in Boulogne were as elegant as Madame Delobel's. We had passed many that were just as I remembered from home. The needs of all ranks were attended to in and around Boulogne. Reille assured me this was the finest to be found.

A few other officers were there in quiet conversations with ladies; they hardly paid us any attention. Seated at several couches were a number of unattended women, who looked at us with a feigned casualness. I felt a nervous spasm in my gut as they watched us.

Some, despite their elegant clothing and makeup, appeared to be rather old, though it was hard to tell in the dim light—yet another reason why these places are generally frequented at night, I suppose. However, several were young and quite striking. One of these waved to Reille and called him by name. She was a stunning blonde, around twenty years of age, with her breasts pushed up for good effect.

We went to her couch, where she sat with another girl. "Bonsoir, André. It has been a long time." The two kissed.

"It has, Lydie." Reille stood back for a moment. "You look well."

Lydie shrugged. "I am well. I'm fortunate to have found Madame Delobel—I could have ended up in a pigsty with every soldier hopping on and off all night for a pittance. It's not a bad living here, and we choose who we see. Who is your friend?"

Reille briefly told her my story and of my three-week-long stint in the French Army.

"He's a bit shy about being here. He got shot with an arrow from Eros over a general's wife yesterday and I thought a visit here might take his mind off her. You should have seen him blush at the mention of this place." Reille laughed.

Lydie smiled at me knowingly. "It's not always easy coming to a place like this, but we all have needs, especially soldiers. I have just the cure for you." She turned slightly and indicated her dusky hued, black-haired companion. In that beautiful face bright blue eyes looked out, so unexpected, they drew you like a moth to a flame. Cleavage shown to full advantage didn't hurt either.

"This is Marie, and like you, she's fairly new here."

Marie stood up somewhat uncertainly. "Bonsoir, Monsieur. Is it true you are from America?"

The way she asked the question made me feel as if whatever I said would be the most important words she had heard. That was her job, but Marie did her job well. She was new enough to the profession that she wasn't too jaded—barely seventeen, and honestly curious.

I forgot Reille and Lydie as Marie and I went to a corner to be alone. I can't remember the details of our conversation but I told her more than I had told any other person since arriving in France, with drinks coming at a slow, steady pace. The drinks were to liven things up, not to get anyone staggering drunk.

At some point, Marie led me to her bedroom. I was surprised how sparsely furnished it was compared to the rest of the house. That didn't matter as we undressed. My only thought was for her, my only desire was for her. I tried to convince myself the look in her eye was because she really wanted me and not just the twenty francs I paid her. Maybe she did.

At dawn I woke up abruptly to someone kicking my foot. It was Reille, dressed and standing over my bed. "Come on lover, let's go, we have to get back to the company."

I dressed hastily. I was still buttoning my coat and adjusting my sword belt when we were out in the street. Reille had already arranged to get our horses from the livery where they had been kept overnight. We mounted and soon were trotting on our way out of town, heading south towards Étaples and Montreuil, where we arrived around mid-day.

We joined Monge in company drill.

CHAPTER 8

July 12, 1804
Montreuil

I was at a firing range with forty five men, around one third of the company. The soldiers had received live ammunition and were practicing their marksmanship, shooting carefully and reloading quickly. This was different from the exercise I'd watched my first day in France, when the soldiers shot and reloaded without aiming. This was more deliberate.

I wasn't just overseeing the men—I was trying my hand with a musket as well. Officers were not exempt from having to use a musket when fighting got heavy.

Sometimes, after firing, I expressed my frustration over the lack of accuracy at longer ranges. I used to be a good shot at home; back in America I had mostly used a rifle for hunting, which was far more accurate.

"Damn it, Sergeant Grenier, I'd be lucky to hit a barn with this from any distance!" I said after firing a musket at a target 150 yards away and missing, though I had hit a target at 100 yards during the previous shot.

Sergeant Major Louis Grenier chuckled behind his giant, bushy mustache. Barrel-chested and imposing, he did not look his forty five years. A veteran with more than twenty-five years-service, he had been in Rochambeau's expeditionary force that had helped force the British to surrender at the siege of Yorktown during the American Revolution. Though we Americans are loath to admit it, we were junior partners in that battle that secured our independence.

"Oh, I think you would probably hit a barn, *mon lieutenant,*" Grenier said smiling. Ever since I'd joined the company, Grenier and I had been good friends. Like many of those who fought in America, he seemed to take a liking to me, and vice-versa. I did not feel so strange in my role when I remembered that, twenty-five years before, he and thousands of his countrymen fought for my country as revenge against their enemies the English. I was repaying the favor for much the same reasons.

"Well, maybe I would hit a barn, but I'd be lucky to hit a man," I said as I reloaded the musket, ramming the ball down the barrel in its paper wadding after the charge of powder.

"One person firing might be lucky to hit someone. But when a line of soldiers is firing, someone is bound to hit the enemy. It's the reason we stand shoulder to shoulder and fire." Grenier spoke to me like a teacher to a pupil, though I outranked him. No officer —especially a junior officer—is worth anything without good NCOs to guide him, and that was especially true in my case. "Don't dismiss the musket entirely. Well loaded and well aimed it can be accurate out to 100 yards, though you are right, beyond that you would be lucky to hit anything. I think you would need more practice if ever you were in one of the shooting competitions."

They often held shooting competitions between the various units in the training area along the coast, though as an officer I likely wouldn't be allowed to enter, anyway.

"I only wish I were able to use a rifle. Then there'd be no question of hitting what I shot at." I primed the firing pan and pulled the hammer back, took my time and shot again, smoke briefly obscuring my target. "Are there units that use rifles?"

Grenier peered at my target, trying to see if I'd hit it. "The officers and NCOs in the *voltigeur* companies of the light infantry regiments carry them, but in general the Emperor does not favor the weapon. It takes a long time to load and it takes much longer to effectively train a rifleman than a soldier using a musket. A waste of resources, he believes."

"But the accuracy..."I began to protest.

"A musket can be loaded three times in the time it takes to load a rifle. In most line combat, facing each other firing, it wouldn't be practical. Your rifleman would fire accurately with his first shot and be overrun before he could reload. They are best used for skirmishing, like the *voltigeurs*. I know the *rosbifs* have a few rifle regiments for just this purpose." Grenier grinned at me. "I think you hit it that time, Lieutenant!"

I started to look downrange to see if he was right when there was a sound of a horse behind me. I turned to see Jomini, his horse lathered from what apparently had been a brisk ride.

"Burns, get your men together on the double and return to camp. Have your officers and senior NCOs meet at your regimental headquarters." Jomini shot the orders out without so much as a greeting. As soon as he was done he turned his horse and headed back towards Montreuil.

Grenier and I exchanged glances. "Sergeant Major, form the men, prepare to march."

Within minutes we were marching down the road back towards town.

A half hour later, Grenier and I entered the regimental headquarters. Reille and Monge were already there, as were Colonel Laplane and *Chef de Bataillon* Ledoyen. There were also two cavalry officers there I didn't know, a light cavalry officer from a hussar regiment and an elegantly dressed officer from a unit I was unfamiliar with. Ledoyen was arguing with Jomini.

"If this is true, we should send the entire battalion, not one company!" Ledoyen said to Jomini. The Swiss wasn't at all intimidated.

"That would attract too much attention, especially so close to the Emperor's arrival in Boulogne. Only one infantry company— Captain Reille's—will go, accompanied by Captain Monteil's squadron of cavalry. Any more soldiers might attract the attention of English spies and we can't take that chance." Jomini looked at the assembled faces and noticed mine. "Ah, Burns, I see you made it. It looks like you may get your chance for some action against the English."

Before I could ask any questions he continued. "As you know, the Emperor is due to arrive in a week for a review and inspection of troops in Boulogne."

I nodded. I was looking forward to finally seeing Napoleon, the man in whose service I had pledged myself.

"Well, Minister of Police Fouché leaked information to known English and Royalist agents that the Emperor and a small guard detail will be at a house along the coast in three days, where he will ostensibly be visiting a mistress before going to Boulogne. In fact, Napoleon will not be there at all. *We* will be there, ready to spring a trap on the Royalists and their British raiding party."

I gasped. "Would they be so foolish?"

Jomini nodded. "If they think they can catch the Emperor, yes. It would be a worthwhile gambit on their part. From what we understand, around ten Royalists and seventy British soldiers will land and meet another group of ten Royalists near the house and try to capture Napoleon. When they surround the house, we spring the trap."

Ledoyen, who had listened to this explanation, jumped back in where he left off with Jomini. "The question we were discussing before you arrived is how many troops do we send? I have been insisting the entire battalion go, this way we will be able to throw a large enough cordon around them so no one will escape."

Jomini shook his head patiently, like an indulgent schoolteacher. "No, one company only will go. I have orders from Marshal Ney and General Savary to conduct this operation as I see fit, and that means determining how many soldiers go. There is a National Guard company stationed in the area and available for the operation."

Again, no sign the major intimidated him, though Ledoyen could have snapped him over his knee. There's nothing like written orders from a marshal of the empire to stiffen your backbone. While he clearly disagreed with the decision, Ledoyen nodded his acquiescence.

Jomini looked around smugly, then indicated the elegantly dressed cavalry officer I had noticed when I first entered the hut. Tall and imposing, he approached the table where we were standing. A heavily mustached *chasseur* of the Imperial Guard, his uniform was spectacular, with tan deerskin trousers, dark green jacket and a scarlet pelisse—a half-cape over one shoulder. One hand held the hilt of a finely crafted saber, and under his other arm he held one of the distinctive round fur hats of the Guard. I hated to think what the uniform cost.

"Lieutenant Charbonnier will, in effect, be our bait for this operation," Jomini said. "He is a member of the Imperial Guard, part of the Emperor's bodyguard. He and his men will be visible near the house, as if they are guarding it. Once they and their distinctive uniforms are spotted, the Royalists and British will attack without hesitation, thinking the Emperor is in there. While they are attacking the house, we attack them. Gentlemen, let us make preparations."

The house was around fifteen miles away, just inland from the village of Crotoy—less than a day's march. Each man was issued fifty rounds of ammunition, packed his bedroll and one day's rations.

I recovered my pistol from the lockbox in our quarters. It was my first time going into action with the army and I might need it.

Within thirty minutes we were heading south. The cavalry squadron, including the Imperial Guard troops, went a different route so as not to arouse suspicion. We were to meet them ten miles south of town.

After a rainy start to the day, just enough to reduce the dust kicked up on the road, the weather had cleared up nicely. All of us, men and officers alike, were excited over the prospect of action. More than the others, I thought I had to prove myself.

After a time, talking ceased in the ranks. Route marching is not strolling. One has enough energy to walk, but conversation is almost impossible. For some reason, however, singing is easier than talking.

The men were in good spirits and began singing an old song popular among French troops for over a hundred years: *Auprés de ma blonde,* "Next to My Girlfriend." The song starts out in the gardens of the soldier's father, where the lilies are in bloom, and moves on to the soldier being captured by the Dutch and his girlfriend being asked what she would give up to get him back. The soldier is worth a lot to his girl, for she would give up Versailles, Paris and Notre Dame. Alas, to no avail.

To save their breath, the soldiers would take turns singing the verses and the rest joined in the refrain. "*Auprés de ma blonde, qu'il fait bon, fait bon, fait bon. Auprés de ma blonde, qu'il fait bon dormir.* "Next to my girlfriend, it's so fine, so fine, so fine.

Next to my girlfriend it's so fine to sleep." Naturally, as is the case with soldiers everywhere, sleeping was the last thing on their minds when it came to their girlfriends.

When we eventually met the cavalry, there was a coach there as well. The Imperial Guard troops were to accompany it to the house to set the bait. Their officer, Charbonnier, pointed to a small wood on the map about a mile east of the house.

"That would be a perfect place to hide your troops until the time comes to attack. The National Guard company will meet you there. Jomini has gone to get them, though they don't know what the mission is yet. You will explain that to them."

Monge spat. "Even if they know it wouldn't do them much good."

Reille nodded in agreement. "We're almost better off without them. They're hardly soldiers, little better than militia. Still, perhaps we can use them to push the English away from the house, while we put our company between the invaders and the sea. Monteil, your cavalry can hit the *rosbifs* from the flanks as the National Guard push from the east, though your primary job will be to hunt down and capture the Royalists. They won't be in uniform, so detain any civilians you see."

The cavalry officer nodded, looking at the map.

Listening to the plans and looking at the map, something was bothering me. "Lieutenant Charbonnier," I said, addressing the Imperial Guard officer.

Eyes fixed on me piercingly with a look that was hardly friendly. "You are Ney's American?"

I was getting sick of being called that. "Yes. My name is Burns."

"What are you doing here?"

I knew he meant it as a philosophical question but I didn't take the bait. "Trying to capture a group of Royalists and their English allies." I saw anger on his face at my answer but pressed on with my question. "Can your ten men hold that house until the rest of us get there? We likely won't start moving until the shooting starts."

My question threw him off guard. "My men are good but there are only ten of us. I don't know."

"Well, if the English take the house before we get in position, they'll know it's a trap and get away."

"Possibly."

Reille looked at us. "What are you saying Burns? Do you have something in mind?"

"I do. Once it gets dark we quietly reinforce the house with an extra twenty or thirty of our men. They should be able to hold out until help arrives."

A smile spread across Reille's face. "An excellent idea, Burns. Are you volunteering?" I must have looked surprised. "It's your idea."

That night, our company was hunkered down quietly in the woods with the National Guard soldiers nearby. They weren't as unprofessional a lot as I'd been led to believe. Their uniforms were similar to line infantry: blue jackets, white trousers, black bicorns adorned with the circular blue, white and red cockades of the Revolution.

Fires were forbidden, as was talking above a whisper. The light cavalry was a little farther away, but they could get to the house faster than those of us on foot. My twenty-five men—taken entirely from our company—were assembled and ready to go. Everything that could make noise was tied down.

"Good luck, Pierre," Reille said, as we left quietly in single file. Jomini watched us leave but said nothing. He didn't offer to accompany us.

There was no moon; the only light was from the stars. We slowly made our way to the house, stopping occasionally to make sure we weren't observed. Once inside, I spread the men between all the rooms of the farmhouse. There were four rooms on the first floor and two on the second. I placed a sergeant and ten men upstairs, the remainder downstairs, including five of the Imperial Guard soldiers. I stationed myself in the room with the main door, as I anticipated that would be the place where the fighting be the fiercest. The rest of the Guard was outside in order to keep up appearances the Emperor was present.

A watch was kept from the second floor. I ordered my men to remain out of sight of the windows—we must not reveal our presence too soon. I slept fitfully, the responsibility weighing on me.

As the sky started to lighten, one of my corporals began crawling from man to man waking them. They quietly lay in place, checking their weapons and eating.

I squatted near a window and allowed myself a glimpse of the fields and woods near the house, barely visible in the predawn light. I absently chewed on a piece of hard bread, washing it down with warm, bitter wine. No movement. I wondered if they would come.

"Lieutenant, come upstairs quickly," came a stealthy whisper. I quietly went upstairs to where my second in command, Sergeant Guillaume Tessier, was standing well back from an east facing window, his shako off, running his hand through his thick brown hair.

"I think I saw movement out there, *mon lieutenant*." The clean shaven Tessier pointed towards the tree line. A handsome, calm-eyed, experienced professional in his late twenties, I had no doubt he saw something.

I stood still looking in the direction he indicated, though I saw nothing.

"I see something over there, too," one of the soldiers whispered frantically from a different window. I moved carefully to position myself by that window and looked again. This time I saw movement, what appeared to be flashes of red along the tree line. A chill went up my spine. Redcoats. My hand gripped the hilt of my sword and I took a deep breath.

"The English are here," I said quietly to Tessier. "Stay out of sight and don't fire until they are very close. We want only the Imperial Guard shooting at first, to convince them no one else is in here."

When I went downstairs I gave the same orders to all the men.

The next ten or fifteen minutes, as the British surrounded the house, were among the longest of my life. I hoped help was already on the way. We had stationed one of the Imperial Guard to the east of the house, mounted and ready to go for help the instant he saw movement. If he were killed or captured, other mounted troops positioned farther away would hear the shooting and raise the alarm.

ART MCGRATH

One of the two Imperial Guard soldiers outside the house suddenly shouted and pointed—he had seen the British troops. There was a sharp report and he dropped like a stone. It was no musket shot, it was a rifle. Some of them had rifles!

The other Imperial Guard trooper made a dash for the door to the house. Several more shots rang out. He staggered at the entrance, but made it inside before he collapsed, dead. We moved the body along an interior wall. I took his carbine and leaned it near a window, thinking I might need it while wishing I had one of those British rifles.

The British approached the house in a loose line. Most of them were indeed Redcoats, Royal Marines in fact, with their distinctive round hats, though there were a handful in green uniforms, who I later found out were riflemen. The Brits fired at the windows, with shots returned by the Imperial Guard troopers.

Already smoke was starting to affect visibility, but my men and I held our fire. The first shots fired in any action are always the most effective. They were loaded when the soldiers weren't under stress and are aimed before the shakes have set in because of noise and recoil.

We held our fire. The longer we waited to shoot, the tighter the noose was being put around our enemies' neck, though the men were anxious to fire. The French are impetuous soldiers. It is hard to restrain them from attacking when their blood is up.

Though the Redcoats were shooting, they were not raining musket balls on the house, just enough to keep our heads down. They wanted Napoleon alive. Some of them were massing to the south of the house, opposite the main door in a clear preparation to charging.

"Now, Lieutenant?" One of my soldiers asked. The Redcoats were only fifteen or twenty paces away and were all around the house. I was next to a window near the door; I had picked up the carbine I had placed there.

I looked around the room to see everyone looking at me, even Charbonnier. My mouth was dry. I tried to lick my lips to speak, though my tongue felt twice as big as normal. I shook my head.

"Not yet, let them try to charge the door. When they open it we'll fire. They won't be expecting so many of us. Once we starting firing, everyone at the windows can fire at will." I placed six men with fixed bayonets in front of the door, ready to fire on the British as they entered.

Outside I heard shouting as British officers were stopping their men from shooting. A voice could be heard above the clamor, shouting at the house.

"Surrender!" A voice called out in French. "French soldiers, lay down your arms and you and Napoleon will not be harmed. Your resistance is useless, no help can reach you. There is no sense in further bloodshed!"

Further bloodshed? Nervy bastards, considering all the casualties had been on our side so far. Two dead Imperial Guards, three more of them wounded shooting from the windows. Time for first blood on their side and make them lose their cool.

"Go to hell, you bloody cowards!" I shouted in English out the window near the door. I shot the carbine at the nearest clump of British soldiers, sure I hit one. "*Vive L'Empereur!*" I added for good measure.

The English started shooting again and their group of twenty or thirty marines opposite the main door let out a shout and charged.

I dropped the carbine, drew my sword and pistol and joined my men by the door. The English were shouting as they neared the door. One of them kicked it open and several tried to squeeze in, jostling against each other in the process.

"*Feu!*" I shouted. Three of my men lined up in front of the door fired and several English soldiers fell, and several screamed in pain. "*Feu!*" I shouted again and the remaining three fired, again to devastating effect. In a confined space the noise was deafening. Acrid smoke filled the room, with the iron smell of blood and urine and shit starting to permeate the air.

From each window of the house, my men began shooting. It was an unpleasant shock for the English.

As more English soldiers tried to clamber over the squirming bodies of their comrades, I fired my pistol into them. It was impossible to miss. You could see the shock on some of their faces at this turn of events. They evidently hadn't expected to run into this kind of resistance.

They didn't give up though, and several pushed their way in. There was no time for my six men at the door to reload, so they charged, bayonets lowered. The remaining British soldiers in the house turned and fled outside. Unfortunately, my men followed. I ran after them to try and call them back. Other British soldiers out there who had not been able to join the pell-mell charge raised their muskets and fired. Half of my six men were struck.

It was now the turn of the English to charge. With a cry of "Huzzah!" they surged forward. I was fighting several at the same time, thrusting and parrying, trying to keep their bayonets at a distance. We were badly outnumbered.

"Back in the house! Now!" I shouted to my remaining men. At least from inside the door we would only have to fight a few at a time. The English pressed us back through the door relentlessly. I managed to thrust my sword into the shoulder of one who dropped his musket and fell back but he was replaced by several more.

We were in the house and still they pressed forward. There was almost no shooting now, except by my men shooting out the windows. Neither side in the melee had time to reload. All fighting had turned hand-to-hand. The house was a storm of red and blue uniforms.

More of the English were forcing their way in. I noticed Charbonnier fighting next to me on my left, wielding his heavy cavalry saber with skill, though the weapon was better suited to slashing from horseback than in the confines of a house. A British soldier was able to push his sword aside and hit him in the head with the butt of his musket, a blow hard enough to knock him off his feet. Charbonnier was on the floor and too stunned to raise his sword to defend himself, and the British NCO was about to bayonet him.

Though I had an opponent directly in front of me, I sidestepped hard into the redcoat, knocking him aside. He was shocked but wasn't off his feet. Now his attention was on me, as was my original opponent.

"Now what'd you go and do that fer, Frenchie? That wasn't polite." Weapon lowered, he advanced cautiously.

I laughed gravely. My blood was up, both French and Scot. "Thanks for the etiquette lesson." A confused look crossed his face for a second. His expression turned from confusion to anger but he remained silent. I baited him again. "You look familiar. Didn't I see your mother in a whorehouse recently?"

Charging, he forgot form and tried to stick me with his bayonet. I blocked his blow, stepped closer to him and kicked his knee. I heard it pop and he screamed, bending to clutch at it. Unable to bring the point or edge of my sword to bear on him because of our proximity, I hit him on the head with the pommel of my sword, knocking him to the floor in a moaning heap.

Without waiting, in a fury I went after my second opponent, who had watched me dispatch his NCO in stunned disbelief. I quickly got through his defenses and thrust solidly into his center. My thrust was near the heart, a killing blow. His expression showed he didn't understand what had happened, and he looked at me in confusion as he dropped to his knees while I yanked my sword out. I was surprised by how much effort it took. As he died he was still looking at me and trying to speak. For a moment I was startled by how young he looked. His face was still smooth like a girl's, he hadn't even started to shave yet.

There was no more time to reflect. My men had been pushed back but were still holding on. Without warning, there was a shouted command in English.

"Withdraw, withdraw! Out of the house! Enemy troops, it's a trap!" The English began to retreat in good order. Outside, to the east there was the sound of drums and shooting. Above that could be a heard the cry, *Vive L'Empereur!* Our reinforcements.

"After them! *Chargez!*" I shouted to those of my men still standing. Of the twenty-five men I'd brought to the house, a little over fifteen were in any condition to join the pursuit.

We chased the English, some of whom had formed a line to face the National Guard troops pushing from the east. Outnumbered, the English were nevertheless holding their own against them, although they were slowing falling back, no doubt intending to retreat to their ship.

We hit them on their left flank, throwing that portion of their line into disorder. It started to crumble, and some of their men began to run, though some turned to face us, to protect their unit's withdrawal.

I had not organized any kind of formation; our pursuit out of the house had turned into a frenzied free-for-all. Through the smoke, an English lieutenant, who appeared no older than eighteen, spotted me and made straight for me, sword at the ready. He seemed more interested in some kind of duel than getting his men out of there.

I soon found myself in a fight for my life with him. For the second time in barely two months, I was being beaten by a superior swordsman.

"Damn it!" I cried in anger and exasperation as he sliced my shoulder (I usually swore in English). I determined if I got through that fight I would practice and practice with that sword until I had few equals.

I fought angrily. I was in trouble and it wasn't likely I would have time to grab a handful of sand to throw in his eyes as I had with Monge.

A thrust low towards my stomach was deflected by the pistol stuck in my belt. With a sudden inspiration I stepped back, took it out of my belt and aimed it at the officer. He stopped and his eyes widened, probably thinking how unsporting I was. Instead of shooting—which I couldn't because I had already fired and had had time no time to reload, but he didn't know that—I threw it at his face.

It was a move he didn't expect, and as he raised his hand to deflect the weapon, I stepped inside his guard and placed my sword tip against his breast.

"Your sword, sir."

Surrender or be killed was his only option, and the look in his eye showed he knew that. Turning his sword around, he handed it to me by the hilt.

"Your prisoner, sir."

By now, the National Guard soldiers had charged and pushed back the retreating British. I assigned several of them to take care of the growing number of prisoners, including my officer, though he gave his word of honor he wouldn't try to escape.

With the remainder of my men, we joined in the pursuit. Ahead I could see the redcoats retreating, some in good order, some merely turning tail and running. Some of our light cavalry were running down the fleeing troops, though I noticed more of them fanned out farther to the south. They were after some of the royalists who had fled in a different direction than the soldiers, hoping to get away in the confusion.

I formed my men in a loose skirmish formation and pushed ahead of the National Guard troops. I may have been only a professional soldier for two and a half months, but I knew my elite light infantry shouldn't be letting militia take the lead, even if we were only a handful. By now the British had put distance between us, trying to get away.

Up ahead, I heard shouting and volley fire. Plainly the English had met Reille and the rest of our company blocking them. We quickened our pace and came within sight of the rear of the ragged British line of redcoats with a handful of riflemen trying to slug it out with my company. They were less than one hundred yards ahead. I doubt if there were forty of the English left standing.

We couldn't fire, my company was just beyond. I turned to my men and the National Guardsmen. I raised my sword in the air. "Come on! *Chargez! Vive L'Empereur!*" I began running towards the rear of the English, not looking to see if I was being followed.

Naturally, I wasn't alone. No one was about to let a new lieutenant, and a foreigner at that, put them to shame and charge the enemy single-handedly. We closed the distance and some of the English turned to face us, clear alarm on their faces. They were surrounded. The fight went out of them and they began dropping their weapons.

My first battle as a soldier of France was over.

We collected our prisoners and under the watchful eye of the National Guard troops sent them back to the vicinity of the house. Monge took a third of the company and, accompanied by some of the cavalry, spread out in the direction of the shore, trying to find any English troops or Royalists who might have gotten through our line.

Others spread out searching the woods and fields in other directions for the same purpose. I didn't join them but took my little band and headed back to the house and scene of the battle. There the prisoners were being gathered, and the wounded from both sides were being treated. Rough bandages were made from torn cloth, taken from the fallen who would not be needing it any longer.

The English had twenty dead and twenty-five wounded. Only twenty-five of them came through the fight unscathed. We had captured ten of the Royalists and killed three more. Seven were still on the loose.

We suffered far fewer casualties. My band from the house— including Charbonnier's Imperial Guard—was the greatest proportion of them, with five dead and eight wounded. The National Guardsmen and the company under Reille suffered light casualties.

I went back in the house, looking at some of my men who'd died, and I wondered whether, if I had done something differently, some would have lived. In my time on ship I had been in fights but never had men die under my command. I began to feel sick and left the house.

I ran into Sergeant Major Grenier who was examining a short musket. Normally he carried only a saber.

"What do you have there, Sergeant Major?" I peered at the weapon.

"Ah, Lieutenant, there you are. This is one of those English rifles, which I understand they used quite accurately when they first attacked you."

I thought back to the first shots fired in the attack, when the two Imperial Guardsmen were killed and we didn't even see who fired the shot. "Indeed, they were able to accurately kill before we knew they were there."

Grenier grinned. "That may be true, but I discovered that up close they fight no better than any other soldier, and die just as easily." He hefted the weapon in his hand and aimed it. "It's much shorter than a smoothbore."

Looking at the weapon, I was surprised it was as accurate as it was. It was much shorter than rifles I was familiar with back home.

Turning from Grenier, I watched the unwounded prisoners, who seemed to be in good spirits despite their defeat and impending imprisonment. They had fought well. The men were a rough lot, with a number of ruffians among them. There were several officers, probably because of the sensitive nature of their mission—all gentlemen who had likely purchased their commissions and never bothered to learn the trade of arms, even after putting on their uniforms. I was always amazed the English soldiers fought as well as they did, considering they were generally led by brave incompetents. Unlike their men they would likely soon be exchanged.

Among the prisoners, I saw the lieutenant I'd captured and walked over to talk to him. It was a good chance to speak my native tongue.

"Are you and your men being treated well, Lieutenant?"

He had been watching some of his men's wounds being treated and turned to see me. "Yes, thank you, sir."

I nodded. He seemed affable enough and obviously a gentleman whose family had spent 1,000 pounds for his commission. "What's your name?"

"Ensign James Miller. Yours?"

"Lieutenant Pierre Burns."

"Ah, a Scot. Jacobite?" He thought he had figured me out. A reasonable assumption, since a lot of Scots had fled to France after the failed Jacobite rebellion fifty years before.

"American, though my grandfather was a Jacobite."

That shocked him. "An American? What the bloody hell are you doing here in that uniform? This isn't America."

I smiled. "I could ask you the same thing. What the bloody hell are you doing *here* in that uniform? This isn't England."

About to answer, he stopped short. "No, but you obviously already know why we're here and undoubtedly knew we were coming."

"Undoubtedly."

"That doesn't answer why an American is in a French uniform fighting for France." His expression was curiosity, not antagonism.

"Why not? One good turn deserves another, as a man I admire said to me. They came to help my country fight the English, I'm here to help *them* fight the English. But, as usual with your country, always interfering in the affairs of others, I didn't even have to travel to England, you came here. Thank you."

Embarrassment covered his face. "Today didn't turn out quite as planned. Was Boney even here?"

"If you mean the emperor, Napoleon, no, he was not."

"Damn. Do you know he plans on invading England?"

"It's why I'm wearing this uniform."

Somewhat taken aback, his expression turned rather grim. "Even if you get there, it won't be easy. We'll fight you every step of the way."

I smiled wolfishly. "I'm rather counting on that."

Our eyes locked and the tension was palpable.

"Why such animosity towards my country?"

"Carrying on the family tradition, you might say. *Sic semper tyrannis.* Anyway, I must see to my men. If you need anything, please let us know. Good day, sir."

"Good day to you, sir."

I left and walked along the line of prisoners, looking at their faces and assessing their injuries. When I passed their stack of weapons, I noticed the sword I had taken from Miller. I picked it up and looked at it. It was a fine weapon, custom made, and possibly a family heirloom. I walked back to him and handed it to him by the hilt. After all, he had given his parole.

"Your sword, sir."

Stunned, he took the sword and slowly put it back in its scabbard.

He tried to say something, then cleared his throat and saluted crisply. "Thank you, thank you very much, sir."

"Good day, sir."

There were still seven Royalists on the loose who had escaped our trap. We would spend the next week scouring the area for them. We found only two of them. Some parts of western France had Royalist leanings and it was easy for them to hide and find sympathizers.

Still, when we marched back to the camp at Montreuil, we considered our mission a success. The rest of the regiment was jealous, as we had seen real action. They had participated in a parade under the eye of Napoleon himself but still envied us.

CHAPTER 9

August 15, 1804

It was the eve of one of the most spectacular military reviews ever held. For weeks we had drilled the troops in anticipation of an awards ceremony when Napoleon would pass out the newly created Legion of Honor to selected officers and men. Uniforms were washed and spotless, boots polished, bayonets and muskets shined and gleaming. Everything had to be perfect and would be. I was splitting my time almost evenly between the company and as aide-de-camp in preparation.

It was late, well after dark when I was called to Ney's headquarters for an errand. When I arrived I was directed to Ney's office. Candles were burning everywhere and the chateau was still a hub of activity. Outside Ney's office there were several officers and men I didn't know, and Charbonnier as well. I hadn't seen him since the fight in the house a month previously. I went over and shook his hand.

"Charbonnier! How are you? How's the head?"

The Imperial Guardsman smiled. "Well, thanks to you. You'd better get in there, you're expected."

I knocked on the door and entered Ney's office. He was there with another man looking at a map on a table. Despite the warm weather, a fire burned in the fireplace.

"Burns, good. Glad they found you so quickly." He turned to the other man. "Sire, this is Burns, the American I've taken on as an aide-de-camp."

Sire? I stopped, stunned, and looked at the other man, who was dressed in the dark blue uniform of an officer of the Grenadiers of the Imperial Guard. It was Napoleon.

He had piercing gray eyes, dark hair, a somewhat dark complexion, and was about as tall as me—average height and build. Despite the English propaganda circulating for years, Napoleon was not short.

Those grey eyes could look right through you and draw you to him. He was like compressed energy, a ton of gunpowder forced into the body of an average man. What surprised me most was how charming he could be. He had charisma like the sun, which he could turn on and off like a spigot. It could leave you cold when he turned it off.

That spigot was about to be turned on.

"Sire." The word was strange on my lips. I bowed slightly then stood rigidly at attention.

"So you are Ney's American." I may have been sick of being called that, but I wasn't about to say a word. He spoke French with a thick Corsican accent that was not at all refined. I found it ironic that of the three of us in the room, I was the only one with French blood and yet wasn't a French citizen.

"I don't know why Ney insists on filling his staff with foreigners, but that is his affair. What I find interesting is you saved the life of one of my Guard officers."

Either Charbonnier or Ney must have told him about the fight in the farmhouse. I tried to downplay the act.

"Yes, sire, though it just happened to be Charbonnier. I was merely protecting a downed comrade."

My answer seemed to please him.

"I also hear you did well in your first action and that you're adapting to your new profession very quickly."

I was ready to fall back on modesty again but thought better of it. This wasn't a man to lie to.

"Yes, sire, I seem to have finally found a home."

Napoleon smiled. "Well, then, we should make it official. I hereby make you an officer."

Confused, all I could sputter out was, "Pardon?"

Instantly Napoleon saw what was wrong and laughed. "Ney, you fool, you didn't tell him?" Ney only shook his head. The Emperor turned back to me. "Only I can make an officer, Lieutenant Burns. A general can recommend appointments but I approve them. You have been a volunteer aide-de-camp, like Jomini when Ney first took him on. Ney has been paying you out of his own pocket, though he'll be reimbursed. He is somewhat profligate sometimes, but in this case I approve. His reasons were sound to take on an American as an aide for the invasion. It is even better you can fight."

Walking up to me, he pinched my ear. This was a great mark of approval, which on the battlefield could bring a hardened soldier, to tears but I didn't know that at the time. I muffled a yelp.

After walking back to a table and taking a drink, Napoleon turned back to me. "So how do they view me in America, Burns?"

Again, I knew I should be honest. "People have mixed views of you, sire, depending on whether they are Anglophiles or Francophiles. Anti-federalists such as President Jefferson have a more sympathetic view than someone like Alexander Hamilton, who is very much an admirer of England. Both sides, though, are content to stay out of the war if that is possible. "

"And your country's purchase of Louisiana?" The year before, Napoleon had sold us over 800,000 square miles of land.

"At first many thought it wasteful, but now they are realizing the possibilities are endless. The last I heard, an expedition was to be sent west this spring to explore the area. It may have already left."

Napoleon looked excited at the prospect and for a moment he did not look like a head of state but like an explorer whose curiosity was never sated. "The reports that will come out of that trip will make interesting reading. What a trip that would be, what discoveries will be made!" He sighed. "Science and exploration has always been an interest of mine, but affairs of state give me little time for that." Napoleon the scientist became Napoleon the emperor again. "Some said I was foolish selling that land, but what good did it do France? We don't have the navy capable of defending it or supplying any troops sent there. What I have done is strike a blow at England by making your country more powerful. I have given England what will eventually be a long-term naval rival." The Emperor looked at the time. "We will probably talk about your country again. Goodnight, Burns."

I bowed. "Goodnight, sire."

I returned to the company to make last minute preparations for the morrow, still excited by having met Napoleon himself. Sleep did not come easy.

August 16, 1804
Boulogne

In our best uniforms, we marched off towards Boulogne before daybreak. As we marched, other units joined our column. In Étaples we joined the rest of Ney's Sixth Corps. Soon, 20,000 of us were marching north towards Boulogne to join the rest of the army.

Two miles past Boulogne was to be the site of the review. Soldiers from all seven corps of the army were staging not far from where the ceremony was to take place. Men looked over each other's uniforms, made adjustments to belts and shakos, or did some last-minute brushing off of weapons dusty from the long march. Sergeants moved men around in formation, removing tall men from the middle of columns where they stuck out like oak trees in a field and bunched them together near the front.

There wasn't a cloud in the sky, and a light wind off the ocean flapped the regimental flags. Tens of thousands of us were lined up along the tops of cliffs overlooking the ocean, preparing to descend to the beach where the ceremony was to begin. Out to sea many French warships were visible, bedecked in flags for the occasion. The English frigates that plagued the coast seemed to have disappeared for the day.

"What a sight," Grenier said quietly.

"Yes," I said just as quietly. Drums were starting to play. We were ready to begin.

The army marched from the cliffs on a road that descended gradually towards the beach. The ritual was to take place in what resembled a giant amphitheatre, with low slopes in back and on each side. Thousands of civilians were lined along these cliffs and hills to watch.

More than 120,000 soldiers assembled in a giant arc inside that huge amphitheatre, with a large platform down near the shore as the focal point. We had our backs toward the cliffs, facing the ocean and the large platform where the Emperor and his entourage would sit.

The platform was adorned with numerous flags and trophies of battles. An ancient, richly decorated wooden throne sat on the top tier of the platform, unmistakably meant for the Emperor.

How do I draw this scene for you, who are used to our fields and endless American forests? It was the greatest panoply of pageantry and uniforms ever seen: the dark blue and white of the line infantry and the Grenadiers of the Imperial Guard; the red and yellow faced blue uniforms of the light infantry; the spectacular, gaudy yet fantastic uniforms of the Guard cavalry units, some in scarlet and ochre, others in sky blue, others in varying shades of green; the cuirassiers—heavy cavalry made up of large men on huge black horses, each man wearing a polished breastplate which reflected the sun like a mirror. The hats of each unit and military occupation had plumes of so many colors it was a like a rainbow.

Overhead, blue skies came down to meet the blue of the ocean, with the white sails of our fleet showing the speed and number of our ships. In the distance could be seen the infamous White Cliffs of Dover, home of the enemy.

Standing there among 120,000 men, I felt a sense of purpose and belonging I had never known, a sense of being part of something much larger than myself, all of us of one resolve, with one will, and Napoleon at our head. These were coming together to draw me into this cause, along with the grandness of the enterprise and my ever-present hatred of the English.

There was far more that kept me there for ten years, of course, but those ties were just starting to develop then—friendship, shared privations, shared victories, shared defeats, and loyalty to friends, to the Grand Armée, and to Napoleon himself.

Something else awoke in me that day amidst that spectacle—*la gloire*, glory. Amidst all the hunger, grime, death and wounds of coming years it was a constant theme and the hardest one to explain here, so far from those battlefields.

Once the army was assembled, the ceremony began in short order. Forty regimental bands played, and close to 2,000 drummers were sounding *Aux Champs*, "To the Field." Napoleon rode slowly between the ranks on a grey horse. Over 100,000 men began shouting, "*Vive L'Empereur!*" over and over again. He was accompanied by eighty generals and 200 aides-de-camp. The uniforms of this grand assemblage glittered in the sun.

At the platform, he dismounted and walked the stairs to stand before the throne. He was dressed in the plain green uniform of a colonel of a Chasseur of the Guard, his famous sideways bicorn firmly atop his head. There was salvo after salvo of cannon fire and drummers and trumpeters played. Napoleon sat down, and in unison,120,000 men presented arms. The Emperor read an oath to be taken by the army, binding us to service to the Republic and Empire, fealty to the Emperor, and to fight against the reestablishment of feudal rule, which would have meant the loss of so many rights gained under the Revolution.

All of us officers had been coached in advance to respond, since it was impossible for everyone to hear the Emperor. Like that day in Montreuil, we shouted "*Nous le jurons!*" We swear it! This time, I shouted as loudly as anyone and meant it. I no longer held back.

Again, we all began shouting "*Vive L'Empereur!*" Bands began playing "*Le Chant du Depart*," The Song of Departure, the anthem of the Empire.

Over 2,000 men received the Legion of Honor in a five hour ceremony. As a soldier's name was called, he walked to the bottom of the platform, bowed and mounted the steps. An aide gave the Emperor the medal and he pinned it on the soldier. As the soldier left the raised area, 1,200 musicians played, announcing a new Knight of the Legion of Honor as we again shouted "*Vive L'Empereur!*"

I think we were all hoarse by the end of the ceremony.

Four men from our company, including Reille and Grenier, received the medal.

After the last medals were distributed, the army closed ranks and advanced to within twenty five feet of the throne. The drums stopped. There was no noise except the wind. The Emperor looked at us silently, as moved as we were. We then marched in review, each unit passing by the throne and saluting the Emperor one last time before leaving the beach.

We didn't get back to camp until after eight o'clock, exhausted, overwhelmed and content. Colonel Laplane and the other regimental commanders made sure there was no reveille in the morning. I took advantage of it and slept like the dead.

CHAPTER 10

August 19, 1804
Montreuil

For the next several days there were many feasts and celebrations, including one the next day for the 2,000 newly honored Legionnaires.

In the chateau in Montreuil, on the third night after the ceremony, Ney put on a ball for all the officers of the VI Corps. It wasn't a soldiers' feast but a true ball, with officers' wives and many unattached young ladies there to capture hearts. Many set out to do just that, brought there by their families to be shown off in an attempt to find officers to marry. Some were ruthless and quite successful in their quest.

The chateau was lit up and sparkling, more beautiful than at any time in my three months there. The walkways were lit by soldiers in dress uniforms holding torches. Notes of waltzes echoed into the fading dusk as Reille, Monge and I walked around a fountain to approach the front door. The laughter of women sounded like tinkling bells.

We quickened our pace and strode through the front door in our finest uniforms. I was putting on a brave face, but if I had felt out of my element when I first joined the army, it was worse here. Dancing was not something I did well, and I was convinced I would be unable to dance and talk with a woman at the same time. I was determined not to find out.

I accepted a drink from a servant and stood along a wall chatting with Reille and Monge. Since our fight, Monge and I had learned to be civil to each other, even if we didn't enjoy each other's company. Not being as inept as I first appeared made it a little easier for that blueblood to put up with me. He was eyeing several ladies in a group across the room and was ready to ask one to dance.

"You're just going to walk across the room and talk to them?" I was horrified.

Monge looked at me with an expression between contempt and bewilderment. "Yes, what else would you do? Afraid, Burns? Stay in the corner where you're safe then, and you won't get bitten."

With that he made his way across the dance floor, gracefully dodging couples who got in his way. Picking the most beautiful of a group of three ladies, he took her in his arms, and soon they were dancing like experts. In a way I envied him his upbringing and the natural grace that seemed to come with it.

"Bastard," I said taking a large swallow of wine.

As I watched them dance, I noticed another group of ladies against the far wall and I froze. In their midst was Marshal Ney's wife, Aglaé, dressed in a radiant light green evening gown. My thoughts had been on her a great deal since I met her, and I was always hoping for a chance to run into her again. Now that I had my chance I began fidgeting and Reille snapped at me, rather annoyed.

"What the hell is wrong with you, Pierre? Don't tell me Monge is getting to you that much. Forget him."

I shook my head, barely able to speak. "It's not Monge." I was still staring but was also straightening out my uniform, working up the courage to go talk to her. I had spoken with her a few brief times in the previous months after our first encounter, and while she was always friendly and radiant, our chats never seemed to last. She always found an excuse to cut them short.

Reille saw who I was looking at swore under his breath. "No! Don't even think it, Pierre."

"One dance can't hurt anything. Just one dance, really." I was pleading, but I'm not sure if I was pleading with him or myself. I never had to answer that question because Aglaé noticed me watching and with her four companions in tow made her way across the dance floor towards us.

"*Merde,*" Reille muttered.

"Shit," I echoed in English.

As they elegantly approached us—they didn't have to dodge dancing couples, couples moved aside for them like the Red Sea parted by Moses—we bowed.

"*Bonsoir, Madame la Maréchale.*" I made a low bow and held it for a moment.

Aglaé smiled a smile that could have lit a room by itself. "*Bonsoir*, Lieutenant Burns."

There were introductions all around and we bowed to her friends.

I wondered why Reille bowed especially low to the first girl, a far from beautiful girl of my age dressed in an elegant yellow gown and unmistakably pregnant. Stupidly, I didn't catch her name, as my attention was on Aglaé. Later I found out she was Hortense Beauharnais, daughter of Napoleon's wife Josephine. She was also the wife of Louis Bonaparte, one of the Emperor's younger brothers. Close by her side was her best friend, Adèle Auguié, who was also Aglaé's sister.

The third friend, Beatrice Fleurette, was another pretty but unexceptional girl in my estimation, but the fourth, Athenaïs Vanier almost literally took my breath away. Around 18 years old, her light brown hair framed a perfectly proportioned face with defined but not sharp features and light blue eyes, which matched almost exactly the color of her evening gown. I bent to kiss her hand, something I didn't even do for Aglaé.

"*Bonsoir, Mademoiselle.* It is a pleasure to make your acquaintance."

She laughed lightly, a laugh that sent a shiver of pleasure down my spine. "Good evening to you, sir. It's a fine night, isn't it?"

I smiled a big, stupid grin. She had spoken perfect English, with hardly a trace of an accent in it.

"Indeed it is."

We began chatting happily. I didn't even notice when Reille asked Beatrice to dance, and soon after Aglaé, her sister and Hortense slipped away. Aglaé, who no doubt knew how I felt about her, was probably thinking her mission to deflect my interest elsewhere was successful—and it was—but it opened up a whole new slew of problems.

"Your English is perfect, where did you learn it?" I was only sipping my drink now—I needed to keep my wits about me.

Athenaïs lightly touched my arm smiling. "The same place you learned your French, at home from my mother." I found out Aglaé had told her a lot about me. She had asked to meet me at the ball and Aglaé had been happy to oblige. I can't blame Aglaé, for while it was clear she liked me, unlike many general's wives, she loved and was faithful to her husband. This was her way of showing affection for me.

"Was your mother English?" Her hand was still on my arm and I was doing all I could not to press her against me. I had to concentrate on her words.

Again the spine-tingling laugh. "Do you always insult girls when you first meet them? No, she was Scottish."

I must have given her an incredulous look because Athenaïs' expression turned serious for a moment. "Honestly. My mother is the daughter of a Jacobite refugee who married a member of the French nobility."

Smiling, I said, "We really are everywhere. My grandfather was a Jacobite too, and fled to France with his wife after Bonnie Prince Charlie's defeat at Culloden. My father was actually born in France. When he was twenty, he and his French bride moved to America just as the American Revolution started. It was an opportunity to continue the family tradition and fight the English as my grandfather had." For a moment I sighed, thinking of those forbearers I had never met but whose purpose drove me as it did them. "Someone told me that many Scots and Irish are in France. I'm starting to see the truth of that."

"But not many Americans. That makes you unique."

I nodded casually. "I suppose so." The way she looked at me and touched my arm made me think she meant it.

She flashed an excited smile. "The land of Chactas and Atala! The land of lost love!"

I looked at her with confusion. Who the hell were they?

The look of disbelief, even pity, on her face was evident. "You haven't heard of Francois-René de Chateaubriand? You have not read *Atala* or *René,*the most popular books in France? Such passion, such romance!"

When I told her that my reading since arriving in France had been strictly about the art of war and history, she promised to send me a copy. She told me the story of the love of the Indian princess Atala and the warrior Chactas, how after she saved him from execution they wandered through the wilderness of Louisiana, Georgia and Florida. In the end, Atala took her own life so she would not break a vow of virginity she made to her mother and God. It didn't sound like cheery reading but I said nothing.

Finishing her drink and putting it on the tray of a passing servant, Athenaïs looked boldly at me. "Are you going to ask me to dance?"

The dreaded moment had arrived. I paused. "But we were having such a lovely time talking..." I didn't finish the sentence because one look told me she saw right through me.

"Why Mister Burns, are you *afraid*?" She put such emphasis on the last word. "You've crossed the ocean, fought at sea, fought on land, and you're afraid to dance?" Her words were not mocking, but she was clearly amused and I could sense the gentle incredulity in her tone.

"I really am not much of a dancer, not at all graceful," I said, indicating several couples passing by.

A hand touched mine and squeezed it gently. "You really have no reason to be embarrassed. Many of those dancers are not that good if you watch them, but no one watches that closely. Besides, usually one is embarrassed by doing something in front of one's friends or people one has known for a long time. You, however, are in a new country, among people who hardly know you. Time to step out there and start anew."

I was sure she was talking about more than dancing, and I smiled, squeezing her hand.

The smile was returned. "Don't worry, I'm an excellent dancer. I'll keep you out of trouble."

We walked out onto the dance floor. Soon we were spinning, back stepping, sidestepping, pirouetting and moving like we were made for each other. Several dances went by quickly and we left to take a rest.

"I'm so hot," Athenaïs said fanning her face.

I looked around and noticed we were near a door. "Would you care to get some air in the garden? Then we can come back for another round."

Arm in arm, we went down stone steps onto a raised patio overlooking a garden with trails. The only light was that pouring from the windows of the house and the stars above us. At first we said nothing but strolled together, looking at the stars and occasionally stopping to look back at the chateau and listen to the music. As we stood there, I slowly pulled her to me and she lifted her face to kiss me, eagerly pressing against me.

Soon, after tidying ourselves up, we strolled back to the chateau, where the ball had not slowed down at all. We went in a different entrance and separated at the door, agreeing to meet near the punch bowls a little later.

I got a drink and saw Reille along the wall with Beatrice. He waved me over and I went to stand near them. We stood in companionable silence drinking.

Marshal Ney was making the rounds of the edge of the room with Jomini in tow and came over to where we were standing. We snapped to attention.

"*Bonsoir, Messieurs.*" Tall and striking, looking every inch a French marshal, Ney was in the finest blue wool coat, with a high gold collar. A wide gold cummerbund was around his waist and a red sash cut across his chest and over his shoulder. Over his heart was a cross-shaped medal: the newly awarded Legion of Honor. "Are you having a good time, Burns?" Ney seemed rather amused.

I was wondering just how much he knew. "Yes, Monsieur le Maréchal, very much so, though it took me a little while to get my nerve up to get on the dance floor."

"Yes, women can be frightening creatures sometimes." There were chuckles all around and all of us nodded. "You look a tad disheveled. You probably should rest from dancing," Ney said with a knowing grin, reaching over and taking a long piece of grass off my uniform jacket. "I was going to apologize for my wife's matchmaking, but apparently it hasn't been too disagreeable."

I wondered if I was blushing, for Jomini and Reille both smiled.

"No, Monsieur le Maréchal, it hasn't. I'm flattered she thought enough of me to introduce me to one of her acquaintances."

A servant came by with drinks. I traded my empty glass for a glass of burgundy, as did Ney and Jomini.

"I think my wife is worried about you. A young man in a strange country can get lonely." While Ney's expression did not betray any other meaning, my mind was racing, wondering what she had told him—not that I ever behaved inappropriately towards Aglaé. "Probably she's trying to keep your visits to Madame Delobel's to a minimum."

I choked on my drink. Aglaé knew about that? Were there any secrets here?

Continuing as if I had not reacted, Ney said, "Not that Madame Delobel's is a bad place. It's clean, and I'm glad you had the sense to go there." Ney looked at Reille. "That was your doing?"

Reille simply nodded.

"Good." Ney turned back to me. "Always remember, Burns, watch what you say in a place like that. Money can buy more than sex. Speaking of Boulogne, you'll be going there soon. English spies and saboteurs have gotten busier over the last few weeks."

CHAPTER 11

August 21, 1804
Étaples

"In the weeks leading up to the Emperor's review, English saboteurs stepped up their attempts to incapacitate in any way possible the fleet we've been gathering in Boulogne, Étaples and other spots along the coast. They've mostly concentrated their attention on Boulogne, which, as you know, is the center of our efforts to prepare an invasion of England."

Jomini was pointing to a map on a table showing the locations of the staging areas for the French invasion fleet. It was two days after the ball at Montreuil and we were in a room of the hotel on the main square of Étaples, taken over for the use of VI Corps. Ney was there as well as Sergeant Major Grenier.

An officer I didn't know was also there. A general of brigade, Savary, wore an elegant but functional uniform. Around thirty years old, dark haired and handsome, Anne-Jean-Marie-René Savary was an aide-de-camp to Napoleon himself and was very much involved in intelligence and countering the various plots of the English and Royalists throughout France. To some he had a somewhat sinister aspect because of his deep involvement in the execution of the Duc D'Enghien, shot earlier that year for his involvement in a plot to kill Napoleon. Certainly he was effective in catching Royalists and foiling their plots, which may have made him appear sinister to his enemies. For truly sinister, I always thought the Minister of Police, Joseph Fouché, who Savary worked with often on these ventures, far more frightening.

Savary remained silent for much of the briefing, letting Jomini take the lead.

"No doubt," Jomini continued, "the English believe the activity here is final preparation for launching the invasion and are doing all they can to stop that. Many acts of sabotage have been prevented, but unfortunately some have been carried out. We have to do something to stop them, if only for morale. It isn't so much the acts—they really haven't caused much damage—but that they have been carried out with impunity, almost under our noses. Some, in between their acts of sabotage, even find time to attend the theater and post their reviews of the shows in the lobby!"

It was a hot day and a cool breeze blew in the window, carrying with it the scent of the sea from the estuary where many of VI Corps' vessels were docked. From our vantage point on the second floor of the hotel we could see many of them.

"We must catch them and make an example of them," Ney said quietly. "They are afraid of the invasion and well they should be. We will call England to account for three centuries of hostility."

"Is the invasion near?" It was hard for me to contain the excitement in my voice.

Jomini looked at Ney before answering. When he did, he shrugged noncommittally. "We hope so. It is up to the Emperor to give the final word to board the ships and sail to England. Much depends on whether the French and Spanish fleets can draw the English fleet away from the coast or hold them off while the invasion fleet crosses the *Manche*. And that will depend on the weather, the preparation of our fleet to set sail. In the meanwhile, we continue to prepare as if it will be tomorrow."

I nodded, making sure not to let the disappointment show on my face. I bent to look at the map showing our fleet, my sword in its scabbard lightly banging the table. "So what is my role against these English spies and saboteurs?"

Jomini smiled wryly. "Simple. Find them and kill them."

I looked up from the map. "That's not very helpful, Monsieur. I'm sure that's been tried."

"Indeed, we've killed quite a few so far. You probably heard about that night in June where ten were caught in Boulogne and executed? They were well dressed and carrying incendiary devices meant to catch some of the ships on fire. No more theater reviews by that band!" There were a few nervous chuckles. "Carry on like that and you'll do fine."

I nodded, trying not to let my exasperation show. "I was hoping you would be more specific, Monsieur. What am I tasked with? What are my geographic limits? What authority do I have? What forces will I have at my disposal?"

Before Jomini could answer, Savary held up his hand to cut him off. My specific questions seemed to impress him and I think Jomini's sarcastic demeanor was irritating him as much as it irritated me. Savary had been the mastermind behind the trap we set for the Royalists and British near le Crotoy the month before, and I learned later it was his idea to assign me to this mission, based on my actions that day.

"You'll have wide ranging authority throughout all the camps of Boulogne, in the town of Boulogne itself and in any surrounding town where English saboteurs are reported to be operating," Savary said. "You'll take forty men of Captain Reille's company, though any forces in the area you need you can call on. Every marshal has given his assent to have you operate where you see fit and has signed orders confirming that."

Savary nodded at Jomini, who handed me my orders, signed by all the corps commanders. "Show this and you'll get cooperation from any unit commander," Savary continued after giving me a moment to peruse the orders. "You'll be given an account to pay informants. Money will lead the way to the English faster than anything. Anyone you catch you are certain is a spy or saboteur you are authorized to execute. If there is doubt in your mind as to their disposition, or if you think they have valuable information, send the prisoner to the nearest corps commander, to the Ministry of Police, or, if I am in the area of Boulogne, directly to me. I'll make sure you're apprised of when I'm here."

I listened in stunned silence. The mandate I was being given was indeed incredibly broad—literally the power of life and death. We were at war, and these men were endangering the lives of thousands and the invasion itself.

"You're right, Pierre, it has indeed been tried," Ney interjected. "We have caught many saboteurs and killed them. Until now, however, no one has been tasked with coordinating all our efforts in the Camps of Boulogne—instead they've been left to the various area commanders. With the English picking up the pace of their efforts, we have to respond more forcefully. You were a natural choice for the job because of your knowledge of the English and your particular animosity towards them." Ney smiled. "We thought you might be particularly motivated."

I was a logical choice, it was true. It was just the type of mission an aide-de-camp might be assigned, and Ney had engaged me as an aide-de-camp to deal with the English in particular.

"When do I leave?"

"Today, as soon as you're ready," Jomini replied briskly. "Choose the men you want and be on your way. Take your horse—you may need to move between camps quickly by yourself."

Since early August I'd had my own horse. Though I was supposed to buy one as an aide-de-camp I couldn't afford to do so, but Ney in his generosity had given me a fine black mare called *Fleur*—Flower. I didn't ride her when with the company, since infantry officers under the rank of major walk.

I saluted and left, accompanied by Grenier. We exchanged looks on the stairs and I exhaled heavily.

"You'll do fine, *mon lieutenant.*" He could tell the enormousness of the task sat heavily on me.

"Thanks, Sergeant Major. I'm glad you're coming."

We had reached the bottom of the stairs. He smiled. "At your service, *mon lieutenant.*"

CHAPTER 12

August 29, 1804
Boulogne

A week later, I rode Fleur along winding streets to the top of Calvary Cliffs on the outskirts of Boulogne, a high point from which I could look at the city, the harbor full of ships, and in the far distance, the coast of England. It was a gorgeous, late summer day—perfect sailing weather. Not far away behind me was Napoleon's field headquarters, an elaborate wooden structure from where he could watch his fleet, the British and his army. He wasn't there today.

Unfortunately the only ones sailing today were the English; two of their frigates were visible in the distance on patrol, well out of the range of our cannon but close enough to remind us who controlled the English Channel, or the *Manche,* as the French called it. I was grudgingly prepared to concede the naming to the *rosbifs*, after all they controlled it, at least for the time being. When night came they would likely come much closer and launch boats, either outside the harbor or elsewhere along the coast and drop off parties of saboteurs. I knew their intentions; stopping them was the tricky part.

Seagulls circled overhead, calling to each other and looking for scraps of food, while from the distance I could hear town vendors hawking their wares. For a moment I thought both sounded very similar. I chuckled at my own wittiness, thinking neither seagulls nor merchants would appreciate the comparison.

After leaving Ney and Jomini, Grenier and I took our forty men to Boulogne. I made sure the survivors of the fight in the farmhouse near le Crotoy were part of the contingent. I rode ahead to see to accommodations and found some just inside the walls of the older part of the city.

At first the mayor was not inclined to be accommodating to yet more soldiers, but my orders from Ney, along with the purpose of my mission, convinced him to make room in the quarters set aside for the city garrison, although most soldiers were billeted outside the city. After all, forty more men among so many thousands were a drop in the bucket.

I looked back towards the town. The ramparts and fortifications here were much more impressive than Montreuil's, as were the castle and the famous bell tower, although Boulogne was much busier. I was ignored by both civilian and soldier alike, even on a fine horse as an impressively dressed aide-de-camp, having donned that uniform in place of my light infantry officer's uniform.

To be honest, I was secretly thrilled to wear it. My blue trousers were more elegant and had more gold braid than before, I had exchanged my commonplace shako for an elegant fur busby, and my long blue jacket was replaced by a short hussar's jacket called a dolman, which had enough gold braid for people back home to think I was the king of Persia! Since I was acting independently as an aide-de-camp I had to look the role. Aides must stand out on a battlefield, thus the colorful, sometimes gaudy uniforms. I certainly stood out.

The sun set lower over the horizon, and for a while longer I watched the harbor, the enemy ships and the activity of the fishermen below the cliffs before heading my mount through the narrow streets of the city to where I would coordinate the night's activities with city officials, gendarmes and military authorities. I was going to do everything in my power to stop any more acts of sabotage. Woe to any English caught in the act who fell into my hands.

An hour or so before dusk, in a tavern near where my men and I were billeted, I met with several of the officers and NCOs responsible for patrolling the streets and harbor of Boulogne. In recent months they had caught a number of saboteurs and were experienced in dealing with them.

An odd assortment of men, they were a mixture of gendarmes, infantry and cavalry officers, and a few in civilian clothes, the latter presumably from the Ministry of Police. I was hoping to learn from all of them and develop a plan to protect the fleet.

As our meal was not yet ready, they stood in various groups, talking among themselves. Everyone looked up when I entered the tavern; a few nodded but most did nothing, preferring to observe for the moment. Among the cavalry officers standing in front of the large stone fireplace, I overheard several speaking English. I decided to join them.

"Good evening, gentlemen," I interjected in English.

A stocky, ruddy faced captain, at least ten or fifteen years my senior, wearing the green uniform of a chasseur, answered in a lilting Irish accent. "And a good evening to you. Burns, isn't it?" His eyes were friendly but there was a definite hardness to the man that spoke of years of experience.

I nodded.

"Ah, Ney's American," said another man, a sergeant, somewhat younger than his companion. He was also Irish.

"Damn it, I swear to God, the next man who calls me that I'm going to call out with my choice of weapons," I snapped, with far more vehemence than I intended. My next sentence was calmer. "You will address me as Lieutenant Burns, or simply Lieutenant. Sorry to snap, Sergeant, but you have no idea how many times I've been called that."

The sergeant, O'Hara, switched to French. "Sorry, Monsieur." The bastard didn't look sorry at all.

"A bit touchy, aren't you?" The Irish captain said.

"Yes, a little maybe. As I said, sorry to snap. I've been called that one time too many, it seems." I looked from one to the other. "By the way, you have me at a disadvantage, Captain."

A look of mock consternation crossed his face. "Dreadfully sorry, I have been remiss in my manners. You have the pleasure to address Nicholas Callahan, poet philosopher and soldier, or would that be poet soldier and philosopher?" He bowed and gave a flourish with his hat.

He may have been playing the joker, but I could tell he was someone to have on your side in a fight. The top of his left ear was missing, with a deep scar on both sides of it. His nose had clearly been broken several times.

"And what brings an Irish poet soldier philosopher to serve in the French army in Boulogne?"

"The same reason you are here, my friend: to fight our age-old enemies across the channel. There be no better place for it. I've been in the French army twenty-five years. I started under King Louis XVI in one of the famous Irish Brigades, the Regiment of Berwick. Saw my first action in the West Indies, and then America in 1779 under the Count D'Estaing. I killed my first Englishman in Georgia at the age of fifteen, so I have fond memories of your country. After the Revolution here, when the Brigades were disbanded, I became a cavalryman and in 1793 joined the Irish Chasseurs of Lamoureux, which was mustered for an expedition to England or Ireland. That fell through and we were disbanded in 1799, just before Napoleon became First Consul. I've served in other units since."

"You weren't part of the landing in Ireland in 1798?" A French force of 1,500 under General Humbert landed in the west of Ireland, drawing thousands of enthusiastic Irishmen to fight under their banner. After some impressive victories against the English, they had been defeated by overwhelming numbers.

Callahan sighed sadly. "No. In some ways I wish I were, but I would be dead now had I gone. While the French soldiers and officers were eventually exchanged or repatriated, the bloody English hung every Irishman in French uniform, no matter how long they had worn it. I was lucky, waiting in France for the word to board ship to sail and reinforce the landing—word that never came."

"And now?" I was enthralled.

"Now I am part of the Interpreter Guides of the Army of England, again mustered for an invasion. We'll see if it happens." He ran his hand through a thick mop of brown hair with more than a little gray.

"Do you doubt it will happen?" It was the first open hint of doubt about the expedition I had heard voiced in some time.

"Oh, I've no doubt Napoleon is serious about this expedition. I've seen preparations for invasions come and go since I first put on this uniform, and this *is* the most serious and well organized without a doubt. It's just that I'm sure the English are doing all they can to prevent it; the Royal Navy is out there waiting and the

English are likely spreading their gold throughout Europe to stir up other countries against us. Ever since they broke the Peace of Amiens in 1802 and reopened hostilities they've been trying to buy allies."

I was familiar with England's violation of that peace treaty, when she refused to remove her troops from Malta after France complied with all the requirements of that treaty. England only viewed the treaty as breathing room until it could start shooting again, whereas France hoped for a lasting peace to rebuild its economy and society. Eventually England seized over one hundred and twenty French and Dutch ships just before declaring war. The fighting was on again, though for the last few years it had been pretty desultory except at sea. The invasion would change all that.

"So you think England will be able to buy allies to distract us from invading?"

Callahan tipped his head back and finished his drink, before taking a bottle off the mantle and refilling his glass. "I'm sure they're trying as we speak. The question is, will they be successful before we can launch our invasion? It's a race, and I think it's even money who'll win."

I didn't respond, just pondered his words. He had spent much more time in France than I and prepared to invade England several times. A few more officers and NCOs came in at that moment and I noticed the tavern keeper signaling our meal was almost ready. I looked back at the mantle and Callahan's drink.

"Just what are you drinking, Callahan?"

He held up the glass to gaze at it. "This? Irish whisky, nectar of the Gods. I have connections with several American ship captains who smuggle me the stuff. I'm not much for wine or brandy and can't stand rum—though I'll drink it in a pinch. Are you saying you've never tried it?"

I shook my head.

Callahan immediately grabbed a glass and filled it halfway. "Here you go, you'll bless the day you met me. Only be careful lad —sip it, or the only way you'll be able to make rounds through Boulogne will be tied to the back of your horse like a sack of potatoes."

We sat around one large table, over a dozen of us. We bolted ourselves into one of the back rooms of the inn, posted a guard at the door and began our talks.

The discussion wasn't entirely fruitless, though it was clear many didn't think I needed to be there. There were many different organizations doing the same job and each thought they were being successful at it. The funny thing is they were right to an extent—they had been successful up to this point. Most saboteurs had been caught and few of their deeds carried out. The problem as I saw it was the lack of communication and coordination.

"What I see as my duty is keeping all of you informed of what is going on along other parts of the coast and be ready to bring reinforcements to a particular area we all agree is going to be the target of sabotage," I said. I took a drink of Callahan's whisky as several officers expounded on what they thought were the most vulnerable areas along the coast. Though Boulogne had the most ships, it was well protected from the sea by emplacements with lots of cannon, not to mention a chain across the harbor that could be raised or lowered from shore to allow the passage of ships. A sentry was posted every fifteen paces along the docks, and on every ship as well.

Some of the men thought other ports, such as Étaples, were more vulnerable, though their relative isolation from larger towns made it more difficult for raiding parties to get close to the ships without being seen.

"What if there is a disagreement as to where reinforcements are needed? How will it be decided where they'll go?" asked Lieutenant Jacques Baudet, a gendarme officer. I could tell by his expression he wouldn't like any answer I gave.

"I will decide. You are in charge of defending your areas, I'm in charge of keeping you informed of danger as I hear about it and getting extra troops to you as needed. One thing we don't lack here is troops." Baudet was about to protest when I cut him off. "There are tens of thousands of our soldiers within ten miles of Boulogne! Manpower isn't the problem, knowing where to put them is the problem."

Despite my orders from Ney signed by the marshals, I knew I was going to have a difficult time getting cooperation. My low rank, my nationality and inexperience were all marks against me.

The men I was meeting with were those directly responsible on the ground, not the officers in charge, who had not deigned to meet with me.

I couldn't blame them really.

We ate in silence. Soon we could hear cracking noises coming from outside. Callahan looked at me in alarm. "Musket fire!"

With one accord we rushed to the door, unbarred it and ran out to where we could see the nearby harbor. Lights were being lit on all the ships and shouts of alarm echoed from vessel to vessel.

Two gunboats, showing French colors, were heading towards some of our docked ships. The chain blocking the harbor had been lowered that morning and had not been put back in place. When these ships had arrived after dark they had passed right through the defensive line of gunboats and on into the harbor without answering any hails. Someone had woken up finally to the danger and the two boats were being shot at with muskets, but no one dared use cannon for fear of hitting other French ships, some of which were packed with gunpowder and ammunition.

One of the two ships struck a sloop and blew up. Both ships went to the bottom right before our eyes, leaving only a fiery mass on the surface of the harbor. Cries of panic went up from some of the onlookers as the other fireship continued on its way towards the docks, where there were many ships and hundreds, if not thousands of people. The ship was likely full of gunpowder, as the first had proved to be.

The musketry aimed at the ship was steadier now, though I wondered if anyone was still onboard. I thought it likely they had aimed it at the line of ships and jumped in the water, though the concussion from a large explosion might still kill them. Maybe they were still onboard and were willing to lose their lives as long as they took many of ours.

Too far away to reach it in time, I stood transfixed by a feeling of utter helplessness as the ship made its way towards the docks. For some reason the vessel was slowing, stopped by some kind of obstruction in the water. Suddenly the ship exploded, a massive explosion like the sun that knocked my companions and me off our feet though we were almost a half mile away. Most of the windows in town were shattered, even people inside their houses were knocked out of their chairs or beds.

My ears were ringing and I lay on the cobblestone street, at first unable or unwilling to move. Eventually I sat up, rubbing my head where it had hit the stone. I would live, but would have a headache. I rose unsteadily, clinging to a hitching post. Around me, others were doing the same. I could hear cries and moaning. Bending over, I picked up my hat and brushed myself off.

"Sweet Mary and Joseph." Callahan was on his feet next to me and we surveyed what looked to be a scene from Dante's *Inferno*. When the ship exploded it rained fiery debris everywhere. Some had landed on nearby ships, catching their rigging on fire, while other pieces hit the docks. Some had flown over us, hitting houses and other buildings. Everywhere people were starting to scramble to put the fires out and contain the damage.

"Hell of a first day on the job," Callahan said grinning.

"Hell of a first day, indeed," I replied, not quite able to return his grin. "Let's go see if any saboteurs jumped ship and lived." The other men with whom we had been eating dinner had already scattered to their units.

Sergeant Tessier, my comrade from the fight in the farmhouse, arrived with twenty men from my company and told me Grenier had taken the others and was already heading to the other side of the harbor to look for anyone who might have jumped ship.

We headed towards the docks, carefully picking our way around burning wreckage. Some semblance of order was starting to be imposed on the scene as officers gave orders, water was brought to douse flames, and soldiers and sailors were using axes to cut away damaged pieces of the wharves. Some civilians had made their way closer to the water and were helping tend to the wounded.

Callahan stopped. "You were wondering if the saboteurs jumped ship, lad. Evidently not all of them did." He indicated something on the ground and moved it with his foot. It was a hand, bloody bones visible where it had been torn from its body.

I swallowed, trying to keep bile down. "One less to find. Let's go."

As we passed where the ship exploded, the damage was evident. The smell of burning wood and the acrid stench of burnt gunpowder competed with the salty tang of the sea. I looked towards the burning wreckage on the water, trying to pick out signs of bodies. Continuing on, we headed towards the mouth of the harbor, ignoring the activity around us. Our job was not to pick up the pieces and repair the damage but to catch those responsible, if they lived. My uniform, with its gold-tasseled, white armband of an aide-de-camp to a marshal, signaled everyone else to leave us alone to stalk our prey.

"Anyone who looks out of place, or looks like they just got out of the water, detain them and bring them back to the castle at the landward corner of the city walls," I said to Tessier. He broke the men into groups of five and they spread out. We were past most of the commotion and walking towards the mouth of the outer harbor along the stone wharves. There were still ships packed together with wooden docks and walkways connecting them, and a great deal of material was stored along the docks. There were houses and warehouses along here as well, though fewer shops.

A group of men were struggling to separate non-damaged barrels of grain from those hit by fiery fragments. Several of them were carrying buckets of water from the harbor to douse embers. Some men were wet, but I thought nothing of it because of what they were doing. We were almost past them when I noticed one was missing a shoe. Of course, he could have lost it in the commotion, but for some reason I didn't think so. His stockings were of incredibly fine material—silk even—and the workmanship of his remaining shoe was exquisite. The man, tall, thin, and distinguished looking, around thirty years of age, glanced at me as we walked by then continued passing buckets. As I passed him I quietly drew my sword and made a gesture to Callahan and Tessier.

"Excuse me, sir, but could you help me for a moment?" I asked him in English.

The man turned. "Of course, I'd be happy..." He replied in English before he even completed turning. He stopped himself almost immediately but it was too late. I had my epee against his chest. Our eyes met.

"Sergeant Tessier, arrest this man." Three soldiers with fixed bayonets took the man back towards the center of town, prodding him along with their weapons.

Our swords out, Callahan and I led the way, accompanied by Tessier and one *fantassin*—an infantryman. Callahan and Tessier both had torches. We walked quietly along the wharves, looking for anything unusual. A few minutes later, Callahan pointed to the ground. There were wet footprints leading from the water to neat stacks of boxes, beyond which we could see the open maw of a warehouse. Whoever had passed this way had done so a while ago —the prints were already fading. We owed this discovery to Callahan's keen eye.

"Where are the guards? I thought the wharves were supposed to have sentries every fifteen paces?" I whispered to Callahan. It was much quieter now, the mayhem was behind us the closer we got to the mouth of the harbor.

"Back there," Callahan said just as quietly, indicating with his head the tumult closer to the explosion. Naturally most of the men here converged there to help fight any fires and look for survivors, though some should have stayed at their posts.

I stared towards the warehouse and the boxes piled all around. We spread out and slowly walked that way, carefully looking around the boxes. There was not much light besides the two torches and some lanterns high up on some of warehouses. As we went through the tangle of boxes, which was more extensive than it first appeared, the infantryman, Minot, called out urgently in a low voice to my right.

"Messieurs, come quickly."

I went over with Tessier. Callahan was kneeling on the ground beside a prostrate form while Minot stood over them, musket at the ready, looking around. As I got closer I could see it was a soldier from a line regiment, his white trousers stark in the darkness, his blue coat all but invisible. He was dead. The body had been hidden behind a crate.

I knelt next to Callahan while he held the torch over his face, which looked ghastly in the flickering light. A puddle of blood pooled behind the soldier's head. "He hasn't been dead long. Head was bashed against the cobblestones."

I peered at the ground around him. "Where are his weapons?"

"His musket is still here. His *briquet* is gone." In addition to a musket and bayonet, many French infantrymen carried short swords called *briquets*. Whoever killed the soldier probably thought he could conceal the sword more easily than the musket if he had to.

Callahan and I both looked at the warehouse and looked at each other. It was a logical place. It was the closest structure, a likely target for further sabotage, and the doors of all the other nearby buildings were closed. I nodded and we stood up.

"He couldn't have gotten too far. I'll take Tessier and go through the front door, you take Minot and see if there is a back door. We'll wait until you've been gone a minute to go in." I looked at Tessier. "Sergeant Tessier, take the guard's musket, I'll carry the torch." It was the only firearm we would have—I wasn't carrying my pistol that night.

Tessier sheathed his sword, picked up the musket, took some cartridges off the body and expertly loaded the weapon. Most sentries on routine duty down on the docks had fixed bayonets but unloaded weapons. The damp air affected the reliability of the weapons and no one wanted nervous sentries firing at every little noise with so much gunpowder around. Minot and Callahan headed towards the back of the building, Callahan holding the torch.

With the weapon at the ready, Tessier looked at me and nodded. I held the torch aloft in my left hand; the palm of my right was sweaty and I tightened its grip on my epee. Sweat ran through the tiny groves of the checkerboard pattern on the hilt. The door loomed before us. Slowly we passed through the entrance. Damp and mold permeated the air. Whatever was stored here had been here too long. Probably accoutrements for the invasion.

We couldn't split up as we had only one torch, and it was safer to stay together anyway. Tessier could wield the musket better using two hands.

I tried to shine the torch into every nook and cranny we passed, and began to realize this could take a while, and we weren't guaranteed we would find who we were looking for. The warehouse was sizeable, about sixty feet wide and 200 feet long, divided by narrow rows, with shelves sometimes stacked to the roof. The entrance was at the narrow end.

Long shadows danced ahead of us and on the walls from the light. The dirt and pebble floor crunched under our feet as we walked. Several times we heard noises off to the side—scurrying rats, disturbed in their hunt for food by our intrusion. Each time one ran off into the darkness we turned towards it, our nerves frayed. For some reason, I felt more fear there in the dark hunting one man than fighting dozens in that house months before. Possibly the darkness cast shadows on the mind and the silence gave us time to dwell on what could be waiting for us, the same fate that met that infantryman outside with his head bashed in.

How long we wandered through that maze I couldn't say. Probably not long, only a few minutes, but it seemed an eternity. A couple of times Tessier and I exchanged glances and shrugged.

"Perhaps he came in the front door and went straight out the back, *mon lieutenant*." He said, the torchlight glimmering on the bayonet of his musket.

Without looking at him I nodded, though he couldn't see the gesture, as his eyes like mine were glued to the darkness. "Perhaps," I murmured.

As we passed through an open area where several rows crossed, there was a movement to my left. I turned the torch to look and was struck by something—someone—with great force. We both crashed into shelving, and the torch fell to the ground and went out. It was complete darkness.

I grappled with my opponent, operating completely on touch, each of us trying to force the sword out of the other's hand. I was trying to use the hilt of my sword to pound where I believed his head to be, while he was trying to turn his shorter blade on me.

"Monsieur, Monsieur! Are you alright?" Tessier was calling out insistently in the dark. He was in complete darkness listening to our struggle, not daring to fire for fear of hitting me. In a sense I was luckier, I knew where my foe was, could smell the fear on his breath, the pungent odor of his body and aroma of seawater still dank on him. Still somewhat wet from the water, he was hard to grip.

As we careened from one side of the row of shelves to the other, he managed to hook a leg behind mine and I collapsed with him on top of me. I screamed in pain as a rib cracked. My sword clattered away in the dark. My left hand was still holding his sword hand, though I could feel him slowly turning the blade against me despite my best efforts. I started pounding my fist into the side of his head, and he replied in kind by a blow with his elbow into my cheek. He now had both hands on his sword hilt and had turned it so I could feel the edge above my neck. He was pushing it down so it would cut my throat like a guillotine. I desperately tried to push him off, reaching for his eyes, but he pulled his head out of reach. Somehow he managed to pull himself up so he was straddling me, practically sitting on my chest, so my blows were ineffectual. I had seconds of life left.

A pain in the small of my back reminded me I still had my knife. I pushed against him with my body, enough to disrupt his aim as he struck at me while I reached under me to pull it from my sheath. I began stabbing him wherever I could. My first was in his calf, and he screamed in pain and surprise. Warm blood began to gush over me from his wound and I stabbed again and again, reaching higher and stabbing him in the side.

His blade stopped descending as he frantically tried to get off me. I leapt up in a frenzy of anger, exultation and relief as I stabbed again and again in the dark, sometimes missing, sometimes connecting solidly. He was weakening but still trying to pull away when my knife hit a rib and I dropped it, so slippery with his blood I could no longer hold it.

Angry, I seized his sword arm and violently twisted it until I heard a bone crack and he dropped his sword. He was begging for me to stop. I felt a rough hand on my shoulder and spun angrily. It was Callahan, with Tessier and Minot. Tessier was relighting my dropped torch from Callahan's.

The three of them stared at me in shock.

"*Mon Dieu,*" Tessier said, barely above a whisper.

"Good God," echoed Callahan, still staring. "Are you wounded?"

"No, not to speak of," I said angrily, "though that bastard was seconds from killing me. Why the hell are you all looking at me like that?"

I must have looked like a sight out of Hell. I was covered with blood—thankfully none of it mine—and had been wildly attacking my would-be executioner when they pulled me off. I can hardly blame them for their shock, but at the time I felt only annoyance. I grabbed Callahan's torch and turned to look at my assailant. A rough, burly man with curly hair, he lay against a post breathing heavily, blood coming from numerous wounds, a few of them mortal. He was holding out his good hand in supplication.

Seeing something twinkle on the ground, I stopped to find my knife. I wiped the blood off on the man's pant leg and stood up. Tessier handed me my sword, which I sheathed.

"Are you sure you're alright, *mon lieutenant*?"

I was about to snap angrily again but saw there was genuine concern on his face.

"I'm fine, Sergeant, just had a scare in the dark. It must have sounded awful to you not knowing quite where we were or what was going on." He nodded. "Let's collect the prisoners back at the castle gate."

Tessier and Minot carried the dying man between them, his unbroken arm flung around one of their shoulders as he sat suspended on a musket. The man moaned in pain as he was jolted along. His complaints were in English, so there was no question about his identity, if there ever had been after he attacked us.

We were walking along the wharves back towards the main part of town, passing more and more groups of soldiers cleaning up the mess after the explosion. The frenzied pace of activity had slowed. Sometimes soldiers stopped what they were doing to stare at us as we passed, both because I looked ghastly and because of our prisoner and the state he was in.

As we walked, our prisoner began begging for water, a common occurrence among the wounded. I was still riled up from our fight in the dark and turned on him angrily.

"You want water, you bastard?" His eyes widened and he said nothing. I grabbed him by his jacket and yanked him off the musket held by Tessier and Minot and dragged him to the edge of the dock. The water lapped below us in the dark, less than ten feet below. "I'll give you water!" I held him so his head was hanging over the edge. I was ready to toss him in the harbor. I ignored his feeble protestations.

"Pierre, enough. Don't do it." Callahan said calmly from behind me.

I turned my head to look at him. "Why the hell not? We're going to execute him anyway, it'll save us the gunpowder!"

"There's no dignity in it, there's no honor in it." He made no move to try and restrain me.

I looked at him for a long moment, then dragged the man back from the edge and left him there. "There's no dignity or honor having your throat cut in the dark either." I straightened up, and Minot and Tessier moved to pick the man up again.

Not long after we stood outside the gate of the castle, which could be entered by a stone bridge over a deep moat surrounded by a low wall. My cracked rib was looked at and a bandage wrapped around me. The opinion of the surgeon was that I would be sore for a few weeks but was fine otherwise.

We had captured five of our attackers who had jumped off the fireships and made it to shore before they blew up. Four of them were British sailors, including my assailant, another was a French Royalist. Their leader was the tall man we captured as part of the bucket brigade. All were in civilian clothes.

I began talking with this man, who identified himself as Lieutenant Richard Soames, of the Royal Navy. A straightforward man, I liked him despite myself. Unfortunately, I had to kill him.

"If you and your men had worn your uniforms when you jumped, you would be prisoners of war. Instead you'll be shot as criminals." This was a duty I did not want to carry out, even if he was an Englishman.

Soames calmly shrugged. "We thought disguise would help us get away once ashore. Do what you must."

I nodded and walked back to where Callahan, Grenier and Tessier were talking. I looked at Grenier. "Sergeant Major, we'll shoot them just outside the walls. March them out."

My entire detachment of forty men escorted them out, our drummer at the head of the little column tapping out a slow march. The five prisoners were in the center, two of them carrying their wounded comrade. They were a sorry looking lot, bedraggled, their clothes still wet from the harbor.

We went out the nearby Porte Neuve gate and immediately turned to the left. The detachment was divided in half, twenty assigned to the firing squad, four for each prisoner, who were lined up against the city walls. A wagon and five canvas sacks in lieu of coffins were nearby.

Torches were driven into the ground all around to light the execution ground.

The wounded prisoner could not stand and an old chair was located for him to sit in. None of them were to be tied unless they struggled. I walked with a corporal to each man to offer him a blindfold. Two accepted the offer, while two, including Soames, declined. We blindfolded the wounded man, as his mumblings were incoherent.

Very precisely, I marched to one end of my column of soldiers and drew my sword.

"Prime!"

Each man held his musket parallel to the ground at about waist level, opened the priming pan, took a paper cartridge from his cartridge pouch, his *giberne,* and bit the end off of it, pouring some of the powder in the pan and closing it.

"Ram cartridge!" Each soldier stood his musket on the ground to his left, butt first, poured the remaining powder in the cartridge down the barrel, followed by the ball wadded inside the paper. He then pulled the metal ramrod out from under the barrel and rammed the musket ball and its paper wadding down the barrel until it was firmly seated. Then they slid their ramrods back in place in the slot under the barrel and brought their weapons to left shoulder arms.

"*Armez!*" The soldiers brought their weapons down off their shoulders in one movement, pointing in the air at a 90 degree angle. I walked down the line of the soldiers, sword to my shoulder, carefully looking at each man and his weapon. At the end of the line, I did an about face, looking down the line of muskets, all lined up perfectly. I glanced over at the prisoners and saw Soames watching me.

I hesitated and he nodded imperceptibly. I nodded in return and lifted my sword.

"*En joue!*" Twenty muskets were aimed as one. Soames still watched me.

"*Feu!*"

Flames and smoke from twenty muskets shot out. The four standing men crumpled to the ground, while the seated prisoner was knocked backwards and rolled onto his side.

I walked over to inspect the carnage. All but two were dead, Soames and another man. The latter was fading fast and wouldn't need a coup de grace. Soames was hit in the shoulder, the stomach, and his leg, which was shattered. The fourth shot missed entirely.

The stomach wound was fatal but could take hours to kill him. He would have to be finished off. Still conscious, he looked at me as Tessier waved a torch close to him. He actually smiled.

"Sorry to be such a bother, old chap," he said coughing up blood.

I sheathed my sword and waved over a soldier whose musket was loaded for such an eventuality.

"It'll be quick," I said, watching as he clutched at his stomach wound, biting part of his shirt to stop from screaming.

He nodded. "Good. I am in rather a hurry."

The soldier was at my elbow and had cocked his weapon.

"I'll see that your grave is marked and your family knows where you are." I took the musket from the soldier and signaled him to step back. "I'll do it."

Soames saw the musket in my hands. "Thank you."

The shot sounded like thunder in the night. I handed the musket back to the soldier and turned to Grenier and Tessier. "Make sure the civilians who bury them put his name on his grave marker. If they don't I'll come after them myself." Both men nodded. "Excellent work tonight. I suspect news of our handiwork will get back to England."

I walked among the formation, talking to the soldiers, complimenting them on their night's hunting.

"Dismiss the men, Grenier. An extra ration of wine for each man, on me."

They cheered me, though I didn't feel very cheerful.

"So, what exactly seems to be the problem, lad?" Callahan said, as he poured me a drink back at the tavern. Along with Grenier, Callahan and I returned to finish his bottle of whiskey, while Tessier and two corporals marched the men back to the barracks. "Don't tell me killing a few Englishmen has suddenly made you reconsider your profession?"

I sipped the drink and watched while Callahan poured one for Grenier, who sniffed his glass cautiously before taking a sip. It was late and there were only a few others in the inn. A low fire still burned in the stone fireplace and a few candles held off the darkness.

"No, I'm not reconsidering, it's just I don't feel like too much of a soldier tonight." I replied, in French, because of Grenier. "Tonight, I tussled in the dark like a common criminal, then put five men against a wall and had them shot without so much as a trial."

"Five men who would have killed thousands here tonight if they could have, *mon lieutenant*—and not just soldiers and sailors would have died, but women and children too," Grenier said, downing his drink appreciatively. He seemed to take to the whisky.

"I know that, Sergeant Major, it's just not what I envisioned doing as a soldier. When I was in the militia back in the United States and in my months here, I pictured myself in a line with thousands of others, shooting at those trying to kill me, charging them with the bayonet, flags leading us on." I twirled the glass around, watching the light brown liquid slosh against the sides and slowly settle again in the bottom.

"Not quite the romantic image you had?" Callahan asked wryly.

I smiled and shook my head. "Not quite."

"*Mon lieutenant*, a battlefield is not as romantic as you envision it, especially after," Grenier said. "There are the groans of the wounded, the stench of blood, death, and shit. Often parts of the battlefield are slick with blood or innards. We do our duty despite all that."

"We fight the enemy where he is," Callahan agreed. "This is war, and if the English are going to send saboteurs and fireships to kill from a distance, then we must do what we can to stop them and make examples of those we catch. You know fighting from a distance is typical of the English—they send fireships to kill with little danger to themselves, or they spread their gold throughout Europe trying to get others to fight for them."

I nodded.

"Think of it as an act of goodwill. You might have saved the lives of several more of our enemies by the example you set tonight." He grinned rather wickedly, I thought. "You'll probably be famous in certain circles in London after this."

I started laughing and soon was joined by Grenier and Callahan. I grimaced as a tendril of pain shot out from my rib but kept laughing. It felt good.

"Are you well, Monsieur?" Grenier, asked, a drop of whisky on his mustache.

I laughed again. "Nothing another drink won't cure." I raised my glass. "To Ireland, the United States, France and the Emperor."

We drank that toast and many others. The sky was starting to lighten when we stumbled back to our quarters.

CHAPTER 13

For the next month or more life settled into a routine. There were no more fireships but almost nightly the British dropped off small groups of saboteurs. Sometimes we caught them, sometimes we didn't. Those we did met the same fate as Soames and his party: muskets against a wall within the hour of being caught. I felt no more qualms, though it helped that none were of Soames' quality. I came to learn quite a bit about incendiary devices, spies, guile and deception.

My military education did not stop because of these duties. Three or four days a week, when I rode to Étaples in my hunt for saboteurs, I met with Jomini and other officers. Ney had set up a school for the officers of his Corps, where they would meet to learn and discuss history, strategy, and tactics. He put Jomini in charge of the school. It seems our talks and the training regimen he set up for me had helped him perfect what he planned to teach. I had been his experiment.

As often as I saw Jomini in the classroom, in the field among the troops I more often saw Ney. He was everywhere among his men, offering encouragement, advice, even demonstrating how something should be done. Never would he hesitate to get off his horse, muddy his boots and uniform among his men, taking up a musket to show them the best way to hold it or thrust with the bayonet. The soldiers of the corps loved him.

As much as possible I would return with my men to Reille's company, where we would participate in these various movements and training exercises. It was a busy schedule.

Because most of my time was spent in Boulogne I was able to stop at Madame Delobel's several times and visit Marie. I didn't quite become a regular customer but they recognized me easily enough.

Marie even helped me catch several saboteurs. She heard some were landing at a particular beach and even what ship they would be attacking. Her information was correct and I didn't ask how she learned what she did in such detail. Some things are better not known.

The two men we apprehended on Marie's warning were shot right on the beach and carted off for burial.

September 29, 1804

Ever since the ball at Montreuil I had remained in contact with Athenaïs, though it was not easy. She could send me letters easily enough, but in order to write her, I had to send my letters through a third party, usually Aglaé, but sometimes through a neighbor of hers.

It was cumbersome but had to be done to keep Jean-Louis, her older brother, from finding out. He was the head of their family since the death of their father during the Reign of Terror, guillotined like so many others. Though the Vanier family was minor nobility, they were still nobility and had suffered under the blade. Jean-Louis escaped France with his twin sister and returned after Napoleon's amnesty, while Athenaïs, her mother and a younger brother and sister stayed in France. Athenaïs had met Aglaé in the same school in Paris, which was also attended by Hortense Beauharnais.

Jean-Louis hoped to improve his family's position. Athenaïs was convinced he would not view friendship, or more, on the part of his sister with an American officer on Ney's staff as doing much in that regard. He was probably intending an advantageous match for her.

Despite all that, Athenaïs was not deterred and insisted we write and meet again. She was visiting a friend near Boulogne and we were going to meet for the first time since the ball. There was a dance being given that night at a house within the city. My assignment to Boulogne made it easy to be there.

It was going to be a dance for mid and lower ranking officers in Boulogne. What few unattached women there were in the city—

and they certainly were at a premium at this time—would be in attendance. Despite the relatively small size of the gathering I hoped to be able to sneak Athenaïs out—if she were willing. Beatrice Fleurette, Reille's partner from the ball in Montreuil, was also in town.

It was early fall and dark came early. I arrived with Reille, who had managed to get away from the company. It was good to see him. While I didn't miss Monge, I did miss Reille. We entered the house together and I looked for Callahan, who was on the other side of the ornate rectangular room, which was well-lit by chandeliers and brass sconces on the walls.

As usual since relocating to Boulogne, I wore my aide-de-camp's uniform and looked—if I say so myself—dashing. After introducing Callahan to Reille, the three of us we were talking by a window when I saw Athenaïs come in the front door, fashionably late. Beatrice was with her, but not Aglaé. A marshal's wife was very much in demand and this gathering was a little below her. That was fine with me. Since meeting Athenaïs, I hardly gave Aglaé a thought.

I couldn't take my eyes off her as the two of them joined a group of elegantly dressed beauties. I wanted to rush over but restrained myself and continued talking to my companions. Our eyes met briefly and she nodded a barely perceptible greeting, and my heart started racing.

I noticed Reille also looking across the room in the direction of Beatrice, who hid her face behind a fan as she spoke to Athenaïs and her other companions. Both of them laughed and Athenaïs shot me another look, this one less subtle. Still I refrained from rushing across the room and waited for the dance to start.

"Do you think they're talking about us?" Reille asked me with a sly smile.

I nodded, a tad nervously perhaps. "I should think so by the way they're looking over here. What do you think they're saying?"

Stroking his mustache, Reille looked at them then turned towards me with a devilish smile. "Comparing notes? I'm sure you're falling short."

I practically choked on my glass of wine. Callahan began patting me on the back. "Are you alright, laddie?" I nodded.

"Our American friend is still a little shy about the opposite sex, or at least talking about them. A habit he brought from his country," Reille said, looking at me with a look approaching pity.

"There's really nothing to be shy about," Callahan said to me, trying to offer fatherly advice. "They usually don't bite, but when they do, you'll love it. Besides, that's when you can bite back."

I said nothing but hid behind my wine glass, hoping I wasn't blushing and that the dance would begin soon. Unfortunately, no such luck.

"It's astounding they manage to breed in his country," Reille continued. "It's the influence of the damned English. I hear the *rosbifs* wear their night clothes when they make love—they cut little holes in them to stick their members through."

Callahan laughed. "I've seen a lot of English women. I can hardly blame them!"

A look of complete seriousness crossed Reille's face, though his eyes were twinkling. "I just hope our friend can recover from those years of English influence. He has a reputation to uphold wearing that uniform."

A look of mock consternation crossed Callahan's face. "Now that is unfair, Monsieur. Our friend is half French and the other half is Scottish, a Celt, by God! Any comparisons your lady friends make I'm sure would be in Pierre's favor."

"Only because of his French half," Reille quipped. "I'm sure it's twice the length of his Scottish half."

The mock argument at my expense probably would have continued but there was a signal the dance was to begin. Not a moment too soon.

A major, an aide-de-camp for Marshal Nicholas Soult, who commanded the IV Corps and Boulogne, was to lead out the dance. Any representative from any other marshal, such as myself, being an aide to Ney, was also to dance the first dance.

Tugging down on my coat and straightening my sword belt, I strolled across the dance floor to Athenaïs. I bowed and kissed her hand. "May I have the honor of this dance, Mademoiselle?"

Athenaïs was dazzling in a pink evening gown, with gold and pearls at the neck and wrists. She gave me a knowing smile as she curtseyed.

"I would be delighted, Monsieur."

The first dance was a waltz, but most of the pieces after that were livelier, fast reels, with the violins racing out a tune. There was much toe tapping and hand clapping. This was not a formal ball, but a gathering of friends and acquaintances, officers connected with the security of Boulogne.

The pieces had a Celtic air to them and were only slightly more refined versions of sailors' jigs or lumber camp reels I heard back home. The veneer of the sophistication of the Imperial Court came off for a while, allowing many who had been merchants or even peasants before the Revolution and the army claimed them to relax again. Though for the last two years many of the old nobility from the *ancien regime* had returned under Napoleon's amnesty, many of the officers and members of the civil service remained from the class established under the Revolution and Consulate. They continued on under the Empire as new nobility, side by side with the old. Each looked down on the other. I always thought the new had the better case—after all, they had earned their titles and positions, often on the battlefield.

Tonight, however, most of those present were not nobility, old or new, simply officers of the empire, and those women trying to lure one in, either for the night or longer.

Athenaïs and I were in a corner talking to Reille and Beatrice. Callahan joined us, an attractive, black-haired woman of about his age on his arm. She had on a wedding ring but that didn't seem to bother anybody, least of all her. The morals of post-Revolutionary France were still taking some getting used to, though I suppose women have always thrown themselves on men in uniform, no matter their station or marital status.

Callahan smiled and shrugged. "Madame needs an escort. Her husband is the captain of one of the frigates protecting the invasion fleet."

Both of them laughed uproariously. Laughter mixed with music throughout the room. Nearby, servants were changing some of the candles on a chandelier during a pause in the dance.

"So, Monsieur Callahan, I hear you and Pierre have become quite close," Athenaïs said. "I hope you are protecting Pierre after that terrible affair in the warehouse on the wharf." She clutched my arm protectively.

Without letting go of his friend for the night, Callahan bowed elegantly. "Mademoiselle, I would protect him with my life."

"As long as his own wasn't in danger," I retorted. Athenaïs slapped my arm.

"Don't listen to him, Monsieur, I hear nothing but wonderful things about you—about both of you." Athenaïs said, including Reille. "I can see it's true."

Reille bowed. "I am honored to be his friend and yours, though as for being protected, Pierre is far from helpless." He took Athenaïs' hand and kissed it. "However, for you Mademoiselle, I will watch him like a wolf watches her cub."

I chuckled and shook my head. "Anything to kiss a pretty girl's hand." Reille smiled and cocked his head in acknowledgement.

"You are most gracious, Mademoiselle." Callahan said, and then looked at me matter-of-factly. "Been telling lies again?"

"Of course, how else could I say good things about you?" Again Athenaïs slapped me, this time a little harder.

I pulled her close to me, our faces barely inches from each other. I stared into those beautiful blue eyes and held her tighter. I wanted her and could see the sentiment was returned.

I turned to Reille and Callahan. "Gentlemen, I think we'll be leaving you."

Reille grinned knowingly (and approvingly, I might add) but Callahan held up his hand. "How about if we all leave? Madame has a house not far away, with well-appointed extra bedrooms."

All eyes fell on Madame Chenier—for such was her name—for confirmation. She smiled a rather happy, drunken smile. "I hardly have any company anymore. I would be glad to have you at my house." She looked knowingly at Reille and me. "You'll find it far more pleasant surroundings for your lady friends than sneaking them into a room wherever you're staying." Reille had rented a room for the night at an inn not far from my quarters, but neither my place nor his was entirely suitable for what we had in mind—though that wouldn't have stopped us.

The six of us slowly made our way towards the door, expressing our regrets along the way, and went out into the cool night air. Madame Chenier's servant was waiting outside the house with a torch to light our way. As we stepped out into the cobblestone street, anxious to make our way to her house, three figures stepped out from the darkness.

Though our hands fell on our sword hilts, we did not draw them. I wondered if it was a message about English spies in the city, though I thought it odd the messenger did not seek us out inside the ball.

"Athenaïs," a male voice called out harshly. I felt her grip tighten on my arm and I instinctively pushed her behind me. I still could not see who was there. The one torch held by Madame Chenier's servant was not shedding much light, though he did turn it so we could see better.

"Who are you and what do you want?" I asked the form.

He stepped forward, a well-dressed man about twenty years old with incredibly handsome features. For a moment I wondered if it was Jean-Louis, Athenaïs' older brother, but there was no resemblance to her. Well dressed and of a haughty demeanor, it was clear he was an aristocrat.

"What I want is for you to get your filthy hands off my fiancée." He took another step forward, as did one of his companions. The third person who held back appeared to be a woman.

"Fiancée?" I said. My question was for Athenaïs, though I never took my eyes off the newcomer.

Before she could reply, he spoke up. "Yes, fiancée. I am Joseph-Marie-Vincent Beaulieu. My family has been friends with the Vaniers for generations and we are betrothed." He spoke fiercely and uttered his name like it was a talisman which should push back the night.

Athenaïs came up next to me again and practically spat a response. "You are not my fiancé. How many times must I tell you that?"

"Of course I am, your brother has given his consent." Beaulieu spoke condescendingly, like he was speaking to a child.

"But *I* have not, you crazy idiot! And I never will! How many times must I explain this to you?" She made an obscene-looking hand gesture, lightly striking the bottom of her chin.

I braced myself for an explosion but there wasn't one. Beaulieu's response was icy. "You enjoy being crude, getting in the gutter and shaming your family, don't you? Probably you were going into an alley to fuck this," he deigned to gesture at me backhandedly, "*soldier.*"

I was about to respond when Callahan jumped in. "No need to fear, they were definitely going to use a bed."

I couldn't help it. I laughed, and so did Athenaïs, Reille and Beatrice. Not just a chuckle but gut-wrenching laughter.

Beaulieu was livid. He evidently was not used to being laughed at and began to look like a kettle ready to boil over. He reached inside his coat and pulled out a small pistol and aimed it squarely at me, clumsily pulling back the hammer at the same moment. I took a half step back, trying to push Athenaïs behind me again, but she refused. She took a step towards Beaulieu though she still held one of my arms with one hand.

"Joseph-Marie, what in God's name are you doing? Put that away!"

"Come with me and I won't kill your *lover.*" The emphasis he put on the word showed the distaste he felt for me. "I brought Elizabeth, your brother's servant, as your escort. Let's go."

The woman, a pudgy, well-dressed, middle-aged woman stepped forward next to Beaulieu's other companion, a mousy looking man who hadn't said a word during the entire confrontation, though he was looking at his friend as if he thought he were crazy.

"No." Athenaïs said quietly, though the tone of her voice led me to believe she was wavering.

Enough was enough. I was getting annoyed at whole affair. "Shoot me if you're going to shoot. But if you shoot me, my friends will cut you down where you stand."

"Aye," Callahan said from behind me.

"It might be worth it, since you clearly have already defiled my fiancée." There was a moment of softness in Beaulieu's face. It was more than family pride, he liked Athenaïs in his way, though obviously the feeling was not returned. Or was it, I wondered.

Behind us I could hear noise in the street as if there were a number of people coming in our direction.

Athenaïs' grip on my arm was starting to hurt as she spoke again. "The only person who has defiled me is you, Joseph-Marie.

Get out of here!" I chanced a glance at her face. The softness in his expression was not returned.

"Put the pistol down, Monsieur." Reille had softly drawn his sword, and swung to Beaulieu's left side in the dark. The point of his blade was touching the side of Beaulieu's neck.

It was unclear how long this standoff would last. Fortunately, the noise I had heard behind us was a patrol of fusiliers from a line regiment looking for saboteurs. They surrounded us.

The corporal in charge lifted his musket at Beaulieu. "Drop your pistol, Monsieur, or you will be shot."

Beaulieu chanced a glance around. An expression of resignation on his face, he slowly pointed his pistol straight up in the air. I stepped forward and took it from him. I blew the charge of gunpowder from the priming pan, removed the flint from the hammer, and then handed the pistol back to him.

"Get out of Boulogne—tonight. These men will escort you out of the city."

In a flash he hit me in the face with the back of his hand, knocking my hat off my head. The blow was hard enough to draw blood from my lip. "You filthy coward! I want satisfaction! Fight me!" Spittle came flying from his mouth as he practically screamed at me.

The soldiers grabbed him roughly and restrained him. I picked my hat off the cobblestones and brushed it off. I walked over to him, where he was struggling against the two soldiers holding him. "Here? Are you insane?" He continued to fight the soldiers. "If you don't stop struggling, you'll be hogtied to a pole and carried out of the city like that."

Beaulieu immediately stopped. "No, not here. Outside the city. The day after tomorrow, an hour past dawn. About ten miles out of the city, on the road heading east, there is a ruined chateau. Meet me in the field behind the ruin with your two seconds. " He indicated Reille and Callahan with his head. "Gaspard will be my second." His mousy companion nodded nervously.

I stared at him for a long moment. Though I had killed men before, I had never been challenged to a duel. I could not let this challenge go unanswered, word would spread otherwise. Despite the emperor's orders forbidding his officers from dueling, I was left little choice. "Very well. Weapons?"

Beaulieu smiled a grim smile. "You are the challenged party, Monsieur. It is your choice."

I nodded. "Swords. I'll see you then." I looked at the corporal. "Get him out of the city."

Saluting, the corporal and his men escorted Beaulieu and his companions out of the city.

I thought for sure Athenaïs would try to talk me out of fighting Beaulieu, but she said nothing and took my arm. The six of us continued on to Madame Chenier's house, where after drinking and laughing for a time in her parlor, we went in pairs to our various rooms. Our room was large and well-furnished, with high ceilings and flowered wallpaper—the finest room I'd spent the night in since arriving in France. Once the door was closed and candles lit, I took Athenaïs in my arms, pulling her to me and kissing her. She pulled my clothes off without urgency as we moved towards the luxurious bed.

There was no need to rush. We had far more time than the time we met in the garden outside the ball. Piece by piece I helped her undress, amazed at how much clothing a woman wears, even in a gown designed to entice and show off cleavage. Those dresses are meant to show off parts of the body, not help you get to them!

She was worth the wait. Her breasts were perfect, and fit just right in my hand. I took them into my mouth like they were ripe fruit, and as she lay down, I began to kiss her, slowing working my way between her legs. She sighed contentedly, running her hands gently through my hair, grabbing a handful involuntarily when I touched a particularly pleasurable spot.

Later, we lay in bed together, touching each other and talking. It was one of the most enjoyable conversations I ever had, mentally and physically. Though we had exchanged many letters, it was the first time we had ever been able to talk quietly—alone.

I was also happy for the first time in a long time—years really. I had a purpose, a home and a profession in the French army, a beautiful woman whom I suspected I was falling in love with. It was certainly better than wandering the world in a wooden ship facing storms that could sink you, eating lousy food which I had to fight the ship's rats for, swinging in a hammock trying to sleep, and the only female company whores in port every few months.

The only thing I missed was the smell of the ocean and the endless night sky at sea. Some moments at night, with the stars looking down, I thought I was looking inside the mind of God.

While that was beautiful, it was remote and cold. I preferred the feel of a warm horse under me, the dust of an army on the march, the banter back and forth of soldiers in bivouac around watch fires, the solidarity of the massed blue columns and lines standing shoulder to shoulder with regimental flags and Eagles leading the way.

More than anything though, I preferred the perfumed smell of Athenaïs, the touch of her skin against me, the feel of her lips against mine, the soft sound of her voice, and her blue eyes looking into mine.

"Why are you smiling like that, Pierre?" Athenaïs was running her hand gently along my arm.

"Was I smiling? Probably because I'm happy, for the first time in a long time."

We spoke in both French and English.

Her fingers touched my cheeks. "Were you so unhappy at home? I can almost see you wandering your wilderness like the savage Chactas after he lost his Atala."

I smiled, reached up and stroked her hand. How she loved Chateaubriand's story. While I read the copy she sent me, I didn't have the heart to tell her I found the story of love and despair too cloying a read. Besides, I had seen too many Indians back home to find any echo of them in a romantic story.

"After my wife Catherine died of fever, I no longer had the heart to stay in Maryland or Virginia where we had holdings. I was getting too many looks of pity from family, friends and acquaintances. Some even tried to get me to court their daughters. I couldn't bear the thought of that. For a long time I never thought I would be able to love again." I smiled and squeezed Athenaïs' hand. "With both parents dead, I didn't even have family to grieve with. Captain Rankin's offer of a position on his ship gave me an opportunity to change my surroundings and travel up and down the coast, seeing most of the major American cities."

"What did you plan on doing after your time on the ship—or did you plan on making that your profession?"

"I never felt any kind of true calling until arriving in France and Ney—and ultimately Napoleon—offered me this position. On the ship I never thought far ahead, but I probably wouldn't have stayed there for too many years; I'm not a sailor at heart. Perhaps —without much enthusiasm—I would have returned to our farm in Virginia or become a lawyer in Baltimore where I lived much of my life." I turned to look at the flame on a candle, staring into its flickering light. "Being on ship did put my mind on the tasks of the moment, able to live each day as it came." I smiled. "And attacking the occasional English trading ship was a benefit I had not counted on—and not just financially." I had stashed quite a bit of money at home from some of our previous trips. "Though my mother brought me up to rightly despise the English, I never thought I would be able to fight them unless the United States went to war against them again. Look at me now. I got a bit more than I bargained for boarding that ship."

Athenaïs looked intently at me. "Do you regret the choice you've made?"

"Accepting Ney's offer and joining the army?"

She nodded.

"It has been a bit overwhelming, and a few times I've wondered if I was up to the challenge of the moment, but no, I haven't regretted it for a second." I smiled. "Not yet anyway."

"What was your mother like?"

Involuntarily my hand touched the crucifix that still hung around my neck. "She looked like a queen—beautiful, cold, brittle. She never recovered from the death of my father, and even though she married my stepfather she never gave her heart to him. It was she who made sure I received a classical education: Latin, French, a smattering of Greek. I was taught by priests, who tried to recruit me to a seminary. My mother would never have allowed that. She wanted me free for revenge."

Athenaïs never took her eyes off me. "What happened to your stepfather?"

I smiled coldly. "Thrown from a horse when I was thirteen when he was stone drunk. It was the happiest day of my life, as he could never put a hand on me again—or my mother." I sighed. "She died five years later."

She changed the subject to my impending duel.. I had been wondering when it would come up. "You really are going to fight Beaulieu?"

"Of course, honor demands it. He left me little choice." She said nothing, just continued looking intently at me. "So what happened between you in the past to cause you such bitterness?"

Sighing, Athenaïs examined the tips of her fingers before looking back at me to reply. "It's not so much what has happened between us, but rather who he is and the full proprietary rights he thinks he has over me because of his name and my brother's approval of his courting me."

I looked at her and was rather alarmed. "Proprietary rights? Has he ever tried to assert those rights? Has he ever..." I couldn't finish the question, my blood boiling at the thought, any reluctance about fighting Beaulieu quickly disappearing.

Seeing my expression, she smiled reassuringly and shook her head. "No, he has never had me, though he tried once at my brother's house in Aubigny."

I was somewhat reassured, but he didn't improve in my eyes at all. "What happened?"

A wide smile covered her face. "I clawed his face. I left scars that took more than six months to heal." She continued to smile, enjoying the memory. "Several servants came running and he had to leave. While my brother scolded me, I know Joseph-Marie also got a dressing down. While he never stopped coming around, he has kept his hands to himself, though that would change if he ever married me. He would take his revenge for those marks before having his way with me." Unconsciously brushing hair out of her face, she sighed. "Despite all that, my brother would still like me to marry him. He is a baron and wealthy. The connection would help our family immensely and probably help my brother in turn gain a bride that would help elevate his status. While my brother has had lovers, he hasn't gotten married yet, waiting for the right breeding stock to come along."

I said nothing, listening and staring in fascination. It was all so foreign to me. I knew wealthy families in Virginia and Maryland maneuvered to marry among each other, but it didn't seem as calculating as this. My expression must have showed disbelief because Athenaïs laughed that spine-tingling laugh of hers.

"That's one of the things I love about you, Pierre, you make no effort to hide your shock at the stale *mores* of European aristocracy. While France put all that behind during the Revolution, Napoleon's amnesty, and especially the return of a monarchy in the form of an Emperor has brought back many of the old ways of the nobility. Napoleon has done nothing to stop it, in fact he has encouraged it, thinking it adds legitimacy to his reign to join the old nobility to the new under his aegis."

While fascinated, I was also confused. I heard nothing in her tone condemning the structure, nor her role in it. "You sound like you are defending the process."

She shrugged, a difficult thing to do lying naked on one's side but she managed it gracefully. "I am neither defending nor condemning, merely explaining. It simply is."

I was quiet for a moment, deep in thought. I made a spur decision and propped myself up on one elbow.

"I love you. Marry me, Athenaïs."

She laughed, a light, beautiful laugh, but a laugh nonetheless. It wasn't the reaction I hoped for. When she saw my expression, she stopped.

"You're serious."

I didn't say anything at first. Had I really just asked her to marry me? I took a deep breath. "Yes, I am serious. I love you and I know you love me."

There was a definite look of amusement on her face, mixed with some consternation. "You know I love you? Isn't that a bit presumptuous?"

Flustered, I replied, "Well, I thought I heard you say it a little while ago..."

She laughed gently. "You shouldn't always take to heart what a woman says in the throes of passion." My expression must have betrayed something because she quickly continued, "Let's say I do love you, Pierre, and God help me, I probably do, but that has little to do with marriage." She cut me off as I started to protest. "You are a romantic. Marriage and love don't necessarily go together, though it is wonderful if that happens. I may not care for Joseph-Marie, but that doesn't mean I will reject other suitors my brother may find for me. I have a duty to him and generations of Vaniers to marry in a way that will benefit my family and bring credit upon it."

"What? Are you saying I wouldn't bring credit upon your family?" I was more than a little annoyed and was wishing I never asked the question.

Athenaïs shook her head. "I'm not saying that at all. I think you would bring great credit upon my family." She touched my cheek. "I've never met a person I would rather have as a husband, but frankly you are an unknown with no name or fortune. My brother would not approve the match and I could understand his reasons. While France has changed since the Revolution, and he might countenance marrying one of the new Imperial nobility, he wouldn't tolerate a marriage with a foreigner four months on our shores."

I lay back on my pillow looking up at the ceiling, angry at myself for proposing, angry at my relative impoverishment, angry at the blasted system which created aristocrats, angry at myself for falling in love—just angry. What made it worse was that in a sense, she was correct. What right did I have in my position to hope for marriage with a woman of her station? Even minor nobility was above me at the moment, though that could change.

Athenaïs moved over to me, naked body pressed against mine. She ran her hands under the sheet and began touching and kissing me. "Besides, we don't have to be married to do this."

I kissed her back.

CHAPTER 14

Just before dawn two days later, I saddled my horse and, accompanied by Callahan and Reille, who had managed to extend his stay in Boulogne for a few more days, rode east for my rendezvous with Beaulieu.

It was a foggy morning and slow going. A number of patrols passed us and let us continue on our way after stopping us briefly. We spoke very little. I was thinking both of the impending duel and of Athenaïs. Her rejection and the reasons behind it stung.

I was intent on punishing Beaulieu for my rejection, though that was absurd, as he had less of a chance than I did of marrying Athenaïs. At the moment though, I wasn't thinking rationally. What I was thinking of was thrusting my sword through his heart, or at least somewhere that would cause considerable pain.

While it is true I had not had much luck during previous combats with a sword—Monge and the English officer—those were two months in the past. True to the oath I swore when Miller almost beat me outside the farmhouse near Le Crotoy, I had practiced intensely every day with anyone willing to cross swords with me, most often with Reille, or Callahan, who, because of his twenty-five years of experience, had a wealth of knowledge he was willing to share with me. Even on the busiest of days I found time between studying and hunting saboteurs to fence, learning every technique I could.

During quiet days I practiced with musket and bayonet and my pistol, but I always squeezed in practice with the sword. Granted, an officer's main weapon is the men under his command and how he directs their use. However, a sword is the symbol of an officer's authority, and he still must be able to defend himself. I would not be humiliated again.

While I was not certain of victory, I was far more confident in my abilities than two months before. When I had first landed in France four months previously, I'd known the rudiments of handling a sword, but now I was starting to know the finer points.

I thought I had the measure of my opponent from my brief meeting with him. While I was certain he received the training a gentleman must have to be able to defend his honor, I thought I detected a certain softness which belied a lack of tenacity required to win.

I was soon to learn, that while I may have mastered the sword, I hadn't fully learned how to appraise people.

About an hour past dawn, we spotted the ruined chateau through the mist. Slowly we rode around to the back of the building and saw two horses tied to an apple tree, which seemed to have survived whatever devastation had befallen the once elegant residence. People must rarely have come here, as apples were left to rot, scattered under the tree where they had fallen.

Dismounting, we tied our horses to the tree also. I took two apples off the tree and gave one to *Fleur*, and began eating the other myself. I had acquired the soldier's ability to eat anywhere during almost any situation. I rubbed the side of her face gently and she nudged me with her nose, whinnying gently.

A very jittery Gaspard, Beaulieu's companion, stood alone watching their horses.

"Where's Beaulieu?" I asked, walking towards him, glancing around cautiously.

"He's in the chateau." Gaspard replied, pointing with his thumb over his shoulder towards the shell of the building. I noticed out of the corner of my eye Callahan taking his cavalryman's carbine off his saddle. Reille moved in the other direction, loosening his sword in his scabbard.

Callahan smiled wolfishly at Gaspard when he looked at the carbine. "Just ensuring there is a fair fight. That's what seconds are for, no?"

There was a scraping noise from the chateau and Beaulieu pushed aside the remnant of a door and walked down stone steps from the house. Callahan swung the carbine towards him but did not raise it. Finely dressed as if going to a ball, the only weapon visible on Beaulieu was a sword.

"There's no need for that, I was just looking around." Noticing my skepticism, he elaborated. "This was once owned by my family. It was burned to the ground with my father inside by a group of peasants during the Revolution. Fortunately we were able to find his body and secretly bury it in the family cemetery nearby." He looked back at the building, a faraway look in his eyes. "We were able to recover the property again under Napoleon's amnesty, but we haven't the money for the moment to rebuild the house."

I said nothing but looked the building over again. I had thought the building a ruin from times long past but on closer inspection I could see the damage was of recent vintage.

"Was he as charming as you? I could see why they might have burned the place down," Callahan said, putting the carbine over his shoulder by its sling and pulling out a long pipe.

Anger flared in Beaulieu's face, his hand dropped to his sword. Callahan looked at him, unconcerned, as he lit his pipe.

I looked at Callahan. "Enough, Nicholas." Turning to Beaulieu, I indicated an open patch of ground nearby. The grass was clipped short; obviously someone grazed their animals here. "Shall we begin?"

He nodded and we walked over together. Each of our seconds helped us take our jackets off. I hung it up on a tree, along with my hat and sword belt.

"Careful you don't spill anything on that aide-de-camp's uniform," Reille said as I moved to position. I smiled nervously as I took my place.

We faced each other about ten paces apart, swords low at our sides. Our seconds spoke briefly among themselves.

Gaspard took a step forward. "This is not a fight to the death—unless someone deals a lucky blow—it *can* end with first blood, at which point either party can yield the fight with honor. *En garde.*"

We formally saluted and moved towards each other. Most fights start out slowly, with each duelist trying to get a sense of the other's abilities. Instead, Beaulieu attacked quickly and aggressively, not hacking wildly but with controlled slashes at my forearms and other places he might incapacitate me. His thrusts were also long and precise, attempts to get a killing blow through my guard. The expression on his face was utter confidence—this was not his first duel. I had misread my man.

He was trying to kill me and was more skilled than his opponent expected.

But so was I.

Though he drove me back, I was able meet each of his blows. I was not overmatched.

I stopped retreating and held my ground. Spying an opening in my defenses, he extended for a killing thrust. I was able to lean to the side and his thrust missed, though it was close—his blade scratched me just below the sternum, drawing first blood. We were now next to each other, our chests practically touching. I grabbed his sword arm and yanked him off balance and punched him in the face with the guard of my sword. He stumbled and looked at me in shock.

I smiled. "That was rather clumsy of you."

Confused and angry, he straightened himself up. I learned much later he had used that move—aggressively attacking at the start of a duel then thrusting deeply—to kill several men in duels. He wasn't interested in first blood for the sake of honor—he was interested in killing me.

Both our seconds stepped forward and looked at us, ready to stop the fight. "Messieurs, first blood has been drawn," Reille said, Gaspard at his side. "You may end this with honor."

Beaulieu shook his head, his eyes never leaving me. I shook my head just as determinedly . "No, André. Not yet."

Though I could see concern on my friend's face, he shrugged as if it were of no consequence. "Very well. Continue, Messieurs."

More cautious now, Beaulieu returned to the attack. He was skilled and fast but lacked stamina and judgment, relying on his speed. I was able to keep ahead of him mentally and knew what almost every next move would be.

He did nick my upper arm and scratched nearly the same spot just below my sternum again—he liked that thrust. While we were both tiring, he was showing it a lot more. I was conditioned from months of training, marching and fighting. I waited for him to make a mistake, and he did—he tried his same killing thrust yet again.

I saw it coming and stepped aside with my left foot, leaving my right in place, in a far from conventional fencing move. As he overextended himself, I sliced at the side of his head, carving off the top of his left ear and cutting into his left cheek. He screamed and instinctively clutched his ear with his free hand. Before he could even turn his sword, I punched the wounded side of his head with the guard of my sword, which caused him to scream even more. I brought my sword down on his upper forearm, cutting it deeply. I generally try to avoid slashing with a sword—it is the point that kills, which is why I prefer straight blades—but we were at too close quarters for me to easily bring the point to bear, and unlike him, I wasn't trying to kill. Unlike many straight blades, mine was rugged enough to sharpen its edge, not just its point.

With a flick of my sword I knocked his weapon out of his weakened hand, then stepped back and put the point of my sword at the base of his neck. The fight had somewhat degenerated into a brawl, at least on my part, but I was learning to use a sword in the army, not a fencing academy. It was effective and not cheating.

Beaulieu's eyes met mine. There was fear and hatred there. I had an enemy for life—slicing off someone's ear can do that, it seems. The question was, would I let him live or would he force me to kill him?

Neither of us said anything for a moment as we stared at each other. "Do you yield?" I pressed the point into his neck just a little. "I will spare your life if you give your word never to talk to Athenaïs again."

His eyes grew red with anger hearing her name. "That whore! Why I..."

Before he could say another word I moved the point of my sword to his right cheek and cut it open down to the bone. The cut went right up to his ear. Now he would have scars from me on both sides of his face—if he lived. He started to scream, but stopped, eyes blazing.

"If you ever speak her name in my presence or talk to her again, I will kill you. If you do not give me your word, I will kill you *now*." I was angry enough to hope he wouldn't give his word.

Something in my expression stopped him from uttering whatever he was ready to say. He simply nodded.

"Say it. Give your word." Nodding is rather ambiguous, especially with a sword at your throat.

Beaulieu swallowed, hatred blazing from his eyes. "I give you my word of honor never to speak to Athenaïs again."

I held the sword to his throat for a moment longer as we stared at each other. Nothing would have pleased me more at that moment than to kill him, knowing I was likely saving myself potential trouble in the future, but I couldn't do it. I had already agreed to spare him if he gave his oath, and honor demanded I not go back on my word. Besides, killing an unarmed civilian after a duel would likely get back to my superiors and see me drummed out of the army or even guillotined.

"A wise choice." I took several steps backwards and wiped the blade of my sword with a cloth before sheathing it. Callahan and Reille helped bandage my wounds, which, while painful, were superficial.

Beaulieu continued to glare at us while Gaspard tried to clean his wounds. "You've won. Get off my family's land."

I slowly put my jacket on and, hat in hand, gave a mock bow. "At your service, Monsieur."

Reille and Callahan were already waiting at the horses. I mounted *Fleur* in a single practiced motion, ignoring the pain from my cuts. I gently spurred her flanks and the three of us trotted around the building and back onto the road to Boulogne.

"That man will not forget," Reille, riding on my left, said as we headed west. "Aristocrats never forget an insult. He will be looking for ways to repay you for humiliating him."

I rubbed *Fleur*'s ears and she shook her head and whinnied happily. "You're probably right, I could see it in his eyes, though why I don't know. He fought well, but lost. It was a fair fight."

Turning his head towards me, Reille rubbed his mustache and smiled knowingly. "It was and you did well. Nonetheless, he'll see it as a humiliation, that someone he views as a commoner beat him. No doubt he's convincing himself as we speak that somehow you cheated."

From the other side, Callahan agreed. "André is right, Pierre. You should have killed him. If you ever see him again, you'll likely have to finish the job." His large bay stallion whinnied and raised his head as if to nod in agreement with his master.

I looked at Callahan's face, trying to see if he was joking. "I couldn't have killed him after he dropped his sword and agreed to my terms."

Callahan shrugged. "Maybe, maybe not. Anyway, what's done is done. Just watch your back if you ever hear he is nearby." He pointed to his own left ear, with its top half missing. "You don't forget a wound like this. It took me five years, but I finally killed the man who did this to me."

I just stared at his mutilated ear as we continued our ride west towards Boulogne, already regretting not slipping my sword into Beaulieu's heart when I'd had the chance.

CHAPTER 15

October 7, 1804
Montreuil

It was a Sunday and I was back in Montreuil. A week had passed since the duel and no one had spoken a word of it to me. Any revenge Beaulieu might have in mind would not involve the authorities.

The next few days after the duel were exciting for other reasons. For weeks English ships had been gathering off the coast, especially near Boulogne, in obvious preparation for attacking our invasion fleet, something they had done several times since my arrival in France.

Their attack on October third was a failure, with light casualties on both sides, except for the loss of one small English warship that strayed too close to a shore battery. That night they debuted a new weapon, called by some a carcass and by others a hogshead. It was a hollow copper ball filled with gunpowder, tied to and buoyed by a large piece of cork. It had a timing device which would allow it to float for a time before exploding. We found a number along the beaches and they were a devil to disarm but ultimately did little damage to the fleet.

The reason for my return to Montreuil was to rejoin Reille's company with my men to take part in an exercise and review near Ney's chateau in Recques northeast of Montreuil. A total of sixteen battalions—around 16,000 men, which was a majority of the VI Corps—took place in the exercise in gently rolling fields and hills not far from the chateau. I was out of my aide-de-camp's uniform and back into that of an infantry officer. It was a confusing existence at times, going from one billet to another, one uniform to another, but no more confusing than my entire world turning upside down five months previously. I was coming to know the army quite well—which was Ney's objective. He believed his officers should know as much about the profession of arms as humanly possible, especially his aides-de-camp.

With the regimental bands playing martial airs behind us and Tricolor battle flags leading us, we practiced various battle maneuvers, especially moving quickly from column formation into line. Sometimes we moved forward with one battalion in line and another in column, just as we might in battle, with the battalion in column ready to exploit a weakened enemy line and attack. We marched straight on, other times marching obliquely, as if we were approaching an enemy line from an angle. At times, all sixteen battalions moved together, like a gigantic living creature with one mind.

The companies took turns in front of the battalion in loose skirmish order, screening the rest of the battalions behind in line and column. When our company was in front skirmishing, I noticed Ney and some of his staff mounted and watching us from not far away. Ney had been joined by the IV Corps' commander, Marshal Nicholas Soult. I didn't have much time to gawk, though, and had to turn my attention to the task at hand. While in skirmish order our soldiers were allowed to fire off some blank practice rounds, and firing erupted up and down from our line.

The Corps' artillery raced just ahead of us, unlimbering and preparing to fire, while on the flanks, the corps' light cavalry regiments attacked at the gallop and the infantry battalions practiced forming squares, used to repel cavalry attacks by facing all the men outward, forming a square of bristling bayonets. Because the men were so tightly packed together, however, it was more vulnerable to infantry and artillery fire than other formations. The three arms, infantry, artillery and cavalry, had to work together to protect each other and complement each other's strengths.

Large maneuvers like this were vital if the Corps was to operate in conjunction with the rest of the army. Each corps was its own little army and had to be able to fight off superior enemy forces until reinforcements arrived. Normally an aide-de-camp would have been in the middle of this on his horse carrying messages back and forth from his marshal, but Ney wanted me to see how things behaved from within, not set apart on my horse.

When the entire Grand Armée was moving into enemy territory we marched as a giant "battalion square," the famous *bataillon carré,* with one corner of the square leading the way— looking on a map like a diamond. Each corps made up a corner of this giant square and stayed one day's march from at least two other corps of the army, with Napoleon and the Imperial Guard in the center. If any corps made contact with the enemy it became the advance guard, and the corps behind it to either side became the left and right flanks and immediately moved to engage the enemy flanks, while the Guard and the far corner of the square moved to reinforce the center. It didn't matter from which direction the army was attacked, even the rear, it reacted the same way.

The system made it difficult, if not impossible, for an enemy to surprise Napoleon for long, but the key was training and practice, which we did until we perfected every maneuver. Waiting in the camps near Boulogne gave the army time to become the best trained, most confident fighting force in the world and was one of the keys to our success in the years to come. And as always, the various units of the army marched, marched and marched many miles, leading to an expression within the army: "The Emperor fights with our feet."

How many days it felt like that!

That exercise and review near Ney's chateau was not so hard on the feet but it did challenge us to stay aligned with the other units, listen for the commands of the company, battalion, brigade and division commanders through words or the drummers, all the while being careful we didn't get trampled by the cavalry or crushed by an artillery caisson rushing ahead. Though I was not with the company every day because of my assignment in Boulogne, I was still a much better company officer than when I first had joined the army. I was learning.

After our company was in front of the battalion in skirmish order, we traded places with another and took our place in the battalion line and formed the company in a three rank line. Soon after, we formed column and one battalion after another passed in review before Ney, Soult and their staffs.

As we prepared to march back to camp, one of Ney's aides, a blond seventeen-year-old named Joseph Vienneau, rode down the line of our battalion until he found our company. "Burns!"

I turned from checking the men's equipment and looked at him.

"Report to Marshal Ney immediately!" He turned around and rode off before I could say anything. I looked at Reille, who merely shrugged.

"Don't look at me, Lieutenant, I'm only a captain. Report to the marshal."

I saluted and headed towards the clump of officers gathered around Ney under a clump of trees a few hundred yards away. I walked by Monge, who sneered as I passed him. We hadn't had much contact since I had been off on assignment, an arrangement that suited us both.

I walked without haste towards Ney and Soult's group. When I was about fifty yards from them, most of the group walked off, leaving only Ney, Soult, Jomini and General Savary to meet me. Savary's presence surprised me because when I saw him it was generally in Boulogne when we were dealing with Royalists or saboteurs. I saluted and stood at attention. Both Ney and Soult returned the salute; Jomini and Savary stood behind them and to one side, about twenty feet away. I waited at attention as both marshals looked at me. It was rather unnerving. Marshal Soult was shorter than Ney, stocky and powerfully built. Somewhat bowlegged, he walked with a limp from a wound he received four years before in Italy and was self-conscious about it. Quiet and intelligent, he was a hard task master, nicknamed "Hand of Iron" by his troops. We were on good terms, as I had met him several times in Boulogne during my hunt for saboteurs. This day, however, he kept his own counsel and watched me silently.

Ney finally broke the long silence, his deep baritone voice carrying despite his low tone. "What did I tell you about dueling?"

Good God, he knew. Nothing was secret near Boulogne, I should have known that by now, though neither Reille nor Callahan would have given up my secret—it had to be Beaulieu or that mousy bastard Gaspard. I was wishing at that moment I had killed Beaulieu, though if I had, it's quite possible I would have been clapped in irons before seeing Ney—if I were lucky.

My mind was racing trying to think of what to say. Ney took a step towards me, hands clasped behind his back, clearly angry, his complexion redder than usual. "What did I tell you about dueling?" He was not shouting but was starting to raise his voice.

I swallowed nervously. "You said I shouldn't be involved in duels, Monsieur."

"That's right! I said you shouldn't be dueling!" He held up his marshal's baton, the gilded caps at either end gleaming in the afternoon sun. "Do you know what this is?"

I looked at the foot and a half long baton, covered with rich blue velvet and emblazoned with gold eagles, symbol of a marshal's authority. Then I looked into Ney's angry eyes. "Yes, Monsieur le Maréchal."

"Well, one wouldn't think so the way you've acted! This baton represents authority, it represents obedience! When a marshal of the French Empire tells you to do something it is *not* a suggestion!! You are an officer in the French Army and I expect you to act like it! If you are unable to do so, then I suggest you take that uniform off now, Monsieur!" Ney was practically shouting and for a moment I thought he was going to hit me with the baton. Staring at me silently for a moment, he continued, quieter than before. "If you are unable to live under the discipline befitting an officer, then leave now. Is that clear?"

I stood as straight as possible. "Yes, Monsieur le Maréchal, perfectly clear. It will not happen again."

Ney was calming down. He had a quick temper but was as quick to forgive, though he took personal breaches of his authority and dignity seriously. He nodded at my answer, satisfied. Stepping close to me, he spoke quietly so even Soult and Jomini couldn't overhear. "Next time something like this happens, come to me first. I understand the need to fight for one's honor—I killed several men in duels when I was younger. I could have allowed it to happen quietly, but I can't tolerate a breach in discipline, *especially* from an officer on my staff." I turned my head sharply to meet his eyes, barely a foot from mine and nodded.

"Yes, Monsieur le Maréchal," I replied as quietly.

Ney circled me and stopped in front of me, a slight smile on his face. "I've thought more than once since we first met that fortune favors you, Burns, and it hasn't deserted you yet. You certainly picked the right person to fight a duel with."

I looked quizzically at him. Ney enjoyed releasing information one tidbit at a time. He nodded at Savary, who stepped forward.

"That man, Beaulieu, whom you fought—and scarred for life from what I hear—was a suspected Royalist sympathizer and a possible English spy," Savary said, a definite look of amusement on his face. "He had been under occasional surveillance for some time. After you wounded him he went to a meeting of known Royalists and from what we understand fled to England after, possibly to join one of their French Royalist brigades, thus revealing his treasonous colors. His comrades here thought he attracted too much attention to remain because of his duel with you."

Ney smiled. "So you see, blind luck or fortune favors you. You might even meet him on the battlefield. I don't need to tell you what to do if you meet the traitor then."

My head was swirling, first that news of my duel had reached Ney, second that I was almost drummed out of the army, then that Beaulieu was a traitor and had gone to join France's enemies—and that I was to kill him next time we met. Things were never simple. Ney was right, I did seem to be lucky. I hoped it would last. "I'll do so with pleasure." I clapped my left hand on the hilt of my sword to indicate I understood. "Was there anything else, Monsieur le Maréchal?"

"As a matter of fact, yes." Ney gestured to Jomini to approach. "Where is that map, Jomini?"

Jomini came over and pulled a map out of a satchel from under his arm and began unfolding it. He shot me a superior, amused look that made me wish I hadn't foresworn dueling. As he laid it on the ground, we circled around it, squatting or kneeling on one knee. For the first time since I had reported to the two marshals, Marshal Soult spoke in his quiet, firm voice.

"In addition to the numerous attempts to disable our ships in the last few months—which Lieutenant Burns has spent considerable time successfully combating—the English have been trying to attack the fleet through more conventional methods. They've made several attacks with their fleet trying to reach our invasion fleet, but to little success. Each time, our ships combined with our shore batteries have beaten off every attack. Winter is coming and they know our opportunity to attack this year is rapidly coming to an end, so it is likely they'll keep trying and maybe do something different, like an amphibious landing against one of the coastal forts to distract us from carrying out the invasion. The *rosbifs* have designed a new craft for landing in shallow waters that can carry far more troops than standard ship's boats. We have information they might want to test them in action —soon."

I looked at the map and the location of the forts up and down the coast. "It would be stupid of them to try and attack any of the forts. Even if they achieved complete surprise, we have so many troops along the coast around Boulogne preparing for the invasion they'd be crushed by a counterattack soon after they landed."

Soult nodded agreeably. "Quite true, if they attacked in the immediate area around Boulogne; however, much of the coast between Bruges and Le Havre has been fortified. Some of these fortifications, especially south of here towards Le Havre are weaker and much more isolated than the forts near Boulogne, which are formidable and backed up by thousands of troops. It's quite possible the *rosbifs* will attack some of these fortifications, or even try a major raid on a coastal city or town. Maybe they'll do both—anything they think might likely get us to reconsider an attack this year."

I watched Soult carefully as he spoke, then looked at Ney, Jomini and Savary when he finished.

"Will it work, Monsieur le Maréchal, will we reconsider an attack this year?" I addressed Soult, since he was briefing me instead of Ney, Jomini, or Savary. Soult shrugged and looked at Savary.

"I would say our chances of attacking this year are slim, wouldn't you agree, General Savary?"

"I can say it is almost a certainty we won't attack this year," Savary said. "We're well into fall, winter is coming and the weather in the *Manche* will soon make any kind of large-scale amphibious attack almost impossible. Besides, the Emperor has his thoughts elsewhere. His coronation is in less than two months and his mind is on that, including welcoming the Pope, who has agreed to crown him."

I felt somewhat crushed and it must have shown in my face because Ney spoke up.

"I didn't say anything before because I knew you would be especially disappointed, but believe me, we all are disappointed," he said gently. "Remember, Pierre, this army has been training in these camps for over a year and a half to invade England, it is on the minds of thousands of men. Though we're not making any general announcement throughout the army, the men will figure it out on their own soon enough when the weather starts to turn."

"I understand, Monsieur le Maréchal." I looked closely at the map again. I knew two marshals of the Empire would not be briefing a mere lieutenant because of my expected disappointment about postponing the invasion yet again. I figured I had a mission connected with the forts and an expected English raid. "What am I to do in connection with these possible raids?"

Apparently appreciating my desire to get to the point, Soult nodded and continued. "Even though I can say it is almost a certainty we won't attack this year, it is not quite a certainty—the Emperor has made no such pronouncement yet—so we can't take many troops away from the embarkation ports to reinforce the forts. Consequently, we will have to beef up our patrols and create a few, sizeable mobile reaction forces moving up and down the coast roads. Any raid the *rosbifs* make will be quick—capture a fort, destroy it and be on their ships again before a counterattack. Their purpose would be for morale at home, to show they are not purely on the defensive. Our response will be to make a point: while they may rule the seas for the moment, the land is ours. Ideally we'll want to catch them on the ground and destroy their landing force. Your role, and that of others we are sending to patrol the coastline, will be to assess any potential threat and bring in those mobile forces quickly."

I was still more than a little confused about my role in the affair. Was I to be a messenger or conduct the defense of any threatened spot? Either the job was below my rank or well above it.

"Marshal Soult, Marshal Ney, couldn't this job be performed just as well by troops and officers already watching the beach and who know the area? I will do the job, of course, but I wonder why I am being sent."

Ney continued where Soult left off. "We are sending a number of officers on this mission up and down the coast with the same orders. Each will have a section of beach he is responsible for and will be accompanied by troops familiar with that section of coastline. All of these officers—many of them are aides-de-camp, like you—are responsible men with cool heads able to operate independently, who won't send a message in panic to the reaction force when they spot a fishing vessel or small English brig. We want to catch the *rosbifs* in the act, not scare them off. While you are a lieutenant, you are an aide-de-camp to a marshal and thus will speak with authority, and our explicit written orders back you up."

To be honest, I was somewhat flattered that these two men trusted me with another independent mission, though I could tell by Jomini's expression he didn't share their view. I didn't much care what he thought.

Using his marshal's baton, Soult pointed to a section on the map just south of the Somme estuary, about twenty-five or thirty miles south of Montreuil. "You will be responsible for a ten mile section along here." The four of us slowly stood up, letting the blood flow back into our legs while Jomini folded the map.

"When do I leave?" I said, looking at the two marshals.

"Tomorrow morning," Ney replied. He smiled. "Oh, and you might be happy to know that the reaction force for the coastline in that area will be the Third Battalion of the Sixth Légèr. Dismissed."

I smiled before I could stop myself, saluted the marshals, and headed off to make preparations for my morning departure. The battalion had already marched back towards Montreuil—I would be walking alone, which I didn't mind.

The early fall weather was beautiful, but evening was coming on and I was walking briskly to get back to Montreuil.

There was a great deal of military traffic going back and forth on the road and no one paid any attention to me, just as I didn't pay much attention at first to a horse walking next to me. I looked up to see Savary looking down at me, his keen eyes visible under the brim of his bicorn. I snapped off a salute, touching the rim of my shako sharply, which he returned just as crisply.

Dismounting, Savary walked with me, leading his gray horse by the reins.

I was practically itching with curiosity, wondering what he could want.

Savary raised an eyebrow as he looked at me. "You don't like Jomini, do you?" It was almost a statement.

I was about to reply but snapped my mouth shut. I had no right to criticize Jomini to a general not in my direct chain of command. Before I could think of anything to say, Savary answered his own question. "No, you don't, though you try to hide it and that speaks to your discretion. It's obvious the feeling is mutual, but he doesn't hide it as well—which doesn't speak well to his." Savary sighed. "He may be a brilliant strategic theoretician of war but he's a pompous ass with few of the skills required of a leader on the battlefield. He's also a poor judge of character. Despite your performance up until now, he doesn't think you're ready for another semi-independent mission. Fortunately for you, Marshal Ney has stuck by his original assessment of you, despite Jomini's constant whispering in his ear. For the record, Marshal Soult disagrees with Jomini, as do I."

"Thank you, *mon général*." A veteran of combat in Germany, Egypt and Italy, Savary was no stranger to the battlefield and had a keen sense of the skills he believed a good officer should have, especially the ability to lead from the front and act independently, without a superior officer always over one's shoulder.

We moved off the road to allow a patrol of green-clad mounted chasseurs to ride by, their officer saluting Savary as they passed. "Ney is right, however, you can't get into any more duels— certainly not without informing him first. You may be half French but you are still an American and are here on a trial basis, so to speak. Ney took a great chance offering you a position with such haste and so far you have more than proved him right. Don't ruin that."

We stopped and I looked at him. "No, Monsieur, I won't do it again."

"Good, because I could tell by the way you and Jomini looked at each other you wouldn't mind getting into one more duel, and I've no doubt you'd easily beat him. You don't need that. You've done an impressive job since you've landed in France, especially in

Boulogne—don't think it hasn't been noticed at the very highest levels." Savary was an aide-de-camp to Napoleon, so that could only mean one thing.

"Thank you, *mon général*."

"It's a rare thing for one of your rank to be able to act so independently and reliably, and your background gives you a unique perspective. If Jomini's whispers finally wear down Ney and you find you are assigned to less challenging duties, remember there are other jobs in the army open to you if you want them."

I didn't know what to say and simply thanked him.

Savary walked to his horse and reached into a saddle bag, pulled out a small leather pouch and handed it to me. It contained a finely crafted telescope. "You'll need this watching the coast. No need to return it, in a sense it's yours anyway. I took it off an Englishman we shot whom we caught fifteen miles north of Boulogne—thanks to information you provided. Obviously he won't need it anymore. Think of it as a prize of war that you earned and you'll need."

I took the telescope and thanked him while he mounted his horse. "Good luck, Burns. Keep your eyes open, and if your instincts tell you, call in the reaction force. We might be able to catch a sizeable force of the *rosbifs* on French soil if we are lucky. And then..." He smacked his riding crop against his boot and his horse whinnied nervously.

CHAPTER 16

October 18, 1804
Twelve miles south of the village of Cayeux, near Ault

It was around noon. As I had for the previous ten days, I scanned the horizon and shoreline for any signs of enemy activity. It was overcast and a cold wind blew off the ocean, which appeared somewhat choppy but still manageable for small boats, especially if handled by expert seamen – and the English were, if nothing else, expert seamen.

I wore the dark blue uniform of the light infantry, complete with shako. My aide-de-camp's uniform was back in Montreuil, as Ney thought I would be less conspicuous patrolling the coast in the uniform of the Sixth Legere.

I snapped the spyglass shut, put it back in my saddlebag, took out a flask with brandy in it and took a draught to keep the chill off. Soult had been right, the weather would soon prevent any invasion until spring and conversely would prevent any large scale action by the English along the coast.

This part of the coast had seen considerable activity over the past year. The area around Cayeux was beaches and low hills and dunes, though not far to the south the Normandy cliffs started to rise up, a seeming wall against the advancing ocean. Less than ten miles to the southwest, Georges Cadoudal and some of his confederates who had tried to kill Napoleon earlier that year had climbed those cliffs when they arrived in France. It was a beautiful, though lonely stretch of coastline, with sparsely populated fishing and farming villages.

Since I started my patrol I had seen little activity, though some British ships patrolled offshore and a few came closer to get a better look at the shore. The last few days, there seemed to be more movement and a few more ships coming closer to land. I had a feeling something was going to happen nearby. This part of the coast was only sporadically defended, though there were sizeable garrisons north towards Boulogne, as well as inland near Amiens, about forty-five or fifty miles inland, and at Dieppe, twenty miles south along the coast.

Those troops were far enough away that a quick raid by a sizeable force *could* get ashore, attack, and be back on ship before an effective counterattack could be launched. Though any raid would be symbolic—there was nothing of military value in the area —my job, and that of others like me, was to prevent the British from getting that symbolic victory.

South of Cayeux towards the neighboring village of Ault, the terrain turned from shingle beach to white chalk cliffs, which could only be scaled in a few places unless there were already men in place at the top of the cliffs with ropes. Otherwise they would have to attack one of the small fishing harbors at the mouths of several rivers, like Ault, which provided access inland. I was patrolling along the tops of those high cliffs today, near Ault.

There were some fortifications along the beaches north of Cayeux, which was the easiest place to land. Those fortifications were meant to repel an attack from the sea, not from land, and the British might try to land somewhere to get troops behind them, unless they decided to attack straight on, which I thought unlikely.

The fortifications were mostly designed to prevent access to the Somme River. Because of this there was a section of undefended beach south between Cayeux and the cliffs near Ault where troops could land, and of course smaller parties could scale the cliffs, as Cadoudal and his comrades had.

Along the beach near Cayeux towards the cliffs there were a number of tidal pools, which would have made it difficult to fortify the spot but still relatively easy for troops to traverse.

"So what do you think, *mon lieutenant*?" The question came from Sergeant Gaucher, a mounted gendarme from the area, assigned along with two of his men to be my guides. We were astride our mounts about thirty feet from the edge of the 200-foot high cliffs.

"I think it's a rugged coast to try and attack but..."

"But it's possible," he said, finishing my thought.

I nodded, taking another draught of the brandy, gently patting *Fleur's* neck. "But it's possible." I returned the flask to my saddlebag and looked at him. "The beaches near Cayeux's fortifications make it a prime spot for boats to land, especially those new ones the *rosbifs* have designed for shallow water." I took the spyglass back out and aimed it an English brig several miles offshore. "So there is more activity these last few days than in recent weeks?"

Having only patrolled this section of the coast for ten days I relied heavily on him for knowledge of the area and previous movements of the English. His blue jacket and yellow trousers and vest were showing the wear of months on patrol, his high leather boots scuffed and splattered with dirt—though his weapons were clean.

As he shifted his reins in his hands, his small brown mare sniffed *Fleur's* nose. "Yes, *mon lieutenant*, quite a bit. There are at least twice as many ships lately, several coming closer in broad daylight than they usually do. There have been reports of increased activity even below Dieppe." Dieppe and its harbor were almost twenty miles southeast. "They haven't launched any boats, but sometimes you can see men on the decks paying considerable attention to the shoreline."

Turning my attention from the sea, I twisted in my saddle and studied the grassy landscape around me, the church in the town of Eu a few miles to the south visible above its other buildings. The walls of the town, sited in a small river valley, had been erected by King Richard the Lionhearted of England 600 years ago; and almost 800 years ago, his ancestor, William the Conqueror, was married near there—sixteen years before sailing to England and gaining that epithet. Sometimes I couldn't get over how much history permeated seemingly every nook and cranny of the countryside. Back home everything was so new. Not even one hundred years before, settlers were still trying to carve a life among endless forests and the constant threat of Indian attacks, a situation that still hasn't changed as the United States pushes west. I said as much to Gaucher.

"I'm not sure if the history is a blessing or a curse, Monsieur," he said, then chuckled. "Of course, during the Revolution we were supposed to pretend there was no history worth remembering before the fall of the Bastille—which is why we started counting all over again and are in the year XII."

I couldn't help but smile at his tone. While officially it was year XII according to the Republican calendar, not 1804, the old system of counting remained in common usage. Few, it seems, were happy with the system. "Why would it be a curse, Sergeant?"

Gaucher joined me in looking at the farms and villages visible around us, his rugged face like a statue as he surveyed the ground from which he sprung. He was from a farming village not far away. "Why? No matter where you go every wall is a memory, every tree has a story, every house has a chain of memory going back centuries. Even with the freedom unleashed by the Revolution the feeling can be oppressive sometimes and make you feel small and insignificant. There are times when I wish to be able to start afresh, build a house that is mine alone, not the abode of generations of my family." He smiled ironically. "I might feel differently if I were an aristocrat in the ancestral chateau, but alas, the Gauchers are farmers. My position as a sergeant in the gendarmeries is a step above my father."

I had never thought of it that way. "Back home, one often gets the sense of being all alone, no past, just yourself and those around you. Some might find it comforting to be part of this long chain of memory you refer to, where every stone has a story to tell."

We sat on our horses thinking in silence when Gaucher spoke again. "Speaking of history, you mentioned William the Conqueror and Eu. Did you know that before he sailed to conquer England, his fleet assembled in the Bay of Somme?"

I looked at him sharply. "The very same bay the fortifications near Cayeux overlook?"

My tone caused him to narrow his eyes and look at me. "Yes, *mon lieutenant*," he said quietly.

I put my telescope back in my saddle bag and signaled Sergeant Sardou to join us. Sardou was a grizzled, thirty-year veteran whose nose looked like it had been broken too many times. He commanded my escort of ten dragoons, there in case we ran into any Royalists or even English soldiers landed in advance of any attack. Each of the brass helmeted dragoons was dressed in their distinctive red-trimmed green uniforms, and armed with pistols, carbines and their long, straight cavalry swords, which I had been eyeing admiringly since riding with them.

"We're leaving, Sergeant Sardou, moving to Ault." He saluted and prepared to form his men in a column, some of whom had dismounted to check their saddles and equipment. "Sergeant Gaucher, send one of your men to Sergeant Major Grenier at Friaucourt, tell him to move the men closer to Cayeux, but not right into the town or the fortifications. Tell him to stay a few miles back from the beach, possibly at that village with the old farm, Br...what was the name of it?"

Gaucher didn't hesitate. "Brutelles?"

I nodded. "Yes, that's the place. They'll be better positioned there to respond to any attack on Cayeux but close enough they can return to Ault or Eu if necessary. I don't think it will be, however, as I think Cayeux is the likely English target."

Gaucher gave the order to his gendarme to ride to Grenier and my men immediately.

Grenier and "my" forty light infantrymen from Reille's company were with me on this mission, kept at what I had thought was a central location in a collection of huts called Friaucourt, a few miles inland from Ault. I had the feeling I wouldn't be able to hold onto the men much longer after this mission. Reille resented having almost one third of his company off somewhere and was starting to make noise about it, that it made it more difficult to train the company as a unit he said—and he had a point. Soon it wouldn't matter anyway. With the onset of winter, my anti-sabotage duties would be over or at least drastically cut back as armies on both sides of the *Manche* settled in for the winter and the weather prevented the landing of saboteurs or the launching of invasion craft.

Then the VI Corps and the rest of the army could concentrate on training for the battlefield without the distraction of practicing embarking and disembarking and learning how to operate boats.

Just as soon as the gendarme galloped off, I raised and my hand and signaled our column north towards Ault, only a few miles away. I wanted to talk to the garrison commander there before moving on to Cayeux. The afternoon was passing and I wanted to get to Cayeux before dark if possible. As we rode off, a handful of gulls that had been fighting over a morsel flew off squawking.

Gaucher moved up alongside me as the column began moving, joined by Sardou, who was naturally curious as to what was going on. Recently we had been concentrating much of our attention on a relatively remote and undefended wooded area south of Ault called the Bois de Cise, which was a small valley that reached right down to the water. I thought the English might find the undefended gap in the cliffs too tempting and land to attack Ault or Eu. Now I had other ideas as to what they might have in mind.

"*Mon lieutenant*, what is it? Where are we going?" Gaucher said, his little mount trotting next to *Fleur*.

"If I am right, to fight symbolism."

CHAPTER 17

October 16, Ault, France

Ault was a tiny town, well protected by seaward-facing fortifications and 24-pounder batteries on the cliffs, all manned by a small garrison. I thought Ault an unlikely target of attack; however, I still needed the garrison's help. I passed St. Pierre's, a checkerboard rock and silex gothic church and went to the garrison commander's house nearby.

The commander, Captain Labrousse, was a pudgy, red-faced officer who had to be at least fifty or fifty-five-years-old and who huffed as he walked, quite out of breath. Fortunately, he didn't resent his backwater posting, which made him much easier to deal with. The food was good, he had a comfortable house and a few servants, which was all he needed. It contributed to a sense of lethargy on his part, but with enough encouragement he was willing to give orders to his staff to help.

I told him of my theory that the fortifications near Cayeux were the most likely spot along my stretch of coast to be attacked because they overlooked the Bay of Somme.

"A blow against that fort would be perfect symbolism on the part of the English, it's the spot from whence William the Conqueror launched his attack against England 800 years ago," I said rather enthusiastically. "If they want to strike a blow against another invasion, picking a vulnerable fortification overlooking the spot the last successful invasion left from is perfect from their point of view."

The bay was not as important as it had been in 1066. There were no invasion ships anchored there, but nevertheless, as symbolism, the spot was ripe. Even worse—or better from the

English point of view—the fortifications were ill prepared to handle any kind of assault from land. Coastal forts were often circular, preventing attack from the landward side as well as seaward. That wasn't the case near Cayeux, where the fortifications were built to overlook the Bay of Somme and the entrance to the Somme River. Though they were well equipped to deal with ships, they were never completed facing inland. On the inland side, the defenses were much cruder, with a rough wood and dirt defensive wall and parapets for defenders to stand on. There wasn't a ditch or even a proper gate.

Labrousse listened carefully to my theory. "What you say makes perfect sense, though I doubt Captain Blandin will agree. However, I will post more men on the cliffs as lookouts—all night as well—and word will be sent to you immediately if they see anything." Many coastal sentries were recalled at night, but after my experience with the English raid three months before, I was certain if they attacked they would try to land before dawn and attempt an attack just after first light.

I had arrived at the fortification in the late afternoon, my stop in Ault only getting me off my horse for barely a half hour, and we were on our way to Cayeux. We needn't have bothered rushing, as Labrousse was right – Blandin would hear none of it.

"If not a ditch, at least cut down some trees and build an abatis. The fallen trees will slow down any attack and break up their formation," I said, frustrated by Blandin's apparent lack of concern.

"I know the purpose of an abatis," Blandin said icily, "and I see no reason why I should waste my men's time having them build one."

Blandin was of average height and build, with a pinched expression as if a rat were constantly biting his ass. Pity the rat if that were the case. The man's blue and white uniform was neither too clean nor too dirty; it was obvious he did just enough to get by, yet wondered why he was stuck defending a beach well away from a major town or the invasion fleet. An officer since the Revolution, he begrudged anyone he felt was rising faster than himself—which was pretty much anyone.

"Furthermore, *Lieutenant*," he continued, "I resent a puffed up foreigner coming here trying to make me panic over some harebrained scheme." We were standing right outside the back gate to the fortification, though I hesitate to call it a gate—opening was more like it—with his second in command and my dragoons and gendarmes watching quietly.

I sighed and counted to ten before replying. "I'm not trying to make you panic, I'm trying to make you take some common sense precautions." He scoffed and I continued. "What the hell else do your men have to do? It'll keep them busy. And I'll remind you this isn't my idea. I'm here at the orders of Marshal Soult and Marshal Ney, who seem to think an attack quite likely."

Smiling condescendingly, Blandin replied, "They believe there might be an attack *somewhere* along the coast. The chances of this being the spot are remote. I suggest you chase your windmills somewhere else along the coast, perhaps with that fat fool in Ault."

It was nearly dark and I was getting nowhere. "That fat fool has some idea of how to defend a coastline, unlike other fools of my acquaintance."

Blandin gripped his sword hilt, anger on his face. I looked at him contemptuously. "Keep your sword where it is or I'll snap it over my knee." Slowly, he withdrew his hand. "Since you've been so welcoming, I'm going to join the rest of my men in Brutelles, but I'm leaving two of my dragoons here. Don't hesitate to send one to me if you see anything worth reporting. But not to worry, they'll be under orders to report twice a day whether you tell them to or not."

Blandin shrugged, though there was still anger in his face. "As long as you're not staying, I'm sure we can find room for two of your men."

I mounted in one swift motion, as did my men. I directed two of them to stay, then rode off into the twilight with the remainder. It was almost four miles to Brutelles, well over an hour's ride at this time of day.

We arrived after dark, and found Grenier, Tessier and some of the men around a cooking pot in a farmhouse in Brutelles. Most of the men were billeted in outbuildings throughout the hamlet, but the NCOs and I were put in part of a house. I took off my shako and brushed some of the dirt off. A puff of smoke from the fire came back into the room before being sucked back up the chimney. I caught the smell of something delicious, went to the pot Grenier was stirring, and sniffed it.

I cocked an eyebrow at him. "What is that you're cooking? It smells good."

Grenier pretended to be hurt. "Don't look so shocked, *mon lieutenant*. A soldier must be able to cook or he'll starve. If you must cook, then it pays to cook well." His turned the wooden spoon towards me to offer me a taste.

It was good. "I notice you haven't told what it is. Is it rat or something?"

"*Mon Dieu*, no, though rat isn't bad in a pinch if you know how to cook it. This is rabbit. There are quite a few around here and quite easy to catch. I bought some eggs and dried greens from the mistress of the farm, and voila!" Grenier wiped soup off his bushy mustache.

"Well, don't stand there all night sampling your own cooking. Give me a bowl, please."

I took the proffered bowl and sat down at a rough wooden table to eat it, joined by Gaucher and Sardou. Tessier was already sitting there, and soon Grenier joined us. For a few moments we ate in silence and watched four soldiers at the other table in the room playing drogue, a popular card game. The loser had a wooden pin on the end of his nose—an incentive to win the next hand.

I explained my theory about why I thought the English would attack near Cayeux for those who hadn't been with me in Ault. They listened in silence.

"It does make sense, given why we're here, *mon lieutenant*," Grenier offered.

It wasn't exactly a ringing endorsement. "I admit it sounds far-fetched." I smiled, filling a tin cup with wine from a small cask the men bought in the area. "At the very least it keeps us busy. We have to do something while we're here."

Sardou agreed. "It doesn't hurt to make preparations just in case. I don't understand why Captain Blandin was so stubborn refusing to improve his defenses."

"Pride, I suppose." Actually I thought it was because he was a jackass, but I was reluctant to criticize a fellow officer in front of the NCOs. Sardou got up to refill his bowl with Grenier's stew. As he returned to the table his sword caught my eye and I decided to change the subject. Since the dragoons had joined me as my escort, I had admired the straight cavalry swords they carried. The dragoons—which were medium cavalry—and the heavy cavalry such as the cuirassiers and carabineers, all carried straight swords designed for thrusting rather than slashing. The thrust kills efficiently, and the French cavalry practiced and practiced the art. Many commanders forbade their men from sharpening the edge of their blades so they would have to thrust. The swords were nothing like the cavalry swords I had seen back home, which were based on the clumsy English cavalry sabers.

"Sergeant Sardou." He looked up at me as he prepared to sit down. "Do you mind if I look at your sword?"

"Not at all, Monsieur." He drew the weapon and handed it to me, hilt extended. Discussion of weapons was commonplace in the army—it was key to our trade, after all.

I took the sword and stood in the middle of the room, hefting it for weight, then thrusting, parrying, riposting and slashing. It was heavier than my sword, not as quick, but still well balanced, so a cavalryman could keep the point aimed and level when trying to run through an opponent. I liked the feel of it.

My infantryman's epee was fine when fighting on foot. I'd discovered I could deflect blows from bayonets and muskets well enough with it and thrust quickly through an opponent's guard. I could also carry it on horse, as I had been for the last ten days, with a belt designed for the purpose. However, if I was going to spend more time on horse during the invasion, at some point I would probably want a sword meant to be used from horseback.

I handed the straight blade back to Sardou. "An elegant weapon, Sergeant."

Grinning as he slid it back in its wooden and leather scabbard, he said, "A damn efficient weapon too. Slides in like butter once you get the technique right of getting it between the ribs. Takes practice though, especially from horseback." He grimaced. "Well, not quite like butter, but it's easier once you have the technique of thrusting and getting the blade back out again. Otherwise, especially if you're sabering a man on foot, your blade can get stuck between his ribs and yank you right off your horse." A look crossed his face which showed clearer than any words that he was speaking from experience.

Grenier and Tessier both laughed at his expression, while he grinned sheepishly. "Did you fall on your ass into a pile of horse shit? What happened?" Grenier said when he was able to get his laughing under control.

"No," Sardou said slowly, "it was four years ago in Italy during the Battle of Marengo. During the pursuit, after the Austrians began fleeing, we were slicing through an infantry battalion. All the men were throwing down their weapons and running for their lives. With a few of my fellows I was in the thick of them, slashing and stabbing. I can't tell you how many I ran through. Then some fool of an Austrian who was running with his comrades turned around to face me as I was about to run him through. Men often do that, I've noticed—they'd rather turn and face death than get it in the back. Anyway, he moved to dodge my thrust and I slipped my blade under his collar bone. As he turned, it got stuck, and rather than me slipping my saber out, I got yanked off my horse as if a giant picked me up. Damn near pulled my arm out of my socket. I was lucky the blade didn't snap." Sardou rubbed his right shoulder at the memory. "Then to add insult to injury I got trampled by several fleeing Austrian infantrymen who were too busy fleeing like rabbits to notice they were trampling a prostrate foe."

Grenier listened with a grin on his face, though his mind had drifted elsewhere, prompted by Sardou's story. Pulling out a long pipe, he carefully lit it with a coal from the fireplace. "Marengo. I was there too," he said taking several puffs. "It was hot there for a while, damn close, until General Desaix showed up with his troops to turn the tide." A thought occurred to him and he looked at Tessier. "You were with Desaix at Marengo, weren't you?"

Tessier had listened silently to the discussion and watched while I tried Sardou's sword. At the name "Marengo" his eyes lit up, and Grenier's mention of Desaix brought back memories, judging by his expression. Pulling out his own pipe, he lit it and took a long puff before answering.

"Yes, I was in the Ninth Legere when we counterattacked and drove the Austrians back," Tessier said, his gaze looking through us into the past. "I was right behind Desaix as he lead that charge —and was shot in the head and killed. He was a good man and would probably be a marshal today if he had lived. I accompanied him back from Egypt as an orderly and convinced him to let me return to a light infantry regiment and fight when we rejoined the army to help Napoleon. He always looked out for his men—it was a sad day when he was killed."

For a time we sat quietly drinking our wine and smoking, the veterans remembering battles from years ago.

I went to check on some of the men before I went to bed, accompanied by Tessier and Grenier. Many of them were sitting around a fire behind a barn, the light of the flames not visible from the coast. They had another cask of wine bought from local farmers and were filling their wooden cups. The sound of laughter and song filled the air. One of the soldiers took my tin cup, which I was still carrying, and refilled it from the cask.

I noticed that even Antonio, one of the company's drummers attached to my detachment, was holding his own with a cup of wine, though several of the men were keeping an eye on how much he drank. The twelve-year-old had been part of the company since it fought in Italy four years previously. He was an Italian orphan adopted by the company after a clash at Romano. Found wandering the battlefield after his parents were killed, he became an *enfant de troupe*, a son of the regiment, looked after by the entire company, soldiers, officers, *vivandières* and *cantinières* alike. Like other *enfants de troupe,* who were sons of *vivandières* and *cantinières,* he was given a uniform, an allowance, schooling, training and a job. Eventually he became a drummer and would likely join the ranks as a chasseur when he got old enough. His dusky hue, raven black hair and big nose made him stand out, and he was tall for his age. Already some of the women were eying him. In a few more years he would be ready to pick up a musket—if he lived. A drummer's job could be dangerous, since they were often the target of sharpshooters.

One of the men, Goussand, an old, half-graying and rather rough looking man, put his arm around Antonio's shoulders and sat him next to him, and told him he had to play a role in a song they were going to sing, *Trois jeune tambours*—Three Young Drummers. It was kind of appropriate, since Antonio was to sing the drummer's role. The young Italian smiled and nodded and took a quick drink of wine from his cup; no doubt he had sung the part many times.

Goussand began to sing. "Three young drummers were returning from war...the youngest with a rose in his mouth." More of the men gathered around the fire, feet tapping out the tune, some joining in with homemade instruments. "The daughter of the king was in her window."

Another soldier gave Durand, a young and rather feminine looking Burgundian, a push to his feet, nominating him to sing the role of the king's daughter. Normally one of the camp-followers such as one of the *vivandières* would play the role, but they were with the main body of the battalion. The men laughed at Durand's annoyance but he quickly began singing. "Good looking drummer, give me your rose!" Durand played the role fully, opening his hands pleadingly as he asked for the rose and the men roared with laughter, me included.

Dropping to one knee, Antonio clasped his hands together as if he were praying. "Beautiful princess, give me your heart!" He was grinning widely, enjoying the moment and Durand's embarrassment.

With a dramatic gesture, Durand pointed back at Goussand. "Good looking drummer, ask my father the king!" Before Goussand could reply, a very drunk private tried to refill his wooden cup again and a corporal, Dautin, kicked the cup out of his hand, telling him he'd had enough. The private tumbled over and almost rolled in the fire—senseless. Two of his comrades pulled him away from the fire, threw a blanket over him and left him there.

The gruff Goussand looked at the scene with disdain, drew himself up straight, trying to take on the mock mantle of a king and continued the song, asking what riches the drummer had, that he could ask for his daughter's hand. After telling the king he had his drums and drumsticks—his majesty was not satisfied with this wealth—the drummer said he had three ships waiting at sea, one with gold, another with gems and the third to carry his bride.

"Handsome drummer, tell me, who is your father?" Goussand, the rough king, asked.

"Sire, he is the King of England."

Goussand gestured at Durand while looking at Antonio, who bowed low. "Handsome drummer, I give you my daughter." Laughing uproariously again, several of the men pushed Durand towards Antonio and they began dancing to the sound of clapping and shouting.

Something caught in my throat and I walked outside the circle of the fire, and stopped, staring off into the darkness. I had never heard the song before and was unprepared for that last twist.

I sensed someone next to me and turned to see Grenier, also staring off into the darkness, puffing on his long pipe. As he took a puff, his rugged face was lit up ever so slightly, even his mustache glowed. His voice barely reached me. "What is it, Pierre?" He rarely called me by my first name. I was an officer, after all, though he knew far more of the art of command and war than I did. He was old enough to be my father and I think in some ways he took on that role.

I shook my head and chuckled. "I don't know, it's only a song, but the thought of giving a child to marry an English prince is..."

I sensed genuine confusion from Grenier. "Is what? Wouldn't a prince be a good match?"

"Not a prince of England!" I spat, a little more vehemently than I intended.

Grenier took the pipe from his mouth and turned fully towards me. "I know you dislike the English, but don't let your hatred blind you, and don't let it control you—especially on the battlefield. Fight with your head, not your hate. And keep some perspective, my friend. That was a lighthearted song to entertain the men, not an excuse to nurse your grudges." He clasped my shoulder briefly. "Let's get a refill for that cup of yours, *mon lieutenant*." Louis Grenier had been replaced again by Sergeant Major Grenier.

I nodded, though he probably could barely see me in the dim light. "One more drink, Sergeant Major."

CHAPTER 18

October 17, 1804
Brutelles, France

Early the next morning, I left with my gendarmes and dragoons to inspect the beach and see if anything had been going on near Cayeux. The weather had cleared. The sun was shining, the wind lighter and from the west and the seas calmer. Perfect sailing weather and perfect weather for light boats.

We stopped atop some dunes just south of Cayeux and I scanned the horizon with my telescope. There were British ships visible well offshore, at least twice the normal number. One, a brig, was making what had become a daily run much closer to shore, practically within range of our guns, either testing them or getting a look at activity along the shoreline. I pulled my men inland and we trotted towards the tiny fishing village of Cayeux.

On the steps of the small church, the village priest, a short, gray-haired man, was sweeping. To me it was a strange sight, seeing him broom in hand, wearing his black cassock. It wasn't the image I generally had of a priest back home in Baltimore or Virginia. My mother would have been horrified.

As we rode closer he looked up, no expression on his face, but fear was in his eyes for a moment. Too many priests and nuns were killed during the Revolution for anyone in religious garb not to look on soldiers with at least a little trepidation. While Napoleon had made France safe for the Church again, there was still a strong Republican and anti-clerical streak that ran right through the heart of the French Army. Neither soldiers nor clergy ever quite trusted the other.

On the other hand, I did not have that background. My father was from an old Scottish family that stayed loyal to the Church and never converted to Presbyterianism. He fought alongside the Catholic Highland Scots and Bonnie Prince Charlie against the English at Culloden during the Jacobite Rebellion and was able to flee the country after their defeat. My mother was from a family that was proud of France's exalted status as "Eldest Daughter of the Church." She brought me up in the bosom of Catholicism, though I have to admit I didn't quite stay there. Even so, though I absorbed much of the Enlightenment philosophy that was so much in the air in those days in Europe and America, I never lost my respect for Rome.

I smiled, touching my hat in respect, a gesture that earned a grumble or two from a few of the dragoons. Then I spoke. "It's a Wednesday, Father, certainly too early to be cleaning up for Sunday Mass."

He still looked at me warily, but my tone and obvious respect must have reassured him and a hint of a smile came to his lips. "This is a house of God, my son, it would be dishonoring Him not to keep it clean. Besides, prayer and Mass are not only for Sundays."

I dismounted. It seemed rude to talk to a priest looking down from a horse. "I did not mean to imply they were." I looked up at the bell tower and back at him. "And certainly God should be willing to listen to our prayers any day of the week—at least I hope so."

With earnest intensity he looked at me. "He is willing to listen to us any time we open our hearts to Him." Leaning his broom against the doorjamb, he met my gaze again, curiosity getting the better of him. "So, Lieutenant, are you here to pray, for confession, or perhaps something else entirely?"

"I was just hoping you'd tell me what kind of activity at sea you and the fishermen have noticed lately the last few weeks and if there have been any strangers around the village, particularly watching the fortifications?"

The priest looked confused. "Why not ask Captain Blandin? He and his men have no doubt watched any enemy ships quite closely."

I smiled again, trying to get cooperation through charm, which was being wasted. "Let's just say Captain Blandin and I would like to have as little to do with each other as possible. Besides, you are in town and speak to the villagers regularly and they would be more likely to confide in you. Captain Blandin, I believe, would not know who was and was not out of place—am I right?"

Father Boucher nodded and pursed his lips as he began thinking. He shook his head. "There were a few wandering peddlers in town, but that was weeks ago. There have been no strangers here since then." He smiled ironically. "Except you, of course." Turning back towards the door of the church, he took up his broom again. "I have heard there have been more ships offshore the last few days all up and down the coast, but," he gestured in the direction of the sea, "you can just look for yourself to see that." Taking up where he left off, he began sweeping vigorously. Stopping in mid-sweep, he looked at me. "I must finish, so unless you wish me to hear your confession, I bid you a good day, Lieutenant."

I was dismissed. With a final nod, I mounted *Fleur* and led the men through Cayeux towards the redoubt for as brief a meeting as possible with Blandin. As we rode, Sardou rode up next to me. "A shame we can't kill the priests anymore," he observed quite seriously. "Still, you don't have to put up with his rudeness. I can send some of the men back to teach him manners."

I think I actually touched my uniform jacket over my mother's cross when he said that. I was horrified, both by the suggestion and the casual manner in which it was made. If he had suggested doing that to anyone else my reaction would have been to chuckle, but as a priest was the target I think I shot him a look of revulsion and incredulity.

Seeing my expression, he shrugged and fell back with the rest of his men. Gaucher remained next to me, silent. He had not said a word of good or ill since we met the priest.

"I suppose you agree with him?" I was still shocked by Sardou's casual reference to killing priests.

Gaucher shook his head. "No, Monsieur. Much good came out of the Revolution but also much that was bad. What happened to the Church and the clergy was horrible. It was worse in Paris and the cities, but the horror spread even here. There is a reason those years were called 'the Terror.'"

Not long after, we reached the batteries and ramparts commanded by Blandin. Our stay was brief. Blandin and I were in rare agreement that while there was more enemy activity at sea, it might mean nothing.

We rode five miles upriver to the old Roman town of Saint Valery sur Somme, where I paused to look at the gothic church and the surviving medieval fortifications. Gaucher was right, every rock, every field and hill had a story. For a moment I was filled with an incredible sense of loss. Every nook and cranny of the landscape had a story, but they were so numerous that most of them vanished from memory.

I spoke briefly to the garrison commander to check for possible spies. A trusting soul, he assured me there were no spies in the area. The town was a port but was far enough upriver I thought it highly unlikely it would be a target of any kind of raid. Any English ships trying such a venture would have to get by Blandin's guns and would be stupid to try, as they would have no room to maneuver. I had to agree: while I thought Blandin a fool, I was certain he could point his guns at ships trying to get by him. I did get a reassuring piece of news: *Chef de Bataillon* Ledoyen and the battalion were reported to be moving that day from Abbeville to a small hamlet about three or four miles south of Saint Valery. I had passed my theory on to him about Cayeux and he thought it sound enough to move his base of operations, making him about ten miles away, instead of fifteen at Abbeville.

Next we headed back to Brutelles. During the overland ride of about six miles, I began thinking of the British activity along the coast and decided that when we got there I would billet the men even closer to the fortifications, or even put them inside, Blandin's complaints be damned.

When we arrived, however, word came from Ault that made me change my mind. It was a note from Captain Labrousse, commander in Ault, that British ships had come quite close to shore near him and even took some shots at shore batteries. The same thing had happened twenty miles further south in Dieppe. He reported seeing quite a number of redcoats on the decks of the ships, which could only mean one thing—soldiers or Royal Marines were onboard, possibly ready to make a landing somewhere along our coast, and it seemed they were concentrating there. It was just as well, I remember thinking, since I couldn't convince Blandin to strengthen his defenses anyway.

Since the enemy was concentrating farther south, I decided not to move my men closer to Cayeux or inside the fortifications. Ault was looking as likely a target now, despite my hunch about the Bay of Somme and William the Conqueror's invasion fleets. Leaving the men in Brutelles kept them well-positioned to respond to either spot.

Late that afternoon, I held an inspection of all my men, the forty light infantrymen and drummer from Reille's company and the eight dragoons present, in a field near the farm where most of us were quartered.

As I walked down the ranks of the infantry, I randomly checked the condition of their Charleville muskets, counted cartridges in their cartridge boxes—their *gibernes*—and examined their shakos. The tall, dark green plumes on the cylindrical headgear pointed jauntily towards the sky, while in the center of the hats, the plates with brass hunting horns reflected the sun. They looked sharp.

As I inspected weapons and uniforms, I spoke to each man individually in formation. The infantrymen and I had been in close proximity for several months. I knew them all by name and even the background of many. More than half were combat veterans, whether it was the Wars of the Revolution, the first Italian campaign in 1796, Egypt in 1798, Germany, or the second Italian campaign just four years previously.

These men knew their business and their professionalism and competence had rubbed off on the newer, untried recruits, and, I hoped, on me. They were a wealth of information and I was always asking one soldier or another about our mutual trade. I learned as much if not more from them—especially Grenier and Tessier—as I did during the formal training put on by the corps, regiment and Jomini.

The dragoons had only been with me for a little over ten days, but they too were a professional lot, not as flamboyant as other cavalry, such as hussars or cuirassiers, but they knew their business.

After the inspection, we got in line for supper, yet another rabbit soup. I made sure I went through the line last.

THE EMPEROR'S AMERICAN

The NCOs and I settled down to a game of cards for the evening. Fortunately I only had two francs on me. I lost it all, though I put up a fight!

CHAPTER 19

October 18, 1804

I woke to my name being called insistently and someone shaking me vigorously. I heard the voices of others being aroused and the grumbling of men still half asleep.

"*Mon lieutenant*, wake up, wake up. The English are landing." That second sentence chased away any vestiges of sleep. In the dim light I tried to focus on the speaker. It was a young corporal from La Rochelle named Pineau. His eyes were wide and he was somewhat out of breath.

I sat up and grabbed his wrist. "What? What did you say?"

"The English are landing about a mile south of Cayeux, hundreds of them." I looked around the room. Tessier and Grenier were already standing and buckling on their equipment.

I swung my legs onto the floor and stood up, reaching for my weapons. I buckled on my sword belt and checked the powder charge in the priming pan of my pistol, which hung from the same belt by a leather strap I had made for the purpose.

"What time is it?"

"Perhaps an hour before dawn."

I looked around. I was tempted to send Gaucher's gendarmes to get *Chef de Bataillon* Ledoyen and the battalion but my orders were specific—I had to assess the threat myself before calling for help. After all, it could have been smugglers landing contraband. I could, however, send my small band where I wished.

"Sergeant Major Grenier, get the men assembled and moving towards the fort—fast. If possible, pick good ground somewhere close to a mile away from it, perhaps in the area of that abandoned farm directly south of the fort. We'll need room to slow their advance. You should have time, it will take the English a little while to land all their men, assemble and start moving. If the English are moving quickly and you can't take up position there, keep moving. Don't let them get between you and the fort. Go!" Grenier and Tessier saluted and left with the infantry. I turned to Gaucher. "Sergeant Gaucher, pick one of your men and send him ahead to rouse the garrison. Tell Blandin the English have landed and to use something to reinforce that gate." It made sense to use Gaucher's gendarmes for carrying messages; being from the area they knew the ground far better than the dragoons.

I looked at Sardou, who simply grinned anxiously. I grinned in return, probably just as nervously. "Don't get your sword stuck in any Englishmen today, Sergeant. In and out like butter."

A tense chuckle was his only reply.

Outside the house was a flurry of activity. A drum was sounding assembly and the infantry were already forming in a column and preparing to move off. There was a clatter of horses as several dragoons led our mounts out, which had been saddled while I was being roused. A single rider galloped away—Gaucher's gendarme.

It was a clear, cold morning. The sky was a blanket of stars and to the east the sky was starting to lighten, though dawn was still a little way off. The English were to the northwest of us—I hoped the rising sun didn't make it easier for them to spot us as we looked for them. It was a chance I had to take.

There was the sound of a muffled command and the infantry began marching. They would get there before the English. No one could outmarch the French.

We mounted and headed off at a trot. I didn't want to stumble upon the English, I merely needed to get close to determine they were indeed English soldiers or marines and try to estimate how many there were.

We rode quietly northwest, occasionally stopping to listen, petting and talking to our horses to keep them quiet. Gaucher, far more familiar with the vicinity than the rest of us, lead the way. It was nerve wracking, as we kept hearing—or at least thought we did —noises every so often.

Eventually we did hear something: voices. We went forward at a crawl. Soon, I could pick out the occasional word—in English.

Just over a rise in front of us, perhaps seventy-five feet away, there was a handful of English soldiers, apparently a patrol sent out to guard the landing area. I dismounted and carefully crept to the top of the small rise, more a grassy sand dune than anything else, to get a better look.

Sure enough, there were three English soldiers at the bottom of the rise, though I couldn't really pick out the color of their uniforms, just three shapes. Beyond, just over a quarter mile ahead along the shoreline, I could distinctly see many shapes and some large boats ferrying what appeared to be troops from ships offshore, which were easily distinguishable in the dim light. Corporal Pineau was right, there were hundreds of them already. Their only object could be the fort. I could see dim shapes moving towards Cayeux already, probably to secure their flank. A group of possibly company size had already moved a little south of their landing area to secure their landing site in case the garrison from Ault made a sally.

I had seen enough. It was time to send Gaucher to get Ledoyen and the battalion and for me to put some distance between myself and the British before racing to the fort. I hurried back to the horses and mounted, then turned to Gaucher and his remaining gendarme.

"Go to *Chef de Bataillon* Ledoyen and tell him to get the battalion here! Now!" It was almost nine miles to the battalion from where we were; it might take more than an hour for them to reach Ledoyen.

Both of them galloped due east for help and as they did I heard raised voices behind me. In my haste I had forgotten the proximity of the English soldiers, and as the gendarmes raced off, they began shouting. I drew my sword and in one motion Sardou and his eight dragoons drew theirs. They formed on either side of me in two ranks. The three English soldiers were between us and the fort—two and a half miles north. It would waste time to try and go around them now that they were alerted, and more would soon be coming.

"We're English soldiers, part of the advance party on captured French horses! Don't shoot!" I called out, then nodded at my men and we began walking towards the rise. "It's Captain Edwards, don't shoot."

"Cap'n Edwards? Who the 'ell is Captain Edwards?" One of the soldiers asked, directing his question at his fellows as much as me.

"How the 'ell do I know? We don't get told nothin'. Don't sound like a frog though."

I decided to keep them talking as long as possible. Even as we crested the rise they might not be able to pick out our uniforms. Our swords were in our hands but low so they couldn't see them. "For God's sake, don't shoot! We have information for the major!" For all I knew, a colonel was in charge of the operation, but there had to be a major somewhere—I hoped.

We were a hair over fifty feet away and I knew our luck could change in a moment. Their muskets were raised but I hadn't heard any hammers cocked yet. Perhaps they weren't even loaded yet after their rough boat ride.

"Halt! Wait there until we can identify you!" The soldier began calling for a sergeant or an officer.

Close enough. I spurred my mount forward. *"Chargez!"* We reached them in seconds. One soldier dropped his musket and dived out of the way just in time. Another was run through by Sardou—in and out like butter. The third was brushed aside by *Fleur* and I hit him across the face with the edge of my blade, cutting open his check and possibly his eye. I didn't dare try to hack or run anyone through with the thin epee from horseback—it would have snapped off.

We were past them and galloping northwest. There was shouting and a shot or two fired from a distance but to no effect. We were already out of range.

The remaining two miles passed without incident. I found my men in rough ground about a quarter mile in front of the ruins I had mentioned to Grenier. I dismounted and went to him.

"They're coming, Sergeant Major." He nodded calmly and looked southwest. I estimated there would be no sign of them for at least a half hour, though now that they knew they had been spotted I felt sure they would send men towards the fort sooner than planned, and possibly before all their men were on the beach. Even so, we were badly outnumbered. There had to be three or four hundred at least, and it looked like more were being shuttled towards the beach. The garrison of the fort had perhaps one hundred twenty-five men, and many of them would have to continue to man the sea-facing artillery as I felt sure English ships would shell them and force them to respond, thus limiting the number of defenders on the back wall. Unfortunately, there was no time to try and move some of the giant 24-pounder artillery pieces to the back wall. They weren't field pieces – they were in fixed emplacements and weren't meant to be moved.

Gaucher probably still had well over a half hour to reach the battalion, so help wouldn't arrive for at least two, perhaps three hours. We had to delay them from reaching the fort and then hold the defenses until help arrived. A grim challenge.

"Sergeant Sardou, there's only a few of you, but you have horses. Make them think there are more of you. Keep moving, try to harass their flanks, keep them from concentrating their troops if possible. Be a nuisance but don't get yourself killed if you can help it, I'll need you to help guide the battalion in." He saluted. "Oh and Sergeant, do me a favor. There's a stable in the fort. Would you put *Fleur* there? The fighting is going to get heavy here and I can't be worrying about her."

I got a cocked eyebrow in response. "To someone in our profession, a horse is a tool, like your sword. You shouldn't be worrying about her, *mon lieutenant*."

I was a little irritated over the lecture, not so much because he was a sergeant but because he was right.

"An expensive tool," I snapped, which earned me another sardonic look, especially as I hadn't paid for her. I wasn't fooling him, I was attached to the horse. I pulled out a handful of oats and gave it to her, and she nudged me appreciatively with her nose. "Just take her, Sardou."

Taking her reins, he led her off in the direction of the fort.

I looked around; several of the men were looking towards me, waiting for directions. Antonio was watching me with wide eyes, his drumsticks loose in his hands. He was scared but trying not to show it. I gulped nervously and looked at Grenier. "You probably should put a few men forward to give us some warning when the *rosbifs* get closer."

"Already done, *mon lieutenant*," Grenier replied.

I looked the ground over and in the direction the English would come from, trying to think how to deploy the men. My mind felt like it was underwater. Before an action is always the worst, once the shooting starts you stop thinking and just react.

"We should deploy the men..." I said quietly and paused, wishing my mind to work, trying to remember every lecture by Jomini and every field exercise I had ever been in. It was times like this when I realized how much I still had to learn—something like this ought to come automatically by training and instinct.

"Yes, *mon lieutenant*, I agree, they should be spread out in files," Grenier said, covering for me. "Probably each pair of men about five paces apart, so we can cover as much ground as possible with our handful of men."

I nodded. "Very good, Sergeant Major." Saluting, he turned to face the men, and gave the command to deploy as skirmishers.

"*Deployez en tirallieur!* By files, five paces apart! Pick your ground well, load when in position," Grenier commanded calmly. There had been no time to load weapons before setting off before dawn, our priority had been to get the men in position. Antonio stayed by my side, ready to pass commands along with his drum— the only way orders could be heard once the shooting started.

I watched the men quietly and calmly pick their spots, then load their weapons, a feeling of pride and apprehension overcoming me for a moment. We had served closely for months and I was constantly trying to prove myself worthy of their competence and respect.

They would fight by files—in pairs—as skirmishers were trained to do. One would fire and then the other would cover him with his loaded weapon until he was ready to fire again, and so on. This tactic could be done advancing or falling back. In this case they would be falling back toward the fort, trying to slow the English and buy time.

As they took their spots and I watched them, the pre-action fog on my mind finally lifted. "Sergeant Tessier, check them from the front, make sure they can't be seen. I don't want the *rosbifs* to know we're here until they taste our first volley."

"Yes, *mon lieutenant*." Tessier ran more than fifty paces in front of our position and began walking up and down in front yelling commands at various men he thought too exposed. The ground dipped where we were, creating several depressions that created perfect cover so the men could fight and load standing up while still protected. From the front it looked like level ground.

Once this spot got too hot to hold, we would fall back to the abandoned farm and eventually the fort. It was possible the English would pass to either side of us but it seemed unlikely. It was a seemingly flat, direct route to the fort, and they would want to get there as quickly as possible.

Soon Tessier ran back and took his position a few paces behind the men with Grenier and me. Each of us was about twenty paces from the other, Grenier to my left, Tessier to my right. We were spaced so we could each watch a portion of the line.

Almost fortyfive minutes passed and we stayed in that position, the men talking at barely a whisper, while some nibbled at food or followed nature's call nearby. They knew, like veteran soldiers around the world, to eat and rest when the moment arose, because you never know when you will be able to again. I dug out my flask of brandy and a chunk of cheese out of a small shoulder bag. Officers weren't issued backpacks, but I had to put my few belongings somewhere when on foot. It contained my flask, a little food, extra cartridges for my pistol and my telescope—everything I needed.

It was just getting light and I began to think the British wouldn't come and was cursing my cleverness speaking English in that recent encounter. They might have realized it was a trap and decided to head back to their ships.

I needn't have worried. Soon, we spotted the two *eclaireurs*—scouts—running back towards us, running low. They arrived excited and out of breath.

"Monsieur, they're coming—straight towards us." My heart started pounding again. Grenier had chosen his ground well, directly in what he estimated their line of march would be. As usual, his judgment was sound.

"How many?" I chanced a glance over the grassy dune in front of me.

The corporal, a young Gascon named Dautin, shrugged, a clear statement he didn't believe it his job to count heads, and likely his grasp of figures wasn't too precise anyway. "Hundreds of them!" I sighed. That much I already knew, but then he said something that got my attention. "They have no skirmishers out and they're marching in column."

That meant they were throwing caution to the wind and trying to get to the fort as quickly as possible. We might be able to inflict a bloody nose on the lead company, shock them and make them deploy into line and send out skirmishers.

"Quick, go to Grenier and Tessier and tell them firing is only to start when I give the word. I want all muskets to shoot in the first volley—well aimed shots. After that each file is to fire at will, standard skirmish practice. After you pass the word, get back here. You and Bernard are to be in reserve." The corporal moved off. He and the other man wouldn't make much of a reserve but I had a small force, I had to make do. I looked at Antonio, who stood nearby tapping his drumsticks together nervously. "No noise. Keep them sheathed until the shooting starts." He nodded and put them in two loops on the drum's carrying strap across his chest.

Moments after the corporal returned, I could see a dust cloud ahead and red forms in the distance. I got the same dry mouth the last time I had seen redcoats and was about to go into action. I checked the flint and charge in the priming pan of my pistol again, then drew my sword. I wiped my hand on my trousers to try and get rid of the clammy feeling and looked at my palm. It looked dry, it looked steady, but felt neither.

A private a few years younger than I was sitting not far away and looking at me, a look of calm fear in his eyes. For a moment I was wondering if I was looking into a mirror. He smiled. "It's always worse just before the shooting starts, *mon lieutenant*. The fear is natural. One would have to be an idiot not to have some fear waiting to face death."

I nodded almost imperceptibly—in theory I was supposed to be reassuring him—then chanced another glance at the approaching column. It was less than one hundred fifty yards away. It looked like the next company behind them was another two hundred yards beyond. I planned on waiting until the first company was between fifty and seventy-five yards away before firing. If I had a larger force, I would have waited until they got closer, but I needed a little maneuvering space to be able to fall back.

At one hundred yards I signaled my men to get ready. Hammers were carefully pulled back, men prepared to pop up over the grassy rises in front of us. I had my shako off so I could peer ahead with less chance of being seen (the plumes on our hats, while beautiful, made them difficult to hide). The English were in a hurry, they still had no skirmishers ahead of their column, just a handful of flankers less than twenty paces ahead of the main body.

They would pay for their haste and carelessness. It was dawn, and a thin light illuminated the ground. While muskets were not accurate weapons, it would be hard to miss at that range.

I looked up and down the line; Tessier and Grenier were watching for my command. Another moment and the main body was just over fifty yards away and I could almost make out the emblems on their shakos. I gave the signal to fire. Forty men stood up, took aim and fired. The roar was deafening. The effect on unsuspecting troops was terrifying to behold. Men all along the column crumpled, some screaming and clutching where the musket balls ripped into flesh. There were shouts of confusion and some of command as officers tried to get the dead and wounded out of the way and deploy their men.

The smoke from our first volley was clearing and my men were calmly reloading as if on a drill field. As the day wore on they wouldn't load as carefully, but the day was young and first blood was ours. It was a good day to be alive. Two of the English flankers who had been ahead of their company were still on their feet and charged ahead while my men were reloading. It was brave, if rather stupid.

One was heading directly towards me, likely attracted by my officer's uniform. I drew my pistol and aimed carefully. Normally hitting a house with a flintlock pistol is a questionable proposition but Captain Rankin's pistol—I still thought of it as that—had a rifled barrel which greatly extended its useful range. As the soldier topped a rise about ten yards in front of me I shot him. I was aiming at his chest but the ball went high and went through his neck, and judging by the blood bubbling from his neck as he fell, through an artery. A cheer went up and down our line and cries of *"Vive L'Empereur!"*

The other fell to a shot from Grenier's English rifle, taken from a dead *rosbif* during our fight at the farmhouse near Le Crotoy three months before.

I tucked my sword under my arm and began reloading.

By this time, shots were ringing out from my men who had recharged their muskets. Each took turns covering the other while his partner reloaded. The British were struggling to get into line, with a handful of men thrown in front in a rough skirmish formation who started a sporadic fire at my men. It wasn't a wise choice. Their entire company should have spread out as skirmishers; in line they were easy targets for my men, who were well protected by the dunes and rough ground. The second British company was moving up at the double but still weren't close enough to help the lead company, some of whose members were wavering and moving back, leaving gaps in their lines.

Suddenly, off to the left there was a cry of *"Vive L'Empereur!"* Sardou and his ten dragoons appeared at the gallop out of a low gully about sixty yards from the English flank. I hadn't even known he was there; he had used cover well to get his small band close. They didn't shoot, they aimed those beautiful swords of theirs at the English and rode like the devil. Sardou twisted in the saddle yelling over his shoulder at imaginary squadrons behind him.

It was too much for the wavering English company. They broke and ran for their lives. Sardou's men sabered a few stragglers, but he checked his men. He knew the support company wouldn't be fooled by a handful of horsemen. Unslinging their carbines, he and his men shot at the fleeing redcoats. Not particularly sporting, but that was a few less we would have to contend with.

As he and his men rode through our lines, we cheered them for their audacity. Grinning, Sardou returned the compliment by saluting with his saber, a gesture I returned, grinning as widely. "Carry on, Sergeant."

Nodding, he and his men headed toward the rear, ready to circle around the enemy flank again.

The second British company, already spread in skirmish formation, came up on the run until less than one hundred yards away. I could see yet another company behind them forming into line and the remnants of the first company was there as well, officers trying to restore some semblance of order and put their men in line. Other units came behind them.

Things were going to get hot very quickly.

ART MCGRATH

The English skirmishers were now sending a fierce fire in our direction. We continued to fire back from cover but they were starting to take cover as well—and they outnumbered us. I peered over the top of the dune, trying to ascertain the enemy intentions and making sure they weren't flanking us. They weren't—they seemed intent on hammering us with numbers, though Sardou's charge apparently had convinced them not to charge us headlong.

I looked up and down the line. Two men had stopped firing, one tending a wound that grazed his head, the other had a musket ball in his shoulder. Both were still on their feet and I gestured that they fall back. I looked down the line of my men and watched the soldier who had reassured me before the fighting lift his musket and prepare to aim. Suddenly he flew backwards as if someone had kicked him in the chest.

I went over to him and saw he had been shot in the face. A musket ball had gone right in his eye, killing him instantly. I looked at his shattered face, took a deep breath—my instinct was to throw up on him—and took his bayonet, then removed the belt across his chest that held his *giberne*, throwing it over my own chest. I sheathed my sword and grabbed his musket. I stood cautiously, looked over the fold of ground in front of me and saw the English continuing to get closer.

"Fall back by files, fall back!" I yelled down the line. Antonio pounded out the order on his drum as we fell back, the instrument bumping against his leg. Every other man ran to the rear about twenty-five yards and took new positions. As they did this, the remaining men fired to cover them, including me. I saw an English corporal about twenty-five yards away taking aim at a man to my right. I lifted the musket and put my cheek in the curved indent in the stock and carefully aimed the musket dead center. The smoke from the priming pan obstructed my view, but I thought I saw him drop to the ground.

I withdrew with the rest of my men to the next position while musket balls whistled past—an eerie sound, especially when you know they're aimed at you.

From our next position we continued firing, and continued to fall back in stages, the drum setting the pace. The English pushed us hard, recovered from their initial shock, but they did not charge. Shooting from off to my left and the occasional glimpse of a horse reminded them—and me—that their flanks were not entirely secure. They were thus content to push forward slowly and fight a running skirmish battle. That was fine with me.

The English had numbers on their side. At best we could keep them deployed as skirmishers, delaying their assault on the fort. We wouldn't be able to prevent it, however. Soon, we fell back upon the abandoned farm. Taking cover among the ruins of the buildings and behind the remnants of a stone wall, we poured heavy fire on our attackers. A second company had joined them as skirmishers and they were hardly slowing down to fire, just pushing forward. The old farmstead was under a mile from the fort and I had planned to use it as a strongpoint to hold for some time, but we had already used up more than half our ammunition (I had issued each man an extra ten rounds on top of the standard 50 round issue) and the English were making the position untenable. Though they didn't dare send men around my left flank because of the threat from Sardou, they were sending well over a platoon around towards my right, which would force me to retire or be cut off.

As I prepared to give the order to retreat, there was shooting from behind me and to my right. I spun in that direction wondering if I was too late and saw about thirty or thirty-five blue coated figures in rough skirmish order falling on the flank of the platoon about to attack my right wing. Hit with this new threat, the English began retreating the way they came. Their advancing companies, seeing their comrades withdrawing, halted their advance, evidently to gauge the new threat.

The thirty men drew even with my line and I ran to greet their officer. It was Lieutenant Felix Roussel, Blandin's second in command. For a moment—and only a moment—I thought Blandin had led the reinforcements himself, but then realized I should have known better.

I smiled in greeting. "Glad you decided to join us. You arrived at an auspicious time. We were about to start running like deer to escape that flank attack."

Roussel smiled, rather sheepishly, though I detected underlying annoyance as well under the brim of his black bicorn hat. "Sorry it took so long. At first Captain Blandin was perfectly willing to let you stay out here and defend us without so much as lifting a finger. Finally I convinced him to let me take these men—all volunteers—out to help. The whole garrison was willing to volunteer, which annoyed him to no end, and he limited us to thirty men."

I nodded with a sigh. It sounded like Blandin. "Were you at least able to bring extra ammunition? Some of my men are down to twenty rounds, even after taking ammunition from the dead and wounded."

Roussel shook his head in dismay. "No, he limited us to thirty rounds per man."

I swore and gripped my musket so my knuckles grew white. "That idiot! If I don't kill him myself I'll make sure General Savary and Marshal Ney hear of his incompetence. He'll be lucky if he's in charge of a kitchen detail on Devil's Island!" Roussel's eyes grew wide but it was apparent he had no sympathy for his commanding officer. "When we get back to the fort, if it comes down to it, look to me for orders regarding the defense of the landward side of the fort—not Blandin." He nodded.

I looked back towards the British. Their flanking platoon had joined the rest of their skirmishers and they started up a fierce fire. It was getting hard to see them as smoke from hundreds of muskets was obscuring my vision. Roussel's men had joined their fire to that of my soldiers but we were still badly outnumbered and more so every minute. "Can your men skirmish by file as they withdraw?"

Roussel grinned. "Are you kidding? Some of my men have never fired those muskets before today and have only shot muskets with live rounds two or three times since putting on those uniforms. These are garrison artillerymen from a coastal fort, not from Napoleon's Boulogne infantry like your men. I think they're doing well under the circumstances."

"Sorry, no offense meant. It's what I thought. Just try to get them to withdraw in a line, and not bolt. We have to start falling back on the fort. There are too many of the *rosbifs* for us to stay here and our ammunition will run out soon enough. I get the feeling they're going to start pushing us a lot harder soon."

Roussel nodded and ran back to withdraw his men.

I was right, no sooner had we begun pulling back than the English infantry began advancing again, swiftly this time. I guessed a senior officer had made his way up to the front and put some fire under his company commanders, who were behind schedule.

We withdrew from the protection of the abandoned farm, protecting each other as we went. We used as much cover as possible and tried to make every shot count. A few times I thought I hit my target—no mean feat with a musket while under fire yourself—though I had no way of knowing what effect those hits had. I would just line the sight on the front barrel band on a target and fire. So far I had only lost a few men, though more were wounded. My goal was to preserve my force for the final defense of the fort, not fritter it away in the open through attrition in a battle with a numerically superior foe. My parsimony paid off. We were within sight of the fortification and casualties remained light.

I looked back at the fort to see what preparations had been made for its defense. I could see the heads of defenders peering over the eight-foot-high wooden and earth walls and many muskets pointing towards the enemy. A makeshift abatis had been constructed—finally—the work, I suspected, of Roussel, not Blandin. The fallen trees didn't completely block access to the walls but they did make it harder for attackers, channeling them into several more easily defensible gaps, though the trees would also provide some cover for attacking troops.

I hoped there would be a sally of troops to help us, though I was fairly certain my hope was in vain; at least we should receive cover fire from the walls. The problem at this point was maintaining order so close to relative safety, as the temptation for the men would be to bolt and run for the fortifications. Some of Roussel's band were already doing that on their own.

"Go, get them there. We'll fall back in good order to cover you." I practically had to shout at Roussel, the musket fire was deafening, as was the cannon from the fort. That meant English ships were coming close enough to shell the fort and the defenders were shooting back.

Shaking his head vigorously, Roussel refused. "You've been out here since the first shot. It's not right."

I pushed him, somewhat rougher than I intended. "Go and get your men to the fort! We'll be right behind you! This fight isn't over, I'm not sending you to safety." He still hesitated, his seventeen or eighteen-year-old pride hurt by the push. "Damn it, Roussel, my men are trained for this. You've done well. Now, retreat, so we can all get in there! The longer you delay, the longer my men have to stay out here."

Finally he nodded and ran back to his men, who needed no encouragement. They ran for cover.

CHAPTER 20

October 18, 1804

As soon as they were behind us, I signaled Grenier and Tessier to send each man for cover as he fired a final shot. I sent Antonio with the first group; he had no musket and I didn't want his blood on my hands. At first he protested but soon he ran with the others.

We were barely seventy-five yards from the fort at this point. I was behind one of the felled trees of the abatis watching each pair of my men fire their final shots and run for cover. One of the last men, Private Minot, was running when he fell, something long and thin sticking out of his leg. It was a ramrod, fired out of one of the British muskets, left in the barrel in a soldier's haste to fire.

"Damn!" I uttered out loud. I liked that young man, ever since that night when he helped Callahan, Tessier and myself search a dark warehouse on the docks of Boulogne.

Minot was trying to get to his feet but couldn't, and was half dragging himself towards us. Only a few of us were left outside the walls at this point, including Tessier and a young Parisian private named Bernard. I looked towards Tessier, who was obviously ready to run back out to help. I nodded and locked the bayonet on my Charleville. When skirmishing, we had kept them off because it was faster to load our weapons without them and there weren't enough of us to engage in hand to hand combat anyway.

I hoped I wouldn't need it.

Tessier was already crouching and running towards Minot. I wasn't far behind and neither was Private Bernard. As Tessier crouched next to Minot, he fired his musket at the advancing British skirmishers barely twenty-five yards away, then grabbed the private's arm.

Over the din I heard a loud command in English. "That one's an officer! Capture him!" In that moment I felt both dread for the danger I was in and annoyance that I didn't realize my joining this rescue might put my men in more danger.

As Tessier and Bernard half-dragged the wounded Minot back towards the fort, I moved backwards next to them, weapon at the ready. Four or five English infantrymen broke from their line and ran towards us, intent it seemed on stopping us, or at least me. I raised my musket and shot the lead man, then drew my pistol and fired at the next one, who dropped, clutching his shoulder.

Holstering the weapon, I began shuffling backwards, trying to put more distance between us, but the three remaining redcoats closed the gap fast and half surrounded me when I was still fifty yards from the fort. I held the musket at the ready. I was not as good with the bayonet as I was with the sword but there was no time to drop the musket and draw it. One *rosbif* immediately began trying to knock my musket aside with his own while another was aiming to stick me in the legs, trying to disable me and capture me.

As I prepared to meet their next charge, I realized with surprise none of the shots from the fort was aimed at my attackers. The soldiers on the ramparts were exchanging fire with the main English body and seemed to be ignoring my skirmish almost literally under their noses. I smelled Blandin.

As my attackers were about to make another go of it, I saw out of the corner of my eye a blue uniform, musket and bayonet. "Would you like help, Monsieur?"

It was Tessier.

I smiled grimly, eyes on our opponents. "It's about time you showed up, Sergeant."

"Sorry, *mon lieutenant*, Minot is heavy, and I didn't realize you were in trouble," he said as he advanced on the three, thrusting and parrying. Tessier was second only to Grenier for skill with the bayonet in our company.

Soon he had two of the English soldiers fighting for their lives, while I concentrated on the remaining man with my musket.

I was lucky—or skillful enough after repeated training with the company—to get my opponent, a rather grizzled looking corporal, off balance after a few heated moments of trying to get through his guard. I blocked his thrust and responded with a horizontal buttstroke to the side of his head. He staggered, stunned. He weakly tried to raise his weapon, but I was able to stab him just below the sternum with my bayonet. He dropped his weapon and desperately grabbed the blade, vainly and feebly trying to pull it out—as was I. He dropped to his knees, gasping and still trying, blood bubbling from his mouth. I twisted the blade to free it, put my foot on his chest, pushed and yanked it free, while he flopped to the ground.

Tessier was just dispatching the second of his foes, pulling his bayonet out of the man before he fell writhing on the ground. We both ran and knelt behind a nearby abatis to catch our breath. He had seen the conclusion of my fight with the English corporal because he raised an eyebrow, a gentle grin on his face.

"Technique, *mon lieutenant*, technique. Twist and pull out immediately. Otherwise, as you discovered, the wound closes around the blade and it's very difficult to extract."

I felt like I was being lectured on the drill field, but couldn't help but laugh. "I'll keep that in mind, Sergeant. Let's get under cover."

We ran like hell to the fort, accompanied by cheers from the walls. As we ran inside the open gate, a group of soldiers started pushing a large wagon onto its side to block it, as the gate had nothing but a flimsy palisade. It worked, but we were going to pay for Blandin's lack of preparation and concern for his command's defenses. He was not far away, gesturing with his sword towards men on the wooden ramparts and yelling at his gunners firing their pieces at the English ships.

I walked towards him angrily and saluted him, very precisely and gravely. It's astounding how much contempt can be put into an act of courtesy. He returned it carelessly.

"Well, I see you made it after all, Lieutenant." The man wasn't good at hiding his disappointment behind that constantly pinched expression.

"No thanks to you, *mon capitaine*. You could have sent out some help or had your men on the walls provide cover fire." I wanted to say more, slap the man, hit the man with my musket, but managed to keep my hands to myself.

"You seem to have managed fine, even saved a man. My priority is keeping those damn English at a distance, not rescuing an impulsive foreigner." He looked around at my men, inside the walls reloading their muskets. "Well, since you're here, defend that wall. Now, I want you to take just over half your men and..."

"No, Monsieur, I will put my men where I believe they are needed." I'd had enough of his posturing and incompetence. He looked at me in shock, mid-word, even lifting his bicorn a tad to get a better look at me.

"What did you say?"

"I will put my men where I believe they are needed, facing the English infantry. You are a gunner, I would not distract you from fighting those British ships. My experience is leading these infantrymen. Let's both concentrate on what we're good at." It was painful to give even a backhanded compliment like that, but this was not the time to fight among ourselves.

I could tell he didn't quite accept my explanation but even he saw this was not the moment to argue. "Very well, use your men to reinforce my men on this wall as you see fit. I leave its defense to you and Lieutenant Roussel." With that, he turned on his heels and headed towards the guns contained within two levels of stone casemates, still gesturing with his sword and yelling.

I looked up and down the two-hundred-and-fifty-foot-long straight wooden and earth enclosure which faced inland. It connected at either end to the stone walls which faced the sea in a half-moon form. If that stone structure circled completely around we would have been in much better shape, just as we would have been if the wooden barricade had been higher, with a proper gate and a ditch in front of it. It's possible that if all that had been done, the English would never have attacked us.

Of course, it was too late to do anything about any of that except curse shortsightedness.

The walls were already lined with the blue and white uniformed artillerymen and National Guard troops assigned to the fort. Almost half the garrison was on the rear walls facing the English infantry; the rest stayed by their cannon to fire at the English ships. My men were still gathered in the open area just inside the gates. They had finished reloading their muskets and were checking their flints and making other checks on their equipment, waiting for orders. I reloaded my own musket and my pistol as well.

All along the top of the wall was the sound of numerous muskets, and smoke drifted in lazy wisps into the courtyard where we stood. A few of the artillerymen fell from the walls, hit by enemy musket fire. The enemy had to be getting a lot closer to the walls and was whittling down the defenders.

Removing the bayonet, I leaned my musket against the wall and climbed up on the ramparts briefly to get a look at the approaching English. Their straggling units had caught up. There had to be almost a complete battalion out there—close to 700 or 800 men I estimated, most in line except for probably a company in front as skirmishers. The red uniforms blended together, and for a moment they looked like a sea of blood. The sun reflected off hundreds of bayonets as they marched in a large two rank line towards the fort. Officers and NCOs ran up and down their ranks, keeping their alignment. I also saw several parties of men between the companies who appeared to be carrying something—ladders, while behind the first line there was a company in reserve, waiting to exploit any breach in our lines.

I jumped off the wall and went to Grenier, Tessier, and Roussel, gathered in a group beneath the wall where I had been standing.

"Roussel, keep your men's fire up, don't let them slow down, especially as the *rosbifs* get closer." I put a hand on his shoulder. "You'll do fine." As he started to leave, I called to him. "There are groups of men between each of their companies carrying ladders. Try aiming at them first. That will slow them down more than anything."

Roussel nodded and ran towards the walls.

It would slow them down but not stop them. They were going to try and overwhelm the wall with sheer numbers and sooner or later they would likely do it, unless help arrived. Something might have happened to Gaucher and his men, or the battalion might have stayed in Abbeville, or even worse, decided to move to a different town, and we hadn't heard about it.

I turned to look at my men, formed into three ranks, standing at attention facing the wall, their weapons on their left shoulders facing towards the sky. A few had been killed, a few more wounded so they couldn't be in formation, but most were still on their feet. The crackling of muskets flared all along the walls and the sound of the enemy's fire grew louder by the moment. Cannon thundered on the walls, shooting walls of flame and balls of iron at English warships. Smoke was getting thicker in the fort and the walls trembled with each shot of the cannon.

I picked up my musket and walked in front of the men. "*Soldats*, order arms!" The men removed their weapons from their shoulders to hold them next to their right legs. I removed my bayonet from my belt and pointed it at the wall. "Our enemies are just beyond that wall, on French soil, killing Frenchmen! They must get no further! Our comrades in the battalion will be here soon! We must hold until then!" I placed the butt of my musket on the ground and locked my bayonet in place. "*Baïonnette au canon!*" As one, the men made a half turn to their right, blades flashed out of their scabbards and were snapped on their weapons.

I lifted my musket in the air. "*Vive L'Empereur!*"

As one, thirty-five muskets were thrust into the air, bayonets sparkling in the sun. "*Vive L'Empereur! Vive L'Empereur! Vive L'Empereur!*"

I split the formation, with Grenier taking fifteen of the men and reinforcing Roussel's men on the walls while I led the remaining twenty and the drummer to plug any gap the English might make, which I was sure they would do. I hoped Ledoyen was hurrying.

Several times the English rushed the walls and were repulsed each time with heavy casualties. It was fortunate they didn't have artillery or we would have been done for. Although we were heavily outnumbered, we possessed the advantages of cover and the wall's eight feet in height.

They attacked all along the wall but concentrated several ladders at our makeshift gate. These were carried by grenadiers, their tall, black fur hats planted firmly on their heads. The overturned wagon at the gate was shorter than the rest of the wall and was a tempting target. On the third try, the English breached the gate. They forced their way over the wagon, fighting their way through some of Roussel's artillerymen and National Guardsmen. With a cheer, about twenty-five of them rushed forward, with others starting to pour over the ladders behind them. The rest of the wall was holding, but if the English could make use of their opening, we were done for.

My men were in three ranks: eight kneeling in the first, seven standing in the second and five men along with our little drummer, Antonio, standing behind them under Tessier's command as a reserve. I stood to the right of the first rank.

"First rank: *feu!*" I shouted. Smoke and fire blazed out from my men and several of the English fell. Nearly every shot was having effect at this range—barely ten yards.

"Second rank: *feu!*" I added the fire of my musket to that of the second rank and noted with satisfaction several more redcoats collapsing at our volley. Now was the time to hit them. "*Chargez!*"

We surged forward, bayonets lowered, while Tessier stayed back with our tiny reserve. The English grenadiers were shaken, but not broken, and met us head on. Though ten of the original twenty-five had fallen, they were joined by several more who had just clambered over the walls. My men fought like demons and tore through the *rosbifs*. They knew the desperation of our situation and the sight of their ancient enemies on French soil burned them.

Soon we were in a melee with them, our lines intermingled. I still had my musket and was trading blows with a private missing his front teeth. He knocked me off my feet and nearly stuck me through the throat with his bayonet while I was down, but I twisted out of the way and his bayonet stuck in the ground. As he withdrew and tried again, I was able to thrust up with my bayonet right into his abdomen. Pushing the blade in deeper, I rose to my feet, while he moaned and started falling. I didn't bother twisting and pulling out the bayonet—per Tessier's reminder. I dropped the musket with the bayonet still in the dying Englishman, drew my sword and waded back into the fray.

The *rosbifs* fought bravely but it was clear their training and experience was not yet equal to the Sixth Léger, who left a trail of broken skulls and dead and wounded English behind them. I killed another *rosbif* private, running him cleanly through the heart, and traded blows with several others as we pushed them back against the gate. While our volleys did not break them, the ferocity of our charge did, and the survivors tried to jump back over the wall. Several were pulled by their jackets back into the fort and killed, though one was taken prisoner.

I signaled Tessier to secure the gate with the reserve before more began climbing the ladders. As I climbed on the overturned wagon to look over the other side, my fear was realized as I saw several grenadiers preparing to mount the ladders. I drew my pistol and shot at an officer at the bottom who was preparing to lead his men in another attempt. Just then, Tessier and his five men appeared next to me and fired at the remaining English, who retreated, though one had the presence of mind to grab the ladder and pull it off the wall before we could bring it inside. We drew the other ladder on the gate inside the fort so it couldn't be used.

I didn't know how long the English would take to regroup, but I immediately set about reorganizing my men. Quite a few of them, who had been fighting for several hours and fired more than their full issue of ammunition, were complaining their barrels were fouled from gunpowder residue. The NCOs were having them clear their barrels the fastest way they knew: having the men piss down them. It looked odd and several men made jokes about the prodigious sizes of their sexual organs, but it worked and soon they were reloading their muskets.

I found my musket with the bayonet still stuck in the corpse of the English private. I yanked it out and quickly reloaded it and my pistol. I popped my head over the wall to get a look at what the redcoats were doing. They were engaged in a fight of attrition with the French defenders on the wall. Balls whistled over my head and made a distinctive "thwack" sound as they hit the wall. I studied their ranks and noted the grenadiers massing together behind the firing line accompanied by a company of musketeers. They were carrying several ladders and no doubt intended to recover the ones left behind at the base of the wall. Another attack could only be a few minutes away. I fired my musket at the grenadier company and prepared to clamber off the wall. As I did so, a gust of wind knocked my shako off my head and back into the fort. I jumped down and picked it up, and saw a hole in the very top. It wasn't a gust of wind but a musket ball. I stuck my finger through and showed it to Grenier, who grinned and commented on my luck. I grinned nervously in return and had him reinforce the gate with some of his men. We were being stretched thin.

I went back to my men, whom Tessier had divided into the same three rank formation as before, sans one dead and one badly wounded man who would soon die. The English attack had failed because they had been spread too thinly and their breach was only made by a few men and not followed by many more. I suspected they wouldn't make the same mistake again.

Looking at my men, I could see little fear, though I could see weariness and faces dirtied from gunpowder and combat. Once the shooting started there was little time for fear. Fear comes in the quiet moments when one is alone in his thoughts. We were too busy trying to stay alive for that. Most of the men were checking their weapons, while others were drinking water or wine from their canteens to quench the thirst that comes from biting so many cartridges in a long firefight. There is so much saltpeter in the gunpowder it can drive some men mad if they don't take a drink, especially as a battle slows. While I wasn't being driven mad—I don't think, anyway—my mouth was dry and I took out my canteen. I had gotten several mouthfuls of bitter gunpowder. I swished the water around in my mouth and spat out several mouthfuls of black water before I dared take a drink. I chased it with a long draught of brandy from my flask. On every battlefield, in every army, alcohol is present before, during and after a battle. While the fighting is going on, the officers try to keep drinking to a minimum, though we all knew—often from experience—the calming value of a drink while lead is flying.

I heard a cheer and walked towards the wall. Men were gesturing and firing more rapidly. Evidently the English were attacking again.

Grenier was carefully aiming his English rifle over the wall. He fired, then looked back down at me. His face was filthy, including his bushy and normally impeccable mustache. There were two clean areas around his blue eyes, giving him the appearance of a raccoon. I chuckled but didn't explain the joke. He wouldn't have known what a raccoon was anyway. "Officer," he said, and made a gesture across his throat.

I shuddered and thought how much of a target my uniform made me. "I thought you said you didn't like rifles. You've taken to that one."

He cocked an eyebrow—he liked doing that—and shrugged. "I said the Emperor doesn't like them. It appears to have its uses." He glanced back at the English, and began reloading. "The *rosbifs* are attacking again."

"So I gathered. Concentrating on the gate?"

A nod was his only reply. I returned to my little formation. The brandy had settled in my stomach and calmed the jitters that had started to creep in during the quieter moments. I took my place at the far right of the first rank, adjusted the chin straps of my shako and waited, musket in hand. They would hit the wall any moment.

A shout from behind got my attention. Several men on the stone walls were pointing excitedly northeast up the beach. I hoped they were pointing at our reinforcements, though the direction puzzled me, as I expected Ledoyen to come from the southeast and try to cut the English off from their ships. I climbed up onto the stone walls and looked up the beach. Sure enough, about a half mile away there were what appeared to be French troops coming up in column, with skirmishers thrown out to the front and sides. The curve of the land meant they could approach without the English seeing them. There weren't that many of them of them, however. At best there were two companies, which meant the battalion had split up or there were no more reinforcements coming. I had a sinking feeling in my gut at the thought but put it aside.

I pulled out my telescope and studied the approaching columns. They were indeed French light infantry—two companies of chasseurs, and the lead company with its skirmishers out was Reille's company, the First Company of the Sixth Légèr. Our reinforcements *had* arrived.

I felt someone next to me. It was Blandin, out of breath. "Well, are they here? Are they ours?"

I glanced at him. "Yes, Monsieur. It's part of the Third Battalion of the Sixth Légèr." I looked again through the spyglass. I recognized some of the skirmishers. As I started to put the telescope away, I felt a hand try to grab it.

"Let me look for a moment." The pushy bastard only asked because he wasn't able to snatch it from my hand. I snapped it shut and put it away.

"Get your own, Captain. I'm going to look landward." I left the walls and ran through the little courtyard past my formation. I hoped the rest of the battalion was coming from behind the English, otherwise the two companies would be on their own outside the walls, though they could form skirmishers and harass the English if necessary. I looked southeast with my spyglass, trying to get a glimpse of our men, but there was so much smoke from hundreds of muskets, French and English, it was hard to see.

My running back and forth from wall to wall had been noticed. The men knew what we were waiting for. All eyes were on me as I looked. Many even stopped firing to watch me—much to the chagrin of their NCOs and Roussel, who kept after them to keep firing. Grenier wasn't far away.

"What is it, *mon lieutenant*? Is the battalion here?"

I looked at Grenier with a grin. "Captain Reille is here with another company." I took my shako off and wiped my forehead, then put it back on and adjusted the straps. "I'm just not sure where the rest of the battalion is."

It suddenly seemed quiet. The fire on the wall had slackened so much the British had noticed and stopped firing. I think they thought we were preparing to surrender.

"What's that noise?" A soldier on the wall said. The National Guardsman took off his bicorn and cupped his hand to his ear as if to listen. Several others began shouting excitedly, and others shut them up so they could hear.

Several said they could hear drums, coronets, even singing. I was frozen, trying to concentrate. It was three hours since I had put out the call for help and it was overdue. I began looking southeast again. With the pause in shooting, the smoke was clearing. I saw dust in the distance just over a small rise behind the English line. Suddenly, all along a front several hundred yards long, troops appeared—French light infantry. First came *voltigeurs* in skirmish formation, easy to pick out because of their yellow facings and collars. Behind them came the companies of chasseurs and the company of *carabiniers*—elite assault infantry with black fur hats, the equivalent of the line battalion grenadiers, deploying from column into line. A mounted officer, *Chef de Bataillon* Ledoyen, appeared in the center near the battalion standard, riding up and down in front of the troops seeing to their dispositions as they formed into line. On either flank there were about one hundred cavalry. I could see the brass hats and green uniforms of the dragoons on one flank and what appeared to be elegantly uniformed hussars in blue and red on the other. I don't know where Ledoyen found the detachment of hussars. Mustaches on all, they were a dashing lot, with green shakos, ornate blue coats with gold piping, and red pelisses thrown over their left shoulder. Unlike the dragoons, they carried curved sabers, but like them carried carbines. I couldn't tell the unit, there was so much variation in uniform color among the hussars, even more than the rest of the French Army, but everything they wore was expensive and gorgeous—which added to their dash.

My heart caught in my throat at the sight of the battalion and its standard. The soldiers who'd said they heard singing had been right. A band was playing *La Marseillaise* and hundreds of soldiers in the battalion were singing it. The men in the fort, and especially my light infantry, took up the refrain.

"To arms citizens! Form your battalions! March on, march on, their impure blood shall water our fields!" No song is more powerful or can send a chill down the spine faster, especially sung by hundreds of Frenchman with the sounds and smells of battle all around. To a small invading force suddenly confronted by the Sixth Légèr singing this song, it must have been terrifying.

The main body of English troops at first did not notice the threat just a few hundred yards behind them, but a company in reserve behind their main line did, and its officers desperately began turning the unit to face the new threat, their drummer hammering out a warning. The company began deploying as skirmishers. By this time word had spread to the main body and cries of dismay echoed across the battlefield. Sergeants and officers shouted to maintain control, while turning the facing of the entire battalion one hundred eighty degrees. I understood their dismay. Stranded on a foreign shore with a superior enemy force between them and their boats would be enough to shake anybody. The famous English sang-froid did not desert them, however, and they completed the maneuver, leaving a company to face us in case we sallied forth. No matter what, their retreat would be incredibly difficult. They were still unaware of the two companies coming from the beach which would hit their flank. I was determined to join them. Despite the weariness of my troops, I knew they wouldn't accept being left behind and neither would I.

I looked at the some of the artillery troops. "Move this wagon and get the gate open!"

As the men struggled to obey the order, Blandin came over. "What do you think you're doing?" He didn't countermand my order, though some of his men stopped to listen to our conversation. Annoyed, I gestured at Grenier, who put some of our men to work on the gate and prodded the artillerymen to continue moving the wagon.

"Rejoining my unit, *mon capitaine*. The English attack is finished, we must join the pursuit."

Clearly he wanted to object, though apparently he could come up with no cause to do so and the wagon was already being moved. There was cheering along the back walls. We went to look and saw that the two companies which had moved up along the beach were marching in front of our walls between us and the English and moving into line. Reille was already striding towards the gate with Captain Jacques Tison, commander of the other company. I went out to meet them, accompanied by Blandin, Roussel, Grenier and Tessier. We saluted, and Reille saluted in return, smiling a greeting at me and extending his hand. Despite a forced march, as always he managed to cut a dashing figure—even his mustache and sideburns looked perfect.

"Glad to see you in one piece, Pierre. You too, Messieurs." His eyes narrowed a tad as he looked at us, glancing at Grenier's blackened face and the musket in my hand. "You look like hell. Rough couple of hours?"

I nodded, then gestured towards the battlefield, as the first elements of the main body of the battalion were starting to clash with the English. "Yes, but seeing that makes it all worth it." Musketry crackled all along both lines. The first volleys of the French were platoon volleys, starting at one end of each company and moving to the other in a dramatic demonstration of precision, but soon the soldiers on both sides were firing at will, as fast as they could reload and fire.

"Indeed. There's still work to be done, though. If you and your men are up to it, get them in line with the company."

I saluted, turned to Grenier and Tessier and told them to fall the thirty remaining men in with the company, then looked at Blandin and Roussel. "We'll be back for my dead and wounded." I shook Roussel's hand. "You did well. Thank you." Giving a contemptuous glance at Blandin, I turned my back on him and headed towards the company.

Soon the men were in line and I was in my accustomed place, center left behind the last rank of the First Company. From there my view of the battlefield diminished considerably. I had to look over the shoulders of my chasseurs to see anything, but essentially the British were forced into a U-shaped formation, with one company of grenadiers in line facing our two companies to their north, their main line of troops facing the bulk of our battalion to the east. At the far southern extreme of their formation, a company had formed square to fend off our detachments of cavalry. We faced them in an L shape. At the extreme right of the French formation, our two companies at the far north formed the small end of the L, the bulk of the battalion faced directly opposite their main body, while the majority of our cavalry was at the extreme left to threaten their flank.

We outnumbered the English, the majority of our troops were fresh with plenty of ammunition, and we had cavalry, not to mention the advantage of being on our own soil. It was a matter of time—and not too much time at that—before the English broke. Their officers had to be trying to figure out a way to withdraw at least some of their men to their boats while holding their line.

Fighting in line, especially as an officer, is frustrating sometimes. At least the men get to shoot; all I could do was watch, listen and give the occasional order. The officers and sergeants in the last rank—the *serre-file*—see the backs of the men, occasionally getting a glimpse over their shoulders.

After a while you are often surrounded by smoke from gunpowder and can see nothing but the men in front of you and perhaps twenty or thirty feet to either side. All the while your ears and head are pounded by the constant noise of musketry and the occasional sound of a musket ball flying overhead or into a comrade. The cries of the wounded or dying are in your ears the whole time, sometimes accompanied by the barking of the dogs which always trailed the army. The skirmish near Cayeux was a tiny affair compared to some of the battles I fought in later, but it was my introduction to the sounds, sights and horrors of the battlefield. I was fortunate to have a gradual immersion.

I was still carrying a musket but there was no way I could wield it while we were in line. I saw to my men's alignment, shouted encouragement and saw that the wounded were comfortable as the unit moved and left them behind. I also had to make sure men didn't stop too long to take care of the wounded. Sometimes in an action a shirker would fall out, using the cover of a noble act to avoid fighting, though there were few of those in First Company. I'd let them see to their comrade and order them back in line.

There was no need for them to linger, as some of the battalion's *vivandières* were following behind the unit tending to the wounded when they could. Not far behind me a stocky woman of about thirty, Louise Cormeau, tended to a wounded corporal. She saw me looking at her and picked her way across the dead and wounded to get to me.

"Brandy, Monsieur?" She practically had to scream over the din of the fight, and gestured to the wooden cask slung on her side. I nodded and got my flask out, refilling it from her cask and taking a draught. There was blood on the sleeve of her makeshift uniform, which was a feminine version of the regiment's uniform, except the skirt of course.

"Are you wounded?"

Shaking her head, she adjusted a pistol stuck into a belt around her waist that kept her skirts from becoming unruly and gestured toward the last man I saw her tending to.

"No, it is his, Monsieur." Her eyes were filled with tears, whether from loss or smoke it was hard to tell. I glanced back towards the front of the line and when I looked back at her she was gone, in the lines among the soldiers to offer drinks, something to wash the taste of gunpowder out of the mouth. The bullets flying by did not seem to bother her at all.

We were pushing hard against the grenadier company that formed the English left flank and it was slowly falling back. The English soldiers knew as well as their officers that some of them would have to stay behind to hold us off while some get away on the boats. The question of who was to go and who was to be sacrificed had to weigh on their minds and affect the morale of many ordinary soldiers. Though the grenadier company in front of us held, some of its soldiers bolted and began running for the boats, over a mile away. Another company, facing the main body of our battalion, tried to withdraw out of line to move to another position, but their withdrawal soon became a rout. *Chef de Bataillon* Ledoyen had kept some of the cavalry behind the center of his line as a reserve and when he saw the English company dissolve, he sent them through the gap, followed by several companies of infantry. It was too much for the English and one by one their companies fell apart or began retreating headlong to avoid being cut off and overrun.

Reille ordered our two companies to lower bayonets and charge. The grenadiers joined the flight and we went after them at the double. We were slowed down somewhat when we hit the village of Cayeux. *Rosbifs* still in good order took cover among some of the buildings and rained fire down on us, but we eventually ran them out of the village and started converging on their landing site from the north, while the other companies of the battalion rapidly advanced from the east. We could see half-full boats already ferrying troops out towards their ships. I suspected once they delivered their cargo they would find an excuse not to come back to shore.

At this point we ran into fresh English troops using dunes for cover, much as we had when we slowed down the English advance hours before. The *rosbifs* had left more than a full company, including Royal Marines, to hold their landing area, troops who had not been engaged until now. The Royal Marines were easy to pick out, as they wore red coats like the infantry but with blue facings on them instead of white, and round black hats instead of shakos on their heads.

The marines and the rest of the rearguard were putting up a furious fight, but they began to crack and we charged, as did the rest of the battalion from the east. The *rosbifs* fled towards the remaining landing craft, whose crews quickly pushed them in the water to escape. Some English soldiers waded through the water and a few even swam to try to get to safety. The crews pulled the nearest ones aboard but then began rowing harder, putting distance between them and shore. While some of the boats were full, a number of the double hulled vessels (which looked like something Captain Cook would have seen in his adventures in the

Pacific) were less than half full, having pushed off in desperation to get away.

With the departure of the landing craft, the remaining English sensibly saw no point in continuing the struggle, and companies began surrendering. They were scattered so much there was no one person in charge anymore. Of the six hundred or so English soldiers who landed, less than three hundred escaped. Many were killed and several hundred captured on that beach south of Cayeux.

As we gathered our prisoners, many soldiers began chanting *"Vive L'Empereur"* towards the English ships and retreating boats, all well out of effective musket range. Surrounded by a throng of cheering French soldiers on the beach, I leaned against my musket and stared at the ships preparing to take the survivors onboard, and for the first time in a long time, I prayed silently for the soul of my father, dead twenty-three years. In that moment, I felt close to him and thought I felt his hand on my shoulder.

Not long after, an ecstatic Ledoyen rode over to compliment me on my role in the day's events. He put me to work interviewing English prisoners, especially officers. Rarely had I combined duty with pleasure as I had on that day.

That evening, as we marched inland as part of the battalion, Antonio began playing *Auprés de ma blonde* and the men joyfully took up the refrain.

"Next to my girlfriend, it's so fine, so fine, so fine. Next to my girlfriend it's so fine to sleep." A cold breeze blew in from the darkening sea and the echoes of singing mingled with the sound of marching feet and accoutrements rattling.

CHAPTER 21

November 2, 1804
On the road between Boulogne and Montreuil

It was exactly one month before the coronation of Napoleon as emperor when I ran into him near Boulogne making one of his surprise inspections.

The weeks since the action against the English had passed relatively quietly for me. About a week after that fight the entire battalion—myself included—was recalled to Montreuil and Étaples, as Ney, Savary and Soult believed the defeat of the English landing force meant we would see no more action along the coast. The English officers in the landing force revealed some especially interesting information to me: there was a price on my head in England. The Englishmen I questioned knew immediately who I was—"Napoleon's renegade American"—and said they had heard talk in London about hiring someone to kill me for my role in executing the English spies sent to destroy our fleet.

When Savary heard this he relieved me from further duties hunting spies—at least for a time. I returned to my duties training with the battalion and attending Jomini's school for officers, with some duties as an aide-de-camp. Frankly I was relieved to be doing plain soldiering. I preferred it to spy hunting, however good at the latter I might be.

The day I met Napoleon again I was on aide-de-camp duty and relaying a message from Ney to Soult in Boulogne. About halfway between Montreuil and Boulogne I moved aside for a forty-strong detachment of cavalry. I immediately recognized the distinctive uniforms of the Chasseurs of the Guard, scarlet pelisses thrown over the left sleeves of their dark green jackets, expensive saddles and accoutrements gleaming, carbines at the ready. They glanced at me as they rode by but said nothing. In their midst was the Emperor, accompanied by Savary, who saw me sitting astride *Fleur* and pointed out my presence to the Emperor. Napoleon ordered the little column to a halt and motioned me over.

On a fine gray horse, the Emperor was the most plainly dressed man present, surrounded as he was by his glittering Guard and various aides-de-camp, including Savary's finery. Underneath his plain gray greatcoat Napoleon wore his campaign uniform, the green coat and white trousers of a colonel of the *Chasseurs à Cheval* of the Guard. That ordinary looking uniform became his hallmark on battlefields across Europe, as capitals fell, monarchs lost their crowns, and armies crumbled before the Grande Armée.

As I approached, I saluted and prepared to dismount to speak to him, but Napoleon gestured for me to stay on my horse. Emperor he may have been, but he tried to simplify things in the field. Among his entourage, not far from the Emperor, I noticed the dark eyes of Roustam, his Mameluke bodyguard, watching me. The dusky Roustam was more elaborately dressed even than the Guard, with his turban, colorful flowing robes, jeweled dagger and scimitar. I wondered if he were cold, though I suppose he had warmer clothes hidden underneath his exotic garb. Napoleon had brought him back from the Egyptian expedition in 1799 and he accompanied the Emperor everywhere, even sleeping outside his door at night.

Napoleon had a house at Pont-de-Briques, a few miles outside Boulogne on the road to Paris. It was perfectly situated so he could arrive from Paris unseen and make surprise inspections of the troops—even his marshals didn't know when he was arriving. He rarely announced his coming and would often appear in the midst of training soldiers, as he did that day.

Napoleon smiled as I approached him, his gray eyes twinkling. "Well, Burns, my 'renegade,' in one piece I see. I hear you helped give the English a bloody nose last month, sent the shopkeepers scrambling back to their island. I suspect we won't see them on French soil again for a long time. You have done well."

I sat straighter in the saddle. "Thank you, sire."

He glanced at Savary and the rest of his entourage. "I hope we can repay them the visit before long." There were murmurs of agreement around him. "When you return to the United States you will have such a tale to tell people might not believe you." He moved his horse closer to mine. "A month from today is my coronation. It will be a unique moment in history. Naturally, I expect you there."

I stammered, not sure how to reply.

Charm like the sun, he smiled again. "I didn't promise you a good view, simply that you'll be there somewhere, a unique observer to a singular moment. Besides, you should see Paris. You haven't yet?"

"No, sire."

"Then you will." I was confused, overwhelmed and more than a little flattered. At the time I didn't know what Napoleon was doing, though in retrospect I can see he was binding me to him, as he had looked ahead and thought I might be useful in his dealings with the United States. Also I had proved I could fight, be ruthless when necessary, and improvise.

By inviting me to the coronation—along with about 20,000 others—he was making me feel like a part of history. It was heady stuff, especially for one looking for a home and a cause. He was giving me both. Some say converts to a cause fight harder and are more loyal than those born to one. I think Napoleon knew this.

Napoleon had a gift of being able to tell the best way to get people to do what he wanted by appealing to their desires. Some could be bought with money, others by appealing to their patriotism, others like Ney by whetting their thirst for military glory and fame. In a sense, I suppose I was being bought as well. He looked into my wanderlust and put an end to it, or at least found a way to channel it as I became part of a venture that turned Europe upside down. I am not complaining, on the contrary I am grateful. What I have seen and experienced few of my countrymen can even comprehend.

The Emperor stared at me with those gray eyes that felt like they could see inside me, then he called a secretary over who was carrying files of paper in saddlebags and was constantly adjusting them so he didn't lose them. "Give me that sheet on those American ships the English captured." The secretary fished through papers and in surprisingly quick order, produced the document, which the Emperor glanced at and handed to me.

THE EMPEROR'S AMERICAN

I read the sheet, a report from a French agent in London. It stated that in one week a few months previously, three American merchantmen had been stopped on the high seas and a total of eighteen seamen taken off and impressed into the English Royal Navy. The American consul had filed a protest with the Crown—which was ignored—and sent a report to President Jefferson. It was an all too familiar story and would remain so for years to come. Many English sailors deserted to serve on American ships, as conditions and pay were far better. The English wanted the men back. The British reserved the right to stop any ship and take off seamen to man Royal Navy ships if they could not prove their nationality, but the problem didn't stop there. Naturalized Americans were seized, as the British government did not acknowledge the right of a man to change his allegiance, and even native born Americans were seized if they could not prove their nationality. Up to 1,000 seamen a year were taken off American ships.

The constant violation of American rights infuriated all Americans and there were occasional calls for war with England, but these were still being resisted by Congress. Many ship owners and leaders of American commerce simply saw it as a price of doing business and President Jefferson—who faced reelection that very month—knew the country was in no position yet to challenge Great Britain militarily, so the violations continued. Napoleon couldn't understand why.

"Why does your country allow this to continue?" He asked me when I looked up from the paper, anger, but no surprise in my eyes. "These are acts of war; your country should declare war on England."

I handed the paper back to him. "Yes, sire, ideally we should. But it would affect commerce, and to many in my country, that comes before almost everything."

Napoleon's eyes grew dark with contempt. "Before honor?"

I paused. "Americans are very pragmatic, sire, and slow to anger as a people. People are outraged at events such as this, especially ship captains and crewmen who see these violations face to face, but there is also a realization that for the moment, the United States is not in a position to do anything about it."

The Emperor was not satisfied by my explanation. "Your country has vast resources. If it marshaled them for war, your countrymen could rout the English and put them on the defensive. How many more events like this before the United States declares war?"

"I don't know, sire." It would be eight long years before the United States joined France in the war against our common enemy.

Shaking his head in annoyance, he handed the report back to his secretary. Suddenly a thought occurred to him and, seemingly forgetting I was there, he began dictating an order to be sent to an architect in Paris about the design of a street and museum in Paris. The city was being built more beautifully than ever before under his direction and his mind was ever on it—as it was ever on so many things. There seemed to be no subject he couldn't master.

"Send this by telegraph. Tell him I want an answer back by the end of the day," Napoleon said. An aide galloped off towards Boulogne with the message. I was constantly astounded at the speed with which messages could be sent back and forth across France using the Chappe telegraph, or semaphore, what some called France's secret weapon. Various series of towers crisscrossed France connecting the major cities, each tower within sight of the next. The towers had large, jointed arms on them. The arrangement of the arms in a certain way created words using a special code. Though the system depended on weather and could not be used at night, a complete message could be sent from Boulogne to Paris—about 135 miles away—in a little over a half hour. It was not unrealistic for Napoleon to expect an answer back from Paris by the end of the day—in fact he could get it much sooner.

He turned back to me. "No country should put up with such outrages, no matter how *pragmatic*," he said, emphasizing the last word with disdain, continuing our conversation as if it had never stopped. His mind was able to work on numerous projects at the same time. "Ending England's dominance of the sea would benefit both our countries. Your country should be at war with England, we are natural allies."

I nodded. "I agree, sire, nothing would please me more."

A slight smile crossed his face and he nodded with approval, glad at least one American agreed with him on the matter. Actually there were many who did, but not yet enough to start a war with England, but I didn't remind the Emperor of that again. "Very good, Burns. We shall have to speak on occasion on how we can convince the rest of your countrymen to join us."

"Of course, sire. It would be my pleasure."

The interview was over. Napoleon and his entourage rode off, Roustam giving me a final wary glance, General Savary nodding familiarly as he rode by. I sat astride *Fleur* as the Guard rode around me as they headed towards Étaples. The troops there were in for a surprise.

CHAPTER 22

November 24, 1804
Recques, northeast of Montreuil

Early on a cold Saturday morning Ney summoned me to his chateau to prepare for the trip to Paris. Napoleon's coronation was to take place on Sunday, December 2. When I arrived, my regalia of an aide-de-camp under my greatcoat, Jomini and General Adrien Dutaillis, Ney's chief of staff, were making final preparations both for the trip and for Ney's absence from the VI Corps. He was expected to be in Paris for several months.

Dutaillis nodded noncommittally at me. We got along well enough, but with Jomini present he was more subdued. The sharp featured, forty-four-year-old Dutaillis was Jomini's superior but at the same time was somewhat cowed by him. Since Jomini didn't like me, Dutaillis thought it best not to be overly friendly to me.

The corps' three divisional commanders were also present and were discussing how to keep the men busy for the coming winter months. Small detachments from each regiment were being sent to Paris to participate in a ceremony on December fifth, in which each battalion and regiment would receive new gold Eagles to top their regimental standards.

General Louis Henri Loison, commander of the VI Corps' Second Division, looked me up and down before continuing his conversation with the other divisional commanders. Loison—of whose division the Sixth Légèr was a part—could be intimidating, especially as I found it difficult to tell what he was thinking. A young man, barely thirty, he was harsh but brave and efficient, though he had a brutal streak in him. It was somewhat subdued today.

"Well, it's our little orphaned American, washed up on the shore like Venus," he said after the divisional commanders received their orders from Ney. "So are you off to Paris?"

"Yes, *mon général.*"

Laughing, he hit me rather hard on the back, practically knocking me off my feet. "Make sure you stick to the clean whorehouses—and there are plenty. I don't need you coming back here and spreading disease among the local whores. If you get the girls at Madame Delobel's sick you'll probably be thrown off the nearest cliff!"

Still laughing, he left with the other two divisional commanders.

Jomini, who had overheard the conversation, came over to me, his aristocratic features all tied up. "Why did you tell him you're going to Paris? You're going to stay here in camp and study and march. You need to study more if you're going to be of any use to us in England."

Blood rushed to my face. In the almost seven months since joining the army I figured I had already seen more action than he had in his entire time wearing a uniform. An impolitic answer was ready to come out of my mouth but Ney's baritone voice interjected before the first word was uttered. "No, he's right, he's going to Paris with us for the coronation, Jomini."

Flummoxed, Jomini looked at both of us. "But Monsieur le Maréchal, he's just a lieutenant, a foreigner barely in the army seven months."

Ney laughed heartily at Jomini's discomfiture. "Indeed he is—as are you—but he will be there all the same. If the Emperor wants him present at his coronation then he'll be present at the coronation."

Jomini looked as if he didn't believe Ney. "The Emperor wants him there?"

Ney stopped laughing, a look of annoyance on his face at the continued questions. "Yes, the Emperor requested he be somewhere present during the coronation—along with 20,000 other people, if you recall. Each time you've criticized Burns I've told you about his almost proverbial luck—which you don't seem to believe in. Well, he certainly seems to have it."

Later that day, Ney, Jomini, Dutaillis and several other officers got into coaches for the ride to Paris. Ney and Aglaé had their own coach; I was stuck in one with Jomini, who was practicing Swiss taciturnity—something I didn't know they were known for—for the entire trip. Over one hundred thirty miles to Paris, a whole day of travel by fast coach and relays of horses, and he didn't say a word to me—which, I think, suited both of us.

Monday, November 26, 1804
Paris

More than six months after my arrival in France I entered the capital of the Empire. The normally crowded city had grown considerably in preparation for the coronation. By the day of the event the population had swelled by an additional million as people swarmed from throughout the countryside to take part in the festivities and get a glimpse of the Emperor.

I had never seen so many people in my entire life. There were almost as many people in the city at that moment as in the entire United States. I looked out the windows of the coach like a backwoodsman, marveling at the crowds, the ancient buildings, the noise and the smell. Everywhere there were signs of construction, some of it in preparation for the coronation but also because Napoleon was rebuilding Paris, intent on making it the most beautiful city in Europe, a worthy capital for the empire. Much of the old city had been torn down and was being rebuilt under his direction. Many mourned the loss of the old character of the city but Napoleon pushed on, straightening streets, building many fountains and bringing water into the crowded and dirty city. It reminded me of Augustus and his rebuilding of ancient Rome, who said he found a city of brick and left one of marble.

Soon after we arrived in city, I was billeted in a house on Rue Saint Dominique with other staff officers not too far from Ney's magnificent new mansion and gardens on the Rue de Lille. It was a showplace residence where he and Aglaé could give parties and be seen—almost a requirement for the marshals and others high up in the new imperial nobility, though ironically all that could be seen of the house from the street was a high wall and a gate. It was on the left bank of the Seine, just a block from the river, near the former Hotel de Villeroy which Napoleon's stepson, Prince Eugene Beauharnais had just bought. The neighborhood was becoming one of the fashionable places to be in Paris.

That afternoon, Ney ordered me to go to the Tuileries Palace, Napoleon's residence and seat of power, and report to the Emperor's aide-de-camp, General Savary. I put on my greatcoat over my uniform, bundled against the numbing cold that had settled over Paris. The palace was barely a quarter mile away, just a brief walk across the Seine and connected to the wings of the Louvre, which housed a museum and administrative offices. I had never been in a palace before, and it was not what I imagined. I had in mind something along the lines of a medieval castle, but the Tuileries was imposing and opulent, not grim and forbidding. It was a richly decorated residence meant to awe with its splendor, not meant for defense like a fortress.

In a room near where the Tuileries and the Louvre palaces joined, I met Savary, who greeted me warmly at the door to a small but ornate office. Inside, sitting in a chair close to a roaring fireplace, was another man, who rose to greet me. Richly dressed in dark green, with a half cape, he carried a cane and walked with a limp, though not because of any wound or old age. His limp came from a club foot he was born with. He was Talleyrand.

I call him Talleyrand because that is how he was known throughout Europe, simply Talleyrand, just as monarchs like Napoleon were known by their first name. Talleyrand was no monarch, though he often wielded power like one. His full name was Charles Maurice de Talleyrand-Périgord, and he was France's minister of foreign affairs and Grand Chamberlain of the Empire, though he would soon acquire other titles. A member of the old nobility, he was a former Catholic bishop who was known for his mistresses even when still in the clergy. He was also a conspirator extraordinaire, member of the Revolutionary National Convention, diplomat, and most of all, born survivor. He was one of the most powerful men in France, and thus Europe. Napoleon once called him "shit in a silk stocking."

Around my height, he was fifty years old, and his graying, light brown hair reached almost to his shoulders. His handshake was gentle yet firm, but there was something in his dark, flinty eyes that was much harder and said he was not a man to be crossed, or entirely trusted. I got a definite chill for a moment. The hardness lurking in his eyes did not reach the rest of his face, however. In fact he was quite charming and elegant. He wasn't Europe's foremost diplomat for nothing. This was quite a casual, even intimate setting for someone of his position to meet an unknown like me. It avoided many layers of protocol and bureaucracy. The question was, why?

"Our American ally, at last. Welcome to Paris, Lieutenant Burns. It is a pleasure to meet you. General Savary has spoken of you quite often, and even the Emperor has mentioned you on occasion." While I was sure Savary had talked about me, I didn't delude myself that the Emperor was casually speaking of me in Paris to his minister of foreign affairs. I didn't say as much, however.

"I'm flattered, *Monsieur le Grand Chambellan,* the honor is all mine." The three of us moved in front of Savary's fire and I stomped my feet to try and get some warmth in them.

"Please, this is not the Emperor's court. Most people call me Monsieur de Talleyrand, or *Monseigneuer.*" He certainly wore his power lightly, he had no need for people to bow and scrape to him. He saw my eyebrow rise with curiosity at his use of the title, *Monseigneur,* which was reserved for princes and prelates.

"I was once a bishop—in essence I still am a bishop in the eyes of the Church. Once you are ordained, you are always ordained. It is an honorific I enjoy hearing and does not take the speaker a full minute to utter," he said, smiling at his own wit. "A beautiful country, the United States," he said, easily switching to English.

Rubbing my hands together vigorously in front of the fire, I looked at him in surprise and responded in kind. "Indeed it is. Have you been there, Excellency?"

Studying me, he nodded. "Yes, I lived there for two years, from 1794 to 1796. I had to leave France during the Terror, and lived in England until the English expelled me because I wouldn't oppose France. I worked in your country selling land in New York and Massachusetts before returning home. I've always been fond of your country, which gave me a home when I had nowhere else to go."

A servant brought in a tray with three glasses of cognac and I sipped mine appreciatively. I had never tried the drink before landing in France but was learning to like it—among a great deal of other things.

"Why did you return to France?"

Talleyrand sniffed his drink, watching it as it swirled in his glass. "France needed me, Mister Burns, beset by enemies on all sides. The United States is far away from its potential enemies—except the omnipresent red man—with a vast ocean between it and the rest of the world's powers. I think sometimes it is hard for Americans, our old allies, to appreciate the dangers we face here—except of course, for someone like you who has been here and seen things for himself."

I nodded, but said nothing, sensing he had more on his mind. I was there for a reason, after all.

"I admire your willingness to join us, to fight for your motherland—in a manner of speaking, and to repay the debt of Yorktown."

I took another sip of the excellent cognac. Savary had taste, but then again, he could afford it. "It is not only repaying the debt of Yorktown, Excellency. My mother was French—she was born here. My father, though a Scot, was also born here after my grandfather fled Scotland. I have two motherlands—the United States and France."

Talleyrand looked closely at me. "And if their two interests come into conflict?"

I returned the look, looking at his eyes to see what might be hiding there. They revealed nothing.

"I pray that will never happen, but if it did, Monsieur de Talleyrand, I would be faithful to both or serve neither."

Shifting his weight on his cane, he closed his eyes and took a slow sip of his cognac, then looked at me again. The barest of smiles touched his lips. "Then, Lieutenant Burns, we shall have to make sure you are faithful to both. You do agree that the United States should be at war with England?"

I took another taste of the cognac; warmth was finally reaching my extremities, a welcome change from the chilling cold. "Of course, Excellency. England's offenses against both our countries should be repaid. I think there would be no better time to reopen the alliance between our countries."

Talleyrand continued to look at me intently. His questions were leading somewhere, I just wasn't sure where yet. "And you would try and convince your countrymen of this?"

"Yes, of course, though I doubt I would have much influence. I am no one, Excellency."

Waving his hand as if he were driving away a wisp of smoke, Talleyrand dismissed the thought.

"You underrate yourself, Pierre Burns, especially in post-Revolutionary France or America. But, I am going to give you a chance to test your influence. Since the Emperor has requested you attend his coronation, I am going to give you a job to occupy your time here in Paris. For a few days before the coronation and during the ceremony itself, I want you to be an aide to General John Armstrong, the new American minister to France. While you are with him, speak of the invasion and the might of our army, of our mission to rid the world of English meddling in other nations' affairs, and that a declaration of war by the United States against England would be repaying her for blows against American honor. You are an American who has joined us in our quest; I think your story and voice might affect him and might influence his future communications with the American government."

For a long moment we stared at each other, and quietly finished our cognac. I looked around. Savary was still standing, listening to the conversation, which had switched back and forth from English to French several times. A servant had come in with three more glasses, which he had left on an ornate wooden table with claw legs. I put down my empty glass, picked up another and went to a window, and pushed the heavy curtain aside, drawn as protection against the cold. It overlooked the ice-covered Seine River, flowing through the heart of Paris and right by the Louvre and Tuileries palaces. To the left, east of where I was, I could see an island in the center of the river, the Île de la Cité, and the very top of the towers of Notre Dame, located on the other end of the island. In less than a week Napoleon would be crowned there.

I turned to Talleyrand. "I will do so, *Monseigneur*," I said. "I will not spy on the minister, nor attempt to pry secrets. I will, however, escort him to the coronation, speak against English perfidy and in favor of the United States declaring war against England, and grant him whatever assistance I can."

If Talleyrand was disappointed, he did not show it. In fact it was probably what he anticipated. "From what I have heard about you, Lieutenant, I would have expected no more—and no less. Frankly, I think just your presence in that uniform, might say more than any words." He lifted his glass of cognac in a toast. "To your health."

I lifted my glass in return. "*Santé!*"

It was just past noon on Thursday, three days before the coronation. The bitter cold had not left Paris and I was hustling along on a street eight or nine blocks from Ney's house on the left bank of the Seine. I was reporting to Minister Armstrong's residence at the Hotel de la Guiche on Rue de Regard to offer my services as his aide through the coronation. Talleyrand had informed Ney I would be occupied for a few days, which didn't bother the marshal, as he really didn't have a lot for me to do anyway.

Since arriving in Paris I had done my best to get in touch with Athenaïs, but to no avail. Her brother had a house in the outskirts of Paris where they often stayed, especially during the cold weather, but all messages I sent—through a circuitous route using a servant who made deliveries to the house—went unanswered. Her silence, while not entirely surprising on account of her brother, was still disturbing and was on my mind as I knocked on the heavy wooden door at the minister's residence, a small but well-kept hotel. No ostentation for the new nation. Armstrong was not known for being a man who lived beyond his means. He and his wife and five children had moved here when they arrived in Paris about a month before our meeting.

A short, stocky man in an ordinary brown coat and trousers answered the door. Around twenty-five years old, with tiny eyes, he had wisps of brown hair going in all directions. He gave me a contemptuous once over and asked me in crude French what I wanted. When I explained, in good French, that I was assigned to assist Armstrong until the coronation, he opened the door and led me to a small parlor to the right with high ceilings, dirty white walls, and a few pieces of good furniture scattered here and there.

Telling me to wait, he began to leave the room when another man entered the room and stopped him.

The newcomer was about fifty years old and balding, with his remaining hair mostly gray. He reminded me of pictures I had seen of George Washington. Though he wore dark brown civilian clothing, his bearing struck me as military. He had a contradictory air of nervous confidence, with a sense of arrogance about him at the same time. I wasn't sure what to make of him.

"What is it, Todd, what does he want?" He asked, looking at me curiously.

"Oh, the bloody frog said something about being assigned to you as an aide during the coronation. Just what you need, Mr. Armstrong, a dressed up peacock helping you."

So this was the America's minister to France. He and his assistant were the first Americans I had laid eyes on since parting with Cushman and the crew. To his credit, the minister looked embarrassed by his assistant's words, though he didn't know I spoke English.

"*Bonjour*, lieutenant. I am Minister John Armstrong." While a little awkward, he spoke French well.

I shook the proffered hand and replied in English. "Good afternoon, sir. Lieutenant Pierre Burns, aide-de-camp to Marshal Ney, on temporary assignment through the request of Monsieur de Talleyrand." The head of Armstrong's assistant—Todd Brown— turned towards me, a look of panic on his face on hearing me speak English.

Armstrong smiled at his discomfort but quickly hid it, running a hand over the remnants of his hair. "Burns, eh? One of those Jacobite families in France?"

I nodded, though my family had left France decades before. "Yes, my family were Jacobites."

"Your English is excellent, Lieutenant, where did you learn it?"

I took a breath, my hand resting on my sword hilt nervously. "Baltimore, Maryland, though I also lived in Virginia."

Armstrong nodded. "How long did you spend in the United States? I can detect no accent other than that of the South."

Time to drop the anvil on his foot. "All my life, I was born and raised there. I am an American."

To his credit, Armstrong did not lose his composure, though the shock was evident if one looked closely. Brown, on the other hand, simply gaped at me. I enjoyed the moment.

"What the hell are you doing in that uniform?" Brown demanded. He looked flustered and angry.

I provoked him, I couldn't help it. God knows I didn't suffer fools lightly. "Serving as an aide-de-camp to Marshal Ney, temporarily assigned to the minister by Monsieur de Talleyrand," I said matter-of-factly.

That infuriated the man and he strode several steps towards me, looking up at me as he approached. I smiled pleasantly, but Armstrong raised his hand. "Brown." He looked at me, rather annoyed. "Mister Burns, I think we both know Mister Brown meant that as a philosophical question. Pray tell, what are you, an American, doing serving in the French Army, especially in wartime?"

I had answered this question so many times I was getting annoyed. Sometimes I didn't know the meaning of the word discretion. "Any excuse to fight the English, and the uniforms are pretty."

My answer was directed more towards Brown, but the minister responded icily and I could hardly blame him.

"Lieutenant," he pronounced the word like one used to command, which indeed he was, "If you will not respond as asked out of simple courtesy, then do so as an officer when addressed by a superior."

I snapped to attention—not to mention my senses—at the rebuke. "Sorry, sir."

Armstrong put his hands behind his back and nodded, waiting for me to continue.

"I was stranded in France almost seven months ago when my ship, the *Bedford*, commanded by Captain John Rankin, was attacked and sunk by a British frigate. After landing, I had the great fortune to meet Marshal Michel Ney and have been in his— and the Emperor's—service since then, serving as an aide-de-camp and training with the Third Battalion of the Sixth Léger. He took me on because as an American I had a better knowledge of the English than most French officers, and he thinks I will be of service during the invasion of England."

Eyes revealing nothing, Armstrong listened attentively, hands still behind his back. "You seem to be doing well so far."

"Yes, sir. And I've seen action against the English twice, including a skirmish last month along the coast."

Armstrong's eyes narrowed; I had gotten his attention. "You were involved in that action south of Boulogne defeating that large English landing?" I could see Brown paying even closer attention.

"Yes sir, I played a role in it." I was flattered; news of the fight had reached Paris, but then again it had to, if it was to be a propaganda victory.

"You've met Napoleon?"

I nodded. "Yes, sir, several times."

Armstrong took his hands from behind his back and walked to a nearby fireplace, putting his hands in front of the roaring fire, trying to warm his hands. He indicated with his head I should join him by the fire, while Brown stayed by the door to the other room. "And what is your impression of the modern Caesar?"

I glanced at him. He was still staring at his hands in front of the fire. "That he is just that. No one like him has appeared since Julius Caesar. Nothing is beneath his notice and no subject seems beyond his grasp. He is unique."

Chuckling, Armstrong nodded. "I agree. I'm also glad there's an ocean between him and the United States."

Though I thought Napoleon had no ambitions against the United States, 5,000 miles of Atlantic Ocean made sure of it. "I think there's little fear of that. There is one thing the Emperor hasn't mastered, or has a firm grasp of, and that is naval warfare. Crossing *la Manche*—er, the Channel—is bad enough, but to cross the ocean is out of the question, especially since he sold Louisiana. I think he would be content with conquering England, or even making a permanent peace with them, but I fear they will make that impossible."

Armstrong turned to face me. "I'm afraid you are right, and that is the assessment of President Jefferson as well. England is intent on restoring the monarchy at all costs." He took in my aide-de-camp's uniform, replete with gold braid, armband on the left sleeve indicating I was an aide, fine leather boots and sword.

"You personally are in a sensitive position, being an American in French uniform, especially with our mandated neutrality. If you are captured I doubt the English will treat you as a prisoner of war. They would probably hang you."

Having shot more than my share of English spies, I knew he was probably right. France recognized me as a dual citizen because my parents were born in France, but the English would not. Besides, my actions in Boulogne had not endeared me to London.

"Minister, there is already a price on my head in England," I said quietly. "There are those there who would love to hang me." Out of the corner of my eye I noticed Brown taking a keen interest in the conversation.

"Well, you'll have to make sure you don't fall into their hands," Armstrong said, smiling widely and clapping me on the shoulder. Suddenly he stopped, his hand still on my shoulder, looking at my face closely, the smile fading. "My God, are you Angus Burns' son?"

For a moment my heart caught in my throat at the sound of my father's name. It was not something I expected to hear from a stranger thousands of miles from home. I searched his face for any hostility connected with the question. There was none I could see, just shock. For a long moment I didn't trust myself to speak and just nodded.

The shock was still evident on Armstrong's face, as he took his hand off my shoulder and solemnly offered it to me again. "When I first shook your hand, it was that of a stranger. Now let me shake the hand of the son of an old friend." Confused, I shook his hand, waiting for an explanation. Instead he turned to Brown and ordered him to bring in a bottle of whiskey. When he returned with a bottle and three glasses, Armstrong dismissed him. Brown eyed the third glass sourly, and left—reluctantly, it seemed to me.

Armstrong poured two glasses, including a rather hefty serving for himself, then raised it. "To Angus Burns." We drank the toast and Armstrong poured another round. I glanced at the bottle; it burned nicely going down.

"Bourbon?" I asked.

He nodded, taking a swig from his glass. "I made sure I brought a supply from home. The French love their wine and brandy and I'll drink it to be polite, but give me a good American whiskey any day."

Though I dreaded it, I turned the conversation back to my father. "How did you know my father?"

"Angus?" He stared at the whiskey in his glass for a moment. "We served together in the Continental Army during the Revolution. I always used to tease him about having such a strong Scottish name, considering he spoke with that French accent of his. He was a hell of a soldier. That's why Tarleton's men did what they did." Pausing to sip his whiskey, he continued. "You've probably heard the story of how Tarleton dug up the body of one of our officers and forced the man's wife to serve dinner to his corpse?"

I shuddered at the thought and nodded my head. My mother made sure no tale of English villainy went untold.

"Well," Armstrong continued. "Your father caught some of the group who did that. They didn't die well. We left them hanging from a tree for carrion birds to eat...." Pausing to take a gulp of his whiskey, Armstrong appeared to shudder, though it may have been from the cold. "Tarleton was determined to pay him back and did. You may have heard, the Tories who captured your father tied him spread-eagle to a wagon wheel and scalped him—while was still alive. They then broke his legs and left him to die, which he did..." he hesitated ever so slightly, "after several days, apparently."

I felt lightheaded and took a quick slug of the bourbon. My mother had told me my father was scalped, she never said it was while he was alive, nor that he took days to die with broken legs. I was not surprised she didn't tell me, and I wondered if she even knew. What returning soldier would give those kinds of details to a grieving widow? She knew enough, however—she had found out he had been scalped and told me. I prayed she hadn't known more.

Armstrong looked at me, and his face softened a tad. "I see you didn't know all of the details. It's no wonder you're in that uniform. Anne would have put her hatred of the English into her very mother's milk."

For a moment anger flashed in me to hear my mother spoken of so familiarly by a stranger, but there was nothing but kindness—and sadness—in the man's face. "I am here," I said a trifle unsteadily, trying to change the subject from my father's death, "because Great Britain continues to be our enemy, stopping our ships on the high seas and seizing our sailors, not to mention the occasional cargo and ship. The ship I served on was destroyed by a British frigate."

Armstrong shook his head. "I know why *you* are here, young Burns, but you overstate the case against Britain, though British actions are often outrageous. The United States wants their high-handed actions on the high seas to stop. More importantly, however, we would like to see peace in Europe and trade with both France and England. As long as war continues, we will remain neutral and friendly with both and allied with neither." He smiled, somewhat ironically. "I knew Captain Rankin, and you have to admit it wasn't entirely random his being the target of a British frigate. His propensity for taking the occasional British vessel as a prize was known on both sides of the Atlantic."

Anger flared up again, perhaps because he had a point, but I would not concede that the English had any justification doing what they did. As far as I was concerned, any English ship, any English soldier was fair game, whether the United States was technically neutral or not. I refrained from speaking my mind, and though I could tell Armstrong knew what I was thinking, he said nothing more. It was a subject I would bring up again in coming days, seemingly with no luck. The conversation turned to the more practical matters surrounding the details of the coronation, and how and when Armstrong would arrive with the rest of the diplomatic delegation.

After I left Armstrong's house and headed towards the right bank of the Seine and the Tuileries, I had the distinct impression I was being followed, though I saw no one. I dismissed it as my imagination.

CHAPTER 23

Sunday, December 2, 1804
Paris, near Notre Dame Cathedral

After arranging to pick up Armstrong and his wife in a coach, we drove towards the Île de la Cité, where Notre Dame was located. The minister was wearing the blue uniform of a brigadier of the American Army, the highest rank he had earned during his time in uniform. It was similar to the blue and white uniform of the French line, except it had yellow facings and was a somewhat different cut. I stopped for a moment when I saw him, because it had been a long time since I had seen one of those uniforms.

A dusting of snow had fallen overnight and there was a light fog over the city that hadn't entirely cleared. Houses and buildings everywhere were festively decorated in tapestries and bright colors. People were hanging out of windows and on rooftops trying to get a better view of the procession approaching Notre Dame, many waving and yelling boisterously as we drove by.

Because of heavy security, few coaches were allowed on the island, for fear of another bombing like the infamous incident on the Rue de St Nicaise on Christmas Eve four years before. Most people, including the diplomatic delegation, had to walk across the ancient stone bridges to the famous church. Mounted soldiers and officers studied us and the crowd, alert for anything untoward. Among them were some of Napoleon's aides on horseback who nodded at me in recognition.

The light snow that had fallen overnight had been cleared off the bridge and road, though nothing could be done about the bitter cold. Perhaps being dressed like a peacock had its advantages, though I'm sure I looked more elegant than warm.

The long white plumes on my busby did nothing but flap in the breeze, but the tall fur hat was quite warm—far more so than the bicorn or shako I wore in my légère uniform. The heavy blue uniform coat and gold lace helped fight off the chill, as long as we kept moving.

For once since meeting Armstrong, the topic of discussion was not war with England but the sights around us. It was a rare change. The day after I had met him we had dined at his house, joined by his wife, Alida, several of their children, and Brown. I had talked more in detail about my experiences with Napoleon's army and some of the people I had met in my time since landing in France. Armstrong's oldest son, fourteen-year old Horatio, took a keen interest in me and my adventures and asked for detailed descriptions of army life, while Armstrong's wife, Alida, an attractive, dark-haired women of forty-five, had no interest in battles but asked for stories about the balls, dances and uniforms, and the young women I had met in my time in France.

Mrs. Armstrong joined us in the coach but would be in a separate area from her husband in the church. I had promised Armstrong I would do my best to get him as a close as I could to see the crown placed on Napoleon's head.

Thousands of troops lined the route to the church, as did tens of thousands of spectators. Around nine o'clock, as we approached the huge church, I looked straight up at the huge twin bell towers looming above us hundreds of feet into the air, the squat shapes of gargoyles visible far above. The building still bore scars of the Revolution's war against religion, when it was converted into a Temple of Reason, statues taken down and destroyed, crowns chiseled off others, gold and precious metals and items stripped off and sold. Even the eleven giant bells in the bell towers were removed to be melted down to make muskets, though only one ended up in the iron foundry. The rest were eventually restored to their rightful places, but not before the building was almost torn down for building material and all but abandoned except to store wine casks.

The contrast between its nadir and the day of the coronation was striking. Right against the western facing edifice of the church was a temporary but imposing and magnificent structure built to look like a triumphal arch, with golden statues of Charlemagne atop it. A giant tent covered the entrance to the adjoining archbishop's palace so that the imperial party need not be exposed to the elements.

Just outside the cathedral we joined another small group of Americans led by James Monroe, then ambassador to England, who unlike Armstrong was in civilian clothes. He had been in France for some of the negotiations surrounding the Louisiana Purchase, though this was my first occasion to meet him. While he had been anxious to return to his post for weeks, he didn't dare go before the coronation for fear of snubbing the French. The compliment had not been repaid, and he was complaining vociferously about the seat assigned to him by courtiers in charge of protocol.

"Armstrong, there you are! Can you believe it? I have been assigned to the third and fourth rank diplomats! This is a deliberate insult directed to an American minister!" Despite his anger, his angular face did not change color, either because of the cold or self-control.

Clearing his throat, Armstrong spoke quietly, trying to calm the normally affable Monroe. "I think, Monroe, that the slight is not meant as such, it's only..."

"Only what man? Out with it!"

"You are ambassador to the Court of Saint James, not to France. I think the French view it as a courtesy to include you at all."

Though he looked like he wanted to say more, Monroe just nodded reluctantly.

"Yes, you are probably right, though they could have made accommodations despite it all." Looking over our party, his eyes fell on me and my uniform. "Ah, is this Napoleon's American? The castaway from Baltimore?"

I snapped to attention and saluted smartly. "Lieutenant Pierre Burns, at your service, sir."

Monroe smiled affably. "Well met, Mister Burns. I don't suppose you could do anything about my accommodations?"

Of course he meant the question rhetorically but I felt obliged to try.

"I will see what I can do, sir." I turned to Armstrong. "With your permission, of course, sir."

I entered the western end of the church with Armstrong and Monroe, and went around an ornately built platform in front of the main entrance. I caught my breath. Despite the light diffusing through stunning stained glass windows, many extra chandeliers had been hung to provide light in the dim church, and the hundreds of glowing candles were a striking sight. Most of the stone floor was covered with rugs, which helped fight off the cold. Much of the gothic architecture was hidden under scaffolding and splendid decoration put up strictly for this day to make Notre Dame look like a Greco-Roman temple. Napoleon was definitely making clear he was heir to the Caesars of ancient Rome. The most obvious sign of this was the giant Arch of Triumph that had blocked our way at the entrance; it took up the entire width of the western end of the nave. A steep set of stairs led to a throne under the arch, with several thrones below the high one. There was no doubt for whom the one was meant.

High up on the arch were words emblazoned in gold: *Honneur, patrie, et Napoléon empereur des Français*—"Honor, fatherland, and Napoleon, Emperor of the French."

Along each wall there were three levels of seating above the ground floor, all crammed with people, 20,000 tor more.

Looking straight up, the ceilings arched towards the sky—towards God—and a long row of decorated columns reached east towards the nave. There was activity everywhere as thousands of people tried to find their places. As we followed others in the diplomatic delegation, a hand touched my shoulder. It was Charbonnier, dressed up in his imposing Imperial Guard ceremonial dress uniform of red, green and ochre. The scabbard of his saber scraped on the floor of the church as he shifted his weight.

"Bonjour, Burns. Look at you, dressed like an oriental monarch," he said, smiling from ear to ear. At a glance he took in my indigo blue aide-de-camp dress uniform, white plumes rising a foot off my dolman, and more gold braid than usual. I even had a little half-cape, like a pelisse, though not as gorgeous as Charbonnier's scarlet pelisse. My sword, however, remained my ordinary, unadorned infantry officer's epee.

I grinned back. "Since when has a member of the Guard been in a position to criticize gaudy uniforms?" I looked more closely at his jacket. "*Captain* Charbonnier! When did that happen?" People swirled around us, trying to get to their places, though it would be several hours before the ceremony was to begin and over an hour before Napoleon and his wife Josephine arrived at the archbishop's palace. Everyone was superbly dressed, jewels everywhere. I was sure some of the outfits, even of the men, were worth more money than I had ever made in a year. I glanced at numerous gorgeous women, magnificently dressed. Despite the cold, I noticed a fair amount of exposed skin and shivering owners. I was glad I was a man, in more ways than one.

"Last month." He looked at me, then at Armstrong and Monroe. "Who are these Messieurs?"

I had forgotten my manners. I introduced my charge for the day—Armstrong—and told Charbonnier of Monroe's complaint and that I was going to try and jostle for a better view for him, indicating the milling crowd in front of the altar in the nave of the church. Thousands of people were already there, which helped fight off the chilling cold in the stone building. Numerous vendors had been allowed to discreetly join the crowd and were hawking their wares, with most officials looking the other way. The smell of fresh bread and sausage was making me hungry. Charbonnier must have caught my glimpse or noticed my famished expression, because he grabbed one of the peddlers roughly by his jacket and yanked him in the middle of our little group, then bought food for all of us.

"Don't stand on dignity, Minister, it's going to be a long day," Charbonnier said, noticing Armstrong's hesitation. We ate the sausage and bread quickly. Fortunately, I had brought my flask of cognac with me; I washed down my meal and slipped the flask back inside my jacket. The warmth helped.

"So you're looking for a closer view of the ceremony?" Charbonnier asked. I nodded but didn't say anything. Everyone else in that room was looking for the same thing and it was getting more and more crowded by the minute, and most people were confined to certain areas, including the diplomatic corps. I didn't hold out much hope. Armstrong was already moving to his assigned spot, which was only a few yards to one side of the high throne on the second level, so he would have an excellent view of the Emperor. Confronted with the daunting view of the crowds, Monroe seemed resigned to accept the slot given him, but before he could go, Charbonnier gestured with his head, his busby pointing towards the nave, and said, "Come." We followed him to the wall and began moving forward.

There were courtiers everywhere checking to make sure people got to their proper places, that protocol was observed and nothing was untoward. Everyone was to be placed exactly according to his station. Charbonnier waved them aside as few could have, since he often commanded the Emperor's personal escort, and we pushed on into the nave and towards the sanctuary at the front of the church. Near the front of the nave, not far behind where the imperial entourage was to sit, a group of at least fifty officers, almost all generals, was milling about grumbling behind a group of seated clergy, who were already sitting down. The group was led by a tall, impressive looking general with dark hair and very sharp, eagle-like features. I didn't know him but he looked like he was ready to lead his men into yet another battle right there in the cathedral.

"Give up your seats, priests, these are generals who have fought on dozens of battlefields for France," he said roughly. "Seeing how tired these men are, you will be performing an act of charity." The men looked anything but tired, though they probably should have, having fought across Europe since the Revolution and before.

The smug looking priest being addressed crossed his arms and shook his head.

The general, who had been holding his hat and gesturing with it, plopped it on his head. "The hell with this. Get up!" He grabbed the priest by his arm, the man's tonsured headed reflecting the dim light, and yanked him right on his feet, almost knocking him over. Immediately the general sat down in his chair. "This chair is taken, Father. Take your prayer beads somewhere else."

There was stunned silence for a moment as everyone around watched the scene, then as if of one mind, the generals waded in and forcibly ejected the remaining priests, who didn't have the sense to scramble out of the way. Charbonnier, who had stopped with the rest of us to watch the scene, grinned widely, his mustache seeming to stretch as he did so. "The fun is over. Come on."

God help me, but I grinned back, then Monroe and I followed him into the sanctuary. The hard marble floor of most of the sanctuary, including the stairs leading to the front of the altar and the floor in front of the ornate altar itself, had been covered in rich blue carpet with little gold bees—one of the symbols of Napoleon's reign—woven into it. We circled behind the high altar, where several other people were milling about, including the Spanish ambassador and the Italian ambassador, and a surly looking man in a turban I was told was the ambassador of Turkey. Behind and above us, large numbers of people were crowding in the galleries to try to see the ceremony when it started. Charbonnier casually made sure Monroe and I were barely ten feet behind the throne where the Pope was to sit and where Napoleon would be crowned, nodded to me, then almost immediately returned to his duties.

We had a long wait, though excellent views once the ceremony began. Various clergy gave us all rather annoyed looks that we were in such proximity to the altar, but said nothing. I think the incident with the generals made all the clergy in the cathedral cautious. It was just as well, as far as I was concerned.

After more than an hour of shuffling and quiet talk, punctured by boisterous laughter among some of the generals, there was commotion near the main entrance of the church as word filtered down that the Pope had arrived.

The doors at the far end of the cathedral opened and hundreds of voices in the choir and the clergy sang *Tu es Petrus* in his honor. I watched Pope Pius VII go around the base of the triumphal arch and advance down the center aisle, dressed all in white, standing erect despite his age. All movement among the gathered thousands stopped as they stopped to watch him walk towards his throne on the foot of the altar in front of me. Even those extremely hostile to the Church—and there were many there—sensed this was a historic moment. It was rare for the Pope to leave Rome. Even Charlemagne, after whose coronation this was patterned, went to Rome to be crowned. Not Napoleon. The Pope owed him a huge debt and he was here to repay it.

Since the consulate, Napoleon had allowed the clergy to return to France unmolested and the Catholic Church to flourish again more or less unmolested, though there was still disagreement over the return of church property. The Church was once again able to freely engage in the battle for souls.

The day of the coronation was not a battle for souls so much as to mark the end of the Revolution and the beginning of a new France, both imperial and republican. Napoleon was to be crowned emperor but would take an oath to the Republic. As Ney had described during our dinner conversation almost seven months previously, it was to be a republic with imperial trappings —or an empire with republican trappings. This was the final transition.

When Napoleon arrived at the neighboring archbishop's palace to change into his eighty-pound coronation garb, cries of "*Vive l'Empereur*" started at one end of the church and worked their way forward. We didn't have much longer to wait.

The Emperor did not enter by the arch and down the center aisle but took a gallery that ran behind the seats, emerging near where the transept met the choir in the center of the church, where the Pope greeted him and gave his pontifical benediction. It was shrewdly done out of the sight of most of the military and senators still attached to the anticlericalism of the Revolution. Emperor he may have been, but he knew he still needed their support.

With the Pope back at his throne in front of the altar, a magnificent march by Lesueur began, and the Emperor and Empress began their slow walk down the center of the choir to their seats. The music that day, with more than four hundred instrumentalists and singers present, was probably the most glorious anyone had ever heard and was enough to transport one towards heaven.

As the Emperor began walking down the aisle of the choir, the fog outside suddenly lifted and the sun shone brightly through the windows, causing an involuntary gasp among thousands. The timing was perfect, as if even the sun were coming out to bless the event.

The Emperor and Empress sat on two velvet covered thrones about ten yards in front of the high altar and facing it, while the Pope sat on his throne facing them. Two ornately embroidered kneelers were in place before the imperial couple's thrones, where

Napoleon and Josephine knelt to receive a papal benediction. They then rose and approached the papal throne to be anointed with oil.

The Emperor was wearing an eighty-pound crimson velvet mantle studded with gold bees and fastened with a gold cord and tassel. The Empress also had a heavy crimson mantle, though not the eighty pounds her husband wore. Her dress with silver brocade was elegant, as was her bodice, which sparkled with diamonds and lace gold.

Though I had met her daughter once, it was the first time I had ever gotten such a close look at the empress herself. Despite the fact that she was forty-one, she didn't look older than twenty-five. Everyone who describes her that day uses that exact phrase, but it's true, she didn't look any older than I did. She was grace in motion, even under all that heavy clothing, with an enigmatic, closed-mouthed smile, dark brown hair and perfect skin.

She looked radiantly happy and had a right to be. Napoleon's family had hounded him to divorce her because she hadn't produced an heir yet and they were horrified she was being crowned empress, yet here she was, albeit not to be empress in her own right but simply as wife of the Emperor. Still, it was too much to bear for some of the Emperor's family. The Emperor's mother, Letizia, even found an excuse not to be at the coronation because of Josephine, but Napoleon altered history retroactively and had her inserted into a painting of the event.

After being anointed the couple went to sit back down on their thrones while the Mass proceeded. Being behind the high altar on which the Pope himself was saying Mass was an odd sensation that tried to reawaken every Catholic bone in my body. I found myself muttering Latin prayers from my youth my mother had ingrained in me. Armstrong, while not a Catholic, had a look of reverent attention, though the marble blocked much of our view of the Pope, as did the six tall candlesticks, topped by beeswax candles almost as tall as a man.

As odd a sensation as it was for us behind the altar, it must have been just as peculiar for Pius VII to be practically surrounded, even at his own altar, by the curious if not reverent. Soon, however, the novelty of the event was wearing off and I struggled to fight off a yawn. I could see the Emperor at his kneeler move his shoulders ever so slightly, trying to adjust his mantle. The weight must have been oppressive.

Soon, after the *Gloria* had been sung, the Pope blessed the imperial regalia on the altar: the crown, scepter and sword, and sat down on his throne in front of it. The Emperor got up from his own throne and courtiers brought these items to him. The diamond-studded dress sword was strapped on and he took the scepter in his hand, before placing it back on a cushion held by a courtier. Then he slowly approached the altar where the regalia lay. Unfortunately Charlemagne's original crown, used to crown French kings from time immemorial, had been destroyed in the tumult of the Revolution, when anything connected to monarchy was a target. A copy of that ancient gold diadem had been made for the coronation.

What happened next has been a source of dispute, at least among those who wish to add more drama to an already dramatic scene, or who wish to slur the Emperor. Napoleon carefully picked up the crown and looked at it, a distant look in his eyes for a moment, followed by a look of supreme happiness, which I could see quite clearly from my vantage point. Time seemed to stand still as thousands of people watched him.

Napoleon turned slowly and carefully (not that he had much of a choice with that eighty pound mantle on his shoulders) and faced the multitude. Nothing moved, no one said a word. With deliberate grace and precision, he placed the crown on his head, crowning himself Emperor of the French. Behind him, the Pope blessed his back, reduced to role of spectator. Though some have said he snatched the crown from the Pope's hands, it isn't true. The Pope was sitting and nowhere near the crown. It was clear Napoleon had worked it out well in advance that being crowned by the Pope would be making a statement that his reign was subservient to the Catholic Church, and that was not a message he wanted to send.

Returning to the altar, Napoleon took off the Charlemagne crown and put on a crown of gold laurel leaves, similar to that worn by Roman emperors, then picked up the Charlemagne crown and walked in front of the altar again, back still to the Pope. Josephine got up from her own throne, approached the altar, and knelt on the bottom of the three stairs in front of it, where the

Emperor stood. The expression on her face was both radiantly happy and triumphant, and her tears were visible from where I stood. The Emperor's family hated her and had fought against this moment. She had won.

Gently, even tenderly, the Emperor lowered the Charlemagne crown on her head, removed it again, and placed it on a cushion held by a courtier. Somewhat playfully he adjusted the tiara already on her head, touching her hair gently. Thus crowned, the Imperial couple went to their thrones to prepare to join a procession up to the high throne beneath the Arch of Triumph.

I heard words next to me and broke out of my reverie and looked over at Monroe. "What did you say, sir?"

"Quite the show the French put on." While his words were casual, you could tell the event moved him as well. I simply nodded in response and turned my attention back to the sanctuary, where the imperial procession was moving away from us, making its way towards the triumphal arch at the other end of the church, with its high throne twenty-five steps above the congregation. There were two other thrones five steps below the high throne, one for Josephine, another for the Pope. After Napoleon was seated, Josephine proceeded towards her throne, Napoleon's three sisters carrying her train. She had gone up the fifth step when, as if with one mind, they dropped it, nearly knocking her backwards. There were gasps, and a few low cries from the crowd. Even from a distance one could see the Emperor's face darken and he said a few inaudible words in the direction of his sisters, who picked up Josephine's train as if nothing had happened. She made it to her seat without further incident.

The Pope slowly and deliberately climbed the twenty-five steps to stop in front of Napoleon and spoke in French the ancient words from the French coronation ceremony, "May God strengthen you upon this throne," then kissed the Emperor on the cheek. Turning to the assemblage, in a loud voice he proclaimed in Latin: *"Vivat Imperator in aeternum"*—"May the Emperor live forever!"

The crowd replied in French, *"Vive L'Empereur! Vive l'Impératrice!"* The enormous choir took up the Latin refrain and began singing *"Vivat, Vivat! Vivat in Aeternum, Vivat in*

Aeternum!" It was freezing cold in Notre Dame that day but I suspect the chills I felt at that moment weren't from the cold.

The Pope returned to his throne near the altar for the rest of the Mass, then just as the Emperor was about to take the secular oath of office as emperor, he quietly left the altar and went into the Ssacristy rather than be present for this part of the ceremony, which confirmed the gains of the Revolution. Hand on the Gospels, Napoleon proclaimed "I swear to maintain the integrity of the territory of the Republic, to respect and enforce respect for the Concordat and freedom of religion, equality of rights, political and civil liberty...and to govern in the sole interest, happiness and glory of the French people."

There was a cheer and in a booming voice, a herald proclaimed, "The most glorious, most august Emperor Napoleon, Emperor of the French, is crowned and enthroned Emperor. *Vive L'Empereur!"* The entire crowd both inside and outside the cathedral took up the cry, and *"Vive L'Empereur"* was echoed by thousands of voices in the ancient stone walls of Notre Dame. Cannons boomed nearby, one after the other, proclaiming the news throughout Paris.

The Emperor left the high throne and to the accompanying sound of music, and the imperial procession made its way out of the church to the archbishop's palace, where the party changed and returned to the Tuileries. Soon after the Emperor left the church, the Pope returned and marched out as well, accompanied by the hymn, *Tu es Petrus.*

The coronation was over. Everyone was exhausted, not to mention cold. The ceremony had taken well over three hours and we had been in the building more than seven, and we were all anxious to get out, which was easier said than done. The order that had been present in the preparation was absent in the dismissal and the 20,000 guests had to jostle and shove and make their way out as best they could. I must admit the crowded conditions were not an entirely unpleasant situation considering the number of beautiful women at the ceremony, but overall, the scene was like a bloodless battlefield or a well-groomed herd of cattle heading for the doors.

As we were leaving, I looked through a press of faces and saw Athenaïs. Our eyes met and for a second there was joy in her expression, but there was panic too. The party she was with—I assumed her brother and other family—swept her off into the crowd before either of us could say a word and I lost sight of her.

Near the doors, a group of officers was leaving and I overheard one say loudly, so that his fellows and many other guests heard. "A lovely show. What a shame that all that was lacking was the half million or more Frenchmen who died to destroy that which was just reestablished."

Darkness was falling as we finally left the cathedral.

CHAPTER 24

December 5, 1804
Paris

The days following the coronation were a series of receptions, parties, fireworks and overall celebration, official and unofficial, and I attended the distribution of the fabled Eagles. Like the Roman Legions, each regiment and battalion of the Grand Armée carried a gold Eagle as its standard. Each unit still carried the tricolor battle flags beneath the Eagles on the poles, but it was the Eagles that counted, not the flags themselves, as the symbol of unit pride that were defended to the death, though the troops nicknamed them, rather irreverently, cuckoos. Sometimes going on campaign, only the Eagle itself was carried as a rallying point and inspiration for the battalion and the flags were left behind in the unit depots in France. We carried them in victory to the capital cities of nearly every country on the continent.

Again I accompanied Armstrong, who was there in his diplomatic capacity wearing the blue uniform of the American Army. Talleyrand had insisted I continue to assist the ambassador; he was not giving up on influencing the man through my presence, though I thought the foreign minister was wasting his time. Armstrong accepted my presence in the French Army, even understood my reasons, but I don't think he was swayed any more towards war with England by my example or arguments.

The ceremony was held on the Champ de Mars—the Field of Mars—a large open field right outside the Military School not far from the Seine on its left bank. Named after the *Campus Martius* in ancient Rome, it was used, like that ancient field, for military reviews and exercises. That December day, however, it might have been more appropriately called the "field of mud," because that is what it was after the thaw which descended on the city right after the coronation.

A huge reviewing stand, covered with red cloth and punctuated by gold statues and columns, was built on the outside of the School and running its length, facing the field, and here all the dignitaries of the empire were seated, including the Emperor and Empress on thrones in the center. At either end of the stand was a large pavilion, one reserved for foreign princes and the other for the diplomatic corps and other distinguished guests. Military bands played and small delegations from each regiment in the army marched on the field, including my own Sixth Léger. My heart leaped at the sight of its standard and of the distinctive uniforms of the light infantry—blue trousers instead of white and shakos instead of the bicorns. I left Armstrong with the rest of the diplomats and went outside the pavilion for a better view.

At the height of the ceremony the troops of all the different units came together in close columns, and marched through the mud right up to the base of the throne, gold eagles and blue, white and red flags close together above the soldiers. The standards in the front dipped in a salute, those behind pointed proudly towards the sky, flags whipping in the breeze. There was silence on the field as Napoleon rose from his throne. Both he and Josephine were dressed in their imperial robes from the coronation, including the gold laurel leaf crown that gave him the air of a Roman emperor.

"Soldiers," he addressed the troops in a loud voice, while those of us farther away strained to hear him. "Behold your standards! These Eagles will always serve as your rallying point and will go wherever your emperor finds it necessary to defend his throne and people. Will you swear to sacrifice even your lives in their defense and keep them by your valor always on the path to victory? Do you swear it?"

The colonels of the regiments and the standard bearers, who were right in front of the throne, replied *"Nous le jurons!"* "We swear it!" The marshals, who surrounded the base of the throne, thrust their batons into the air and joined in the oath. The rest of the troops on the field repeated it and I joined in like the rest. The Eagle standard bearers took their places among the troops, either joining their regiments, or, if they weren't present (most of the army was at Boulogne and elsewhere), then the regimental delegations formed small units of their own.

The army passed in review before the imperial couple, and was dismissed for further celebrations. Armstrong went to a grand reception and dinner at the Tuileries that night. I was not invited.

January 17, 1805
Paris

Much of the rest of the month of December was taken up with more celebrations and parties, many of which I attended, many which I didn't; either way I spent a lot of time with Armstrong. When the festivities slowed down after New Year's I began to spend more time on my military duties with Ney and his staff present in Paris, especially when discussions of invading England came up. The marshal was anxious to get back to Boulogne and the VI Corps; all the parties and the rarified atmosphere were taking their toll on him—and quite frankly me as well—and he wanted to be among the troops again.

If the truth be known, I think that's where Napoleon wanted to be as well. Life was simpler and had fewer layers of protocol in the field. Being emperor had its price. Outside the view of the public Napoleon lived far more simply and had far fewer levels of ceremony and ostentation than any other monarch, but in Paris he wasn't out of the public eye for long. That was my impression of the man. Not that I saw the Emperor much during that month, though a few times he stopped in to visit Ney and his staff. Once he asked me about the American minister and the likelihood of getting him to support war against England—something I told him was unlikely.

The varied schedule had me running back and forth between Ney's house, my residence, and Armstrong's house, which fortunately were less than a mile apart. Though I made the occasional foray over to the Tuileries to report to Savary, I generally stayed on the left bank of the Seine.

Several times since my first visit to Armstrong's house I had the distinct feeling I was being followed but never was able to determine if this were so, or if so, by whom. During my walks back and forth between the various places the feeling continued. There was so much activity on the streets I wasn't able to pick out who it might be, nor could I imagine why I would be followed by anyone. I mentioned my feeling to both Armstrong and Savary, whose reactions were similar: they shrugged and said Paris was a hotbed of spies from many countries—including France, and that it would be almost impossible to find out who it was.

When I arrived at Armstrong's house that day around noon, he was buried in papers over various claims American ship owners had made for ships seized by French privateers. American merchant ships were preyed on by the French as well as the English, both looking for money to fund their war, but in France the Americans had a recourse they didn't in England. As part of the agreement for the Louisiana Purchase, $3,750,000 was to be paid by the French government to settle claims of ship owners whose ships had been seized and cargo confiscated. Only a few months in France and Armstrong was right in the middle of it and it was a mess. As he said to me once after a particularly bitter negotiation, "There's more than just honor at stake, my boy, there's money too." Money trumped everything, something I remembered trying to explain to Napoleon about my countrymen. To the Emperor, money was simply a tool and a secondary consideration.

Armstrong's office was looking less sparse. Books had been unpacked and shelves built to hold them, and he had bought more furniture. Several boxes sat next to his large wooden desk and were overflowing with stacks of papers. The minister looked flustered as he ran a hand over his bald head, shuffling papers with the other. His wrinkles were more evident than usual. Looking up, he put the papers down, seemingly glad for a rest, and gestured to a chair.

"Well, how is Bonaparte's American today?" He began reaching into a desk drawer for a bottle and two glasses, part of his precious store of bourbon emerging.

I sat down, looking at him with a smile. "As much as I regret to be insulting, you're starting to sound like an English officer, sir. It's rather disconcerting."

He looked up from pouring and smiled whimsically. "Well, coming from you that isn't a compliment! I think an explanation might be in order before I share some of my already dwindling stock of whiskey."

"You called the Emperor, 'Bonaparte.' A monarch is always referred to by his first name. Using his last name is a mark of disrespect and can even call his legitimacy into question." I adjusted a plume on my busby that I was holding on my lap, giving it a long look and wondering if I was being too much of a prig. "The French are a bit sensitive about that."

Pushing my glass across the table towards me, Armstrong picked his own up. "Really? Brown said he thought in a republic with a monarch, as France purports to be, it was fine to refer to the Emperor as Bonaparte, though obviously not in his presence."

I shook my head. "Brown is a fool. You are a diplomat, sir. You must be careful, especially in your language."

Brown's position as Armstrong's assistant had been only a temporary arrangement. The minister's permanent private secretary, the Reverend David Bailie Warden, a naturalized American who had fled Ireland six years before, had arrived from America a week after the coronation and taken on most of the official duties required of Armstrong's assistant, but Brown still performed some tasks, including recently escorting Armstrong's two oldest sons to a school in Nantes. I got along much better with Warden, who had the Irish wit and was a keen intellect.

Brown had been on one of the ships seized by the French, and Armstrong had hired him to keep him from penury while he was waiting for his case to be heard by the three-member American Commission which, along with a French bureau, decided how the $3,750,000 was to be divided.

If Armstrong was annoyed at the correction over the Emperor's name, he didn't look it. Raising his glass to me, he proposed a toast. "To the Emperor Napoleon and President Jefferson. Cheers."

"Santé!" We downed our whiskey, then Armstrong poured two more, which we savored slowly. I looked at the glass and at him. "It's barely noon, sir." I had learned to be direct with Armstrong, he hated obsequiousness and because of his fondness for my parents he treated me as family.

"Aye, so it is. I didn't see you turn down the drink," he said taking a gulp.

I smiled, slowly taking a sip, feeling the distilled corn, malt and rye burn pleasantly on the way down. "That would be rude, sir."

An almost mischievous grin appeared, making him look years younger. "And the second whiskey?"

"Again, sir, my manners would prevent a refusal."

Laughing, he raised his glass again. "You are indeed a gentleman, Pierre. I wish I could say the same for some of these ship owners." He gestured at the stack of papers on his desk.

I looked at the papers covered with figures, cargo manifests, and various claims concerning seized ships. "Having a rough time with those cases?"

He laughed mirthlessly and picked up a stack, gave it a glance and tossed it back on his desk. "Rough? It's similar to being shot at but without the honesty. Though the commission and the French agents make the decision, I still must make my recommendation. No matter which way I turn there's a dagger in the form of quill and ink aimed at me—or bribes." Taking a sip of his whiskey, he continued. "Then there's Brown—the 'idiot' you just spoke of. I've had to recommend against his case."

I looked up sharply. "Really? Why?"

Armstrong couldn't keep a look of dismay off his face. "It seems Brown's ship was partly owned by an English shipping company. It wasn't a small part, the company owned close to sixty percent of his vessel, the *Hudson*. The French would never agree to reimburse funds an English company lost and I can't say I blame them."

"I see." I slowly took another sip. I could see why Armstrong got the whiskey out so early. "How did he take it?" I knew the answer to *that* question.

"Not well." He shook his head. "He stormed out of here some time ago, raving mad about everything, even you."

I was puzzled. "Me? What do I have to do with anything?"

Smiling grimly, Armstrong shook his head. "I don't know, lad, he's disliked you from the moment he set eyes on you. That uniform hasn't helped."

I shrugged. "Well, that can't be helped." I adjusted my sword's scabbard, which was pressing against the arm of the chair into my side, then brushed a spot of dust I noticed on the sleeve of my uniform, a little self-consciously and protectively perhaps. There was silence in the room except for the ticking of a clock on a mantel over the roaring fire.

Putting his glass down and leaning towards me, Armstrong nodded, intensity in his expression. "Perhaps it can. I can arrange for you to go home."

For a moment I didn't know what he was talking about. "Home?"

A look of exasperation crossed his face. "Indeed, home! Virginia, Baltimore, Maryland, the United States of America. You remember those places?"

"Yes, sir, of course I remember." For a moment in my mind I could see the streets of Baltimore, the fields and forested hills of Virginia, which I hadn't given any thought to in some time.

"I *am* rather occupied at the moment," I said gesturing to my uniform with a flourish.

"Aye, in a foreign country's uniform in a foreign country's war," Armstrong said impatiently.

I sighed. I truly was getting sick of explaining myself on this matter. "I don't recall Lafayette being sent home when he came to aid us in the Revolution, nor your good friend Kosciuszko, sir, not to mention my father," I said, looking Armstrong evenly in the eye. I thought it would be hard for him to argue after the mention of his friend, Tadeuz Kosciuszko, the famous Polish patriot who had fought alongside Washington during the Revolution, and who returned to Poland to lead a gallant but unsuccessful struggle to free his country from Russia and Prussia. Now he lived in exile in France; I had met him twice at Armstrong's residence. "Besides, as I never tire of telling people,"—Armstrong's patrician hauteur did not allow him to recognize the sarcasm—"I am half French, and both my parents were born here. Although I could leave at any time, I have no desire to. I have a home, a cause, and have discovered I am quite good at what I do."

Anger flashed across his face and his cheeks grew red. "Dammit, Pierre, you are not Lafayette or Kosciuszko, two idealists who crossed the Atlantic at great risk and expense to join us in our Revolution. You washed ashore and practically stumbled into that uniform. Go home where you belong."

Anger was rising in me as well and I sat up straighter. "Sir," I said very crisply, "I did not stumble into this uniform, I am an aide-de-camp to a Marshal of the Empire, Marshal Michel Ney. It is a singular honor that I strive to be worthy of every day." My tone softened. "It may seem like I washed ashore and fell into this uniform, but Marshal Ney seems to think I am favored by fortune, that I have Napoleon's luck and washed up at precisely the right moment."

Armstrong frowned, a crease furrowing his forehead. "Bah! Superstition!"

I nodded agreeably. "Perhaps, but it's hard to argue with the fortune of my circumstances."

Seeing this was going nowhere, Armstrong tried a different tack. "Since you are so intent on soldiering, I'm certain I can get you a commission back home in the American Army."

I smiled. "Not that I don't appreciate the offer, sir, but the opportunities there are somewhat limited by comparison. I've been in divisional exercises far larger than the entire American Army, let alone in exercises involving the entire VI Corps." I paused. "Come to Boulogne and you'll see why I'm not tempted. Besides, whom would I fight if I accepted your offer? Indians at best. Most likely it would be garrison duty." I leaned forward a bit and my voice hardened. "Here I have an opportunity to strike at England itself. What my father wouldn't have given for that chance." Armstrong nodded at the reference to my father and I raised my glass to him, tipped my head back and finished the whiskey in an overly dramatic gesture.

I saw defeat in Armstrong's eyes. I don't think he was surprised, but I suppose he thought he had to try. He poured himself another whiskey and held up the bottle to me. I shook my head and stood to go. "I can't stay, sir. I just came to tell you that I'm being reattached to Marshal Ney's staff, as he is likely to want to return to Montreuil and his corps soon." Paris and the life of a courtier was not agreeing with Ney. I think he wanted mud on his boots—the honest mud of a soldier—not the ever present winter mud of Paris' streets which splashed on him going from ball to fête. "I'll try and stop in before we leave."

Armstrong stood and held out his hand. "It has been an honor meeting you, Pierre. I'm not sure if you're doing the right thing or not but I think your father would be proud of you. Good luck."

I shook his hand, came to attention and saluted him, then left for Ney's residence, a lump in my throat.

That same evening there was a knock at my door in the rooming house on Rue Saint Dominique. One of the house servants, a timid old woman of about sixty, gave me a note she said had been dropped off a few moments before. She didn't know the messenger. I watched her candle disappear down the hall and heard a door shut. Darkness filled the corridor and I closed the door and sat down by a candle. I opened the paper and instantly recognized Athenaïs' handwriting. She said she would be at the side door in an hour and for me to let her in.

Instantly my heart started pounding and sweat beaded on my brow, despite the cold room. It had been three months since I'd last contact had with her, except for the glimpse I caught of her during the Coronation. I had tried to contact her in the month and a half since I arrived in Paris—to no avail. Now here she was about to visit me in my room practically without warning. I looked at the note, stunned.

The hour passed slowly, like being tortured. It was almost midnight when I went downstairs and let Athenaïs in. Her stunning face, lit by the most radiant smile I ever saw, was framed by the fur-lined hood she wore, attached to an elegant white cape, and for a moment all I could do was stare at her. I was startled by a noise behind her and got a glimpse of her small carriage leaving, hooves scraping on the icy cobblestones. I shut the door and pulled her to me, slowly drawing down her hood. Reluctantly we drew apart and I led her up to my room. As I latched the door, she drew close to me with a serious expression and seemed as though she wanted to say something.

I looked at her curiously. "What is it?"

She shook her head. "It can wait." Taking my hand, she led me to the bed.

We lay under the covers, our love spent for the moment. There had been an intensity, almost franticness to our lovemaking that disturbed me, though I didn't know why. As we lay there we talked about everything that had happened since we last saw each other. As I suspected, her brother had prevented her from having any contact with me, something she was far more accepting of than I. Part of me sensed something else she was not saying; I couldn't figure out what it was and tried to press her on it.

She laughed, that spine tingling laugh of hers. "There *is* something I'm not telling you and it's serious."

I smiled, running a hand on her shoulder, barely visible in the light of the two candles I had lit. "You love me."

Her expression changed, though the smile didn't completely disappear. "Yes, probably. What of it? I said this was serious; serious people don't worry about such things." The features of the Athenaïs I knew were replaced by that of Athenaïs the aristocrat. I didn't entirely believe her, and looking in her eyes I don't think she entirely believed it herself, but I didn't press the matter and waited for her to continue. "You're in danger, Pierre."

I raised my eyebrows at her, a grin on my face. "Because I love you?"

I could see her exasperation. She hit my chest. "Real danger! Listen for a moment! I overheard a conversation during a party at my brother's house tonight. Two men I didn't know were talking about the American minister and how his murder would affect relations between France and the United States."

A chill filled my body. "His murder? Who is going to kill him?"

Athenaïs looked at me, holding my hand. "You. They said you would, or that blame would fall on you."

I stammered, unable to say anything for a moment I was so stunned. The shadows in the dark room seemed to grow darker and the wind seemed to grow stronger outside. "That's ridiculous. How and where? Who will actually do it?"

The worry on her face was palpable. "I don't know. I think they feared I could hear them and they changed the subject. I came here as soon as I could."

I sat up, the chill air racing in under the blankets, my mind thundering like a racehorse; Athenaïs sat up next to me, her arm around me, saying nothing. I didn't know what to do. I could go to Savary or Talleyrand, but without more proof than an overheard conversation by a girl, I would probably be laughed out of their office and jeopardize my career if nothing happened. Fouché? No, I had heard enough horrid whispers about the minister of police that I wanted to stay out of his sight. Ney would be little help. He was a soldier, as straightforward a man as ever lived and wouldn't know the first thing about responding to such a crisis—he likely would direct me back to Savary or Talleyrand. I certainly couldn't go to Napoleon, I wouldn't get past the first ring of courtiers and court officials. My only other choice was go to Armstrong directly, though I wasn't sure what I would tell him or whether he would believe me. I looked at Athenaïs.

"Do they really think anyone will believe I killed Armstrong?"

Nodding, she continued. "They said the two of you had an argument today and that would convince both American and French authorities that you did it."

The chill I felt had nothing to do with the cold room. "My God, it was a minor disagreement. How could they even know about that? They have spies under Armstrong's own roof?"

Smiling gravely, she nodded. "This is Paris, there are probably almost as many spies here as there are whores, and no doubt many of the whores are in both professions."

That was likely true, I thought, as I recalled Marie at Madame Delobel's and how she had helped me catch English saboteurs.

"Did you happen to hear when it would happen?"

She nodded. I think she felt somewhat helpless. "They said within the next two nights, most likely tomorrow."

I relaxed a little. I thought I had a better chance of convincing Armstrong in the light of day. I was glad I wouldn't have to beat down Armstrong's door at this time of night and I rubbed the stubble on my chin. Something Athenaïs had said was suddenly at the forefront of my mind, the danger to Armstrong forgotten for the moment.

"You said you came as soon as you could. God knows I am happy to see you, but I have been trying to reach you for more than a month. Where were you?" I watched to see her reaction.

She looked me straight in the eye. "In and around Paris. I got your messages. I had to ignore them. I cannot be seen frolicking around Paris with you; my brother would never hear of it and would likely try to lock me in the chateau if I did. He does not approve of you, you are a figure of controversy and yet a patriot, the opposite of an *émigré* like him, which he probably believes reflects badly on him for fleeing France. Besides..." She sighed. "He is always looking for a suitable husband for me and you could jeopardize that."

I looked at her with fear in my eyes. "I hope I do. Is he planning your wedding?"

Laughing at my discomfiture, mischief in her sparkling blue eyes, she shook her head, flipping her light brown hair to one side. "I have many suitors, but no husband yet."

"Yet."

Though eighteen, she let out a world-weary sigh. "Oh Pierre, my dear, moral, naïve American, what we have is wonderful and could continue in spite of any husband Jean-Louis might find for me. That is the way of things, but I am not sure you could accept that. My duty to my family must come first."

I found it bewildering to be called "moral" and "naïve" while lying naked in bed with a woman not my wife and found it just as odd she could accept such an arrangement so easily. I changed the subject.

Only a few hours later she started to get dressed. "I have to leave, I will be missed if I am gone overnight." I watched her, wanting her to stay and knowing there was nothing I could do.

"So you came here to save my life. Thank you."

Something in my tone made her frown as she looked at me. "I was planning to see you before you left Paris—when the time was right. The time happened to be right."

As she put her cape on around her, I stood in front of her. "When will I see you again?"

All elegance, she shrugged and brushed a strand of light brown hair away from her face. "I do not know. I think you have more important things to worry about."

CHAPTER 25

January 18, 1805
Paris

Brown looked at me with undisguised contempt in his tiny eyes when I asked for Armstrong. It was just past eight the next morning on another gray day and I had rushed over to Rue de Regard as early as possible and begun knocking on the door of Hotel de la Guiche, Athenaïs' visit still foremost on my mind. When I explained it was urgent and the minister's life might be in danger, Brown actually laughed, wisps of his unkempt hair waving.

"Get along to your frog masters, Burns. The minister in danger? That's the most ridiculous thing I ever heard." Brown started to close the door but I placed my foot in the door jamb so he couldn't shut it.

"Please Brown, I beg you, this is serious." Staring at me closely, Brown reluctantly opened the door and looked at me with distrust. "I won't have anything to do with this lunacy, tell him yourself. He's with a private wine merchant picking wine for a party, just a block away at 26 Rue Saint-Placide. Go to the back entrance, there is a door to the cellar. That's where you'll find him." He stared darkly at me. "If you tell him I told you where he is, I'll deny it." He slammed the heavy door in my face before I could even thank him.

I walked around the corner onto Rue Sainte-Placide. The street was quiet, in keeping with its name, with only a few people on the streets, apparently servants on errands and a bulky ox-cart carrying barrels going in the opposite direction. When I reached number 26, the tan stone house looked empty; it didn't look like an active wine merchant's house, but then again Brown said it was

267

a private sale. I saw the arched side-entrance he mentioned down a narrow alley and followed it. A heavy open door led down into a dark wine cellar, with a few stone steps visible in the faint light in the alley.

I stuck my head in a little ways. "General Armstrong? Minister?" Seeing nothing, I stood there a moment listening. I thought I heard voices and something falling. Hurrying down the stairs I was halfway down the steps when I fell headlong over a dark rope strung across the stairs, invisible from the outside. I crashed heavily into some wooden boxes. As I unsteadily tried to get to my feet, I heard footsteps behind me, there was a bright light in my head and I remembered no more.

How long I lay there, I don't know. Voices brought me to almost instant consciousness but I did not open my eyes or stir, despite the excruciating pain in the back of my head. My face was against the cold dirt floor facing away from the voices. They spoke English and their accent was decidedly British, except one: Brown. Including him there were at least three, perhaps four men. What a fool I had been to trust him! But while we despised each other, I never imagined he would be involved in a plot to kill Armstrong.

I could feel the hilt of my sword digging into my stomach. They hadn't disarmed me yet, and I still had my father's knife hidden under my jacket—after that night in the warehouse I never went anywhere without it. If they were going to kill me on the spot I was determined to rise and sell my life dearly, though I had no illusions about my chances. I was wounded, stiff, and they might be able to kill me before I could even rise, especially if one of them had a firelock. It is no easy thing to rise and get a sword out of a scabbard, especially when one is lying down on it and has taken a blow to the back of the head. I didn't move, kept my eyes shut, and lay there listening to try to find out what they planned.

"Did you get his hat?" It was Brown's voice. I almost exclaimed in surprise at the question, which could have been fatal. My hat? What could they want with my hat?

"Yes, I have it," said a voice with an educated, if not cultured, English accent, a sharp contrast to Brown's nasally New England tones. "It will complete the uniform and I will drop it at the scene in my haste to escape. Combined with your eyewitness account when you look out the window and see Burns kill Armstrong, it will be irrefutable evidence of his guilt. His unique position in France will make it easy for both sides to blame the other for the murder."

Brown laughed, a nasty sound that grated up and down my spine. I wanted to kill him. "The minister will be coming home in less than an hour. Make sure you kill him right in front of the hotel."

"Do not worry." There was a pause. "It was a fortunate coincidence that Beaulieu's sister overheard us last night and ran to warn Burns," the Englishman continued. Anger filled me that they had used Athenäis, but at least it was unwitting. "We couldn't have arranged this better. I doubt they would approve of our methods if they ever heard about this in London, but they will not argue with the results: no alliance between the United States and France, and possibly even war." I heard a door open and felt a cold draft. "Burns should be unconscious for a while longer. A shame we can't bring him to London to hang, but that would be too much of a risk. I suspect after Burns kills the minister he will feel a great deal of guilt for the act and will want to take his own life. There's already a noose on that beam, a chair in the corner. Wrap him snugly in that blanket, except his head and neck. He can't have marks showing he was tied. Remember, the poor man is committing suicide in a fit of conscience, not being murdered. You can take the blanket off once he's dangling in air. Take nothing of value off the body, he must be found as he is. Don't do it until you hear the shot, just to make sure everything goes as planned."

"Aye, sir," came the low response.

There was noise on the stairs and the voice grew fainter. "Let's go, Brown. Once on the street, go right and I'll go left. I'll be there when Armstrong arrives..."

To be perfectly candid, I don't think I've ever been as terrified as I was that moment. I've faced death in many ways, I've killed many men in battles in numerous countries but I had never heard my own death discussed so casually, nor felt so helpless. I was overcome with a great sense of injustice by the utter foulness of the act. It is one thing to die in battle, it is another to be swaddled like a baby and hung up by the neck to die kicking and choking in the dark. And my name would be disgraced by Armstrong's death in the minds of Ney, Reille, Callahan and so many others I served with.

One ray of hope shone on my predicament: the number of my captors had been cut in half to only two men, though I still faced the same difficulties. I was wounded, how badly I didn't know, and stiff from lying on the floor. I had one advantage—desperation borne out of the knowledge of their plan and contempt for it. I had to hide that until the right moment.

Groaning loudly, I sat up as quickly as I could, while holding my head and complaining in French. I glanced around the room, separated from the rest of the cellar by a wooden wall. It had a dirt floor and stone walls that were part of the foundation. Wine casks were against the walls, so there was a sliver of truth to Brown's ruse that had led me there. The only light came from the door open to the outside and a candle in a sconce on the wall. The ceiling where I had fallen wasn't much taller than I was, though part of the room was deeper than the rest. That, apparently, was where they planned to hang me.

The men made no move to stop me as they watched me rise and lean against the boxes behind me. I looked at them as blankly as I could. "I must have tripped on those stairs and hit my head," I continued in French, not wanting to let them know I knew what was afoot. "I was looking for General Armstrong, the American minister." I appraised both men. They looked dangerous. They were burly types with dark brown hair, dressed roughly like workmen or sailors. One appeared to have had his nose broken a number of times, judging by the odd slant to it, the other had a nasty old scar across his forehead. I saw no weapons displayed openly, though I thought I caught a glimpse of the round brass butt of a pistol under a jacket of one. No doubt they carried blades out of sight.

The taller of the two, with the many-times broken nose, nodded and replied in Dutch accented French. "Yes, Monsieur, we found you not long ago when picking up some wine and were going to call a doctor. Are you alright?" He took a step forward.

I nodded. "I think so, though I'm freezing. I don't know how long I was on that floor."

The man stopped. "Would you like a blanket to help you warm up, Monsieur? I have one." I almost laughed, he was so obvious, but instead smiled gratefully.

"Yes, thank you." As he moved to get the blanket the other man with the scar on his forehead—Hyde, I believe—looked at the other and nodded almost imperceptibly and began moving towards me. I had to keep them separate for a few more moments. "Would you have anything to drink? Wine? Brandy?"

They both stopped and looked at each other with almost comical looks. There was nothing funny about the situation yet I was almost overcome by a sense of the absurd. I think in moments of danger humor can be a refuge, but it can be distracting as well. I pushed it aside.

The thought must have occurred to both of them that I would be easier to catch off guard and possibly easier to subdue after drinking. "Get him a drink of brandy," the taller one with the blanket said, and his companion responded by going to the far corner where there was a bottle and a crude wooden cup on a small table. As the one with the blanket approached me, I bent over a little and held my head with my left hand. My sword was plainly visible to him in the faint light, which was my plan, as I had no intention of using it. When he was steps away, I slipped my right hand behind my back under my coat, slowly drew my father's knife, and kept it close to my body.

Everything seemed to slow down. There is nothing like danger and the immediate prospect of death to concentrate the mind. When he was upon me, I groaned, "Thank you" and grabbed his wrist as if to steady myself. I stared at his chest and saw my right hand thrust the knife forcefully just below his sternum, angled up and to the left. He grunted in surprise and looked at me in terror as I smiled and whispered one word in English. "Die." I twisted the knife out and thrust again just as hard.

I called out loudly as he began to slump and I struggled to keep the body standing, the life rushing out and quickly becoming deadweight. The warm blood on my hand wasn't making it any easier. "Hey, what are you doing getting sick on me? What's wrong with your friend here?"

His companion was approaching with a wooden cup of brandy. With a heave I pushed the body forward towards him. It fell practically on his feet and his eyes widened as his friend rolled onto his back, a bloodstain darkly evident on his shirt. Before he could react I let out a blood-curdling cry and stepped over the body, thrusting with my bloody knife as if it were a sword. He moved the hand with the cup of brandy in front of him to block the blow, which protected his chest, but I cut his fingers to the bone, making the hand practically useless. Brandy splashed over both of us. Shouting in pain and terror at this sudden turn of events he turned and bolted for the stairs. I pursued, yelling a war cry right behind him. As he was on the second step I grabbed both his legs and pulled. He fell flat on his face on the stone steps. I heard a crack—his teeth hitting the stones—and moaning, as I yanked him back into the cellar as hard as I could, his head bumping against another step. Groaning, he tried to lift himself onto his knees and I stepped on his wounded hand, grinding it into the ground with my heel for good measure. Screaming through a broken mouth, he reared back onto his knees, and gripping his other arm I twisted it behind him as far as I could.

"Wrap me in a blanket and hang me, will you?" I pulled his arm even further behind him and he began begging piteously for mercy as we stood up in the middle of the room. "How many others in your plot besides Brown and the man dressed as me?" The escape from death, while a relief, did nothing to improve my mood. Anger and bloodlust coursed through me. I twisted even harder, the stink of the man's fear and sweat filling my nostrils.

Gasping in pain, he could barely respond. "One! Just one!!"

"One?" I pulled on his arm more.

"Yes..." He moaned. "Yes, sir. I swear just one!" Blood dribbled from his mouth and he was having trouble speaking through his broken teeth.

"Where?" He hesitated and I twisted his arm and brought it farther behind him. "My patience is about to run out..."

"At the corner..."

"What corner?!" I was ready to rip his arm out of its socket, I was so impatient and angry at his dissimulation.

"The corner of Rue de Regard and Rue du Cherche Midi, a lookout to watch for Armstrong! Mister Edwards will arrive on a horse a few minutes before and wait in front of Armstrong's house." Edwards. It was the first time I heard the name of the

English agent who orchestrated this whole affair. I had to stop him, kill him if necessary, though admittedly he would be more useful alive, as he might be able to provide information about other spies.

"Thank you." I twisted even harder, pulling the arm up as hard as I could until I heard bones break and he screamed horribly. I shoved him amongst the boxes I'd crashed into when I fell down the stairs. He fell into a heap, unconscious. I had no time to try and secure him. Disabling him seemed the quickest course of action, or so I tried to convince myself, though it was not mercy that propelled him with such force into those boxes.

There was no time to get help. It would take time to find someone and offer explanations and return. I wasn't sure where Armstrong was returning from, so I couldn't intercept and warn him. I had to stop Edwards myself. Quite possibly just appearing alive in the street near Armstrong's house would be enough to scare him away, but it might impel him to intercept Armstrong and kill him on his way home. It might also get me killed unless I could get close enough to Edwards unobserved.

Looking around the dirt and stone cellar, my eyes fell upon my attackers.

Not twenty minutes later I was shuffling down the Rue de Regard near Armstrong's house, dressed in an assortment of clothes stripped from my would-be assassins.

I was wounded, tired and sore, which all contributed to my disguise. Wrapped in a blanket and thrown over my shoulder like a heavy burden was my sword, while under my jacket was a horse pistol I had taken off the man I killed. It was the only firelock I could find on either of my assailants.

Up ahead, in front of the minister's house, I saw a brown horse. Standing next to it there was an officer in the uniform of a marshal's aide-de-camp. Edwards, I presumed, though suddenly I realized I didn't know for certain. I had never seen the man, only heard his voice in the cellar. It was possible it was an officer sent to find me, or there on another errand, though I didn't think so, since the uniform looked very close to mine. Still, I could not attack him without knowing who he was, which meant I had to wait until Armstrong arrived before doing anything. In the minutes until that happened I had to get out of sight, yet be close enough to intervene. There weren't many places to do that, as the houses came right up the narrow street. There was an alley that led to the back of the house next to Armstrong's residence. I was about to turn down it, but at the last moment continued on past the officer. In the alley was a short, dark, shabbily dressed man who appeared to be a mason, judging by the way he was measuring stones of the building, though he looked oddly familiar when he looked at me.

I passed the alley by, looking down and not making eye contact with the officer, who didn't spare me a second glance. At heart he was a *rosbif* aristocrat who would see no danger from a workman. Slowly walking into another alley between two stone houses farther down the block--and fortuitously closer to the direction from which Armstrong came—I looked in the direction of the Rue de Cherche Midi. A man walked in the middle of the street down at the corner, took off his hat, and kept walking. It was, I guessed, a signal,, for not long after, I saw Armstrong in the blue uniform of an American brigadier general, an old-fashioned three-cornered hat perched on his head, walking down the cobblestone street. He had been on the right bank near the Tuileries sitting for a portrait. As he got closer his steps echoed on the quiet street. From my spot in the alley, I noticed the officer wave at Armstrong, then open a saddlebag as if he were preparing to take something out. I was at a loss; the man wouldn't try to kill Armstrong until the minister was right up to him, but that was past my spot in the alley. Just as Armstrong passed, I determined to get him off the street. If the waiting officer had ill intentions, he would have to follow him in the alley where he would be vulnerable. If he was there on an errand he would likely wait where he was.

"General!" I whispered urgently, still out of sight of the possible assassin but visible to Armstrong. Startled, he turned, hand on his sword, and looked at me, his eyes growing wide with recognition under his hat. "Get off the street quickly!"

"Burns? What in blazes are you doing in there dressed like that? Come man, get out of that alley and explain yourself. For the life of me, I thought that was you in front of my door!" He said, gesturing towards the officer in front of his house and speaking loud enough that I had no doubt the sound of my name carried. Unfortunately the minister wasn't moving anywhere of his own volition. There was no further time for ceremony or Armstrong's dignity for that matter. "Off the street, sir!" I stepped out from the alley and grabbed his arm. As I did, the approaching officer— Edwards, I was now certain—raised a pistol and aimed it at us. I yanked on Armstrong's arm and forcibly pulled him into the alley just as Edwards shot at us, the ball ricocheting off the stone wall. That woke Armstrong up.

"Who the bloody hell is shooting at us?"

"An English spy is trying to assassinate you!" I dropped the blanket I had wrapped my sword in, pulled out the horse pistol and leaned around the corner. The fire sparked in the priming pan, followed by the charge and ball, blocking my view with smoke, but I knew I hadn't hit him. A smoothbore pistol is inaccurate at best and the hard trigger pull threw my aim off, though I heard his horse scream, one of the most bloodcurdling sounds imaginable. I dropped the pistol and ran down the alley with Armstrong, our swords in hand. Being shot at had curbed the minister's tongue.

The prudent thing for Edwards to do would have been to flee. The plot was foiled, but with English stubbornness he pursued us down the alley, determined to kill us. We were like sheep in a pen, hemmed in and prepared for slaughter. The alley was a dead end, with heavy wooden doors to the left and right leading into the two stone houses. Armstrong and I leaned against one of heavy doors, pushing with our backs, but to no avail. It would have taken a battering ram to open it. In seconds Edwards was upon us. We stood facing him, our backs to the door, swords in front of us. I moved to get in front of Armstrong; Edwards had only one pistol left; the minister would at least have a chance sword to sword.

I could see in his eyes that Edwards knew what I was thinking and he smiled unpleasantly, throwing aside the empty firelock and drawing his sword, more than happy to oblige. He raised the remaining pistol and pointed it at me, judging me the best use of his bullet.

As he began to cock the hammer, the alley echoed with the thunder of a gunshot. I had been anticipating the discharge from Edwards' pistol but saw confusion and fear in his eyes as he stumbled and spun around, falling to his knees as he did so, blood on his back and dribbling from his mouth.

Standing behind a cloud of smoke was the familiar looking little man I had thought a mason near Armstrong's residence, pistol in his hand. Edwards tried feebly to raise his own pistol, but the man walked up to him and twisted the weapon out of his hand. He forcefully lifted Edwards's head by the chin and looked at him carefully.

"Edwards," he said, almost whispering. "I should have recognized you." The newcomer looked at us, dark eyes narrowing as he examined us. "Minister Armstrong, Lieutenant Burns, is either of you hurt?"

I think we were both so stunned from this unexpected rescue we were unable to say anything, and only shook our heads.

Our benefactor nodded and turned at the noise of hooves at the end of the alley. Half a dozen elite gendarmes in blue and yellow uniforms appeared and rode towards us, carbines at the ready. Their sergeant saluted Armstrong, then looked at our rescuer, calling him by name. "Bonjour, Vignon. What spy work does Fouché have you doing today that requires you to shoot up Paris?"

Vignon smiled grimly. "Our old friends, the English. They decided to kill the American minister in broad daylight. They came close." As I listened, I stripped the workingman clothes off that covered my uniform, buckled on my sword belt and roughly took my hat off Edwards' head. The sergeant noticed my transformation and saluted me. Before another word was spoken there were running footsteps from the street and Brown appeared, out of breath, a look of counterfeit concern on his face.

"General Armstrong, Burns, what happened? I heard shooting."

With a guttural grunt of anger, I drew my sword and stepped forward, prepared to kill Brown, but before I could get within ten feet of him, Vignon raised his hand with a gesture that said, 'step no further.'

"Monsieur," he said, like it was a command, and it was. I stopped, sword still in hand. Looking up at the gendarme sergeant, Vignon gave him his own command, indicating Brown with a nod of his head. "Sergeant Doucet, arrest that man him and keep him out of sight. He is to be held for questioning." He turned towards Edwards, who had slowly slipped to the ground, his labored breathing loud in the quiet alley. "And try to keep this one alive as long as possible, at least until he can be questioned."

Brown looked shocked and tried to back around the gendarmes, but they blocked off the little alley with their horses to prevent escape. One of the soldiers used his horse to gently push Brown against a wall while another dismounted and began shackling him. "I've done nothing wrong, why are you arresting me?" he demanded. The gendarme ignored him and continued shackling him.

Armstrong stepped forward, starting to recover his wits and composure. "There must be some mistake, Monsieur. Why are you arresting my assistant? What's going on?"

Vignon was deferential but not backing down. "There is no mistake, Monsieur le Minister. He is being arrested for being involved in a plot to kill you."

The color drained from Armstrong's face. "What? No. Brown, try to kill me? That's ridiculous, it can't be." He looked at me, the sword still in my hand and a look of unbridled hatred directed at Brown. "Pierre? What is happening?"

I sheathed my sword and glanced at the minister. "I heard it from his own mouth today, sir. Brown was involved in a plot to kill both of us; I barely escaped with my life from a cellar a block from here where two of his compatriots were to kill me and make it look like a suicide. Edwards was disguised as me to make it look as though I killed you. They were even going to leave my hat at the scene to implicate me." I scrutinized Vignon. "What I would like to know is, how did you find out? Who are you and how do you know who I am?"

A mysterious smile touched the corners of Vignon's mouth; he was obviously a man who enjoyed secrets. "Forgive my manners, Lieutenant Burns. You are a man quite familiar to me, and you have seen me before, many times. You don't remember, though I see you find me familiar. Alas, that is the nature of my business." There must have been a look of utter confusion on my face because he laughed gently and bowed. "I am Alphonse Vignon, of the Ministry of Police. I—and a few of my comrades—have been your shadows since your arrival in Paris."

"My shadows?" My suspicions I had been followed were right. "*You're* the ones who've been following me? Why?"

Vignon shrugged disarmingly, as if he was not a matter of great concern, and perhaps it wasn't to him. "We follow many people, Monsieur. You must realize you have attracted your share of attention since your arrival in France. Minister Fouché wanted to know who you have been in contact with since arriving in Paris. There was even some concern the *rosbifs* would try and kill you, since there is a bounty on you in England. It appears that concern was warranted." He looked towards the prostrate form of Edwards, who was being put on a makeshift stretcher by some of the gendarmes.

Just at that moment a dark-eyed, nondescript man in civilian clothes passed between the mounted gendarmes, approached Vignon, and whispered something in his ear. Vignon's eyes widened ever so slightly and I thought I saw him surreptitiously glance at me. He nodded, and the man left.

I was still more than a little confused and starting to get annoyed. "How long have you known of this plot? Why didn't you do something to stop it?"

"I believe I just did," Vignon said.

"I mean *before* they tried," I said annoyed.

"Ah, I see your confusion. We knew there was possibly a plot but we didn't know when it would happen or where until just a few minutes ago. Today I was following you as part of my routine when you went down the Rue Sainte-Placide, and into the cellar of a house. Not long after, Brown arrived, and then the two of you left together, going in different directions. At least I thought it was you, but as has been revealed it was Edwards. He fooled me because I didn't see his face." He paused, self recrimination taking over for a moment at his professional failure. "Knowing the two of you despise each other, I should have known something was wrong at that moment."

I nodded. It made sense. "I was attacked by two of Edward's accomplices in that cellar. One was still alive when I left, though I can't vouch for his condition any longer."

There was a look of grim amusement on Vignon's face. "Yes, we found them. The man is alive, though how long he will remain so, I don't know. I was told you were quite thorough." I started to say something in protest but he cut me off. "I'm not faulting what you did; on the contrary, you did what was necessary. Anyway, he thought you were returning and was babbling incoherently in fear. I hope we can get some information from him before a fever takes him in his weakened state."

Armstrong turned to me and held out his hand. "I owe you my life. I hope someday I will be able to repay you." We solemnly shook hands, drawn close by our shared brush with death.

Both Edwards and my attacker from the cellar died of their wounds within several days, but not before revealing much about the English and Royalist spy network in France. The unwounded Brown lingered considerably longer; Fouché showed a reluctance to kill an American who had worked for the American minister to France, even if he had tried to kill that very minister. Armstrong duly filed his protests and tried to save Brown, but it was as a matter of form rather than conviction, and soon the protests stopped. Brown was guillotined by the end of the year. I wished to see him off, but, alas, was otherwise occupied. No man deserved the blade more.

Before leaving the capital there was one person I had to see. I had a final interview with Talleyrand. I reported on the attempt to kill Armstrong and my efforts to convince Armstrong to pressure the American government to join the war against Britain.

"Well, Lieutenant, you have done well, more than I could have hoped for. Stopping an attempt on your ambassador's life and linking it back to the English was a stroke of luck."

We were sitting in a parlor in Talleyrand's elegant residence on the Rue du Bac. The setting was typical Talleyrand, opulence mixed with an air of relaxed intimacy. The parquet floors gleamed like glass, reflecting the chandeliers above us. When I entered the room and looked down, I saw my reflection looking back at me. It was rather disconcerting, as was Talleyrand, who was disarming, yet chilling too.

"Thank you, *Monseigneur,* though as you say, it was a bit of luck. I was fortunate Minister Fouché decided to have me followed."

Talleyrand smiled oddly, glancing at one of his servants before answering. "It is a rare man who can consider himself fortunate to have had one of Fouché's ruffians spying on him. Rare indeed."

Talleyrand was speaking from experience, as he and Fouché each had spies in the other's household, always looking for ammunition in the constant struggle for power among the upper echelons of the Empire.

"Unfortunately, *Monseigneur,* I must report that my efforts to induce the ambassador to advocate for war with England were a failure."

Talleyrand shrugged gracefully, not easy to do while sitting. "Hardly a failure, Burns. Expectations were that he would not be convinced. The effort was made and perhaps a seed was planted. The English attempt to murder him can hardly have induced Armstrong to view them favorably."

"True, *Monseigneur.*"

In response to the slightest of gestures, a liveried servant came to us bearing a tray with two glasses of cognac and a small wooden box on it. He wore an old-fashioned powdered wig. We each took a glass and Talleyrand indicated I should take the box. Raising our glasses, we toasted the other's health.

"*Santé!*"

I glanced at the glass appreciatively. The liquor was supple and smooth. Talleyrand noticed the look and smiled a genuine smile.

"It is a rare vintage, from the age of Louis XV. I have a private supply from a vintner in Champagne."

I swirled the caramel colored liquid in my glass, sniffing it gently and taking another sip. "It is the finest I have tasted since arriving in France."

Talleyrand nodded.

"I am pleased. In that box is something else that may please you. A little gift to remember the coronation and the services you rendered here."

I opened the small wooden box. Inside, cushioned in blue velvet, was a silver watch on a chain. It had a beautifully painted front, with what looked like two warriors in ancient armor, one standing over the other, vanquished on the ground with a hand up in supplication.

"Taken from a painting by David, *Minerva triumphing over Mars*—a reminder that when one fights, the mind is a more important weapon than brute strength."

ART MCGRATH

Inside the cover was an inscription which included my name and the date of the coronation in the French Revolutionary calendar, *Pierre Burns, 11 frimaire an XIII, Sacre de l'Empereur Napoleon., Vive la France, Vivent les Etats Unis.*

Echoing the sentiment in the inscription, Talleyrand raised his glass and made another toast, "Long live France and the United States."

Less than a month after the attempt on Armstrong's life, Ney was making final preparations to return to Boulogne. He was to send me on ahead with General Dutaillis, his chief of staff, ostensibly to help him make preparations for Ney's return, but I got the distinct impression it was to get me out of Paris. Trouble seemed attracted to me since the attempt on Armstrong's life— including several duels, which I promptly reported to Ney— although my escape from death and thwarting the attempt on Armstrong only reinforced Ney's belief in my luck.

"Burns, my boy, good, clean soldiering will be a relief after all this diplomatic nonsense in the capital," Ney said, the red sash across his gold braided indigo jacket almost matching his red hair. He clapped me on the back, his eyes twinkling, as I was getting ready to leave his house and get in a coach with Dutaillis. "I envy you. The smell of horses, gunpowder and campfires will be a welcome change from the smell of intrigue." I knew it wouldn't be long before he would follow, as soon as he could make arrangements to have Aglaé's things moved to their chateau.

Soon our coach was rattling down the cobblestone streets, mud splashing in all directions from the puddles we drove through. Dutaillis, one of his aides, and I were the only occupants of the coach. It wound through the city and the outskirts of Paris, heading north to Boulogne. I'd been in the capital a little over two months, and though I still gawked out the window at what I saw, I was more discreet and possibly a bit jaded. Ney was right. It would be good to be back with the army.

I did not see Athenaïs again before leaving Paris, though I got a brief note expressing relief at my survival. Not seeing her again was my one regret when I left Paris. As the carriage left the outskirts of the city, I read and reread her note and thought in frustration of my inability to be with her. She had charged back into my life for one night, warned me so I was able to save Armstrong, and I couldn't even thank her in person.

CHAPTER 26

February 15, 1805
Boulogne, France

The return trip took several days, longer than the grueling trip over when Ney had paid to have fresh horses waiting at intervals along the way and insisted on not stopping. I slept fitfully for much of the ride back. I awoke to feel my head banging against the wall of the coach and to the sound of gunfire, music and horses outside. Looking out the window to the right I saw a sea of blue uniforms: at least a division of infantry at maneuver. One brigade was smartly forming the *ordre mix* formation—the mixed order, with some battalions in line and others in attack column formation. In front of the infantry, eight- and twelve-pound cannon moved ahead between the battalions and began unlimbering.

The coach stopped and the three of us got out to watch, happy to stretch our legs and even more so to observe the maneuvers. It was Loison's Second Division, with my Sixth Légèr in the center of the First Brigade. I had woken up in the outskirts of Montreuil.

There was light snow on the ground, though the day was not cold for the time of year and the sun was shining. A hint of spring was in the air. Under the snow the ground was still frozen, ideal for marching. I scrutinized the First Brigade carefully. Its two battalions were stacked in two marching columns, one company behind the other. On command from the drums, each battalion formed an attack column two companies wide; the lead company stayed in place and the one behind it moved next to it to its right; the third company stopped and the fourth moved next to it and so on, so that the entire battalion of eight companies was stacked two companies wide and four lines deep. The *voltigeurs* and *carabiniers* were in the last line. After advancing for a time in attack column, the brigade was signaled to move into line. The first two companies stopped, while each line of two companies behind them split in two, going to the left or right of the companies in front. The last two companies, the *voltigeurs* and *carabiniers,* formed the left and right of the battalion in line. In the center of each battalion I saw the new gleaming Eagle standards with their battle flags beneath.

The VI Corps' own light cavalry was in position on either flank of the division, and a regiment of cuirassiers, weapons gleaming in the sun, was mounted on black horses behind the center of the division. These cuirassiers were heavy cavalry and were usually attached to Marshal Joachim Murat's Cavalry Reserve, which formed its own corps and was stationed farther inland. General Loison must have been persuasive to have convinced Murat to let them go for the exercise, especially since Murat and Ney despised each other.

The entire divisional maneuver, consisting of eight battalions and thousands of men, was a giant precision movement, a textbook maneuver according to the Regulation of 1791, practiced countless times by each battalion in the army around Boulogne. It was an impressive sight that I didn't get to see often as an observer —usually I was in the midst of it—and one that could take one's breath away. It would be terrifying to be on the receiving end.

As the brigades completed their maneuvers, the artillery thundered, shooting live ammunition at large hayricks set up as targets five hundred yards away. First they fired solid shot, some of the rounds hitting the ground and rebounding towards their targets, which could have a devastating effect on enemy ranks. They followed these rounds by two shots of explosive rounds. After a final volley consisting of canister, the guns grew silent and drums signaled the infantry forward. The blue lines advanced, first at a walk, then the drums signaled the *Pas Accéléré*, and the soldiers quickened the pace. About fifty or seventy-five paces from the hayricks, the line stopped and the battalions began firing by platoon, starting at the right and moving left so that from each company a constant rain of fire fell on the enemy. After two volleys, the drums sounded the *Pas de charge* and the entire line moved forward singing *Le Chanson de l'Oignon*—the "Onion Song"—a favorite of the soldiers under fire. Despite uneven terrain, the white legs of the line and the blue legs of the légère moved in unison to the refrain, *au pas camarade, au pas camarade,* "in step comrade, in step comrade," looking like a giant, many-legged bug.

At what must have been a prearranged point, the line stopped and drums signaled the 39th Ligne—the 39th Line Regiment, the Sixth Légèr's sister regiment in the First Brigade—to retreat, leaving a gap in the division's line. Bugles blew and the cuirassiers, with a spectacularly dressed, bareheaded officer at their head, raced through the gap, falling upon an imaginary enemy, while the remaining infantry advanced and the light cavalry raced in from the flanks. It was beautifully done.

The regiments began forming to return to camp, and the division's commander, General Loison, rode with the commander of the cuirassiers to join us where we stood near our carriage. We saluted, and General Dutaillis took a step forward, addressing the bareheaded officer first, who was patting the neck of his fine black charger and calming it down, apparently excited by the action. "Bonjour Marshal Murat, General Loison. A fine exercise. The cuirassiers looked in fine form."

I looked at the bareheaded officer. So this was Marshal Joachim Murat, the most famous cavalry leader in Europe, who soon would become a legend. Not for his strategy—Napoleon said he was an idiot concerning anything outside his immediate view—but for his ability to inspire men on the battlefield, part of which had to do with his dashing appearance. He looked the epitome of gaudy splendor, from his fine long brown curls down to his tiger skin saddle blanket. His fur busby was tied to his saddle. I think he took it off because he thought he looked better leading a charge like that, hair streaming behind him in the wind. He probably did. Tall and athletic, with an open, handsome face, many women thought he looked like a god from antiquity. Murat never lacked for female companionship.

I must have seen him at the coronation but everyone was gaudily dressed that day so he didn't stand out. Here he did, as he did on the battlefield. His horse reared slightly as he responded to Dutaillis. "Of course they're in fine form. They wouldn't be French cavalry if they weren't. Is your master still in Paris?"

I think Dutaillis winced at the term "master," as it wasn't meant to be complimentary, but he ignored it. "Yes, Marshal Ney will be returning to Montreuil within a week. I came in advance with a few of the staff to see that things are in order."

Murat nodded, not really caring what Dutaillis was saying, not an uncommon reaction, I'm afraid. Dutaillis was a decent enough sort but a non-entity as general of brigade and chief of staff, which was why Jomini had slowly become the real power on the staff. He looked the rest of us over, his eyes settling on me. "I don't remember you being on Ney's staff. Who are you?"

Loison had remained silent up until that moment. "Ah, that, Monsieur le Maréchal, is our orphaned American, washed up in front of Marshal Ney, who has since put him to work. I hear he even saved the life of the American minister to France a few weeks ago."

I nodded to Loison but said nothing.

Murat's eyes grew more interested and he laughed. "I heard of that. You've also gotten quite the reputation as a duelist. I understand you even found time in Paris between your duties to fight several."

I turned cold. While I had told Ney about the duels because I promised him I wouldn't fight without his permission, I didn't think word had spread beyond him. They were minor affairs with infantry officers from another corps and one with a civilian I met at a ball, all fought in Paris' Boulogne Forest—Bois de Boulogne—a common location for duels. I won all four, and fortunately no one was killed, only a few scratches inflicted on humiliated opponents.

My expression must have betrayed me because he laughed again. "Such affairs rarely escape the notice of the cavalry. There are some among my staff who I am certain would gladly give you another opportunity to test your sword. Farewell, Messieurs." With that he turned to ride off, returning our salutes as he did so, still bareheaded, hair blowing behind him. For all his faults, the bastard did look magnificent. As he trotted away, one of his staff officers, a handsome young hussar in a stunning uniform, with sharp eyes and a long elaborate mustache, stopped his horse in front of me and threw a gauntlet at my feet with almost feigned indifference. "Tomorrow morning at seven by the edge of those trees over there. There is a small clearing just inside the woods.

Adieu, Monsieur." Quickly he galloped to catch up with Murat, who was heading north, probably towards Boulogne.

Loison dismounted and slapped me on the back, practically knocking my busby off my head, his sharp, cruel eyes enjoying my predicament. "Only an hour after you've returned and you already have a duel. Well done! Be sure to get some sleep tonight, the honor of the VI Corps is at stake—and Marshal Ney."

I shook my head. "I cannot, I promised Marshal Ney I would only duel with his express permission. He isn't due back here for almost a week. I could forfeit my commission. And *mon général*, no insult has been given."

Loison stopped short and shook his head, half bewildered, half angry. "No, you *will* fight. In the absence of Marshal Ney, I think the permission of a general of division will suffice. Isn't that correct, Dutaillis?" The look he gave Ney's chief of staff brooked no contradiction. Dutaillis nodded in return.

"If it was any other duel, Burns, I would tell you to wait, as Ney's orders to you are widely known within the Corps and there would be no loss of honor. But General Loison is right: the honor of the VI Corps is at stake. That was a deliberate insult to the Corps, from Murat to Ney. You have been chosen to answer that insult. Considering the challenge came from a member of Marshal Murat's staff, and that Murat and Ney despise each other, you *must* fight this duel. Ney will approve—just make sure you win."

And with that, I was committed to yet another duel. Often hot-tempered and proud, the French are a dueling people, albeit not to the absurd extent of the Spanish or Italians. Affairs of honor are quite common and were even more so in the Camp at Boulogne. It is amazing how many duels were fought among officers in what was soon to be called the Grande Armée. Since they weren't fighting the enemy they decided to fight each other. It was common, almost routine, for officers of different regiments and battalions to fight each other for their units' honor. Napoleon despised the practice and tried to stop it several times; more wounds were being inflicted on Frenchmen by French swords than by English musket or cannon.

The Emperor's orders tempered the practice—thus Ney's orders to me to receive his permission—but could not stop it entirely, though rarely were they allowed to be to the death.

THE EMPEROR'S AMERICAN

Sometimes that couldn't be helped. Such was the danger one faced.

February 8, 1805
Near Montreuil

The next morning I was at the agreed upon spot, a clearing just inside the woods, joined by Reille and Captain Jacques Tison, commander of the battalion's Second Company, as my seconds. Lieutenant Monge was left back at camp—he likely would have been cheering my opponent, honor of the Corps or not. Trees bereft of leaves reached to the sky like skeletal hands, sending a chill down my spine at the image.

There were quite a few other officers there to observe as well, both from our Corps and others. A fight—or rather, practice, if any official inquiries were made—between Ney and Murat's staff officers apparently was not an event to be missed. Though senior officers studiously avoided the affair, they would be briefed as soon as it ended.

I looked up, and striding from the small crowd was Callahan. We shook hands vigorously. He was as glad to see me as I him. His eyes were twinkling and his scars looked deep and dark in the early morning light. "Well lad, not even here a day and already getting into duels. I came to offer my services as second, if needed." He spoke in his uniquely accented English, his Irish lilt tinted with more than a hint of French after twenty years in the country.

I accepted his offer as second, allowing Reille to take over as president of the duel, whose job it would be to oversee the affair.

Reille smiled, his mustache moving as he spoke to us. "Burns is not boring, that is for certain. He has made my life interesting over the past year." He cocked an eyebrow. "Sometimes more interesting than I would like, I'll admit."

Three cavalry officers walked over to us in the center of the clearing, two mustached chasseurs in green and a cuirassier, complete with breastplate. They were the young hussar's seconds. The man I was fighting—Lieutenant Dominque Vinot—was not far away, jacket and pelisse off, practicing with his epee, having put his cavalry saber aside. It was after all, my choice of weapons.

The cuirassier, a captain, spoke. "Monsieur, I must ask you to apologize and admit Lieutenant Vinot is the superior swordsman. That would be satisfactory and we can dispense with the whole affair. He has killed or wounded several men in duels and there is no need to add your name to his list. After all," –his voice dropped conspiratorially—"this was not really your doing."

I handed my hat to Callahan and began taking my jacket off, the cold biting. "Apologize for what? For accepting this contrived match? No, *mon capitaine*, that would hardly be satisfactory. I never laid eyes on Lieutenant Vinot before he threw his gauntlet down before me. If anything, he should apologize for playing Marshal Murat's game. And besides..." I roughly thrust Vinot's gauntlet into the cuirassier captain's hand. "He has yet to prove his superior swordsmanship."

Bowing, the cuirassier withdrew to join his charge. I drew my sword and made a few perfunctory test jabs and parries.

"Are you sure, Pierre?" Reille asked quietly, visibly concerned. "Callahan was telling me of this lieutenant's reputation. He is quite the swordsman, that captain was not exaggerating. It is not worth it, this is not truly an affair of honor."

I smiled at his concern but my voice was sharper than intended. "It is now, André. Would you have me *apologize?*" I emphasized the last word with scorn. "Besides, I think perhaps you underestimate my skill." I stepped towards the center of the clearing before he could reply.

I hoped I wasn't overestimating my skill. I hadn't neglected my swordplay while in Paris, in fact I had made it a point to practice daily with several masters at the École Militaire—the Military School—that wasn't far from where my quarters had been. I also attended an Italian fencing master's school off the Rue de la Mortallerie, on the left bank of the Seine within sight of Notre Dame. It had proven expensive, but finally—after six months of letter writing—I had been able to get money from my holdings back home through a draft with an American company. I wasn't quite the pauper I had been when I landed, though my losses from the sinking of the *Bedford* hurt. No one on the ship but Captain Rankin had known my family owned a share of the *Bedford*. I had written my business agent in Baltimore that I was alive and enjoinied him to continue to watch over my interests, and to make sure I had access to funds. This also gave me a safe way to stash money, in the unlikely event I came into any, besides my one hundred forty francs a month pay, which barely covered my expenses.

I stopped about ten paces from my opponent and studied him. Like all hussars, Vinot had two long, thin braids of hair that ran down either side of his face from his temples, and a well-groomed mustache. The rest of his black hair was pulled in a queue behind his head. Despite the hardness of his expression, his face was exquisitely formed, almost feminine, though I had no doubt of his skill just by the way he moved and handled his sword. He looked to be the epitome of the dash and verve of the light cavalry.

Our seconds stood together, off to the side, ready to interfere if anyone ran or there was ungentlemanly conduct. The cuirassier captain raised his own sword and lowered it as a signal to begin. We raised our swords and saluted, then advanced slowly, thrusting and parrying, testing the other's skill and looking for weakness. Light sparks flew off the blades, the raspy sounds of metal colliding breaking the morning quiet. With those first blows I kept in mind the advice of my fencing masters: hold back, reveal little, while learning as much as possible. Unlike personal combat on the battlefield, a dual usually starts quite leisurely. The purpose of the initial moves is to test an opponent's skill and reaction. My Italian master compared it to the slow, deliberate moves of seducing a woman, though in some ways it is more intimate, as the end result can be death. Some men try to use these opening moments to show off and intimidate—a stupid tactic, as it makes the opponent's task easier.

It seemed my opponent was actually going for the stupid tactic. This was not a true fight of honor for him either, it was a task to be accomplished and one he was ready to dispatch perfunctorily. That impatience was a weakness I intended to exploit. I deliberately botched a parry, slowed one of my thrusts and made sure its aim was off, in an attempt to make him overconfident and careless. After he parried, he responded with a combination of a high slash, a low thrust towards my right side followed by a half slash towards my upper sword arm. The last move was a feint meant to weaken my guard of my vitals. Rather than finish the half slash he was already thrusting towards my center, but anticipating the move I had already half moved and caught his sword tip on the foible of my own. I turned my wrist, passing the blade along to the forte, and pushed well outward away from my body as I thrust towards his side. I drew blood, a good slice to his side, and there were calls of "First blood!" from several sides. Our seconds began to step forward.

"Messieurs," called out Reille. "Blood has been drawn, honor is satisfied. Do you agree?" If Vinot looked like the ideal of the light cavalry, Reille more than represented the élan of the light infantry and was a commanding presence.

"As the challenged party, I am satisfied," I replied, sword still half at the ready, hoping it was over.

"Monsieur?" Reille looked at Vinot. His seconds were already heading towards him to dress his wound, but he shook his head angrily and waved them away.

"I am the aggrieved party and I am *not* satisfied," he said. There were several cries of dissatisfaction and guffaws at the word "aggrieved." Everyone knew the reason for the fight. "I am *not* satisfied," he said again, almost a growl.

Reille shook his head, an expression of disdain on his face. "Very well. Are you ready, Monsieur?" Vinot nodded. "And you, Lieutenant Burns, are you ready?"

I sighed. I did not put the uniform on to fight Frenchmen but the English. However, reason would not win out. Honor is a prickly thing. I adjusted the grip on my sword and nodded.

"Begin." Reille stepped back.

Immediately Vinot leaped to the attack with a fury, almost as if the fight had never stopped. His anger was giving him a burst of strength and speed, while I did my best to detach myself and concentrate on the motions of the fight, continuing to observe his patterns and movements but always watching his eyes. He liked the three movement attack, with a double feint and a thrust, and though the feints were different, I could usually guess where the hothead's next thrust was going to be. I stopped retreating, blocked his blows and waited for my moment. It came with a feint in the form of a high half slash, a low thrust followed by a determined thrust meant to go over my blade and straight for my heart. I deflected his blade to the right, and thrust, trying to slice almost the same area as before, to force him to quit. As he tried to knock my sword off course, he forced the point inward. I felt my blade sink deep into his side, just below the ribs, and his forward momentum pushed the blade deeper. It looked like a killing blow.

Shock was on his face, which turned a shade of gray. He stumbled, dropping his sword, and fell backwards, though he managed to land sitting rather than on his back, holding his side. People rushed from both sides, including our regimental doctor. I stood there numbly, bloody sword still in hand. Reille and the cuirassier captain walked over.

"Well fought," the cavalryman said grimly. "I think you had no choice; you did what honor required of you."

I stared through him towards the ground where I knew the young man lay, his life draining out of him, a doctor trying desperately to save him. "What a waste. We should be using these swords against the *rosbifs*, not each other."

The Captain nodded at the sentiment, but didn't entirely agree with it. "Ideally, yes, but honor requires us to fight our own sometimes to protect our reputations. And it was he who declared that honor was not satisfied. *Au revoir*, Monsieur." He spun on his heels and walked back to where his friend lay.

It was ironic. I had been training every day for months to be able to protect myself, yet my reputation with a sword was drawing more people to challenge me, requiring me to fight more often. Nonetheless, it was important that I honed that skill. While an officer's main weapon was the men under his command, he still had to be able to defend himself on—and alas off—the battlefield.

I left with Reille and Callahan to get drunk on wine and cognac at the Sixth's regimental mess. I was almost senseless by midnight, trying to get the image of the bleeding hussar out of my mind.

Vinot died the next morning. There were no repercussions, only praise from Ney.

Despite my guilt, it was far from the last duel I fought.

CHAPTER 27

May 11, 1805
Montreuil, France

Months went by after the duel with little happening of note. Winter turned to spring, flowers bloomed and grass turned green, only to be tramped down by thousands of marching feet as the army stepped up its training. Each battalion drilled and shot, held bayonet practice and drilled again, either by itself or as part of its larger mother units. We went from column to attack column, into line, into square, formed skirmishers, or did combinations of the above, sometimes firing live rounds, often dry firing, sometimes fixing bayonets and charging an imaginary enemy. The only real foe visible was the occasional English man-o'-war off the coast which would exchange a few desultory shots with coastal batteries, generally with no effect on either side. We practiced embarking and disembarking on the vessels assigned to the VI Corps and there was a lot of activity getting them ready to go to sea. I hoped our moment was arriving soon.

My studies and practice had continued through the winter into spring. I was starting to train more on the back of *Fleur,* riding as I would on the battlefield, drilling with some of Ney's other aides, and with members of the cavalry like Callahan, racing through practice fields full of scarecrows, impaling and decapitating straw enemies, always victorious. Now that I had my own money, I tried to repay Ney for the gift of the horse, but he wouldn't hear of it, a gift was a gift. I used the money to buy a smoothbore horse pistol with a saddle holster, giving me two pistols, including the weapon Captain Rankin had given me. While less accurate, the smoothbore was more practical. It was easier to load and ammunition was quite easy to get, as French cavalry pistols fired the same size ball as the standard infantry musket. I had to have balls for the rifled pistol specially made.

I also bought a proper sword to use from horseback. Ever since handling Sardou's sword before the skirmish near Cayeux I had kept in mind the straight cavalry blades carried by the dragoons and cuirassiers. My epee was fine for fighting on foot, but on a horse one needs something a bit more rugged; however, I still wanted a weapon meant for thrusting, as it is the thrust that kills.

Around the time of the coronation I had gone to a fine sword maker in Paris who forged weapons for cuirassier officers and had a sword specially made that was similar to theirs but lighter and a tad shorter. Like the cuirassier swords it had a guard on the hilt that protected more of the side of the hand than did a standard saber, or even that carried by the dragoons. Though it was a thrusting weapon, not primarily meant for slashing, its edge was indeed sharp. It was well balanced and could be used on foot if needed, though I still kept my epee for days I knew I wouldn't be on horseback.

I learned to turn my mount with the barest of touches on the reins, or if need be, with just pressure from my knees, all the while managing to handle my sword and sometimes a pistol—not an easy feat, trying to be precise with one's weapons while keeping hundreds of pounds of horseflesh under control.

It was a beautiful spring day, a year exactly since I'd landed in France, and we were in line practicing volley fire as a company in a field south of Montreuil. The soldiers were standing shoulder to shoulder and I was at the captain's post, epee in hand, at the far right of the front line giving the commands to put them through the twelve steps of loading, followed by three steps of firing. Now the men were loaded and ready to fire. I spoke the commands to the first rank.

"*Armez!*" Each man of the front rank held his musket vertically in front of him and cocked it. Then the front rank knelt.

"*En joue!*" As one their weapons lowered and they aimed at the targets ahead of us.

"*Feu!*" Like a crack of lightning and smoke, the line exploded.

"Second rank—*armez! En joue!*" I paused. "*Feu!*" Before the smoke even cleared I was barking out the next command. "Second rank, kneel. Third rank: *Armez. En joue! feu!*"

I looked off to the right where Captain Andre Reille was surveying and timing the exercise on his watch. He nodded approvingly. "Better than four rounds a minute. Very good." I saw to his side a man wearing a sideways bicorn hat, red trousers and blue coat—the uniform of a French naval officer. "Lieutenant Burns, please join us. Lieutenant Monge can continue the exercise," Reille said.

I put the men at order arms and passed the command to Monge, who glowered as he went by but said nothing. He had been much more polite since I'd killed that hussar in a duel. I walked over to Reille and the newcomer, saluting them both.

Reille smiled. "Of course, Pierre, you sped things up by substituting your own step, that's why you were at almost five rounds a minute."

I knew just what he was referring to. "I know having the second rank kneel and having the third rank fire over their heads is not in the Regulation, but passing muskets back and forth is clumsy and the men are reluctant to do it. No one wants to give up his personal weapon and hope it gets passed back to him in the heat of battle." According to the Regulation of 1791, the second and third ranks were supposed to exchange muskets after the second rank fired. The second rank would fire the third rank's weapon while the men in the third rank reloaded, never actually firing themselves. I never met an officer who liked this system, let alone any soldiers who did. It was rarely done in combat.

Sometimes the third rank was sent out as skirmishers or just waited as a reserve, stepping in to fill holes in the line as men fell. I knew Marshal Ney would have cringed to see the second rank kneel—he didn't even like having the first rank kneel, he thought it was hard to get the men back on their feet again ready to charge. Though I admired the marshal as I did few men, I disagreed with him on that.

Reille nodded. He didn't need convincing. "Anyway, Pierre, this officer wants to speak to you." With that he left to oversee Monge.

I looked at the newcomer, wondering what a French naval officer could want with me. Uniform immaculate, he was a tall, slim man with longish brown hair and intelligent eyes that looked like they missed nothing.

"Hello Lieutenant Burns, I am pleased to make your acquaintance. I am Captain Nathan Haley." I blinked and said nothing for a moment, unsure of how to respond to the man's perfect, New England-accented English. I took the proffered hand and shook it blankly. I think my shock must have been evident because he smiled. "Did you think you were the only American in French service?"

I smiled in return and shrugged. "I don't know, sir, I suppose I did."

"My coach is over there; I have a fine bottle of red wine and another of cognac that needs drinking, and a freshly cooked hen that needs eating. Join me, please, Lieutenant." He gestured over his shoulder at a coach with a team of four fine horses. In addition to the driver there were even two footmen. He certainly traveled in style.

Soon the coach pulled up near a stand of trees on a low hill that overlooked Montreuil over a mile to the north. The ramparts of the walled town looked like a picturesque medieval fortress, while the whitewashed soldier huts and lower town at the base still had that feeling of transience they did when I first set eyes on them a year before. Near them I could see blue masses of infantry in columns and lines, drilling. Haley's servants began setting up a small table, complete with the best breads, cheeses, and of course the chicken. Everything was served on the finest china. I looked at the preparations and up at Haley suspiciously; he answered my question before I could say it.

"I like my comforts, Lieutenant, no matter where I go—something I've learned in France." I nodded slowly. It may have seemed effete but I knew better, having met enough officers who liked the finer things life had to offer, while still being able to fight like Satan himself and suffer deprivations without complaint. A contradiction, but a true one nonetheless. In this circumstance what was in essence a picnic seemed a bit strange.

"Also," he continued in English, as if in answer to my unspoken question, "no one can hear us talk. Every inn, every tavern and restaurant likely has spies lurking. Here we cannot be overheard."

Dismissing his servants out of earshot, we paid equal attention to our meal and conversation.

"I have been in and out of French service almost since the beginning of the Wars of the Revolution," Haley said. "After the Revolution broke out I left my home in Stonington, Connecticut to come here to fight the English. The French needed all the help they could get with their navy, and still do, frankly. During the Revolution a great many French naval officers left the country because of their Royalist sympathies, some quite willingly, others driven out. The shortsightedness of the Revolutionaries deprived the fleet of many of its best officers and captains, men who did quite well against the English when they aided us during our Revolution."

I took a long sip of fine Bordeaux—he did have taste—listening carefully. His desire to fight the English I certainly understood, though his talk of the French need for good naval officers worried me. I didn't know if he was trying to recruit me.

"Since that time I have served on various warships and as a privateer. My most recent mission took me out of uniform to England, where I actually received a commission from an English shipping company to go on a trading expedition to the United States with several ships." He smiled, undoubtedly enjoying the memory. "With a picked crew I took my ships right to a French port, selling the cargo and ships quite reasonably. That is one thing about fighting at sea: there is a profit to be made."

After idle chatter about our experiences in France, I asked him what he wanted with me, making it clear I did not want to serve on a ship again. He assured me that was not his intention. "When I was told of you, I was told of your desire to stay ashore and I respect that, though if Captain Rankin trusted you, I'm sure you would be a fine officer. However, the sea is not every man's calling, though I hope you are not averse to a little more time on deck. After all, to make the crossing to invade England you will have to get on a craft of one kind or another."

In fact I had made several brief forays out to sea on the VI Corps' vessels, as we practiced embarking and disembarking and testing the seaworthiness of our vessels. We rarely strayed far out of range of the protective guns of shore batteries, however, to Ney's embarrassment. There were a number of problems facing the invasion, not the least of which was the unsuitability of most of the invasion craft for any but the calmest weather on the *Manche*. It would take three high tides to launch all of the invasion fleet from the various harbors, which would use up precious time during which the Royal Navy could swoop down. This was why it was so essential for the French and Spanish fleets to draw them away from their patrol.

Somehow, I didn't think Haley was referring directly to the invasion fleet when speaking of my feet on a deck. I thought he had something specific in mind.

"The purpose of this visit, Lieutenant Burns, is twofold: first I wanted to meet a fellow American in the Emperor's service. I've heard quite a bit about you, from your fight in the dark in a warehouse in Boulogne, your part in the skirmish in Cayeux, to your saving Minister Armstrong. In case you were feeling rather alone, I wanted you to know of other Americans serving and to let you know you're representing us all rather well."

"I'm surprised General Armstrong didn't mention you to me. Are there others besides us?"

Haley finished the last of his chicken, washing it down with a generous draught of wine. "I don't think Armstrong is aware of my existence yet; he hasn't been in France very long and I have been out of the country. I will have to call on him in Paris soon, however. As for others, yes, I am aware of some, a few officers, a number of enlisted men. Some are adventurers, some are idealists repaying France for its help in the Revolution. Some are both—like you."

I looked up at his assessment of me. His eyes met mine, judging my response to his words. I did not think of myself as an adventurer, more an idealist. I think I had deluded myself that my motives were entirely pure, though on reflection one can hardly call hatred of an entire nation pure.

"One particularly noteworthy individual comes to mind whose motivation was similar to yours. Colonel William Tate had the honor—or misfortune—to lead the first, and until our coming invasion the only large scale landing on British soil. Seven years ago Tate led a few thousand French Revolutionary troops in a landing in Wales, where they were speedily captured. His family had been killed by Indians in the pay of the English during our Revolution and he hated them and wanted to pay them back."

I felt a little lightheaded and took a drink of wine, the story sounded so familiar. "What happened to Tate?" My heart was racing at the similarity in our stories.

"I don't know. He was eventually repatriated to France along with his troops. He was quite old and I heard he was sick." He shrugged. "I think he may have died, but I am not sure."

Haley waved one of his servants over and the man took our plates away, leaving the bread and cheese, a bottle of cognac, and two glasses. A noisy magpie was calling from a branch of a tree nearby, and Haley took a piece of bread off the table and threw it towards the bird, which flew down to the ground to peck at it hungrily. He watched the bird squawk and eat.

"And the other purpose for this visit besides meeting a fellow American, sir?"

Smiling, Haley swirled the light brown liquid in his glass and stared as it slowly ran back down its sides. "To speak to you of a brief mission, which I have already been authorized to conduct by the Emperor and Marshal Ney. In a small, fast ship we are to reconnoiter part of the shore and inlets of the English coast opposite us in preparation for the landing. If we see a safe opportunity we are to land at night and explore one of the coastal fortifications, but that is secondary to exploring along the coast."

My heart was pounding—this was what I joined the French for, to strike at England itself. This meant the invasion truly could not be far off. I had so many questions. "Why am I picked for this mission? Why you? Who will command the ship?" After all I had heard and seen about the French navy, I was surprised they would risk a single ship so close to the coastline.

Haley laughed pleasantly at my enthusiasm. "Calm down, Lieutenant, one thing at a time. First: why us? I have recently been to England, I know the coast, I speak the language. You are going because you are an aide-de-camp to a marshal, you speak English and have a special motivation when it comes to fighting that nation. There will be several other aides-de-camp from other Corps representing other marshals, though no one of particularly high rank; too much of a risk apparently." Haley smiled, not entirely pleasantly. "As foreigners, we are more expendable than native Frenchmen. As for captain of the ship, I will be in command, but the ship's master will be one of Surcouf's privateer captains."

Robert Surcouf and his men needed no introduction to me. Captain Rankin had spoken of him all the time and we even sailed under one of his letters of marque once. Surcouf—dubbed King of the Corsairs—was France's most successful privateer with over fifty English ships to his personal credit. It was said English ships automatically lowered their flags when they realized they were facing him; his taking of the forty-gun English East Indiaman *Kent* with his own little eighteen-gun sloop *Confiance* was legendary and inspired songs. While the French Navy was of poor quality, their privateers were second to none and wreaked havoc on English shipping. I often thought they should take over the Navy, or at least its training. Surcouf was in semi-retirement but had started his own privateering guild, building his own ships and training his own crews and captains.

CHAPTER 28

May 25, 1805
The *Manche*, off the coast of southern England

Sergeant Tessier had thrown up over the side several times and still seemed to have more in his stomach. Several officers who accompanied us were also in the same condition. Though I had swiftly regained my sea legs—and stomach—watching so many others turning green made me a tad queasy. The waters of the *Manche* were pretty rough, though it hardly seemed to slow down our sharp-bowed schooner aptly named *L'Ombre*—Shadow. Copper bottomed for speed like a warship and lightly armed, it was meant to outrun other ships, not fight them. There were only a few light guns, meant more for repelling boarders and boats rather than combat ship to ship, though from a distance we appeared to be an English man-of-war, with painted gun ports to look like we had sixteen guns. We flew an English ensign—a common enough practice at sea. Our blue uniforms only added to the subterfuge as they appeared like British naval uniforms, except Haley's, who traded his red trousers for white. The crew was good, if a rough lot.

We raced along the southern English coast from east to west looking at every cove, inlet and fortification we could see with our telescopes. A few times I scrambled up into the rigging to get a better look, the only non-seaman to do so.

Tessier—whose stomach regretted volunteering—and ten other men from the First Company accompanied me in case there was to be a landing party, if the naval officers determined a landing warranted. We were to be joined by a group of fifteen line infantry from Marshal Soult's IV Corps, who had accompanied another officer. I hoped the men weren't too sick to be of any use if we did have to land.

There was one point of coastline that seemed more interesting than most, near a small peninsula on which was located a round, forty-foot tall stone tower like a castle turret with a cannon on the top. Captain François Tulard, an engineer captain from Soult's staff, pointed to it.

"A Martello tower. I heard the English were building some of those to repel our invasion. It's a design they copied from a tower we held in Corsica that they had one hell of a time subduing—their ships couldn't make a dent in it. Apparently they were so impressed they copied it." He took a long look at it with his telescope, as did I. I could see a few redcoats casually walking on the top, including one, an officer, looking at us with a telescope. "There is a platform up there so that gun can face 360 degrees. From what I understand the towers are almost impervious to artillery but do not have sizeable garrisons and don't seem to have many places from which soldiers can fire out from. A closer look at one would be invaluable." The engineer looked over his shoulder at Haley. "What do you think, Monsieur? Is it possible we can get a closer look? It would be helpful if we could look inside. Is there somewhere nearby we can land after dark?"

Haley glanced at the sky and then his watch before looking down the coastline. "We should be able to swing back just after dark and lay anchor at a cove a mile or so west of the tower. Your opinion?" The question was directed at me and a captain from Marshal Nicholas-Louis Davout's III Corps. Davout's troops had recently started arriving from farther north in Belgium, a sign to most of us the invasion truly was near. Like most of "The Iron Marshal's" officers, the captain was a serious man. Davout, who would prove himself to be the most capable of Napoleon's marshals in coming years, was a no-nonsense man and expected the same from those under him. The captain, Jean Thévenet, looked at me. "It is dangerous, but the intelligence might be worth the risk."

I turned to look at the tower and the land around it, already disappearing to the rear as we headed west, angling somewhat away from the coast. A gull swung low over us and turned leisurely back towards land, crying impertinently that no food was to be found on our deck. I shrugged, trying not to show how nervous I was at the idea of landing.

"I agree getting a closer look at the tower would be useful; but all the same, I don't like it. I don't relish the idea of landing after dark on a strange coastline with no one there to guide us. A mile through strange terrain in the dark is a long way. Then we have to deal with the garrison."

I remembered the problems faced by the English landing parties I had intercepted in France, and our party would be much smaller than those. "I'm not sure of the wisdom of this. We would be extremely vulnerable, especially if they are alert. Once we get to the tower only a thin, easily defendable strip of land connects it to shore, and there's a small rise just beyond. We don't know what's beyond that. There could be a barracks there containing a couple of hundred men. We could be trapped between them."

Haley shook his head. "I don't think so. I traveled along much of this coast recently, ostensibly looking for a crew for my ship. Not too many barracks are so close to shore, though no doubt there are a great many militia units that could descend upon you if you're discovered. Be quick, take the tower, prevent word of your presence from getting out, and give Captain Tulard a chance to look at it. With luck you should be out of there undetected just past daybreak."

I nodded, sparing another glance for the shoreline. "With luck."

Three or four hours after dark we dropped anchor in a small cove under low cliffs west of the tower. A cleft in the cliffs led right up to the top where the terrain was mostly level and open, with a few scattered stands of trees. There were thirty-five of us total: me and my ten men, Thévenet, the fifteen line infantry, along with Tulard the engineer and ten men from the ship's complement of forty, whose job was to help take and guard the tower and guide the ship to the rendezvous in front of the structure.

We stumbled slowly through the dark, stopping at the slightest noise. Some of the men, especially the sailors, were clumsy and made more noise than a rutting moose. I thought it a miracle the whole countryside didn't turn out, especially when we passed a farm whose dog barked briefly. We were apparently undetected by human ears, however, and soon a light glow could be detected ahead of us. I went forward with Tessier, Thévenet and Tulard. We squatted at the top of a knoll overlooking the tower a few hundred yards from the west. The light we had seen came from torches around the base of the structure, especially along the back where a thin strip of land connected the little fort to shore. Along the shore stood two sentries, and I could see another on the top of the tower. There was nowhere to hide anywhere near the shore, though the dark could hide men until they got fairly close. The only way I could see to get closer was to bluff our way right to the door.

I pulled out the watch Talleyrand gave me in Paris and peered at the time in the faint light. It was well past midnight. Our stroll through the woods had taken far longer than predicted—as I had known it would. We had no time to waste.

"Do you either of you speak English?" I asked the two other officers.

Tulard answered in heavily accented English. "A little." Thévenet shook his head.

"Damn." Tulard's accent would reveal him immediately, though it gave me an idea. Our blue uniforms could pass for Royal Navy uniforms in the dark, though the blue trousers of my light infantry uniform would give them pause if I didn't keep them talking. I took the cloth off the lock of pistol that protected it from the elements, checked the priming charge and told them my plan.

Not ten minutes later I was briskly walking with Thévenet and Sergeant Tessier towards the torches and sentries. Tulard, the engineer, stayed with the rest of the men until the tower was secure. After all, he was the reason we were taking it. Tessier had left his musket and cartridge pouch, his *giberne*, with the rest of the men, the bulk of whom were stealthily following us fifty paces behind us in the dark. Our light infantry shakos would have marked us as French, so Tessier and I each borrowed a bicorn from one of the line soldiers, making sure to take the tricolor cockades off them. There was a chill in the air which I couldn't decide had to do more with the situation or the season.

The only door to the tower was around ten or fifteen feet off the ground and was reached by a ladder that could be brought back inside—as it was at that moment. We had no scaling ladders, and in any event the door was probably heavy enough to resist our efforts for some time even if we could reach it. We needed to convince the sentry to give his compatriots the word to open the door and lower the ladder.

The sentries heard our approach. The one to the left called out to us while the other on the right grabbed a torch to get a better look at us. Though the redcoats had fine, even expensive uniforms, by their demeanor they appeared to be militia rather than regulars, which would make things easier all around.

"'Alt! Identify yourself!" The challenge rang out in the night.

I took a deep breath, trying to make my accent sound more English. "Lieutenant Bryce, Lieutenant Sweeney, and Midshipman Wilde, Royal Navy. Bring us to your commanding officer. We are here to inspect the tower."

I could see them squinting in the faint light. "Advance and be recognized!" He brought his musket to the ready, half pointed at us. I wished the fool would keep his voice down. We didn't need anyone coming out of the tower before we were ready.

As we approached I put all the arrogance in my voice I could. "What kind of greeting is this, soldier? Surely you knew we were coming?"

I could see the soldier with the musket shake his head. He was doing all the talking while his comrade held the torch and watched us. "No, we ain't 'eard nothin' 'bout any kind of inspection. You'll 'ave to wait here while I get the lieutenant."

I took a step forward, starting to move to the left of the man, then stopped. "What is your name?"

"Corporal Adams."

"Sir." I left the word hanging there.

"Eh?" His dull, piglike eyes watched me uncomprehendingly.

I took another half step towards him. "Goddamn *militia*." I spoke the word with utter contempt. "Corporal Adams, you will address me as 'sir,' or I will have you flogged, do you understand me?" It was an utterly foreign threat in the French Army, where the barbaric practice was long banned, but English soldiers were all too familiar with the lash.

The man gulped, fear in his eyes, his attention riveted on me, as was his companion's. He nodded vigorously. "Yes, sir."

"Good. Now then, Corporal, you will take us in to see your commanding officer. I will not wait out here in the cold because of the mistake of some incompetent who failed to inform you of our arrival."

Adams quickly agreed, anything to get as far as possible away from the threat of flogging. He scuttled ahead on the rocky jetty, and I followed close behind. His companion with the torch came next, several steps behind us, leading Tessier and Thévenet. I prayed to God he didn't say anything to them or we would be revealed.

The heavy door was open but the ladder was inside—a sensible precaution. A man was sitting just inside, able to either lower the ladder or close the door. The corporal called out to him. "'Ey, Jones, let the ladder down, there's some officers 'ere to see the lieutenant."

A face peered down. "That you, Adams? What are you talking about?" At a glance he took in our group. "I'll get the lieutenant."

Before I could say anything, Adams protested. "Just lower the damn ladder, Private Jones, then get the lieutenant. These gentlemen 'ave come a long ways and don't want to be left waiting in the cold." His obsequiousness, not to mention his throwing his rank around, was almost sickening but worked to my favor.

"Alright, 'aright, but I'm goin' to get the lieutenant as soon as I do."

Adams nodded his head. "Fine, fine." He looked at me apologetically. "'E's only a private and a Welshman, can't 'spect much from 'im, sir."

There was a scraping of wood and a light wooden ladder was lowered down. The corporal gestured to it. "If you please, sir." I glanced at Tessier and nodded almost imperceptibly, gestured with my head towards the other soldier, and began climbing up. In a moment I was at the top, in a white painted, half-moon shaped room that took up more than half of the floor of the tower. Arched ceilings, meant to resist cannon blasts, rose above; while in the center, almost flush with the wall, was a giant masonry column that reached up to the ceiling. It supported the weight of the cannon on the roof above.

The room was damp, despite being ten feet above the ground; moisture beaded down the walls and it smelled dank. It was lit only by a candle on a table near the door and another in a sconce on the opposite wall. There were around twenty beds in the room crammed along the walls, most of them filled with sleeping men, while there were tables and benches in the center for the men to eat. At the other wall next to the sconce were two doors. Through one I could see a stone staircase that led to the roof. The other portal had a painted wooden door, currently open, beyond which I heard voices—Jones waking up his officer. I had to move quickly. I doubted our uniforms would fool him.

There was a noise behind me as Corporal Adams reached the top of the ladder, unslinging his musket as he did so. I moved as if to help him, but instead wrenched the musket out of his hands and pushed him right out the open doorway with my shoulder. I saw a look of confusion on his face as he fell backward, landing with a loud thud more than ten feet below. I looked down and saw Tessier finish him off with a quick blow from the butt of the musket he had already taken off the other guard. Thévenet was moving up the ladder and in the darkness up on the beach I could see and hear movement as our men rushed towards the fort. We needed numbers quickly.

Thévenet entered the room, looked around and stepped to one side to make room for Tessier, who was reaching the top of the ladder. At that moment, two shapes came out the door at the other end of the room. A groggy, young, redheaded lieutenant, still fastening on his jacket, started walking towards us and stopped, sleep not quite dulling his senses. He must have seen the musket in my hands and noted Tessier coming in with another—and taken a closer look at our uniforms, barely visible in the faint light.

"Good evening," I said, trying to buy precious seconds. "I take it you weren't informed of our scheduled arrival. We were delayed. I'm dreadfully sorry about the hour."

"Those don't look like Royal Navy uniforms." He didn't even offer the barest of pleasantries.

There was noise outside at the base of the ladder—the fastest of our men had reached it and began to climb. At that moment there was a shot outside: the sentry on the top of the tower must have finally detected something amiss.

I raised my musket and pointed it at the officer, hoping the charge was good after the damp night air. "You are prisoners of the French Republic. I ask you not to resist, sir." Outside there was a flurry of musket shots as our men fired back at the sentry and the first of them, a private from my company, clambered up the ladder into the room. A few of the sleeping soldiers sat up, others—sounder sleepers—stirred.

"Go to 'ell!" Jones, the private who had woken his lieutenant, exclaimed, raising his musket towards me. I pointed my musket at him and pulled the trigger and nothing happened—a misfire. Another shot rang out to my right as Tessier fired. The noise was like a cannon in that confined space and all the men in bed woke with a start. "The French—at them, men!" The lieutenant yelled, drawing his sword.

Thévenet drew his own sword and yelled out the door at the remaining men to hurry. *"Vite! Vite!"*

The man closest to me started to get out of bed and I knocked him down with the butt of the musket and one of our soldiers finished him off. I stepped over his bed to thrust my bayonet into the man beyond him, who was desperately reaching for his musket, which was leaning against the wall next to his bed. Initially we were sorely outnumbered, but we were armed and awake and as our reinforcements came one at a time through the door, they rapidly turned the balance.

Our men had loaded muskets, which they fired at the English as they entered the room, before entering the fray with the bayonet. A few English soldiers were able to fix their bayonets but most simply used their muskets as clubs—or anything else they could grab for a weapon.

Near the middle of the room, I tossed my stolen musket aside, drew my pistol and sword and made my way towards their officer, who was still on the other side of the room. It was my first time going into action with my newly made cuirassier sword. Two English soldiers barred my way.

One, who tried to club me with his musket, I simply shot. He fell back, clutching a shattered arm, while I flipped the pistol around to hold it like a club, using it to block blows coming from the left.

The English lieutenant and I crossed swords, the ringing of the blades lost in the cacophony. Over a year of constant practice paid off and I swiftly drove him back towards the wall. With a quick succession of blows, I knocked the sword out of his hand and held the point not far from his breast. "Surrender, sir. Stop any further bloodshed."

A quick glance at the room showed his men were losing. He nodded. "We surrender, sir." I lowered my sword and let him take a step forward where he shouted out to his men. "Stand down! Lay down your arms! Stand down!" A few of the English looked over their shoulders but didn't dare comply while fighting for their lives.

I called to my men. "*Assez!* Enough! Stop fighting. The *rosbifs* surrender!" Our words slowly got through and NCOs began pulling their respective men apart, the English laying down their weapons as they did so, under the watchful eye of my men. I ordered the weapons collected and the prisoners to sit down on the wooden floor in the center of room while their wounded were tended to. They had five killed and eight wounded. We lost no one, though there were some bruises, sore heads, and a few wounds form bayonets that needed dressing. Such is the difference the advantage of initiative can make.

While several of our men went to secure the roof and make sure no one was in the powder magazine below us, I took aside the English officer—Lieutenant Fleming was his name—and returned his sword after he gave his parole. Questioning him briefly I placed him under guard separate from his men. While we wouldn't take the men back with us as prisoners, we certainly would keep the officer. I questioned several of the men as well to confirm what I learned.

I saluted Thévenet and Tulard, who had just entered and was eagerly examining the tower. "Messieurs, the tower is secure. It is ours—for a few hours at any rate. There is a hamlet less than a half mile inland and a larger town a few miles beyond which is the headquarters of a militia infantry battalion and squadron of cavalry. It is likely they will learn of our presence soon. One of the sentries on the roof sent up a signal rocket before he was killed. One of our men reported seeing another fire light up on a hill east of us. They must have an observation post there. They must also have heard and seen the shooting and sent a runner for reinforcements. It's likely we'll see them no more than an hour after dawn."

Thévenet nodded and turned to Tulard. "How long will you need to look over the tower in daylight?"

Tulard thought for a moment. "An hour past dawn should just do it. I'll get to looking at what I can inside by torchlight and candle before that." With no further ceremony, he turned and pulled a notepad out of a shoulder bag and began examining key points of the structure, sketching and taking notes as he went along. We watched him for a moment; he was already completely absorbed in his work.

"Well done getting us into the tower, Burns." I turned to see Thévenet scrutinizing me.

"Merci, mon capitaine."

"We'll be here some hours yet. We have to prepare to spike and destroy the cannon and blow up the powder magazine." Thévenet glanced around the building and the activity around us. " Hopefully there will be enough to destroy this structure, or at least make it unusable for some time. As soon as more of the ship's company comes ashore to guard the prisoners, I want you to post a few men at the top of the little hill overlooking the tower, then take the rest of the infantry and move inland, perhaps as far as that hamlet but no further. This is a raid, not an invasion. Watch for the approach of any enemy, delay them until we destroy the tower, but don't get cut off. Is that clear?"

I certainly didn't need to be reminded not to get trapped in England. *"Oui, Monsieur*, perfectly clear."

"Go, good luck."

I saluted and joined Tessier near the door, where there was a pile of captured English weapons. With such a small force, every hand would need a weapon, including officers. I looked over several of the Brown Bess muskets until I found one I liked. It was not as well made a weapon as our Charlevilles, especially these battered specimens, which were old enough to have seen service in the Seven Years' War. The notch in the stock for the shooter's cheek in the Charleville made it an easier weapon to shoot and the bands around the barrel made it more durable, especially in hand to hand combat. The angle of the priming pan also made it easier to prime the weapon during the loading drill. That being said, while our muskets were better, the English gunpowder was far superior and burned cleaner. A few of our men had already emptied some of the English cartridge pouches for the powder, tossing the balls away, as they were a different caliber and too large for French weapons. I grabbed a full cartridge pouch and belt and slung it over my shoulder, then began loading both musket and pistol.

Without looking up from loading my weapons, I spoke to Tessier. "Get all the infantry assembled outside, we're taking a patrol inland in fifteen minutes. Have ten of the men each take one of the English muskets in addition to their own weapons, we may need them."

Not fifteen minutes later, I led a small column off the beach. After leaving four of the line infantry at the top of the little hill where they could observe in all directions, my patrol slowly began following a road north, and inland. We spread out and walked slowly, stopping to listen every so often. It was about an hour before dawn, perhaps less. In the east, the sky showed the barest hint of light. Birds were already starting to wake in the trees, spreading their songs across the landscape, oblivious to the carnage man sought to wreak upon his fellow man. Mostly the landscape was open pasture for sheep, with some crops scattered about. There was the occasional stone wall, which I noted would be good for defense.

We had not gone far when we came upon a wood and thatch cottage not far off the road. A dog barked wildly in the yard as we approached and light showed in a window. The farm was just starting to wake up. Cattle were lowing and sheep bleating. It was probably almost time for them to be milked and led out to the fields.

A door opened and a man and a boy came out. The boy held aloft a torch, while the man held an old fowling piece. "'Ey! Who's there?"

One of the soldiers, a massive Norman, stepped to the man's side and grabbed the barrel of the ancient weapon, wrenching it up and away. The hammer fell as he did so. Nothing happened. One of the soldiers guffawed as he tossed the ancient weapon off into the darkness.

"We are soldiers of France," I said, answering his question. "Where is the nearest village?"

Their eyes widened but it was the boy who spoke first. "I told you I 'eard shootin, from the tower! Boney's comin' here! They'll eat us!" His father whacked him on the back of the head.

"Not more than a five minute walk up the road, sor." He had taken his hat off as he spoke, trying to show as much deference as possible. "But it's just three or four houses, hardly a proper village." He smiled. The gap where his front teeth should have been appeared much larger in the shadows.

I nodded. "Thank you, my good man. Now, go about your business. If you leave us alone, you shall be unmolested, and the army will pay you for any provisions it takes. If you interfere, we'll burn your farm to the ground and take your animals. Understood?"

Head bobbing fearfully, he said he did.

With that we moved off down the road. I had no doubt that one of them would race ahead to raise the alarm, though by now word would have reached the militia anyway. It was safer for us they think we were simply the vanguard of a much larger army, otherwise we could face swarms of farmers with scythes descending on us.

It didn't take long before we crested a rise that overlooked the tiny hamlet. The man was right, it wasn't much. There was just a handful of houses, two of wood and one hovel of stone. There was also the smallest of chapels, which I was certain didn't have its own vicar. The road led through the center of the hamlet, crisscrossed by a much fainter trail, more like a cow path.

The sky was lightening as we slowly entered the village, spread out in a long skirmish line. I turned to Tessier and Sergeant Danton. "Clear out the houses, send the people elsewhere, but there is to be *no* looting. Word could spread and make our invasion more difficult—when it comes. I will post myself in the church tower." We were standing near the churchyard where several dozen moss- and lichen-covered headstones were mute testimony to generations of yeoman farmers who had lived and died in the vicinity.

"'Some mute, inglorious Milton here may rest, some Cromwell, guiltless of his country's blood.'" Knowing Callahan would approve of the sentiment, the words of Gray's "Elegy in a Country Churchyard" came out in a moment of melancholy.

"What did you say, Monsieur?" Tessier, standing nearby directing men to one of the houses, asked.

I paused in confusion for a moment, unaware I had spoken out loud. "English poetry about a small church graveyard just like this one, and how fleeting is glory." Tessier simply nodded. A soldier who had seen as much action as he had didn't need to be reminded of mortality and fleeting glory—he had lived it, though few could equal how Gray expressed it:

The boast of heraldry, the pomp of power,
And all that beauty, all that wealth e'er gave,
Awaits alike the inevitable hour;
The paths of glory lead but to the grave.

I shook the feeling off, pushed the words out of my mind and climbed the church tower. I didn't have the luxury for melancholy or meditation, especially about mortality, as I would likely have vivid reminders of it soon enough.

I didn't have long to wait. It was dawn and I could see a long distance down the road inland. There was movement—horses. The militia cavalry squadron of about fifty men was on its way down the road, doubtless doing reconnaissance work for the infantry which couldn't be too far behind. At first glance they looked French. Their uniforms were blue with yellow facings, but they had fur hats of a type I had never seen before. They were well mounted and well equipped, from what I could see, but there was an unease about them that spoke to their militia status. They made no move to check their advance and scout our position. We were in buildings and behind stone walls, invulnerable to cavalry, yet they seemed determined to continue on into the village.

"Sergeant Tessier!" I called down from the bell tower. "We'll let them get close and really bloody them. Pass the word, everyone hold his fire until I shoot!" My musket was leaning against the wall. I picked it up, checked its priming charge and waited.

The cavalry came trotting down the road. There were a few cries as they spotted a few of my men scrambling for cover yet they stupidly kept coming. On command—in an admittedly impressive motion—they drew sabers. Not fifty yards away they leapt to the gallop and charged, swords held in front of them, bugle sounding the charge. It was an impressive sight—the first enemy cavalry charge I ever witnessed—but it was essentially an impotent move against fortified troops. It was time to show them how impotent.

I aimed not at the first rider but at his horse—a huge brown gelding—and fired. Smoke blocked my vision and I waved it away to see what effect I'd had. The animal reared screaming and kept going backwards, falling right on its rider, who had no time to escape. The horse right behind careened into it while its rider desperately tried to check his advance. Suddenly fire erupted from all sides: from windows, doors, walls and fences as French infantry shot round after round into the milling and confused English cavalry. Their way forward was blocked by dead and dying horses and men.

Within moments, without a signal or command, the remnants of the English cavalry fled the way they came, leaving ten of their compatriots dead or dying, while several more who lost their horses had to scramble away on foot as fast as they could. We let them go; we had no means of taking care of prisoners, besides which their return on foot would add to the English morale problem. We caught two of their horses, thinking they might come in handy.

Perhaps four hundred or five hundred yards away the English stopped to regroup. I watched through my spyglass as officers and NCOs did their best to calm their men, keeping them busy checking on their animals, weapons and equipment. They spread out in a loose line and waited, probably for infantry, which had to be marching as hurriedly as possible towards the scene.

While we were waiting one of my men climbed the tower to give me a piece of bread and some kind of gruel found in one of the huts. He also handed me a dirty cup with cloudy ale in it found in a cask in a nearby barn.

"It's not much, *mon lieutenant.* We wanted to butcher a sheep we found but Sergeant Tessier said there was no time..." The soldier left the statement hanging there, hoping I would contradict Tessier.

"This will do, *Soldat* Fortin, *merci*. Sergeant Tessier was right, there is no time. We should be falling back to the ship in less than three quarters of an hour." The soldier left me alone in the belfry and I leaned against a post eating and looking north. Both bread and porridge were fresh, probably prepared for that morning's breakfast and not unpleasant going down, especially with the ale.

From my vantage point, I saw Tessier not far away personally distributing the ale, giving each man just enough to wash down his breakfast and nearly knocking down one who tried to take too much. When he was done he smashed the cask with the butt of his musket. Several of the men groaned loud enough for me to hear them from the bell tower and I'll admit I grimaced at the sight myself, but it was a reasonable precaution. We didn't need anyone getting drunk. Each man had to be able to fight and run when the time came. Any who straggled would be left behind in England and captured.

Probably another half hour passed before I saw movement to the north beyond the cavalry. Red-coated infantry were arriving— more militia. They were of battalion strength at least, more than five hundred men. As more troops arrived they milled around with no sense of order, though soon their officers put them into a line four companies wide, with more in reserve. It would be like dropping an anvil on a fly, especially once they realized how few we were and not the advance of a larger force. I watched one who appeared to be their commander—a corpulent, gray haired man on a magnificent, spirited charger, who was getting red shouting orders. I suspected he was paying for the entire unit's equipment out of his own pocket and expected control over every action his men took.

I scrambled down the rough wooden ladder out of the bell tower and left the church. Tessier was there, as was Fortin. "*Soldat* Fortin. You can ride a horse." It was a statement rather than a question; he was no cavalryman but he knew the rudiments of riding from growing up on a farm. "Ride to the beach and give Captain Thévenet my compliments. Tell him the English are here in large numbers, and that I will be compelled to fall back to the beach quite soon. He must finish what he is doing. Ride back here as soon as you're done."

"Yes, *mon lieutenant*." Climbing into the saddle of one of the captured English mounts, he galloped off. I knew the English would notice his departure and it would worry them, wondering if he was summoning reinforcements. Once they advanced in force we would have to retreat quickly. When we did, I planned to provide some kind of cover or distraction and hit them hard enough so they would hesitate. I explained to Tessier what I had in mind and climbed to my vantage point in the belfry again.

Before long the anvil began moving forward to crush the fly, though they didn't know the odds, otherwise they would likely have charged immediately rather than advance cautiously. They had no skirmishers in front—likely they weren't trained for it—but moved forward in line, their commander in the center on his spirited animal. They marched steadily enough, drums marking time. When they were within fifty yards I slowly aimed at the commander's horse, pulling the trigger gently. The musket slammed back into my shoulder, smoke from the priming pan obscuring my view as I placed the butt of the weapon on the ground and began reloading.

Again my shot was a signal to commence firing and from windows and behind walls my soldiers shot at the English line, concentrating their fire in the area where the English commander was located. His horse was bucking wildly and screaming, whether from fear, pain or both, I couldn't tell.

I saw several men in their line fall, hit from our fire, which at fifty yards was quite accurate.

The horse was still bucking wildly, unable to be controlled. It turned and began running in the opposite direction, its rider clinging on for life, while first the color guard, then the rest of the English line stopped in confusion.

At our next volley, first a few, then dozens of English soldiers began breaking formation to flee after their commander.

At first I didn't believe my eyes, and when I did—I couldn't help it—I stopping firing and began laughing. While trying to catch my breath I noticed I wasn't the only one, laughter had erupted from all our positions. Some of it was nervous laughter, we were after all quite vulnerable, but at the same time seeing the vaunted *rosbifs* running from a handful of French soldiers was worth the trip and the danger. The cry, *"Vive l'Empereur,"* came from soldiers up and down our line.

As the guffaws died down, something in the sight of fleeing redcoats awakened my Scottish blood. "Culloden! Culloden! Culloden!" I yelled without explanation to my comrades.

Of course our good fortune didn't last; I saw the commander bring his wounded horse under control and some of their cavalry stopped the fleeing men. As they were herded back towards their respective units an idea occurred to me and I left the bell tower. I stopped in the sanctuary of the church and took a white cloth off the altar before joining Tessier at his position behind the central house. The remaining captured horse, a tan gelding, was tied there and I mounted it, tossing my musket to Tessier.

"Get the men ready to retreat the moment I return. If I don't return, take them back to the ship right away." I drew my cuirassier sword and thrust it through the altar cloth. For a moment I hesitated before doing it, then shrugged. It was only from a Protestant church after all.

"Where are you going, *mon lieutenant*?" He propped my musket against a wall and leaned against his own.

I smiled. "To offer them terms of surrender."

Tessier couldn't hide the shock from his face. "We are *surrendering*, Monsieur?"

"Not us Sergeant, *them*. I am going to ask them to surrender— on very good terms, I might add." Before he could reply I spurred my horse forward between two buildings onto the road out of the hamlet. My sword arm was raised above me to show my white flag. I rode slowly towards their line then stopped until my flag of truce was acknowledged.

A pimply faced young officer—I doubted the lad was more than sixteen—approached me on a white stallion and led me to the commanding officer, a colonel, who was watching his wounded horse being tended. His uniform was as grand as a field marshal, with more braid than a courtier at the Emperor's court in Paris. It was the same red-faced, corpulent officer I'd shot at earlier. His resemblance to the pimply faced officer was uncanny— undoubtedly his son.

I dismounted and saluted. "Sir, are you the commander of these...militia?" I deliberately paused over the word, uttering it not quite as an insult but not much above one either.

"I am Colonel William Fitzgibbons, commander of this battalion of His Majesty's troops, Monsieur," the colonel said, responding in French. Apparently he wanted to limit the number of eavesdroppers, either that or show off his French.

I bowed slightly and continued in English. "My compliments, sir. I am Lieutenant Pierre Burns, an aide-de-camp of Marshal Michel Ney. I must ask you to surrender. You cannot possibly stand against us. We are prepared to offer you generous terms if you immediately agree to lay down your arms." I glanced around me, at faces both nervous and angry. "Your men are not soldiers and we are prepared to let them disperse to their homes on parole as long as they swear not to take up arms against the French Army."

There was angry grumbling, but surprisingly some favorable remarks from men in the ranks about accepting the terms. It was stupid of the colonel to receive me so close to his men.

Face turning red, he practically shouted out his answer. "Absolutely not! We shall defend our native soil to the death against the Corsican ogre and Jacobite toadies such as yourself."

"Very well, I regret that is your choice." I took several steps to my mount. From the saddle I looked at my watch. "We shall recommence fighting again in fifteen minutes. Agreed?" I held my breath waiting for a response.

"I think that should be adequate, Monsieur," the colonel replied coldly.

I spurred my mount and cantered back towards the village. As I left the English lines I could see a horse galloping from the direction of shore with a blue coated figure on it. Once in the village I discovered it was Captain Thévenet. He was watching me with a bemused expression. Tessier evidently had told him what I was doing.

"I beg to report, *mon capitaine,* that the *rosbifs* have declined to surrender. They agree hostilities should recommence in fifteen minutes." I was barely able to keep the smile off my face.

"I see." The normally severe Thévenet could barely keep the grin off his face either. "That should be more than enough time.

ART MCGRATH

The cannon on the tower has been overcharged and will explode any moment. The rest of the gunpowder will be exploded in the magazine soon after. Unfortunately there wasn't enough to blow up the entire tower. Evidently it was just built and doesn't have its full supply yet. Even if it had, Tulard isn't sure even the full ton and half it was supposed to have would have been adequate. It is a well-made structure. However, the explosion will likely destroy much of the wooden floors inside, wrecking the place for some time. Start withdrawing, I'll see you there."

He headed back towards the beach and I pulled the men out of their positions. As they withdrew, I had them set fire to two buildings—a hayshed on the north side of the village nearest the English, and what appeared to be an abandoned chicken coop on the south side. The smoke would somewhat mask our movements from the English and would occupy some of them putting out the fires, I hoped. I had taken great pains to avoid burning dwellings or even those containing livestock, as I didn't want rumors spreading that the French would burn English villages when we returned during the invasion, though no doubt the story would spread anyway.

As the men reached the small rise overlooking the village I stayed on the back of my captured horse, watching the English with my telescope. They were observing our withdrawal just as carefully, and I saw the glint of telescopes from the little group around Col. Fitzgibbons. Evidently they were counting our numbers, for suddenly I saw him lower his spyglass and start shouting orders, gesticulating madly, realizing he had been tricked. Orders were reaching the companies, which began moving forward, slowly at first. Behind me, from the beach, there was a thunderous explosion—the cannon on the tower being destroyed. Seconds later there was an even louder blast—the tower's powder store had caught fire. Our work was done.

Noting Fitzgibbons was looking at me through his telescope again, I snapped my own glass shut, took off my hat with a flourish, and did a half bow from horseback in his direction. I then spun my mount around towards my men, already a few hundred feet ahead.

The gelding was a powerful animal and covered the distance in moments. Tessier and several of the men looked up.

"The English are just starting to move, they won't catch us," I said in response to the question in their eyes. "But don't dally."

We crossed open fields in the half mile stretch that separated us from the beach and passed the farm whose owner had threatened us with his ancient weapon. He and his son were fixing a fence that held a small flock of sheep. I waved. The son, who appeared about eight years old, carefully waved back. From ahead I could see smoke, evidently from the sabotage done to the tower. I looked over my shoulder to see smoke rising behind us as well, as the buildings we torched in the village burned more fiercely. The first English troops were just coming up over the rise, more than a quarter of a mile behind us—too late.

We were almost to the rise overlooking the beach when to the right just ahead there was movement. Out of the depression not seventy-five yards away rode a group of ten blue uniformed horsemen, probably from the squadron that attacked us in the village. It's amazing what can be hidden in what appears to be flat ground. Their commander must have sent them to scout our rear.

Normally when facing cavalry, infantry will form a square, but we were twenty men—except me, still on horseback. Hardly enough for an imposing square. My sword flew out of its scabbard. "Form two ranks, in a half-circle. Front rank—kneel!" I trotted my horse to the right of my tiny formation as the men packed together shoulder to shoulder. Already the cavalry were at the full gallop charging us.

"Steady, steady, *mes enfants,*" Tessier said calmly. It was ironic he called them his children; he was not any older than many of them, but at that moment in a sense he was their father, as was I. It was our responsibility to get them safely back to the ship and to France. "Aim for the horses, *soldats,*" Tessier continued. "Stand your ground and you will be safe. First rank, plant your musket butts on the ground with your bayonets facing out after you fire." Of course such reassurances are easier said than done with a line of thousands of pounds of horseflesh galloping at you, but Tessier had practically grown up on a battlefield.

At fifteen yards I gave the command for the first rank to fire. Smoke and flame shot out from ten muskets. Horses and men fell in a writhing, bloody mass. The second rank followed with a volley moments later and more English cavalry fell. While the survivors milled about in confusion I spurred my horse forward and rather stupidly charged among them. Ducking under the saber of a young NCO, I stuck my blade in his side, twisted and pulled it out. Clutching his wound he toppled off his horse. I parried the blow of another cavalryman and almost ran him through as well but he gave his horse some rein and bolted. The other survivors followed suit. Only one mounted man had reached our lines and sliced open the throat of one of the soldiers from the line regiment before being pulled off his horse and bayoneted.

I looked north and saw that while we had been fighting, the English had made good time. The English infantry was advancing practically at the run, and even worse, their remaining cavalry was out in front coming at the gallop, seemingly joined by another squadron. The time for tactics, indeed for fighting, was over.

"Run!! Back to the ship!"

No one needed to be told. The men ran towards shore, some of the NCOs taking up the rear. We came over the small rise and saw the smoking ruins of the tower, mostly intact, though the cannon was just a jagged piece of metal on the top. Not far out to sea our ship was at anchor. It chad made its way back towards the tower right after dropping us off up the coast. There were several boats waiting at the little spit of land connecting the tower to the beach, their crews ready to push them in the water, while Thévenet and a detachment of sailors stood by with muskets ready to protect them. Tulard was nowhere in sight—already aboard ship. We ran headlong to the boats, where sailors started hastily directing us aboard. I dismounted, cut the saddle off my mount, threw it in the water, then slapped the animal on the rump and it ran along the beach to safety. I noticed a number of barefoot redcoats running along the beach away from us—the garrison of the tower, who had been released. Nearby I saw the other horse lying on the beach, a bloody wound in its head. I looked at Thévenet, who shrugged.

"Like spiking the gun on the tower, I destroyed war material."

Though I understood his reason, I couldn't have done it so easily—not to a perfectly healthy horse, especially not after riding him in action. There was no further time to reflect, however. Barely were the words out of his mouth when I heard cries of alarm and looked at the rise overlooking the tower. The first

English cavalry appeared there. They didn't advance any further but started forming a line at the top of the ridge.

"Guillaume." I nudged Tessier, gesturing towards the English musket one of the soldiers had been carrying for me since the village, which he handed to me and I loaded.

A musket shot rang out from one of the sailors, but Thévenet slapped down several other musket barrels. "Hold your fire unless they approach."

He looked at me. The last boat was ready to go—the others were already rapidly making for the ship. "Ready, Lieutenant?"

I smiled. "Indeed, *mon capitaine.*"

Sailors and soldiers began pushing the boat into the water, while behind us there were shouts as some of the horsemen charged. We were in the water, the oarsmen putting all their strength into getting us to the ship. The first of the horsemen in the meanwhile had reached the base of the tower. A few of them had carbines and fired shots towards us. I returned fire, as did a few others. No one on either side was hit and the horsemen withdrew a little ways up the beach and sat astride their mounts watching us.

Haley and Tulard were waiting at the top of the ladder when we climbed aboard. Haley held out his hand to me with a grin and spoke to me in English. "Glad you decided not to stay."

The smile was infectious—I was relieved we got away so lightly. Besides a few minor wounds the only casualty was the soldier whose throat was cut open by the English cavalryman. We inflicted much greater losses on them, not to mention the loss of material and the damage to their morale. I shook Haley's hand in return. "We'll be back soon enough, and in much greater numbers."

Haley nodded, and turned to give orders to run up the British flag again and get the ship underway. As the soldiers moved to get out of the crew's way I noticed a white bundle strapped to one of the men. It was a white lamb, legs tied together and thrown across his chest like a haversack, with a cloth over it to hide it. How he held onto it during the running fight I couldn't imagine, though the ingenuity of soldiers to acquire and hold onto provisions was a never ending wonder for me.

"*Soldat* Fortin."

The soldier began pretending he didn't hear me, then thought better of it. He stopped. "Monsieur?"

I lifted the cloth and looked at the lamb, which seemed resigned to its fate. "Where did you get this?"

"In the village, *mon lieutenant.*"

"Did you pay for it?" I had ordered any provisions be paid for, either by paying someone outright or leaving money, if no one was available.

Fortin began looking at the deck and started stammering. "Well, um, no, Monsieur. I didn't know what to pay for a lamb, and, um, didn't have much money on me."

I lifted the animal's head, looking from it to him. "I should have you toss it in the water. Maybe it can swim back."

His look of disbelief was comical. "But Monsieur, what a waste that would be..." The words died in his throat.

I stroked the lamb's chin before dropping its head. "Indeed it would, especially as I am not sure it could make it to shore. Instead, you will bring it to the galley where it will be butchered for my supper." Dismay on his face, Fortin started to leave but I wasn't through. "When we get back, you will donate four francs to the orphanage in Montreuil. You will also donate another two francs to Saint-Saulve church." I grinned unpleasantly; I knew of his anticlerical bent and chose the punishment for that reason. Disobedience to an order would not come as easily next time.

Face turning red, he was barely able to control himself. "I understand the orphanage, but please Monsieur, not to a Catholic Church. My brothers fought to free us of the priests in the Revolution."

"And the Emperor has made peace with the Church. Religion is once again welcome in France. Be thankful I don't force you to attend a Mass." He started to protest and I cut him off. "You will now donate four francs to Saint Saulve. Speak again and it will be six francs." He was now forfeiting the better part of a month's pay. No further words came from his mouth. "Get to the galley. I am getting hungry."

I turned to see the captured English officer, Lieutenant Fleming, watching the entire affair. Unlike the last time I saw him, he was fully dressed, right down to shiny shoes, shako and polished sword hilt. At least he was allowed to finish getting dressed before being brought aboard. I smiled. "Lieutenant, allow me to extend to you the hospitality of the French Army, Navy, and the corsairs of Robert Surcouf. Captain Haley's cook will do wonders with that fine young English lamb for our midday meal. It should be at least six or seven hours before we set foot in France. We may as well make the best of it." The ship was getting underway and we made our way aft.

We were joined by Haley, Thévenet, Tulard, and one of the corsair officers in the captain's cabin. We slipped by the English naval patrols without incident and I had one of the best meals it was ever my privilege to eat on board a ship. I ate and drank ravenously, buoyed by the events of the day. I was glad to leave England but anxious to return to its shores again with to the entire army.

CHAPTER 29

August 20, 1805
Montreuil, France

In the two and a half months since the raid on the English coast I worked feverishly towards returning with the invasion—as did thousands of others, but unlike most, I had had an appetizer, in a manner of speaking.

Though I still lived with the company and the Sixth Légèr, pretty much all my time was occupied in staff duties for Marshal Ney. Much of it involved carrying messages, always a role for an aide-de-camp, but I also spent time poring over English maps, translating documents, and interviewing the occasional English prisoner, spies either from around Boulogne or from naval actions. Saboteurs and incendiaries still tried to damage the fleet but their activity was far less than it had been the year before. There was so much more activity and our vigilance so much greater I think they thought it a waste of men to try.

I was still a lieutenant. Ney promised when I first joined his staff I would be promoted to captain when the invasion was imminent, practically when we were boarding the ships. That would be my own signal we were leaving.

Since the raid, Marshal Davout's corps had arrived just north of Boulogne, at Ambleteuse, which added to the sense our moment was near, especially since summer was almost over. We embarked and disembarked numerous times and even launched the fleet away out from the coast before turning back. The army was ready, but we were waiting on the navy and good weather. Admiral Villeneuve was to take the French and Spanish squadrons out of Cadiz and either draw the English fleet away, or hold the *Manche* against their attacks while the invasion fleet crossed.

THE EMPEROR'S AMERICAN

We never knew but any moment the fleet could arrive off the coast to drive the English away, so we always had to be ready. Of course, this did not prevent us from enjoying ourselves when we found the moment. Shooting tournaments—complete with prizes for the best soldiers—fencing, dances, balls, plays and other diversions kept both men and officers entertained and broke up the monotony of camp. Napoleon even brought a theater group from Paris, promising them they would soon be performing in London.

After a hard day of training, there was a particularly memorable ball at Ney's chateau in Recques for officers of the VI Corps that lasted all night and well into the early hours of the morning. Like the ball almost exactly a year before when I met Athenaïs Vanier, the chateau was lit up and music livened the air. The night reminded me very much of her, made all the more poignant since I hadn't heard from her in many months, only one brief letter since leaving Paris.

Though I arrived with Ney, Jomini and others of the staff, I was off to the side talking with the ever dashing Reille, over our third round of wine. Monge was there as well, in better spirits than I had seen him in a long time. With my increasing absence, he finally moved into the sous-lieutenant's slot in the company which he felt—with some justification—was due him. Callahan was absent that night, though since he was not in the VI Corps it wasn't entirely a surprise. He had been attached to Marshal Berthier's staff for some months, as had many of his guide unit. As a result, while on staff duty I actually got to see him quite a bit, and Marshal Berthier, when he was in Boulogne.

It was past midnight. Double doors opened at the other end of the room and through them came several gorgeously attired women, among them Ney's wife, Aglaé, in a sky blue dress. My heart jumped at the sight of her, and I searched the faces of her companions, hoping Athenaïs was among them. She was not. However, Aglaé saw me from across the room and, leaving her companions, walked to me across the dance floor, an image of radiance, a path opening for her among the dancers. Couples steered around her or stopped to let her by. I bowed as she approached. She smiled, though the smile did not entirely reach her green eyes, which held a touch of sadness.

"*Bonsoir*, Pierre."

Reille bowed as well and she nodded in return, smiling.

"*Bonsoir*, Captain Reille." She brushed her brown curls away from her eyes in a gesture as charming as it was innocent. "Several of my companions over there have expressed a desire to dance with you, if you are available."

It was a polite but clear dismissal.

Without hesitation, Reille bowed again. "Of course, Madame la Maréchale."

As he left, I looked curiously at Aglaé, at the expression in her eyes. "Is something wrong? Has something happened to Athenäis?" A sick feeling twisted my stomach.

"In a manner of speaking." The panic must have been evident on my face because she quickly reassured me. "She is fine, Pierre, but there is a reason you have not heard from her in some months. She asked me to tell you she has gotten married."

I felt lightheaded and moved to steady myself against the wall and stopped myself. Instead I took a long draft of the burgundy still in my hand. It was a long moment before I could speak again and when I did my voice was toneless. "Married? To whom?"

"Andre-Louis Beaulieu." Her eyes watched my reaction carefully, for she knew there would be one.

"Beaulieu?" The last name was familiar but not the first. The sick feeling returned. The shadows on the walls cast from many chandeliers seemed to perform a mocking dance. Even the walls were laughing at me.

Brushing her hair from her face again, she nodded. "Yes, the younger brother of the man you scarred in a duel last year. Since his brother fled the country, he is now baron and head of his family." She smiled sadly, but this time the smile reached her eyes and she took my hand and squeezed it. "I'm sorry, Pierre, but you knew her brother was trying to arrange a match for her."

"I know but..." Words failed me for a moment as I fought anger, despair, confusio—all trying to get the better of me. "...a Beaulieu. That makes it worse, I think."

Glancing around, she nodded. "I understand why you would think so. To be frank, I was surprised too. I thought the rift between their families was permanent after last year's affair.

Apparently not. Oh, before I forget," she pulled out an envelope from her sleeve and held it out in front of her. "She asked me to give you this."

I recognized the neat hand on the front as Athenäis'. I took the envelope numbly, hardly noticing Aglaé as she gently squeezed my hand again and kissed me gently on the cheek before joining Ney, who was speaking with several officers, including Jomini and Loison. A small circle of admiring women were with them and Loison and Ney were laughing boisterously, Ney's face getting almost as red as his hair at some joke or another. As Aglaé approached, Ney held out his hand to her and the officers bowed.

I stopped watching and moved to a more remote corner of the room, pulled out the letter and began reading. It was short and mostly in English, except the salutation. My heart jumped at seeing her precise, handsome script, though I dreaded reading it.

Mon beau amoureux,

My handsome lover—I liked that, despite myself. Take that, Beaulieu brothers.

Aglaé will have told you by now of my marriage, long a *fait accompli* by the time you read these words—I am even due to have a child in a few months." The wounds just kept coming and coming. "I married Joseph-Marie's younger brother the week after I saw you last in Paris. I didn't have the heart to tell you when I saw you. I knew you wouldn't understand.

Don't hate me, my love. I have a duty to my family and my brother, though you are in my heart before all others. I hope you remain in France. You have not lost your Atala. This need not be the end—with discretion our love can continue for many years.

I expect to hear many great things about you, and I suspect you will soon get many chances to prove yourself. You might be interested to know Joseph-Marie is not longer in England, he made too many enemies there. He has joined other émigrés in either the Austrian or the

Russian Army. He still hates you, though I suspect you'll soon be too busy in England soon to worry about that.

With all my love,

Athenäis.

My eyes were starting to water, making it difficult to see the page—smoke from a nearby sconce. I read the letter again and smiled grimly at Beaulieu's plight. He had a talent for making enemies. How I wished I had killed the man, how I wished I could kill his brother.

I winced at her reference to Atala. For once I didn't think poorly of Chateaubriand's tale of despair and love. I sympathized with the Indian warrior. Athenäis said our love could continue despite her marriage, but that was not my way. I did not mind occasionally cuckolding a husband, that was the way of the soldier, but I could not share Athenäis. As far as I was concerned her letter was one of farewell.

As I put the letter in my jacket, several officers entered the room, disheveled and dirty, evidently after hard riding. One of them was Callahan. Outside I could hear the sound of shouting and horses and carriages galloping off. Everything in the room stopped, even the music as they strode to the center of the room.

"Everyone get to his unit! The Emperor is embarking all the troops! We are going, the invasion begins!" For a long moment, no one said anything, then cries of *"Vive l'Empereur!"* went up from many of the officers. Dance partners were abandoned where they stood, some without even a farewell. The room emptied with astonishing rapidity; I started to go, and then realized my first duty as a staff officer was to Ney. I looked and saw he was still talking to Jomini and Loison, seemingly unconcerned. The circle of women around them had not diminished. I walked over and stood by discreetly.

Ney looked up.

"Orders, Monsieur le Maréchal?"

His sharp green eyes held that old hint of amusement that was there the first day I met him. "Anxious, Pierre?"

I tried not to smile. "Yes, Monsieur le Maréchal. It has been a long wait—I wish to return to England. They have much to answer for."

There were murmurs of agreement from the other officers.

"I think you should wait, Monsieur le Maréchal," Jomini interjected. "It could be another of the Emperor's practical jokes."

A similar ball earlier in the summer had been interrupted by another officer, informing everyone present the invasion was starting. Soon after the Emperor had walked in laughing, enjoying the stir he caused. That joke was only played on the participants in the ball, however; it didn't involve the whole army, as this did. I told the marshal as much.

"You are not here to offer your opinion," Jomini said when I finished.

I glanced at him contemptuously then returned my gaze to Ney.

"Where is Dutaillis?" Ney asked, looking around him for his chief-of-staff.

"Already heading to Étaples to coordinate the movement of the Corps," one of the officers said.

Ney nodded, thinking. "Pierre, go directly to Boulogne. Find the Emperor or Marshal Berthier, find out what is going on and report back here." He took in at a glance those around him. "In the meanwhile, the ball will continue, though I think a game of cards may soon develop."

I saluted and headed for Callahan, standing at an unattended table, drinking deeply straight from a bottle. He never even took his shako off, and his green uniform was speckled with dirt.

"Not letting anything go to waste, I see."

He turned and laughed. "Of course not, lad, especially not cognac." He handed the bottle to me, the formalities of the ball having been dispensed with.

"Barbarian," I said before tipping the bottle and taking a long draught. "I have to find the Emperor or Marshal Berthier. Can you take me?"

Corking the bottle, he clapped me on the shoulder and we left the still brilliantly lit chateau.

A few hours later, about four o'clock in the morning, we arrived at the Emperor's field headquarters on the cliffs overlooking Boulogne and the *Manche*. The very elite of the army, Grenadiers of the Imperial Guard surrounded the headquarters. Each a veteran of ten years or more, these imposing, six-foot-tall men with mustaches wore huge bearskin hats that made them seem even taller. Their dark blue uniforms contrasted sharply with their white trousers in the darkness and created an image that made them seem like ghostly creatures of legend. Callahan and I were known to them and went unchallenged.

There was a bustle of noise and activity as aides came and went bearing orders, horses whinnied nervously, and men spoke in groups, all watching a few tables under a large awning outside the headquarters where the Emperor's staff was standing. The Emperor himself was lying on the ground outside on a huge map, concentrating intently on it, occasionally making a mark on it and taking measurements. He was never a man to avoid getting dirty if he had to. Soldiers and aides stood around him holding torches and a few oil lanterns, while he moved a candle in a covered brass holder to light where he was writing.

Marshal Berthier noticed us and walked over. The ugly, big-headed Alexandre Berthier was Napoleon's chief of staff, in many ways the Emperor's right arm, a man who knew the intricate details of every unit in the army: who commanded it, where it was, and how to get orders to it—no matter what hour he was asked. This man was able to translate every wish, every order of the Emperor's, into a comprehensible order that would almost unfailingly reach its destination. A man of limitless energy, during one campaign his staff said he went thirteen days without sleep.

Though he was a brusque man, he treated me decently enough, I think because of Jomini's antipathy towards me. He knew the Swiss officer and I despised each other, and since Jomini and Berthier felt the same way towards each other, it was a case of having a common enemy.

Also, like many others I met in the army, Berthier had served in Rochambeau's army at Yorktown and elsewhere in the United States fighting the English, where he rose to the rank of colonel.

We saluted as he approached us. "You found Marshal Ney and his staff at the ball in Recques." The statement—for statement it was and not a question—was directed to Callahan.

"Yes, Monsieur le Maréchal."

Berthier looked at me, then beyond me, squinting at figures in the darkness. "Burns, where is Marshal Ney?"

I took a deep breath. "Monsieur le Maréchal, he remained at the ball with some of his staff and sent me here to look over the situation and report back to him." I hesitated and continued. I knew Berthier and the Emperor would find out what happened anyway. "He was concerned it might be one of the Emperor's practical jokes. I am to determine if this is real and report back."

Instead of exploding or getting angry, Berthier shook his head in quiet disbelief. "I see. Was this his idea or did it come from his staff?"

I could see where he was heading. "The suggestion came from Jomini, Monsieur le Maréchal. General Dutaillis is at the corps headquarters in Montreuil getting the troops to the ships."

The barest of smiles bent up the corners of the marshal's mouth. He had a weapon he could use against the Swiss, though he had to use it carefully, as the Emperor liked Jomini and his book about war. Nearly everyone around the Emperor competed against each other for position and influence. Such is the way with power.

"Berthier!" The Emperor had looked for his chief-of-staff and found him missing. I saw grey eyes flash up from his spot on the map and rest on me for a moment before turning back to Berthier. "Where is Ney? I want him to look at this map."

The marshal replied. "Still at his ball in Montreuil. He thought this might be one of Your Majesty's practical jokes."

Napoleon slammed his pencil down and jumped to his feet and stormed over to us. "He thought! I didn't make him a marshal to think but to carry out my orders! The fool, it would serve him right if the army left without him!" The Emperor fumed for a moment longer in front of us without saying a word, and then the anger drained away from him face as if a plug had been pulled. "Burns." Pausing for just a moment, he continued. "Return to your marshal, tell him the moment of decision is upon us, if not tonight then at most a matter of days. Tell him I expect him here now and any other time the army is mustered. Tell him," he paused again for emphasis, "tell him there are any number of generals I could give that marshal's baton to." He lightly slapped my arm. "Go!"

I bowed. "Yes, sire."

I turned and walked into the darkness and as I did so I almost bowled over three approaching officers. General Savary was foremost among them. He was accompanied by Captain Thévenet from my raid on the English coast. The third was Marshal Davout, who was assessing me coldly in the faint light. When I first met him that cold stare unnerved me but I soon came to realize that it wasn't me, the Iron Marshal was like that with everyone; his personality, what there was of it, was reserved for his family. The most brilliant of Napoleon's generals, his appearance was the least martial. Average height and balding, he often rode his horse with a pair of special, thick eyeglasses strapped to his head. Despite that, no man could assess ground better or more accurately determine what was needed to rout an enemy "Marshal Davout, you remember Lieutenant Burns, Marshal Ney's American aide-de-camp," Thévenet said, squinting at me in the flickering light from the tents.

"Monsieur le Maréchal," I said, saluting.

No smile, no expression as he looked at me. "Yes, I recognized him immediately. I've heard about your landing in England. Well done, Lieutenant Burns."

"Merci, Monsieur le Maréchal."

Without another word Davout left, trailed by Thévenet. Savary stayed behind.

"I think he likes you, Pierre."

"How can you tell, *mon général*?"

I saw the white of his teeth in the dark as he smiled. "He spoke to you, didn't he?" For a moment he looked towards the activity at the Emperor's headquarters. "I'd better get over there. A few more days at most and the army moves."

THE EMPEROR'S AMERICAN

It was mid-morning on a beautiful late summer day and the army was gathered all around the city. From the hills surrounding the ancient port I could see the thousands of ships in the harbor waiting to take us on board. Those to carry the VI Corps were south of us at Étaples, their customary berthing place, yet we were gathered outside Boulogne. If this was the day for the invasion, and it certainly seemed possible, we would have to march south to embark our own vessels. It seemed odd.

The Emperor and his staff had ridden by several times; he was looking the troops over. Occasionally he would stop to talk to an officer or soldier. For several minutes he stopped to speak to Ney.

Towards mid-day, a courier came from the Emperor with a written order. Ney read it, his face darkening in confusion for a moment, then lightening with relief. He snapped out commands that the Emperor's order be read out to the entire Corps, after which his staff was to converge at the Emperor's headquarters.

The Corps was assembled, thousands of us in formation. I was in a group of mounted officers with Ney in the center. Ahead of me I could see the colors of the Sixth Légèr among those of all the other units, regimental standard snapping in the breeze beneath its Eagle. Bands played the imperial anthem, *"Le Chant du Départ."* All of us faced forward to listen to the order as it was being read. It was being repeated by several heralds, as one voice would not carry across the entire field. There was excitement mounting everywhere, with men whispering excitedly to each other. "This is it, we're going."

England—at last, I thought.

Silence fell as the order was read. It would echo across Europe for ten years.

"Brave *soldats* of the Camp of Boulogne! You will not go to England! British gold has seduced the Austrian emperor into declaring war on France. His army has crossed the line which he was to have guarded and has invaded Bavaria. *Soldats*, new laurels await you beyond the Rhine. Let us hasten to conquer those enemies whom we have defeated in time past!"

There was silence on the field. Ney took off his hat, held it above his head and stood in his stirrups. *"Vive l'Empereur! Vive l'Empereur!"*

The cry was taken up, at first desultorily, then with enthusiasm. The men had prepared for years to invade England; to abandon that goal had never been in their thoughts. It was action, however, an end to sitting and waiting, and going against an old foe without having to get in leaky wooden crafts to get at him. I did not join the cries. I sat on *Fleur*, shocked, disappointed, confused. I looked around at the cheering Corps, at the army around me that had become my home. What role did I have here if we didn't invade England? Was I still needed or wanted? Furthermore, what quarrel did I have with the Austrians? I was barely sure where Austria was on a map.

A thought flashed through my mind—I did have one enemy among the Austrians. Beaulieu, my sworn enemy, was likely in the Austrian, or possibly Russian Army. As enthusiastic as I could get at the thought of killing him, it was hardly reason to want to wage war against the entire country, though I supposed it was a start.

The Corps was already heading back to Étaples and Montreuil to break up the encampment, its home for several years. I followed Ney and the rest of the staff to the Emperor's headquarters overlooking Boulogne. The meeting was in the council chamber that was part of the pavilion like headquarters. Inside there was a large table and a single chair—for the Emperor.

Inside the room in the center were the staffs of Marshals Ney, Soult and Davout, whose troops were located near the city. We milled about, some talking among ourselves, the only other noise the creaking of leather accoutrements and the scraping of scabbards on the floor. I looked up at the ceiling, decorated with golden clouds and in the center the imperial eagle, lightning in its talons. The eagle was flying towards England guided by a star—the Emperor's guardian star. I half expected to see the picture turn around of its own volition and start heading east.

"Well, I suppose this will be the last we'll see of you." I turned to see Jomini, a wry grin on his face.

Though I had been thinking the same thing, I didn't say it. "Why would you say that, Monsieur?"

Sparing a glance around, he turned back to me and chuckled. "What possible use can you be now? Do you speak German?"

Hardly a word, I thought. "Not much, but I can fight, I can ride. I've spent more than a year in your classrooms—for whatever that's worth."

Face turning red with anger, he was about to reply when silence fell on the room as the Emperor entered, accompanied by Savary, Berthier and several other officers. Though not physically imposing, his presence and personality dominated the room. Electricity filled the air as after a summer lightning strike. Walking to his chair, he stopped but did not sit down. He was dressed, appropriately enough, in his green campaign uniform. Dark eyes, framed by dark hair, looked out from his intense dusky face.

"*Bonjour*, Messieurs. You have heard the order. No doubt many of you are disappointed."

Slowly he studied the faces in the room. For the slightest of moments his eyes rested on me.

"*I* am disappointed. Conquering England would end most of our problems in Europe. Unfortunately, it is not to be. Admiral Villeneuve's French and Spanish fleet is nowhere to be seen. What is worse, the English have convinced, through their liberal sprinkling of gold throughout Europe, both the Austrians and the Russians to join them in a coalition against us, though we have no quarrel with either country. Already a large Russian army is marching west to join forces with their Austrian allies somewhere in central Europe," he said, sparing a glance for the map of Europe laid out on the table.

"In the meanwhile, the Austrians have violated the neutrality of our ally Bavaria while other Austrian forces in Italy are tying down Marshal Massena. They are convinced they will be able to overrun the German principalities and invade France before we can react. They think because they are seven hundred miles away they are safe." Smiling, he shook his head. "They do not remember just how fast the French can march or how easily we have beaten them in the past. Well, Messieurs, we shall remind them. We will smash the Austrian Army before the Russians can join them, and destroy the Russians if they give battle."

Walking slowly among the marshals he looked at each in turn. The feeling of energy, of an electrical storm that accompanied him into the room, only increased as everyone got caught up in what he was saying. "This army, the greatest Europe has ever seen, is no longer the Army of England, it is now called the Grande Armée. The Grande Armée shall march east in two days, each corps advancing on a route to parallel to the other. Over the summer, in the event I couldn't keep the Austrians and Russians out of the war, I had supplies staged across France along the route east, which will help each corps to maintain a pace of thirty miles a day until you converge near Strasbourg, where you will receive new orders." Stopping, he looked completely around the room again. "That is all. You have much to do."

The Emperor slowly moved through the crowd as the officers began dispersing. As he was passing he saw me and stopped. "Don't be too disappointed we are not going to England, Lieutenant Burns," the Emperor said quietly. "This is typically how the English fight—by paying other people to fight for them because they are not strong enough on land to do so. They knew we would crush their army if we landed in England. By fighting the Austrians and Russians you *are* fighting the English almost as directly as if we had crossed the *Manche*. Their gold started this, we must finish it." Moving a step closer, his eyes held me.

"Remember, if you defeat their plans, you defeat *them*."

"Yes, sire!"

If I had any thoughts of not staying with the army, they disappeared in that moment. Where else would I go?

Nodding curtly with approval, Napoleon continued on with his staff.

Outside the headquarters pavilion I looked towards the *Manche* and the Cliffs of Dover with a sigh. Ney was standing nearby with Jomini and Dutaillis. He called me over. "Burns!"

Saluting, I looked up at him, a red-haired giant of a man, a warrior at last going back where he belonged.

"Yes, Monsieur le Maréchal?"

Eyes full of life, he looked exuberant to be heading to battle. "Jomini tells me you plan on staying with the army, though we are not going to England?" When I confirmed this he laughed boisterously, while Jomini tried to change his look of disapproval into one more neutral. "Excellent! I knew I chose well when I made you an officer. Unfortunately, since we are not going to

England, that promotion to captain will have to wait. Fear not, promotion runs across the battlefield like a whore in debt, eager to share her favors with everyone. Your chance will come."

August 27, 1805
Montreuil, France

Two days later, not long past dawn, I sat astride *Fleur* near Ney and the rest of the staff watching thousands upon thousands of troops march by, muskets gleaming in the sun. In two days the camps that had been the soldiers' homes for two years—many of them essentially small cities—had been dismantled. Soldiers were told to travel light, anything extraneous was packed away to be stored in depots.

The men were in excellent spirits, many cheering Ney as they passed. Finally they were doing something, going towards battle. While many were disappointed they were not going to England, the Austrians and Russians were old foes preparing to wage war against France and had to be dealt with. They had confidence in Napoleon and themselves to do just that.

I caught a line of a song as a company of grenadiers passed.

"On va leur percer le flanc..." "Let's go stab them in the side..." I shivered despite the growing warmth of the day and patted *Fleur* gently.

Ney looked over his shoulder at us, the early morning sun catching him in its glow like a halo, making his red hair seem like it was on fire. "Let's go, Messieurs, immortality awaits." Spurring his mount, he broke into a trot alongside the endless columns of soldiers, the rest of us hastening to catch up to him.

The Grande Armée marched east and I marched with it.

THE END OF BOOK ONE

HISTORICAL NOTE

Much of this novel is based on historical fact. One fact that may jump out at readers is Napoleon's height. The Emperor was about 5 foot 7 inches tall, about average for his time. For centuries English caricaturists have painted him as a dwarf of about five foot inches two, which is true—by old French measurements, which made him 5'7 by English reckoning. Two centuries of English propaganda has painted him as the short Corsican ogre. The truth is far different.

The training of the Grande Armée, as experienced by Burns in the VI Corps, was much as described. Unlike the stereotype that has come down in English histories and novels, the French army, especially in the Camp of Boulogne, was a well-drilled combination of veterans and recruits that indeed practiced regularly with live ammunition and conducted large exercises with an entire corps, with infantry and artillery using live ammunition on a scale and precision not seen until the twentieth century. No army throughout the entire Napoleonic Wars, French or Coalition, was as well-led, well-trained, or could fire as rapidly as that which marched out of Boulogne in August of 1805.

The main French battalion Burns is attached to for much of this novel, the Third Battalion of the Sixth Légèr, was indeed a real unit, but I have taken the liberty of activating it a few years early.

When first writing this book I had to decide whether to attach Burns to a wholly fictional unit or an historical one, with all the limitations that brings concerning its real history. I compromised, activating it early, which gave me the freedom of a fictional battalion with the gritty sense of real history connected with an authentic unit.

The Third Battalion at this time was still a depot battalion and did not see field service until after Austerlitz.

THE EMPEROR'S AMERICAN

The English landing near Cayeux is fictional. Though there were English raids on the French coast on occasion, they would not have been as foolish as to land a sizeable force near the main French Army, for they would have easily been pushed into the sea, as were my fictional attackers. For dramatic purposes, I made them more foolish than they really were.

My inspiration for Burns' location during Napoleon's coronation came from Jacques Louis David's famous painting of the event, which shows Ambassador Armstrong in the spot behind the altar where Burns and future U.S. President Monroe are standing. While in reality Armstrong was kept by protocol to a spot near the high throne, and not the altar, David put him close at hand to the key moment. I have changed that a little and put another famous American who was present at the ceremony, James Monroe, in Armstrong's spot. He was indeed unhappy about his placement during the ceremony and I have given him the opportunity for a better view.

Now the years of wars begin—instigated by English gold—that will take Burns across Europe.

Many readers will have noticed the more frequent use of the term English rather than British throughout the book. I do this to echo common French usage, especially at the time, possibly because the word British encompassed the Scots and others who were historical allies of France and the French had no desire to insult their old allies.

We will see Pierre, Ney, Reille and the others again in Central Europe in the next book.

ABOUT THE AUTHOR

ART MCGRATH

Art McGrath grew up fascinated with all things Napoleonic. When he was little he reenacted the Battle of Waterloo with toy soldiers—always making sure Napoleon came out on top!

He spent four years on active duty in the United States Marine Corps; and in 1987, while in Egypt during Operation Brightstar, the words of Napoleon to his men when they caught sight of the Great Pyramid came to mind: "Soldiers, forty centuries of history are looking down upon you."

After the Marines he returned to Vermont for college, getting a bachelor's in English and a master's in history. Even while working as a reporter for a small weekly newspaper in northern New Hampshire he still read all he could about the Napoleonic era. After running across references to Americans serving in the Grande Armée, he became frustrated there was so little written about them. Thus *The Emperor's American* was born.

"I wrote this as a way to discover how an American could end up across the Atlantic in French uniform fighting the Emperor's enemies," McGrath said. "It was discovery through writing, and while it may sound like a cliché, it was as if Pierre Burns was standing over my shoulder telling his story. He wanted to be discovered."

McGrath is a reenactor and a proud member of the Brigade Napoleon and the *3me regiment infanterie de ligne*—the French 3rd Infantry Regiment of the Line. He became a reenactor after he began writing the novel.

"In order to really describe it I needed to be able to taste the gunpowder, hear the drums and volleys of musket fire, feel the wool of uniforms. Reenactors bring history to life."

The Emperor's American is the first in a series that will follow the adventures of Pierre Burns through to Waterloo, with a hiatus between Elba and the Hundred Days for part of the War of 1812.

In addition to being a novelist, McGrath is the editor of three weekly newspapers in northern New Hampshire. He lives in the Northeast Kingdom of Vermont with his wife and two sons.

If you enjoyed this book—you'll love...

Sir Arthur Conan Doyle's
Complete Historical Fiction Series
by
Fireship Press

Many people do not realize that Arthur Conan Doyle, the creator of Sherlock Holmes, was also one of the finest historical novelists of his day. Between 1888 and 1906 he wrote ten historically-oriented books...

The entire series is now
available through
Fireship Press!

Sir Nigel and the White Company: (Combined) Two tales of the Hundred Years War
The Refugees: A Tale of the Huguenot persecution
Micah Clarke: A Tale of the Monmouth Rebellion
The Napoleonic Trilogy: In one volume!
    Uncle Bernac
    The Exploits of Brigadier Gerard and
    Adventures of Gerard (Combined)
    The Great Shadow
Rodney Stone: A Tale of the 19th Century Prize Ring
The Tragedy of the Korosko: A Tale of the Desert
Around the Red Lamp: Tales on a Victorian physician

For more information about these and other
fine Fireship Press books please visit us at:

www.FireshipPress.com

All Fireship Press books are available
directly through www.FireshipPress.com, amazon.com

THE CORSICAN
The Virtual Diary of Napoleon Bonaparte

Edited by
R.M. Johnston

Napoleon's Diary?
**Napoleon didn't keep a diary—
that's what makes this book
so interesting**

We know that Napoleon Bonaparte did not keep a
diary. But what if he had? What would it look like?
American historian, Robert Matteson Johnston,
decided to find out.

Working from memoirs and collections of
correspondence, he painstakingly pieced together
the items that likely would have appeared in
Bonaparte's diary—had he kept one. Reading
Napoleon's story, arranged in this way, is a
fascinating and curiously addictive glimpse into the
mind of one of the major figures in history.

WWW.FIRESHIPPRESS.COM

For the Finest in Nautical and Historical Fiction and Nonfiction

WWW.FIRESHIPPRESS.COM

Interesting • Informative • Authoritative

CPSIA information can be obtained at www.ICGtesting.com
Printed in the USA
LVOW01s0908190814

399801LV00018B/390/P